ILL

GOTTEN

GAIN

ILL GOTTEN GAIN

A NOVEL

RALPH E. JARRELLS

WordCrafts

You will devote their ill-gotten gain to the Lord.

Micah 4:13

Cursed is the man who is hung on a tree.

Galatians 3:13

PROPHESY

Running … running … running down the ancient street. The uneven stones turning and twisting my ankles. The pain is unbearable. My calves and thighs are on fire. The people looking … no, staring. All around me, hideous faces. Their ugly mouths wide open, screaming. Their stinking breaths hot in my face. Shrill voices fill my ears, their hate a living thing, reaching out, stabbing at me, looking to destroy me.

I run blindly through the masses. My breath comes in gasps, the pounding of my heart is deafening. But run away I must. Run faster. I have to escape. I must get away from them.

Away from here.

Gasping. Gasping for air. Breath … ragged in my throat.

"Why me? Why me?" I demand. "What have I done? I've done nothing wrong. Nothing, you hear. Nothing! I love my Lord. He'll come out on top of this. You'll see. My Lord is the next King of the Jews."

But I know, I know better.

Hot air dries my mouth, burns my lungs. My heart races.

"God help me, please help me."

But, no one answers. No one is there to help. No one.

There. There is a stable. I'll lose them through it.

The pleasant, earthy smell of hay mixed with the stench of animal dung makes breathing even more difficult. Hiding in a stall, I peer out to see if they have followed.

No one is there.

The rope. I'll need the rope.

Running out through the back of the stable I grab the rope. No time to think now; later, when I'm safe.

My feet are torn and bleeding. All I can feel is the pain. I can't stop running. I must get away. They're still there. I know they are, even though I can't see them. I hear them. Their chanting echoes in my ears.

"You! You!"

They're there. I know they're there. All around me, pointing their bony fingers.

Outside the city now. That way, through the olive grove. That's the way to escape. The brush and small trees will hide me.

Sharp branches and thorns tear at my skin. So much blood. I'm tired. But no stopping. I must run; must disappear among the trees. I still hear them. Their anger and hatred stings like burning arrows piercing my back.

Oh God, I'm so tired. My legs are numb with the pain. Fatigue invades my bones, making me weaker. But I must escape.

My face is covered with dust and blood, mixing with the sweat that is burning my eyes. My head is splitting. And the voices, those damned voices are still there, getting louder.

I must get away. There's a turn in the path, an exposed root.

"Oh, no!"

The fall rips the breath from my lungs. As I scramble to my feet, I stumble and fall again. Screaming in agony, I know I can't stop. I must get away from them. Staggering through the heavy undergrowth my mind reels. My vision blurs.

Rest. My body cries for rest. Pain screams from every muscle, every joint and the voices get louder.

The acrid, almost antiseptic smell of the olive grove digs into my nostrils. It's a comforting, cleansing odor.

There. The tree. Now I see my escape. It's the only way.

As I climb on the stump, I look back. Curse them, why are they still after me? I don't see them, but they're there. I know they are. Why won't they show themselves?

"Stop it," I scream. "Stop it. Leave me alone. I didn't mean it."

I must be free of them. Throwing the rope over the branch, I know it's the only way out. No one will blame me. It's my absolution.

The rope feels rough on my neck, rough yet comforting.

This is it … my way out … a way to quiet those cursed voices, the pounding in my ears.

Jump!

Seconds of uncertainty followed by the jerk of reality. Struggling to get free, but … "No, don't struggle," I tell myself. "This is the means of escape."

The pounding is still in my ears, the fire in my lungs, but the voices are fainter now. Fainter even yet. The light is fading, too.

Finally, yes, the voices are gone!

I've done it. I've escaped … at last. No more struggling.

Calm approaches. A warm, comforting darkness envelops me like a soft, warming blanket … but … there's no air. I can't breathe.

Choking, gasping for even a breath of air

"Can't breathe," I try to yell.

Something's wrong. It's too dark. The voices, they're returning. No. No. Not again. No.

Please, no! Oh God …

CHAPTER 1

Thomas Edward Garrett III struggled to awaken and found himself in a cold, inky blackness ... as black and chilled as the last feelings of death that lingered from his *oh, too real* dream. Straining his eyes, not really sure where he was, he tried to focus on something, anything, but he might as well have kept his eyes shut.

In those first moments of disoriented consciousness, the fear that gripped his chest and left him gasping for breath assured him that death was imminent. The moments that followed seemed like an eternity. He felt the icy fingers of death slip around his heart and begin squeezing the life from his body.

"A dream. Only a dream," he told himself as he struggled to move his arms. "Yes. Only a dream," he said aloud as he began to feel the life awaking, but he felt his neck just to be sure.

"Thank God." Softer, "just a dream."

As he moved to turn on the bedside light, he felt the soaking wet bed sheets. His body was wet and clammy; his hair, wet and matted to his face and head. It may have been just a dream but at this moment Garrett wasn't all too sure.

He groped for the light on the bedside table, knocking papers and books to the floor. Cursing, he managed to find the switch. The metallic click echoed through the room. The shaded light cast a warm, somewhat comforting glow, reducing the inky blackness to shadows.

"God, what a nightmare," he heard himself say aloud.

His tongue, feeling like a clump of wool, moved sluggishly in his dry mouth. Stumbling into the bathroom, he yanked on the cold-water faucet, splattering water everywhere.

Garrett didn't care.

The shock of the icy water on his face helped to shake the lingering effects of his brush with death, albeit through his dream. Pausing, somewhat more awake, he looked in the mirror and groaned.

"Jesus Christ, Garrett. Look at yourself," he said loudly, "you look like hell. Ashen face, bloodshot eyes, those overnight bags under your eyes. You look awful. Get hold of yourself. Good God man, it was only a dream."

The words did little to shake the sense of death that lingered deep in the core of his being. Every nerve in his body was alive as if charged with tiny electrodes. His hands trembled like they would had he awakened from a three-day drunk. Shaking his head to clear the haze that clouded his thinking, he gulped down some water from his cupped hands.

God! My throat hurts, he thought.

"Hope I'm not getting a cold," he said aloud, an effort to find some plausible reason to the lingering dread of the all too real dream.

He splashed more water on his face and walked back into the bedroom. His bed looked particularly uninviting even though it was still an early morning hour. Knowing that continued efforts to go back sleep would be futile, Garrett slipped into his jogging shorts and t-shirt. It was 4:30 a.m. as he made his way downstairs and into the cool autumn morning.

Jogging down the uneven cobble stones of Church Street brought back momentary flashes of his dream. An early morning fog hung closely to the light along the street shrouding their attempts to pierce the early morning darkness. The filtered rays cast a surreal glow to the street, its buildings and the entire setting. Even the smiling military faces painted on the fire hydrants along Church Street took on the menacing look of some evil militia.

"Shit! I thought I left this place in my dream," Garrett's words echoed off the silence, as he hurried his pace leaving Church Street.

His normal jogging route took him down Church Street to South Battery. He always ran around White Point Gardens at the Battery, past the old Fort Sumter Hotel and up onto the top of the Battery wall. It was there that he was able to inhale the fresh, ocean breeze. Yes, there was the faint smell of the marshes, an odor that visitors often referred to as the stink of Charleston, but to him and most of the Charleston population, it was the fragrance of home. It always caused his brain to link his conscious mind to warm, nostalgic thoughts of his youth.

Ending his nostalgic pause, he continued his jog down the Battery wall to East Bay Street past some of the most beautiful homes in the city. History dripped from these magnificent structures. Their much-publicized ghosts could fill volumes.

Past Rainbow Row's multi-colored stand of three story houses, probably the single most photographed and illustrated feature of Charleston, pacing himself, Garrett's stride was still measured and consistent. Turning onto Broad Street, he passed an array of *old-line* attorneys' offices, miscellaneous buildings and St. Michael's Church. Finishing his morning jog with a sprint down Meeting Street to the South Battery and back to #13 Church Street, Garrett was eager to find his warm shower.

Only slightly winded, Garrett ran up the steps and opened the front door. Bounding up the stairs to his third floor living quarters, he made his way into the bathroom for a shower.

Fifteen minutes of stinging heat in the hot shower and the morning run helped Garrett feel more like himself. The cold bite that ended his shower cleared his head of most of the leftover thoughts of his dream. A vigorous rubdown with a rough towel released the tension from his stiff muscles and made him ready to face the new day.

But, try as he might, he was unable to shake the nagging memories of that horrible dream. Like a chill that reached to the marrow of his bones. Again, looking at himself in the mirror he said, "Dammit! It was just a bad dream. That's all. Just a bad dream." His voice trailed off in volume and confidence. "You've been working too hard. That's all. But that will change very soon. Very soon, my man. Very soon."

His voice changed as his confidence began to rise and a broad smile spread from ear to ear.

"Very soon, they will know about my treasure. Very soon, I'll have the respect I deserve. Then everything will change."

Garrett walked across his bedroom and stood at the window

that overlooked the Battery. It gave him a strangely titillating feeling, standing there naked, flashing the entire city, even though they couldn't see him. He posed, shifted, turned, then pressed his cheeks against the window glass. The chilly glass on his bare behind brought a quick end to his discrete exhibition. But, it was a statement, none-the-less.

The fall gardens of Charleston were almost as beautiful as the spring gardens. Looking down from his window he had a view of the back garden of #8 South Battery, now a bed-and-breakfast inn. In this section of town, the back gardens were often the more spectacular than their much-touted front gardens; that was true from Garrett's view.

Turning back to his room he caught sight of his reflection in the full-length mirror. At 43, he had kept himself in reasonably good shape. No bulging muscles accented his 5'10" frame but little excess baggage had found its way to his middle, either. Jogging, exercising and forcing himself to stay on a sensible diet were responsible for his present condition. His tendency to put on extra inches where they were least appreciated, especially since he was eating out more often, had become a major problem for Garrett. That, together with his passion for good food had resulted in many mental battles. For Garrett, logic customarily won out over passion.

He began to stare at himself in the mirror. He tried to find something unusual about what he saw. Something that made him special.

"Average," he said to himself, "simply average, John Edward Garrett, simply average."

His friends had told him that his deep-set, brown eyes with the intriguing flecks of glittering green and gold were his best feature. A straight nose accented his face, a little on the long side, but not too bad. The braces he'd hated so much as a teenager had done their job well. Lips, a little on the thin side, but again, not too bad. All in all, there was nothing about Edward Garrett that would make him stand out in a crowd.

"Average," he mumbled as he turned away from the mirror, "but that's changing."

Glancing at the still rumpled bed, a momentary twinge of fear shivered its way down his back. Striding purposefully across the room, he picked up his favorite robe. Slipping into the robe, he decided to begin his day with breakfast. Coffee, eggs and toast, maybe even some bacon.

"To hell with the diet, for now," he muttered aloud.

CHAPTER 2

As he waited for the coffee to perk, his mind drifted back over the years of his life. His list of acquaintances in Charleston was long and interesting, many politically and socially positioned. Garrett was, for the most part, considered an outsider. He was born in Charleston to a prominent orthopedic surgeon who, unfortunately for the younger Garrett, was originally from Boston.

Dr. Thomas Edward Garrett II had moved to Charleston with his young wife, Marlene, then 6 months pregnant with their first of many hoped-for children. Thomas Edward Garrett III was born in the same house in which he now lived and operated his antique store. Marlene didn't live to see her new baby. His birth had been too much for a fragile woman — she died only a few moments after Garrett's first cry of life.

Garrett's father did what he could to raise his young son. Early grief over the loss of his much-loved wife resulted in devoting more and more time to his practice. As years passed, this workaholic tendency had become a matter of habit that kept the two Garretts separated. An unexpressed resentment for the young boy was balanced, to some degree, by the elder Garrett's desire for his son to achieve as he had.

Edward Garrett was an average student, not interested in sports, and spent many hours daydreaming. This lack of achievement caused problems for his father. As a result, disappointment joined with the resentment to drive an even bigger wedge between the two. The young Garrett couldn't understand why, unlike his friends, he had no mother and little or no time with his father.

Garrett learned to be independent at a young age even though his father provided people to take care of him. Queen Ester, the rotund black housekeeper, a direct descendant of African slaves had retained much of her Geeche accent, lived in the basement. Robert Storey, the combination gardener and handyman, who was white but Geeche from the top of his curly head to the bottom of his flat feet, lived in the carriage house. They became his real family.

Queen Ester had taught him right from wrong, how to keep his room straight, and the polish of a "proper young man of Charleston heritage." She policed her training with a yard stick from the hardware store. Her training had proven valuable in the social circles in which he occasionally revolved.

Storey, on the other hand, had taught him some of the *earthier* things of life. Most of what he learned about sex and the opposite sex came via Storey's jokes, answers to his questions and Storey's wonderful collection of nudist magazines. It was through those magazines that Garrett got his first rudimentary road map of a woman's body. Storey was also the source of many of Garrett's superstitions.

With the elder Garrett's death, a little over fifteen years ago, Garrett's over-riding feeling was one of regret. Not regret at losing his father but regret that he had never measured up to his father's expectations. It was a cross he continued to bear without recognition.

Dr. Garrett had seen to it that his son did the proper things to be accepted as a part of the Charleston society. He was sent to Porter Gaud, the *proper* military and educational prep school. Garrett had been accepted and attended the Citadel. He had hated the tough, military discipline and lack of personal independence and had dropped out after only one year.

He finished his business degree at the College of Charleston, the other socially accepted institution of higher learning in Charleston. Nonetheless, he was never really accepted in the social circles since there weren't three generations of his family in the Charleston Social Registry, a fact he knew and tried to dismiss as unimportant. But, it still nagged him even today.

He could never accept nor understand a social structure where lineage was more important than individual success.

A good antique business had kept him much more than comfortable. It allowed him to travel abroad three or four times a year and keep hours of his choosing. Antiques may be the only thing he shared with his father. Both relished their deep love for antiquity. But even that had not developed into an area of mutual respect prior to Dr. Garrett's death. It was only a source of competition.

Garrett loved his antiques and the antique business as well. The quality, workmanship and craftsman's pride was obvious in each of his pieces. As Garrett had often explained his theory to customers, a part of the soul of the craftsman went into each handcrafted piece and remained there. It was something intangible that no mass-produced item could have. Each antique had a history. A stability that was also lacking in modern furniture, art, buildings, or people, for that matter.

He often caught himself fantasizing about the history of a particular piece. *What stories could it tell? Who had owned it? What were they like?*

Garrett's antique business was successful primarily due to his hard work and careful selections and his understanding of the tastes of the Charleston bluebloods. As a result, his clientele read like the Charleston social register. The Pringles, the Ravenels, the Tradds, the Pinckneys, the Heywards, the Petigrus to name only a few and many others whose fortunes had long since been exhausted.

Charleston was a place where living in the past was not only practiced but unquestioningly accepted. He had often rented antiques to "socialites" for their galas so they could keep up appearances — many of them he had bought from them - another discreetly and socially accepted practice. Garrett furnished them what they needed, yet rarely received invitations. He wasn't sure he would attend even if invited. However, it damn sure would be nice to have the satisfaction of turning them down.

CHAPTER 3

The warming rays of autumn sun splashed into the kitchen and along with the pungent odor of freshly-perked coffee, interrupted his daydreaming. His mixture of coffee and cinnamon sticks added a sweetness to the scent that he liked. As if on cue, the prepared coffee set Garrett into motion. Today was to be a big day and only breakfast stood in the way of his exploring the treasury he knew was there.

Eggs and bacon were cooked in the same pan. "What the hell. They'll be mixed up in my stomach," he thought. He finished eating and stuffed the soiled dishes in the dishwasher. Looking out the kitchen window he saw the siennas, ochers and browns had begun to replace the pinks, reds and greens of spring and summer.

Sunday morning's lazy pace had its grip on the Charleston denizen as it did on most Sunday's. Today would be different for Garrett, however. All over town, people were moving about their normal activities and not one single person knew about his treasure.

"If they only knew," he mused aloud, "if they only knew."

As he slipped into jeans and an old sweatshirt, Garrett went over the events of last evening in his mind ... again. Fate had finally stepped in and smiled with favor on him. He and Storey had been busy digging in the basement to make room for the new vault he was going to build. They had accidentally opened an underground room. He and Storey had been doing the work, themselves, to save money. And then, this. They had no idea what they had found.

For his part, Storey wouldn't enter the cave-like room — full of "haints," he said. Garrett had told him later that there was nothing of importance in the earthen cave; just some old boxes with junk and broken dishes in them. Worthless, he had said.

But what a find!

How long had the room been there? He could only imagine. As the day unfolded he found the trove was full of old trunks and aging wooden boxes. All the items pre-dated the Civil War. Some were certainly much, much older.

One of the smaller trunks was full of gold coins, mostly Spanish doubloons. Another larger trunk contained silver coins. There were other chests, some large, some small, some full, some empty. One unusual greenish chest looked like wood but felt like stone. Since it was empty, it was put aside in favor of more interesting items.

Swords, daggers, and other metal weapons appeared to be in reasonable shape. Wooden relics had, for the most part, survived extremely well since the room had remained watertight.

There was a large number of silver antiques, trays, tea and coffee services, goblets and a variety of individual pieces. He noticed the coveted Revere hallmark on a number of pieces but most of the silver bore much older English hallmarks.

Because of the array of items and their age, the room had obviously been considered a safe place for family treasures during the turbulent years of Civil War Carolina. To fool the invading Yankees, groups of families often pooled their valuables and hid them to protect them from the looting that accompanied the invasion. For whatever reason, the owners had never returned to reclaim their treasures. As for Garrett, he was certain the Find would be the long-awaited vehicle that would carry him, not only to fame and fortune, but also to the acceptance he so desperately sought.

His years of experience and training guided him in his efforts as he began to retrieve, catalog and evaluate the items in "the Find," as he had begun to call his new treasure. Many of the items were easy to both identify and establish values. Many others, however, would require specialists to set their true values. He knew he would require some outside help but it was important that very few people know about the Find — certainly, no one in Charleston — except Lee, of course.

He would look for help from New York; London, maybe; Christie's or Sotheby's. He knew the credentials had to be impeccable.

That was for later, for now there was much to be done.

It was late afternoon before he stopped his fevered search of the precious articles. Lunch had been forgotten. Even at that, he had adequately catalogued only a small part. This was due partly to the large number of unique articles and partly to his short attention span. He acted more like a child on Christmas morning, jumping from one thing to another, than a well-trained professional taking inventory of valuable antiques.

Dirty and tired from so many hours of bending and being on his knees in the cramped room, Garrett crawled out and slowly stood. Stretching his knotted muscles, he suddenly remembered his luncheon plans with Ashley. He recalled the ringing of the phone while he was working on the treasure. Now, he was sure it had been Ashley trying to find out where he was.

For the moment, the present became more important than the past. Even with his call and a promise of a complete explanation at dinner, Ashley's tone left Garrett uneasy about his forgetfulness.

CHAPTER 4

Ashley Cooper Barrineau, or Lee as she preferred to be called, was accustomed to Garrett's somewhat eccentric behavior at times, but never had he been so inconsiderate. She knew plans could change, but no call? That simply wasn't at all like him. Surely there would be a good reason, just as he had said on the phone.

At 7:00 p.m. sharp, Garrett rang the doorbell. The ride to Poogan's Porch was short, but the silence was long and heavy. She noticed a guarded nervousness in Garrett that she had not previously seen in him. He was moody at times and that had caused them some problems, but tonight he was different. Could her father have been right after all? True, Garrett was a workaholic — self-centered, at times — introverted, but he had never been spiteful where she was concerned. He had always been considerate, loving. He was a little distant at first, almost shy. But she had sensed that underneath his aloof, erudite demeanor was a gentle and fun-loving heart that simply needed a little encouragement to break out of its shell. And she had been right; at least she thought she had been.

She had argued with her father.

"Something's not right," he had said. "He's never fit in. Neither did his Yankee father. And remember, he couldn't cut it at the Citadel. A man would have stuck it out."

He always used the Citadel argument. He would never accept her feelings that Garrett was a sensitive, caring person. Her argument that Garrett's choosing not to put up with the crap at the Citadel did not lessen his manliness fell on deaf ears.

Her father would merely chuckle and tell her, "Time will tell, my dear. Time will tell." Would she be wrong and her father right, again? She wasn't ready to face that.

Arriving at Poogan's Porch was a relief for both of them. Poogan's was an old house converted into a restaurant, as was the practice in that section of town. It was, however, deceptively large. The carriage house, servants' quarters and a courtyard had been connected to the main house and served as additional restaurant seating.

Entering the glassed-in front porch from which Poogan's Porch got its name, was like entering a tropical garden. Tom Bass, *Poogan* to his friends, had quite a green thumb and he tended the plants personally. Many guests preferred seating at the tables artistically-placed among the plants on the porch.

Because the people at these tables were the first seen, Garrett preferred to be seated in the Grand Room. Service was better, he had often said. He began requesting a particular table in the Grand Room. It was in the back corner, across from the main entrance. From there you could see everyone entering the restaurant, and be seen as well. It soon became known as his table among the help at Poogan's, and Tom Bass took note and arranged to seat him there whenever he made reservations.

Bass had furnished the restaurant with top quality antiques, many on loan from Garrett's shop. Other than the Grand Room, there were five rooms in the main house for serving meals; the Formal Parlor, the Sitting Room, the Dining Room (often used for private parties) the Music Room, and the Library. The Carriage House and Servants Quarters boosted the seating capacity to well over 200. All the rooms were, however, tastefully decorated and comfortably arranged.

Poogan's was one of Charleston's better-known restaurants. Like Robert's, Perdita's, Henry's or the Marketplace; but it was quiet, the food was good and the service excellent. In addition, Garrett was treated as if he were the very best customer, and he liked that very much.

"Tom, good to see you," Garrett greeted Bass with a warmth reserved for few people other than Lee.

"Mr. Garrett. It's good to see you as well and I am pleased to see you here. Good to see you again as well, Miss Barrineau. I'm afraid we have people sitting at your table. I'm sorry, we didn't expect you tonight," Bass wanted to leave his message without alienating a good customer. "I believe I have an ideal substitute, however. It's quieter and out of the rush of the main dining area. How's this?"

"It's just what I wanted, Tom. We wanted some privacy tonight, anyway," Garrett assured his friend. "This will be just fine."

"In that case, I'll see that your order is taken immediately and I won't seat anyone else in this room," Bass said as he bowed slightly and left the table.

Garrett was about to stop Bass and tell him it wasn't necessary for that much privacy but the gesture made him feel important. And, for him, tonight was a night to be important.

"William! Hurry into the Library and take Mr. Garrett and Miss Barrineau's selections for dinner and please make sure he has the utmost privacy tonight." It was Bass's voice Garrett heard from the other room. William was the oldest employee at Poogan's Porch.

The white-haired black man had been a waiter for as long as Garrett could remember. Garrett's father had said that William was the best waiter in the state. The elder Garrett always asked for William when he took his son to eat at Henry's Restaurant before he joined Tom Bass at Poogan's.

That's where Garrett first remembered William, at Henry's. How long ago was it? Thirty years. Garrett was nine. It was his ninth birthday. It was his first "adult" birthday party. His father had selected Henry's. Garrett was allowed to invite 14 of his school friends. Only ten came. Now he didn't even remember who they were but he did remember William.

All evening long he was called *Master Garrett* by William. (Not *Edward* like his father and friends called him.) It was William that brought the biggest birthday cake Garrett had ever seen. He smiled. It was funny, he could remember William and the cake even though he had forgotten the names of his friends who shared the evening.

It seemed that, from that day on, William had played a role in Garrett's life. Throughout his youth, Sunday was the servants' day off. Dr. Garrett would take his son out for the noon meal every Sunday, usually at Henry's. William always did something special for Garrett. Cookies with his ice cream. Candy bunnies on Easter. A cake on subsequent birthdays. No one ever told William when the special days were. At least no one as far as Garrett knew.

The ritual continued until Garrett went off to the Citadel. It wasn't until after Dr. Garrett died that Garrett found out that his father had arranged for all these little extras that he credited to William. Still, William remained a special person to Garrett. He was the only black at the Elder Garrett's funeral. Garrett wanted him to sit with the family, but William elected to sit in the last pew. William had lived his entire life in Charleston. He knew the old ways had not died in the city. It was his preference not to cause his friend any embarrassment by sitting in the front of the church.

"Good evening, Mistah Garrett. How are you and your lady tonight?" It was William's slow, soft voice that brought Garrett back to the present.

"Fine, William. Just Fine." Garrett answered William's question without thinking.

"You remember Louis, don't you, Mister Garrett." William was gesturing to the younger black man assisting at the table. Louis, filling the water glasses, was William's youngest grandson and currently an apprentice waiter at Poogan's.

"Why, yes, William. Of course I remember Louis. How are you, Louis? I see that you are following in the steps of your grandfather." Garrett was talking as he noticed that Louis was not as thorough as William in his attention to the details of a properly presented table. William, however, made the adjustments making the table perfect.

"Andre' will be here with the wine list in a moment, but, if I may, let me suggest the Red Snapper steaks tonight. Chef has prepared a new dill and hot sauce. From what I hear, it should be quite good." Garrett knew that William's suggestions usually turned out to be worth taking.

"Certainly sounds good to me, William. How about you, Lee?"

Ashley's preference was poached oysters but she smiled and agreed with Garrett's choice. This would be a time to listen, she told herself.

"That makes it unanimous, William. It's the snapper for both of us. Andre', nice to see you again." Garrett had turned his attention to the wine steward. "Tonight is special. Bring a bottle of your best champagne."

"Very good, Mister Garrett," replied Andre' as he left the table. "I have an excellent bottle of Dom Perignon. A very good year."

Andre's choice was far from the house's best champagne, but Garrett's reputation for frugality was well known in the restaurant. The last thing Andre' wanted to do was to cause a problem with the owner, Tom Bass, by bringing the $800 bottle. To do so would mean certain dismissal.

With the table set to perfection, the water poured, the champagne ordered, the awkward silence that had accompanied them to the restaurant had returned. Seconds seemed like hours. Andre's return with the champagne was a relief. The bottle was opened and served with Andre's usual flourishes. Two glasses properly poured, Andre' excused himself.

"To fame, fortune, and the future," Garrett's toast followed a few more seconds of the awkward silence. As he spoke he hesitantly picked up his glass and extended it toward Ashley.

"To answers and explanations," Ashley shot back without touching her glass, her voice showing far more of her anger than she had intended. "Listen to me Edward Garrett. I want to know what's going on. I called you today. And called and called. I know you were home. I drove by. Your car was parked out front where you always park it. You didn't come to the door when I knocked and you had the dead bolt on the door so I couldn't even use my key. We had a date for lunch, I'll assume you forgot since I had no phone call. I believe an explanation is in order. Not some meaningless toast. I can't remember you being so damned inconsiderate. I tried to make excuses for you, but now I'm just plain mad."

Garrett took a quick sip to clear his throat and set the glass he had awkwardly been holding back on the table. He launched into his story of Saturday night's find. Ashley listened quietly as much from relief as from interest. She was amazed. She could not remember Garrett being so excited, not even during their bedroom activities. He was so excited he looked like he had just found the long-lost map to Atlantis.

His excitement was contagious. Soon Ashley was engrossed in

his descriptions of some of the items in the Find, especially the silver pieces bearing the Revere hallmark. Happiness had replaced the question marks and anger from before. To Garrett, he wasn't sure what he had seen in her eyes during the earlier part of the evening; he was now sure that the beautiful spark had returned.

"You must promise me, Lee," Garrett pleaded. "You can't tell anyone. Alright? Not until I'm ready."

"OK, Edward," she agreed, "but you must realize that if this is what you say it is, it could be your big chance. But you must play it right. After all, you've always said you wanted the opportunity to prove to the Charleston establishment. This could well be your chance."

"I know, Lee. And you are right. I want this to be perfect in every way. I'm sure there are real treasures in that hole. Treasures beyond belief. This is my chance to make your father and his *yacht club* buddies notice I'm here. And, it's an opportunity to show those ne're-do-well socialites that I deserve a place in this city's social structure, no matter how many generations of Garretts have lived here. And the others, all of the others, I'll show them."

It had always seemed exclusionary to Garrett that membership in the yacht club required someone to have three generations born in Charleston. He knew he was as good as any of them; better than some. It wasn't until Ashley had caught Garrett's attention with a finger to her lips that he realized he had raised his voice well above his normal talking level.

"I'm sorry. I guess I'm a little excited. But not a word to anyone, alright, Lee."

His insistence made her promise, and he seemed to calm down, somewhat. Their conversation drifted back to the Find and to individual pieces Garrett remembered. His memory was like a picture book. He described many items in great detail. He strained to keep his voice low.

Garrett had always had a reserved air about him. When they first met she considered it to be shyness. But she detected more, she thought. It seemed to be a conscious effort on Garrett's part to exclude people from becoming too close to him. She noticed it the first night they met. In fact, it was the reason she had refused to see him after their first date. She had considered him one of those persons it was easy not to like.

He had persisted and she had seen time change him, at least where she was concerned. It was almost like he was afraid of people. She hadn't been able to find out why. He wouldn't talk about it. But, there were occasions when Lee could feel the hatred almost oozing from Garrett. Especially during confrontations with someone from the old Charleston society.

She knew Garrett felt he was unfairly excluded. But, as one of the insiders, she knew that he had been accepted far faster than others she knew about.

Still, it wasn't enough for Edward Garrett. He was an accepted member of Charleston's business community and, as of late, he was invited to most of the social events. It was Garrett who usually failed to accept. Maybe he had not been afforded the same courtesies as someone from a family that had been a part of the city for many generations. But then, much of Charleston's society had been more concerned about a person's family three or four generations back than the modern-day representatives.

She had observed this at an early age and she didn't like it very much, but it was still a fact of life. Garrett, on the other hand, never seemed to accept this, no matter how many times she tried to explain.

Maybe 'the Find', as he called it, would change things for him, she thought.

William's return to clear the table and suggest dessert brought Ashley back to the present and ended Garrett's description of the Find.

"The pecan pie is especially good, tonight, and so is the cheese cake, Miss Ashley," William suggested. "The special topping for the cheesecake is strawberries in vanilla brandy sauce," he added.

"No thanks, William. We must watch our girlish figures." It was Garrett's feeble attempt at humor. Neither William nor Ashley bothered to laugh. "Just the check, please William," Garrett mumbled after a short agonizing pause.

As William left the table, Garrett turned to Ashley.

"It's still early, Love. Let's go back to the store, you can see the Find for yourself and maybe there'll be some time to play hide-the-baloney," Garrett smiled, anticipating some bedroom fun.

"Keep it up with your crude humor in public and I'll tell you where you can stick your baloney, and I don't think it's where you had in mind."

Before Garrett could pursue his point, William returned with the check. As they were leaving the restaurant, Garrett again pressed Ashley.

"#13 Church Street?"

"Not tonight, Edward. I'm exhausted. You're exhausted. I'm sure it'll all be there tomorrow. I have an early breakfast with the editor and the Washington bureau chief at the newspaper. I must be rested, you know what a pain the D.C. guy is. I'll be at your place tomorrow at six o'clock with sandwiches. We'll make an evening of it, in the basement and the bedroom, ok?"

Garrett started to argue, but thought better of it. Lee was right. A good night's sleep would do them both some good.

"I only hope I can sleep tonight," Garrett's feeble try for a little sympathy was wasted on Ashley. Since she didn't answer him, he continued to himself, "No dreams tonight, I hope."

It wasn't until he got home that he realized just how tired he really was. Between the Find, the dream and Sunday's search of the treasure, he only had three hours sleep in the past 38. He was tired. He longed to have Ashley in his arms but, *After all*, he thought, *as Scarlet O'Hara said, tomorrow is another day*. And, with that thought, he snuggled into his bed. The cold sheets sent shivers through his body. He began to think warm thoughts, the beach, the warm sun, Ashley. With the thought of Ashley, he began to recall their first meeting, awkward and yet so wonderful.

CHAPTER 5

It was her beautiful blue-green eyes. They reached out and grabbed him, even from across the room. Those eyes could look right through you, seemingly reaching into your very soul. They could nail you to the wall or melt you with a single glance. Hazel-green, ringed by a halo of aqua-blue, flecked with gold that appeared to flash with reflected light. Her eyes were haunting. He learned later that they would change colors depending on her clothes, room colors, her mood, even the season of the year.

It may have been her eyes that caught his attention, but it was this aristocratic lady's body that caused him to break from his self-imposed shell of no involvement. However, it was her openness, her lust for life, her adeptness with people (all the things he lacked) that had made him consider a lifetime commitment.

There was something about her, everyone agreed. An aura. A feeling. A presence. Something. Some of his acquaintances had told him — almost warned him. Ashley had broken more hearts, they said. Mostly theirs, Garrett later found out. Garrett didn't listen.

Not breathtakingly beautiful, she was short, well-proportioned and athletic. Her straight dark hair framed an elongated oval face. A saddle of freckles hung subtly across the bridge of her nose as if cinched to her high cheekbones. She looked at home in jeans, but wore formal clothes with an easy grace that left little doubt that here was someone well accustomed to the demands of social entertaining. Someone from a family of wealth and position.

Although Garrett had tried to picture her at the obligatory social debut, he was sure she would have looked much more at home astride her roan stallion than all decked out in lace and silk.

Garrett relived how hard it had been to ask her out that first night. She was so young and could have been with anyone she wished ... always the center of attention wherever she went. He was much older, 13 years, at least. Age differences had never mattered to Ashley. She was vivacious and open — he quiet and reserved.

It had been at a political fundraiser for Mayor Pinckney's re-election effort. It was hosted by Ashley's father, Senator Bradley Cooper "Brad" Barrineau, *the Senator* as his friends called him, mostly to his back. As the ranking state senator, Brad was second in political power to the Governor. Because of his Chairmanship of the purse-string holding Ways and Means Committee, he was considered by most to be more powerful, in the areas that mattered, than the Governor.

Garrett hadn't planned to attend. Most social functions were boring to him. They were attended by people he disliked, people who handled themselves with ease in groups, unlike Garrett. People who were accepted in the Charleston social structure, unlike Garrett. But on this occasion, Mayor Pinckney had called with a personal invitation and he was a good customer. So, Garrett accepted. Maybe it would be good for business.

Ashley was there, of course, even though she maintained to her close friends that she was bored lifeless by all the brouhaha that was politics. That night she looked anything but bored.

On most social evenings, the Senator was seen in the company of his daughter, rarely in the company of Mary Ellen Boggs Barrineau, his wife. The commonly held story was that Mary Ellen and the Senator had long ago acquired separate bedrooms. With much of the Senator's love focused on his pride and joy, Ashley, Mary Ellen had a sort of self-imposed incarceration in their home on the South Battery. She had even dropped out of most of the clubs and associations that had been much of her life. Mary Ellen now spent most evenings with her close friend, Jack Daniels. That's how it was the evening in question.

Men hovered around Ashley like drones around a queen bee,

each vying for a smile of acceptance, a touch of recognition. For almost an hour, Garrett watched with growing admiration as Ashley treated each man as if he were something very special. In her own way, she made each one feel important to her, but most of all, to her father.

He watched her. She was so beautiful, so self-confident. She moved from one group to another with such grace. Ever smiling, ever witty, and just a little bit bold and flirtatious. He watched, discreetly at first, while he was talking to his customers and other acquaintances. He was certain, however, to keep her in sight as he, too, maneuvered around the large room.

He made no effort to talk to her. This frustrated him resulting in a number of trips to the bar. Maybe it was the alcohol that made him so bold. He began to stare. *She is beautiful. Everything a man could want, everything this man wants.*

He wanted to be with her, to talk to her, hold her. But he was afraid she would treat him like all the others, warmly but at arm's length. He couldn't handle that, he thought. After all, most of the other people at the party were more important to the Senator and as a result, to her. Garrett's obsession with Ashley kept him at the party far longer than he intended.

Maybe it was the extra alcohol, maybe not, but before he knew what was happening, a plan began to take shape in his all too inebriated mind. It was now or never he surmised. He turned to the bar, *for one final drink,* he thought. Gathering his courage and thoroughly fortified, he turned his attention back to the room only to find her nowhere in sight. His heart dropped. He had finally worked up enough courage to talk to her and now she was gone. Garrett turned back to the bar and scowled into his drink cursing his lousy fortune to himself.

"Mr. Garrett," the soft voice paused as he turned around. "That is it, isn't it?" The voice was light with a faint touch of huskiness.

"Yes?" Garrett turned quickly almost spilling his drink on the bar, and found himself face-to-face with Ashley Cooper Barrineau.

"I, uh, yes. That's my name. Edward Garrett," he managed to stammer.

"I know," she smiled doing her best to overlook Garrett's

ineptness. "I asked Mayor Pinckney. He told me who you were. I don't think I've seen you at these functions before. You've been staring at me for some time. What's the matter? Is my slip showing?" Ashley's tone was serious, but her eyes danced with mirth.

Garrett wanted to tell her that he had been totally taken with her beauty and grace — her sparkling eyes. He wanted to say that he would, very much, like to get to know her, make her laugh, as all the other men in the room seemed to be able to do with such ease. But, being glib wasn't one of Garrett's strong suits.

"I wasn't staring ... I mean I'm sorry if I was rude. I didn't mean to stare, actually, I wasn't really staring ... I," he continued to stutter.

"Oh, it's all right, Mr. Garrett ..."

"Edward," Garrett interjected.

"It's all right, Edward," she continued, "really. I didn't mean to infer you were leering at me or anything like that." The low-pitched laughter in Ashley's voice made Garrett feel even more uncomfortable. He would have given anything at that moment to have been transported very far away from Charleston.

"I understand you sell antiques," Ashley began, noticing how uncomfortable Garrett was; empty glass shifting from hand-to-hand, unsteady voice, eyes not quite meeting hers. Ashley was adept at handling awkward situations and even more skillful at making whoever she was talking to feel as if they had known her for years.

Even with all the people milling around the crowded room, Garrett had been remarkably easy to single out. He seemed to be the only person having a truly miserable time. She couldn't really say what first drew her attention to him. He was certainly nothing special to look at, although his face held an unusual sort of attractiveness. His staring had begun to annoy her. At first, she was convinced there was a challenge in that stare. And Ashley Cooper Barrineau was not one to back away from a challenge.

Ashley's question about his antique business flooded him with a sense of relief. At least it was a topic he could talk about with her and talk he did. For the next half hour Garrett had a captive, yet willing audience. At various times, he realized he was doing most of the talking but that didn't matter to him. All that mattered was that she was there; listening to him, smiling. Her well-placed questions served to fuel his monologue. She seemed anything but bored. He could tell from some of her comments that her knowledge of antiques was more likely a result of a true interest.

"Would you like to stop by the store, sometime?" Garrett asked, half expecting a polite, yet unmistakable, refusal.

"I think that would be nice, Edward."

Garrett could not believe his ears. Ashley Cooper Barrineau, girl of his dreams this evening had just said yes.

"I would love to see your shop. #13 Church Street; that's the name, right. Isn't it?" she asked.

"That's it. #13 Church Street and the address as well."

"Are you open tomorrow?" she asked.

"Certainly, till 5:30, but if you'd rather you could come a bit later, say 6:00. I'd be glad to pick you up." Garrett was surprising himself with his boldness.

"I appreciate the offer, but that's not necessary. I'll stop on my way home from the newspaper then. Six o'clock, it is." Ashley smiled and was about to say something else when the Senator called to her from across the room.

"Please excuse me, Edward." she began, "I'm afraid I've been neglecting my duties as hostess. I've enjoyed talking to you. You're quite a fascinating man. Thank you for saving me from a totally boring evening," her voice had dropped to a conspiratorial whisper and with a happy smile she moved toward her father, "See you tomorrow," she called after her.

As she walked to her father's side, Garrett smiled. He had been anything but perfect, and yet, he was delighted with how the evening had turned out. He was very pleased with himself as well. That was three years ago.

CHAPTER 6

Morning arrived for Garrett with warm, bright sunshine streaming in his bedroom window. The bedroom of the house at #13 Church Street seemed to vibrate as the sunbeams danced off shiny surfaces in the room. The dancing sunlight brought the room to life adding a warm, comfortable feeling to it and to Garrett.

He looked around the room. "This is going to be a good day. I can feel it," Garrett said aloud. Dreamless sleep left him refreshed and ready to start the day. He realized it had been almost a week since he last jogged the usual mile and a half around the neighborhood. It was unusual for him to break his routine like this, but this had been a couple of unusual days. Today was the day to start again.

Garrett slipped on his well-worn Nikes and his Boston Marathon t-shirt and shorts. A friend in Boston had sent him the t-shirt, but it made him feel good when other runners passed noticing the memento. Only a small deception, he thought.

He locked the house as he left for this morning's jog. He would soon find out that this was only one of many ways the Find would change his routine and his life.

The sun may have been warm in his room but the autumn's chill had begun to creep along the South Carolina coast altering the early morning temperature. Garrett considered changing into his running suit, but, he reasoned with himself that he was a man, he could handle a little chill. Leaving his front steps, Garrett jogged down Church Street towards the Battery. His side street was still in shadows, unwarmed by the suns rays. The cold piqued at his bare arms and legs.

It was only a short block but it made him appreciate the warmth of the more sunlit streets.

Like his bedroom routine, he jogged the route he had begun years before. Garrett found comfort in the routine.

Physically and mentally refreshed by the run and a warming shower, Garrett made a cup of hot coffee and prepared to start his day.

Time seemed to slip into slow motion for Garrett. The more he tried to concentrate on his antique business the more he wanted to be downstairs with the Find. He knew that others were aware of his dependence on routine, so he didn't want to call undue attention by adjusting his business routine. He didn't want to alert anyone, not until he was ready. So, work had to look like it was normal. The day dragged on. He could close the store, but, he reasoned, it must be business as usual at #13 Church Street for his good fortune not to be suspected. Plans on how to take full advantage of the treasure began to form in his mind as the hands on the many clocks played their slow-motion game of tag with each other. Nothing would be suspected.

Finally, the hands on the big grandfather clock assumed their position ... 5:30 p.m. had arrived and none too soon for Garrett. He was quick to place the 'CLOSED' sign in the window and lock the front door. He took the stairs to the third floor two at a time, changed into his 'grubbies' and bounded down to the basement room, completely forgetting about Ashley's impending visit.

Ashley arrived about 10 minutes after Garrett had engrossed himself in the Find. The unanswered rings of the doorbell left Ashley standing on the front porch for some minutes. She began to look around at the old house.

#13 Church Street was a beautiful old home. The architecture was definitely 'Old South.' But it had the faint overtones of a graceful Spanish mansion. The Desassure House, as it was called by the historic society, was built in the mid 1700's by Alexander Desassure, a wealthy rice & indigo plantation owner. Its colorful history knew no specific allegiance to the South or to Charleston, for that matter. It had served as a hospital for British troops in 1781-82 and as headquarters for federal troops in 1867.

The house had elegantly withstood two wars, an earthquake, a fire and numerous hurricanes. It had maintained the look of a stately matron who was the self- appointed representative of the family of many generations.

The family gardener, Robert Storey, had maintained the look of 'old Charleston' with well designed English gardens on both sides of the house. The Chinese garden in back was Garrett's addition. It had not made Storey happy to change his handy work but he had ... with some urging from Garrett. Now his pride and joy was the back garden. Tradition was almost as much of a god to Storey as was superstition.

Unlike many of Charleston's fine homes, the main level of Garrett's house was the second floor. The second-floor entrance made the house ideally suited for his antique business. #13 Church Street, he called it. One of his college marketing professors had said a business' name should be simple, easy to remember and help guide a prospective customer to it. What better name, then, than the address? It had seemed to work well and it also had helped Garrett get by the city's stringent signage and business codes in that area.

Three unanswered rings ... she used her key. She had refused the idea, at first, but having the key had come in handy on a number of occasions, like today.

Hand-carved, 14-foot-tall, teak wood doors opened into a large entry foyer. Garrett had positioned his display rooms on the second floor. Additional stock and lesser-priced items were placed in rooms on the first floor. Each of the second-floor rooms was decorated much as it would have been if it had been in a private home. The major difference ... everything was for sale. Although each room would be termed eclectic by definition, each did have a basic theme in both period and style.

As she entered, Ashley thought how perfect it was for Garrett to be in the antique business. His excellent taste and feel for presentation was evident in the placement of each piece. Each looked as if it were in its natural place.

She wandered through the rooms as she waited for Garrett.

The formal parlor, on the left, was a large and stately room. The major pieces of furniture were Louis XV and extremely expensive. Although far too gaudy for her utilitarian taste, not so for Garrett's more flashy clientele. He had found Louis XV was where much of his profit was made.

A tasteful and complementary "Oriental" rug formed the background against which the furniture was placed. Period chairs and a matching settee formed a conversation pit around the front of the fireplace. Glass and porcelain statues and other accent pieces dotted the cocktail table and side tables. A Louis XIV desk and matching chair, complete with period carved marble desk set and quill pen, was centered on the far wall. A variety of highboys and two chests were on other walls but, their placement was tasteful and logical. A tea caddy was on the right as she entered the room. The ornate hand-hammered silver tea service had been traced by its hallmarks to a silversmith in France and had been made around the same time as #13 Church Street was built. Paintings and a couple of French clocks completed the look.

Across the foyer was a less formal parlor. Furnished, mostly in Eastlake, the furniture offerings of this room were of a more reasonably priced nature. The accent pieces, however, were not. The simplicity and grace of the Oriental accents were greatly enhanced by the somewhat busy and angular setting provided by the Eastlake furniture. Color splashes were provided by the Oriental rugs and the Nauking and Peking glass, Jade carvings, cloisonné pieces and a large collection of netsukes. All-in-all the atmosphere was one of affordable warmth and subtle elegance.

Queen Anne furniture was reserved for the formal dining room. The graceful curves of the dining table and chairs made an ideal surface for a setting for 12 of R. S. Prussia dinner wear in the "Four Seasons" pattern. Garrett had told her that the dinnerware was the most valuable presentation in the room. Two of the 11" serving bowls were valued at almost $5,000 each, the entire set well over $100,000. Garrett's price $195,000. He had picked it up from a yard sale at the house next door for $200. The red makers mark was the reason for the inordinate value and acted as a guide for connoisseurs. Corner cupboards and matching sideboards completed the furniture in the room.

The other rooms each included at least one major piece around which the room was decorated. The music room's centerpiece was a museum quality Chickering grand piano, but a collection of Regina music boxes usually drew the attention of most visitors.

Another room, probably a former study, was decorated as a bedroom. A large four-poster, tiger oak bed with matching chest and side tables were the only effort on Garrett's part to show American furniture. Their prices were lower than the European furniture and much less in vogue with the Charleston collectors. A number of rooms on the first floor contained a collection of American oak furniture for customers who wanted it. There was no need for Garrett to clutter his limited floor space with these less expensive items.

A number of rare Pairpoints gave warm, inviting light to the rooms while other accent pieces bore names like *Limoge, Lalique, Tiffany, Wedgwood.*

The rooms seemed to flow into each other. It made keeping track of customers simple for an unobtrusive observer and it helped encourage customers to completely tour the offerings of the floor.

Extremely valuable items, silver, gold, jewelry and the like were kept under lock and key in safes on the first floor. Only Garrett had access to this room and showings were by appointment only.

The sound of Garrett's footsteps on the stairs from the basement interrupted her tour.

"Lee, is that you?" she heard him call out.

"Yes, Edward. Were you expecting someone else?" She paused, when she got no answer she continued, "I was just walking around. You've made some changes since I was here last week."

"I had to do something today," he said somewhat sarcastically. "Time seemed to move as slow as a 'darky' in December."

Ashley ignored the racial comment. She and Garrett had had a number of discussions on the subject. She decided tonight was not the time for another argument.

"Come on upstairs," he said as he turned for the stairs to the third floor, "I've got to find some reference books in my study."

Garrett had been able to keep his living area totally separate from the business area of the house. He had graciously decorated his living area. Most of the furniture in his area were antiques as well. Some he considered permanent but most would be moved back down stairs and placed for sale when he tired of them.

He had made his parents room into an office and gallery that housed his valuable paintings and sculpture. His "private collection." It was the largest room in the upstairs. He had considered making it his bedroom but he felt more comfortable in the room he had had as a child. The focal point of the big room was his grandfather's large, S-curve, mahogany roll-top desk which Garrett still used. The bookcases on either side of the desk were filled with books on antiques. Research had been the key to Garrett's success. Much of what he knew about the business was from the hours he spent reading and his photographic memory.

The room had been divided through an interesting furniture placement. There were clear breaks establishing an office, a sitting room and a gallery. Paintings, however, lined all the walls of the room. Few people were ever invited into this room. What visitors there were to the third floor were usually entertained in the parlor at the other end of the hall. Formerly the Nanny's quarters, the room was easily converted to Garret's current use.

Paintings were Garrett's first love. He had been successful in selecting works of new, local artist before they became famous. Also, he had made a number of lucky finds in area yard sales and from dealers with less knowledge.

As he continued to look for the right books, Ashley wandered from the office/gallery to his room, down the hall. It, also, was a large room for a child's room. His re-decorating had removed all of the 'little boy' look from the room. Certain happy memories were retained, however, and embodied in an old train set and a few old model airplanes placed indiscriminately on a bookshelf.

The room was off white. Walls, ceiling, drapery, bedspread. The monotone background focused attention on the large brass bed and the roll-top desk that accompanied the bed. The lack of any kind of chest was obvious. It called attention to the only radical alteration to the old house. Garrett had taken one of the extra bedrooms and created a large dressing area adjacent to his bath. Everything was built into the walls. This one expression of modernity seemed grossly out of place, but it suited Garrett.

Ashley walked through Garrett's bedroom, a room she had come to know very well. She opened the French doors that led to the third-floor veranda. She had stood there many times before, looking out toward the Battery. She could see that the trees of White Point Gardens had begun to drop some of their leaves.

Others had completed their colorful metamorphosis, soon to cut loose their bonds and float earthward like a host of brown butterflies. Spring and summer had been so hot. She looked forward to winter and a change of temperature. She looked past White Point to the Charleston harbor and Fort Sumter. There, just beyond the jetties was the point where the Ashley River and the Cooper River come together to form the Atlantic Ocean. The thought of that old local saying brought a smile to her face.

From the veranda, she could see the back gardens of #13 Church Street. Like most of the other Charleston houses, the formal gardens were in the back of the house. Unlike most Charleston houses, Garrett's were of Oriental extraction. For this reason, his house was never featured on the historical society's annual Christmas garden tour. Storey had done a superb job with the gardens.

In addition to his garden responsibilities, he assisted in moving the antiques in the house and took care of most of the restoration. His quarters were in the carriage house at the back of the property. Its primary entrance was by way of the alley that divided the block by running parallel to Church Street. Although he had been considered a part of the family when Garrett was growing up, he had always kept to himself. Other than the two weeks of vacation he spent with some faceless family in Asheville, North Carolina, Garrett was aware of no social life engaged in by the illusive gardener. He liked it that way. The gardener was there and available from 7am to 8pm and rarely seen at other times. "Lee! Lee, where are you?" It was Garrett calling her name that brought Ashley out of her own thoughts.

"Out here, on the veranda," she replied.

"I didn't know where you were," he said, slipping his arm around her and hugging her close to him, "I must have called you a half-dozen times."

"I was just thinking how beautiful Charleston is in the fall. I really am happy to see fall come." Her voice drifted off into the resounding "clip clop" of one of the horse-drawn carriages that moved past the house on Church Street.

"The city is somehow warmer to me during the cold times of year. Charleston is a very warm city," she added.

"Yes, I know what you mean. I guess," Garrett was anxious to get back to the treasure and answered only to pacify her. He had never considered Charleston to be a warm city even when the temperature was over 100 degrees. But, at least for Garrett, other things were warming up.

"Let's go inside, there are some very special surprises for you," he added with glee.

They made their way down to the first floor of the house. Ashley stopped briefly on the second floor long enough to pick up the basket of food she had brought.

Garrett had cleared one of the rooms at the back of the first floor and had moved some of the uncataloged chests and boxes into it. Well over half the room was taken up. He had set aside certain boxes he wanted Ashley to see. It was fully an hour before they had gone through these special boxes. It wasn't until then that she mentioned the picnic meal she had brought. And it wasn't until then that Garrett realized he had not stopped since breakfast that morning. Food sounded good to him.

The sandwiches and wine, fruit and cheeses could have been organized by one of Charleston's greatest chefs and Garrett wouldn't have eaten any more voraciously. As they ate, Garrett looked at the beautiful girl/woman seated cross-legged in front of him. She was very much an enigma to him. As he looked, he let his mind wander over the many stories he had heard about this woman and the Barrineau family.

CHAPTER 7

Even though she was an only child, the relationship she shared with her father was one usually reserved only for male children. She had grown up placing major emphasis on masculine things. Her father, Senator Bradley Cooper Barrineau, was her strong role model. She had learned to hunt and fish while other girls her age were learning the finer points of being a proper lady. Her social graces and entertaining acumen had not suffered, but most everyone agreed, she was different.

She had little in common with her mother and saw little value in most of the things her mother considered important. She was down-to- earth and direct, like her father and took great pride in pleasing him. This single-mindedness as well as the similarities with her father caused frequent differences of opinion with her mother.

In most cases, Brad supported his daughter in these little tiffs adding to the widening rift between the two of them and Mary Ellen.

Garrett knew that Ashley Cooper Barrineau came from a long line of wealthy Charlestonians, but she carried few of the pretensions of the Charleston society. Her parents were not so disposed, however, especially Mary Ellen.

Mary Ellen Boggs Barrineau reveled in the social environment that was "old Charleston" from the time she was old enough to participate in it. She had become a member of the Women's Club, the Historic Charleston Society, the Hibernian Society, the Church League, the Music Society, Friends of the Ballet — it was safe to say that Mary Ellen was an active participant in every organization that counted. It wasn't unusual for her to hold offices in half a dozen of these clubs at one time. She kept herself busy to help ease the strain of an otherwise empty life.

Mary Ellen Boggs had spent most of her formative years competing against older siblings: two older brothers, the sons of which her father was most proud; an older sister, the beauty of the Boggs, as she was called; and a much younger sister, the much-pampered baby of the family. Because Mary Ellen had the misfortune to be born in the middle of three girls, she was often ignored by her parents.

As a child, she possessed no outstanding qualities or talents to get her noticed. Her childhood was spent mostly dreaming of becoming an adult. High school provided her first real stage on which to perform that all-important extra-circular activity: club membership.

She found she was a natural in this milieu. Conversation was light and rarely ever on subjects that required her to read or have an opinion. She made certain not to offend any of the other members. She was popular as a result. She dressed well with considerable help from the junior buyer at Boggs Department Store, the family business. In fact, it was through her father's business that she and Brad Barrineau met.

The Barrineau Law Firm handled all legal work for Boggs Department Store and most of the other profitable enterprises in Charleston, both public and private. The legal profession was the only acceptable career for the Barrineau men.

Mary Ellen met Brad for the first time when she accompanied her father to the Barrineau law offices. Brad was there visiting his father. He was a senior at the Citadel, co-captain of the football team, tall, good-looking and above all, a Barrineau. All it took was one look for Mary Ellen to fall "puddle happy" in love. A crush, her friends called it. After all, he was a college senior, she was only in high school. What possible future was there for such a relationship? Mary Ellen wouldn't listen — even though she rarely saw him, her world revolved with him as its axis.

Five years passed.

Brad returned a hero from Korea and began law school to carry on the tradition of the Barrineau barristers. Mary Ellen completed college, joined her father's business as a buyer and was recognized as an active member of many clubs and associations promoting Charleston.

The chance meeting at a beach party at nearby Isle of Palms would result in the fulfillment of Mary Ellen's dream, but not her fantasies. Each was there with someone else, but from the moment Mary Ellen saw Brad, she could think of no one else. In that casual atmosphere, she was able to maneuver herself to a group that included Brad. The same skills that made her a good club member aided greatly in her quest. She exuded a sort of open naiveté that attracted Brad. Although she was not as pretty as many who had occupied of the younger Barrineau's stable, Brad was attracted to the soft, pretty, open young lady.

She asked him what it was like to be a hero. He answered shyly, but his ego brimmed and his cup ran over. Her other questions resulted in Brad being the center of attention for most of the evening. He felt an entirely new level of personal importance with Mary Ellen around, although he wasn't sure exactly why.

It was a feeling he enjoyed — a feeling very close to power. Although they each left with their original dates, Brad had decided he wanted to spend more time with the young source of such ego building.

Dating quickly fell into a pattern for them — parties and group functions — at each, Mary Ellen provided the backdrop for Brad's performances. Sex, if one could call it that, for the adventurous twosome was confined to occasional wrestling matches in the back of Brad's '55 Olds. These encounters left Brad frustrated — Mary Ellen nervously embarrassed. With each new effort, Brad became more bold, Mary Ellen less restrained.

It was three months after the beach party. A solitary car parked at Lands End Point. A beautiful summer evening, the moonlight made the ocean shimmer like a large black hand filled with diamonds. First hands then lips meshed. Brad was more insistent than usual. Mary Ellen, more enchanted by the setting and the closeness of the love of her life. They shared the treasure she had kept intact for him. A part of her fantasy had come true. But, the back seat was cramped. She couldn't figure out what to do with her legs. Brad's haste made him less than gentle. Love was lost in passion and Mary Ellen had lost control.

Things ended much too fast. Although somewhat experienced, Brad had never made love to a virgin. The girls in Korea were different — they knew what to do, in more ways than one. Mary Ellen felt deprived. Her fantasy, her dreams seemed destroyed and she didn't know who to blame. Certainly not Brad, her Prince Charming. It must have been her, she told herself. She just knew she had lost him.

For days, Brad's calls went unanswered. Requests to see her were turned down. Finally, she went out with him. They walked on the beach and talked about their last evening together a month earlier. Brad's insistence that things had not changed between them made her feel better, still somewhat soiled, but better. They were together more often, but no more repeat performances in the back seat of the car. Weeks passed as the uncomfortable feeling of hurt and disappointment faded from the couple's happy time together.

The realization came in an odd way. Mary Ellen was walking through Boggs Department Store, much as she had a thousand times before. Upon entering the baby department, she stopped cold. "No!" she gasped. "It couldn't be." She had had no period for almost two months now. It hadn't crossed her mind that there might be a reason until now. *God, it just can't be true.*

Dr. Seeward proved her worst fears to be fact. One brief moment of carelessness would destroy her entire life, just like her mother had said. How would she tell Brad? What would he do? How could she face her family? Guilt and uncertainty dominated the rest of her week. Brad was in Atlanta on business.

Friday arrived as did Brad ... both too soon for Mary Ellen.

It was early morning before the reality of the situation sank in. Their talk had been stilted and strained. What could they do? Brad's future was at stake and now he had lost control of it. His initial suggestion was met with a shower of tears. He then assured Mary Ellen that everything was alright. He would do the right thing. But what would he really do?

"Get a hold of yourself," he told himself after he had taken Mary Ellen home.

"Sort it out and analyze it like you would a legal case."

He began to consider all facets of the situation. He wanted a political career. This could ruin it for him if he made the wrong choice. But there was, after all, a positive side. Mary Ellen was plainly pretty. She was fairly intelligent, carried herself well in a crowd, dressed well, and she was from a reasonably good family. She could be an asset. After all, his father had said that if you want a career in politics, you have to be willing to make some compromises. Maybe this would be one.

For the rest of the night and the next day, Brad weighed all sides of the situation. Saturday night, Brad met Mary Ellen for a dinner they had planned earlier. The stilted conversation of the previous evening carried over. Finally, Brad raised the topic uppermost in both their minds. For a list of "good" reasons, Brad thought they should get married as soon as possible.

It wasn't the perfect love affair Mary Ellen had dreamed of by a long shot, but the important part of her dream had come true. She would soon be Mrs. Brad Barrineau. Plans were made that night.

Brad told his father the entire story when he got home. The elder Barrineau saw through the problem to the potential. Mary Ellen was a much better politician's wife than those flashy girls Brad had dated. If flashy girls were what Brad wanted, he could have all he desired on the side if he were discreet, a situation Brad's father pointed out to him from personal experience.

Brad's mother got an abbreviated version of the story. Her innocent enthusiasm was catching and helped make the evening somewhat more festive. Weddings meant grandchildren to her, no matter how soon they were likely to arrive. Brad asked Mary Ellen not to say anything that evening. There was still the formality of asking for her hand — humorous as that may be, it was a formality. She agreed and Sunday afternoon, Brad met Mr. Boggs in their formal parlor and officially asked to marry his daughter. Although approval was a foregone conclusion, Mr. Boggs listened politely to Brad's request and gratefully accepted him as a soon-to-be member of the family. Mrs. Boggs was informed and the date set six weeks off. Mary Ellen pleaded with her mother for a small ceremony held right away, but Mrs. Boggs wouldn't hear of it. It would be the social event of the year. At least six weeks would be needed, if not more. Mary Ellen agreed, at least that way she wouldn't have to tell her mother of the events leading up to the marriage until well afterwards.

Invitations were mailed. Anyone who was anyone was invited. All the arrangements were made. A dress selected. Mrs. Boggs saw to it that this wedding would be an event to be remembered. After all, her daughter was marring a Barrineau.

As the day drew nearer, Mary Ellen became increasingly more apprehensive. Her morning sickness became difficult to hide and explain, but it did help keep her weight down.

The big day arrived, the event of the season. The dress was snug, but not obvious. Mary Ellen was radiant, Brad subdued. Both mothers cried. The reception at the Carolina Yacht Club lasted too long and Brad had too much to drink. On her wedding night Mary Ellen sobbed as Brad snored.

The happy couple settled into their routine shortly after the honeymoon, two weeks of soaking up the Caribbean sun, two weeks of satisfying Brad's desires with little attention paid to Mary Ellen's.

Six months later, Ashley was born. A seven-pound, six-ounce "premature" baby girl. Delivery complications would prohibit Mary Ellen from having the son Brad wanted so much, but she was determined to be a good wife, nevertheless.

There were other stories about Ashley's parents but Garrett accepted this one as probably true since he had heard it from a number of different sources. It would also help explain the relationship between Ashley and the Senator and the indifference of Mary Ellen. But it didn't matter. Ashley was considered to be his lady now and that was all that mattered.

CHAPTER 8

They continued to work for some time after their portable meal was eaten. It was largely Ashley's idea that they number each piece and use a page in the notebook for its description and a 3 X 5 card with the same number indicating its location. It was after they had gone through one pile twice that she had taken charge of the project.

Garrett was pleased. He was still so excited about the treasure that he might have spent hours cataloging the same items, over and over. It was also thanks to Ashley that he decided to take pictures of each item as it was cataloged. He recognized the value of the photos in evaluation only after he had lost the argument over how much it cost.

Eleven o'clock arrived far faster than either had expected. As they locked the door to the room that was the home of the treasure, Garrett asked Ashley to rub his shoulders for a little while. She agreed and the twosome returned to Garrett's bedroom. Ashley's soft yet strong hands soothed much of the tension that had been building in Garrett for days.

As the tension eased, Garrett's body began to respond to Ashley's rubbing in a more familiar manner. As she moved closer to him and they embraced, she recalled the feelings she had experienced early in their relationship. They had always seemed to fit so well to each other. His early tentativeness had been replaced by practiced artistry. Garrett had become not only accomplished but a good and gentle lover. Ashley had been a patient and willing teacher.

Tonight's lovemaking was tender and fulfilling for each. But as the hour approached midnight, Ashley decided, over Garrett's objections that, she would return to her bed tonight. She kissed him one last goodbye kiss and reassured him of her happiness with his Find. As Garrett slipped into his bed, the feeling of completing another good day nudged the tired from his body as the "sandman" tossed double-handfuls in each eye.

On her way home, Ashley began to analyze what all of this meant to her. At first, she felt only happiness for Garrett in his good fortune. But then, the importance of the Find became more evident. The Find could catapult them to heights even he could not recognize. This could be her way to show them all just how right her decision to date Garrett had been.

What had attracted her to him? At first, she admitted to herself, it was curiosity. She had seen him a couple times before the fund-raiser where they had officially met. But they had never talked. Their social circles may have been concentric but they never seemed to move in the same circle ... both growing up in Charleston.

That night, she was actively fulfilling her role as hostess. She knew she must spend an adequate amount of time with each and every guest. It was a role with which she was both familiar and completely accomplished.

She would have spoken to Edward Garrett, the antique dealer, much earlier had she not noticed him staring at her. At first, she was concerned that her slip or something else was showing. Assured she was properly attired, she decided to see exactly what this new admirer would do. Her years of hosting for her father had exposed her to almost every possible line and line reciter. She had a more than adequate level of experience in dealing with would be lechers in a most firm and friendly manner.

Garrett's lack of even a hint of practiced subtlety, assured Ashley that he would be easy to handle. So, she decided to play her favorite cocktail party game; at different times she had called it "What's My Line", "Blind Man's Bluff", "The Game of Life", and "Pick-up Chess." No matter what she called it, she was an accomplished player of the Game.

Even his early attempts to be unobtrusive had been obvious to Ashley. She began counting his trips to the bar. It soon became certain that to be remembered she would have to make the first move or she would be talking to a stiff. Even in his overly inebriated state, there was an open naiveté that made him different from most of her friends and suitors.

This curious meeting began an even more curious love affair. A love affair that had been questioned by her friends and her father. She was well aware that no one would meet her father's standards, but her friends' concerns that he was not a part of her world, not a part of the true Charleston had, at times, concerned her.

As she drove home that evening, Ashley secretly hoped that the treasure would be the "abracadabra" that would alter Edward's future. The key to his entrance to the society that readily accepted her and currently excluded him. And, her vindication.

CHAPTER 9

For Garrett, the rest of the week was a carbon copy of Tuesday. It was work as usual during the day and he and Ashley working late into the night cataloging, filing, photographing and placing the items. These late-night sessions fortified Ashley's hopes. The treasure contained some truly valuable collector's items. Items that, if properly organized and presented, would make Edward Garrett internationally known. A plan began to develop in Ashley's mind.

Garrett worked by himself Thursday night because Ashley had an engagement with her father. Very little was accomplished that evening because Garrett spent much of the time going back and admiring pieces he particularly liked.

Saturday morning, Garrett slept late. It was noon before he rose. A gray blanket was tucked under Charleston's chin. It draped the uppermost points of the Cooper River Bridge and hung off the foot of the slow-moving peninsula. Its silky edges submerged in the ocean. It totally kept out the sunlight and muffled the sounds of the city. It was a day for sleeping. There had been no rain, but it looked like it would, at any minute.

Ashley was involved with more family obligations, so Garrett decided this Saturday would be spent away from the Find and away from Charleston for that matter. He would drive to Columbia to see the new exhibit at the art gallery. The drive up was quiet and uneventful. The exhibit interesting.

Leaving the gallery, he walked into an old college friend. The invitation for drinks at a local club was accepted, and their reminiscing lasted longer that Garrett would have liked. It was already dark before he started home.

As Garrett's BMW settled into the arms of the super-highway that lay between Columbia and Charleston, the rhythmic thumping of the tires on the seams became more hypnotic than annoying. He almost dozed off three or more times. He was more tired than he expected. He was never more relieved when he drove up in front of #13 Church Street.

He didn't even take the time to call Ashley. Sleep descended almost immediately, but his sleep was light and he tossed and turned much of the night.

I told them, "If you think it best, give me my pay; but if not, keep it." So they paid me thirty pieces of silver.

And the Lord said to me, "Throw it to the potter"—the handsome price at which they valued me! So I took the thirty pieces of silver and threw them to the potter at the house of the Lord.

Zechariah 11:12-13

So they decided to use the money to buy potter's field (they called it Akeldama in their language, Field of Blood) and so it is called today.

Matthew 27:7
Acts 1:19

PROPHESY

It's dark outside, so unbelievably dark. As I peer through the slats in the shuttered casement, I can barely see the front gate only a few feet away. Nothing moves; everything sleeps, everything except me ... and them.

No moon tonight; a perfect night for thieves, curse them. I know they're out there. Lurking in the shadows. Waiting. Watching. Waiting for it to be my turn. The light from my small candle shines, bravely; maybe they'll know I'm still awake. Shadows of the unseen grow on my walls. I must put out the candle. Dark outside, dark inside — as it should be.

A twig snaps. Was it a twig? Or my mind finally snapping. I feel them nearer.

I huddle in the corner, covering myself with a blanket. The dark makes me cold. So dark. So cold. I can't even see the shadows now, but it doesn't matter. Nothing matters, anymore. They're all dead. My son, his wife, my grandchildren. Nothing matters, anymore. Time passes so slowly. How long have I been here, under this blanket; hours or minutes?

Something disturbs the night. Suddenly there are loud noises all around. Could it be the wind rushing through the trees, making the leaves crash together. The noises are loud and hurt my ears. Terrible demons fighting for the right to be the first to violate my home, my soul, trying to make me tell them where it is, forcing me to ...

"In the name of all that is holy, leave me alone," I shout at the top of my lungs. "Leave me alone."

What have I done? Silence has been my protection. Maybe they didn't hear me, I think. Maybe I only thought I screamed.

"You didn't scream," I tell myself. "It's only your mind —

you're an old man with an old brain — it's your mind playing tricks on you. That's all."

Safe, assured. Moments of silence follow. The fibers of the blanket begin to scratch and irritate my skin. It's uncomfortable. Is it time to come out of hiding? They're not out there, after all. It's late. I'm tired. Time to go to bed, get some rest. Maybe tonight I can sleep. So tired.

Cracking timbers crash through the silence. What was that? My mind? No. Thieves. It must be! They have broken in the door. They have come for me. I shrink into an even tighter ball under the blanket. Darkness fills my soul. I can hear them now. One gruff voice is giving orders. Then the sounds of pottery breaking, furniture being destroyed, my home begin torn apart. But, I am safe as long as they don't find me. The voices are closer now, but it's still dark and I'm still safe.

A blinding flash of light. A torch almost in my face. I can feel the heat from the flame burning my face singeing my beard. I can smell the sickening odor of burning hair, my hair.

The leader grabs, jerking me to my feet, shaking me like a child's plaything.

"Thought you could hide from us, did you old man?" he yells, his eyes burning like coals in the reflection of the torch, the stench of his foul breath almost making me retch. "Thought you could fool us, eh?" he laughs cruelly. "Where is it?"

"Please, don't hurt me. I'm old and I wish you no harm. Please, leave me alone," I plead with him.

"Hurt you? We will not hurt you, old one, not unless you refuse us." His face an inch away from mine; his breath, still foul in my nose; his thick fingers clutching at my robe, bunching it against my neck. "All we want is the money, the coins, where did you put it?"

Shaking me again and again, making me lightheaded. "I don't know what you mean, I have nothing of value, I'm poor and old," I continue to plead with him.

"Liar!" he screams, shoving me into the arms of one of the others. "Do you wish to die, you cursed old fool? If you do not tell us where you have hidden it, you'll beg me to kill you."

"Please, I know nothing of what you seek, nothing I tell you." I must convince him, make him believe me. Make him leave.

Cursing me, the leader orders the others to continue the search.

"Look old man, we will find the pieces of silver, I know they're here."

A wicked sneer spreads across his ugly face. Again he moves so close to my face that I can feel the stinking air rush from his mouth as he says the words.

"And when I find what I am looking for, I'll take great pleasure in squeezing all the life from your wretched old body."

The whispered threat sends chills through my body.

"Here! You see to him while I continue the search," he snaps to one of the band.

For the moment I am left in the care of one of the younger thieves as the others continue their search. His hold is not so tight, not so rough as the other's. I relax momentarily, but as the search continues, I know there is little chance of escape.

From the sounds, I know there will be little left of my house or my belongings. The noise and cursing continues for some time, then silence. The harsh, ugly one faces me again, grabbing me by my hair, forcing my head back — the pain blinding me.

"Listen, old one. Tell me where you have hidden the coins or I'll squeeze your scrawny neck until your eyes pop from your skull. You, with those devil eyes, one blue, one green. You cursed old fool. Where is it?"

"You have searched my house. I know nothing of what you want," I whisper, hoarsely. "Please leave me alone."

His hands slowly move to my neck. He curses me again and begins to squeeze. Harder, harder, his fingernails digging into my neck. The pain is unbearable but he will never find the coins nor the box that contains them. Never.

"I'll kill you, old man, if you don't tell me where they are," his voice hisses in my ear.

But I say nothing. He'll never know.

I can't breathe now. The room is growing darker. The noises fading. Did some of the torches burn out? I can't see his face. A cool, comfortable, flush sweeps through my body. His voice is only a soft whisper. His iron hands are still choking me and still he asks where it is. But he will never know, I will not allow the curse to be released, even if it takes my life. Even if I ...

Shivers racked Garrett's body; sweat soaked his face, ran into his ears, burned his eyes. Groaning, he slowly sat up in bed using the top sheet to wipe the sweat from his face.

"Oh, Jesus! Not again!"

Feeling a sudden overwhelming fear of the darkness, he quickly leaned over and turned on the bedside light. For one odd moment, he half-expected to be someplace else — an old stucco room — but it was his bedroom, nothing else. Certainly not the house of death in his dream.

His body felt like a limp, much-used rubber band as he struggled to stand up. He shuffled off to the bathroom and began splashing cold water on his face. *Just like last Saturday night,* he thought.

"What the hell is going on with me?" he asked the reflection in the mirror. "What the hell is going on?" he asked again, only softer as he buried his face in his hands.

Moments passed. He moved his hands from his face and again faced the reflection.

"Why am I having such horrible dreams? So damn real. Why do I feel as if I am these reluctant victims? Why?"

The first dream could be explained away as just a nightmare. But, now, he wasn't so sure about this one. Feeling completely drained, his brain a mass of questions, Garrett walked back into his bedroom and stood at the foot of his bed.

"Sleep! I've got to get some sleep," he said aloud. "Too much vodka. Yeah, that must be it, too much to drink." He was mumbling to himself as he crawled back into the bed. But not before he made a quick check of the room; what he was looking for, he had no idea.

"Go to sleep, Edward Garrett," he said aloud again.

Punching his pillow into a more comfortable shape, he glanced at the luminous numbers on the clock at his bedside. It was 3:00 a.m. He wanted to go right to sleep. But, no more dreams.

"Please, God! No more dreams."

CHAPTER 10

6:00 a.m. The harsh buzz of Garrett's bedside alarm clock jarred him from his short, restless sleep; not yet totally awake, not quite asleep. At first he didn't even recognize his surroundings. It was his room but the dull early morning light made the familiar things in his room seem gray and ghost-like.

Garrett clenched his eyes closed, not sure. *Is this a continuation of my nightmare?* The unrelenting sound of the alarm finally reached out and grabbed him. He again opened his eyes. With his conscious mind more in control, it was his room ... he was certain it was his room. This was not a dream. The lump of fear that had massed in his chest began to fade. He reached to turn off the alarm.

Aaaah, silence at last.

Slowly, Garrett made his way to the bathroom. A flick of the switch flooded the room with bright light. The intensity made him flinch. Squinting, his eyes grew accustomed to the brightness. He looked at the image in the mirror.

"We've got to stop meeting like this," his weak attempt at humor didn't make him feel any better.

He continued to stare into the mirror in a detached manner. It was as if he were out of his body looking at the pathetic home of a disturbed soul. Looking at the lines and bags that the past few weeks had been added to his visage. The paleness that had begun to take hold of his skin. A deep, dark color of foreboding that was lodged in his eyes. His body was showing signs of something that his mind wasn't willing to accept.

He continued to stare.

"What's the matter with you, Edward?" Garrett asked in

earnest and paused as if he expected the mirrored image to answer him.

"What's happening to you? You look awful. No sleep. Not eating. Nightmares. Are you totally crazy or just cursed? How much longer will this go on? Can this go on?"

More moments passed as he continued to stare at the face in the mirror. He was vaguely aware that there was something different about the face. Something he couldn't put his finger on.

Garrett continued to stare.

He concentrated his stare on his eyes. They seemed to be the source of the mysterious change. He had heard someone say that the eyes are the mirror of the soul. As he stared at his, he could believe it. He saw conflict, dread, worry, death and a complete lack of control in his eyes. Could all this be deeply locked in the recesses of his soul? It was a look of fear. A fear that had its grasp on his inner self. A grasp that ...

"Bullshit!" his angry voice shattered the silence. "This is bullshit, all of it. You're not crazy. You're just overworked. Christ, you're 43 years old." He was shouting at the mirror. "It's those damn dreams," his voice had dropped to a whisper. "Those damned dreams."

Tearing himself from the mirror, he jumped into the shower. The hot water ripped at his skin, digging into each pore, washing out the toxins that were poisoning his body. He watched the little whirlpool made as the water slipped down the drain. The noise of the water splattering on the shower walls and the motion of the whirlpool were soothing, almost hypnotic. More relaxed, the old Edward Garrett began to take hold.

It was a few moments before the silence registered. It was like a quiet pall that even muffled the splashing or the shower. The silence made Garrett realize that he hadn't turned on the bathroom radio. He always listened to the local news and weather while he showered and shaved. Always. It was his habit. An integral part of his morning routine. For some reason, it had been overlooked this morning. It was the dream, for sure, but that too made him concerned. So many things were happening now, things that were interrupting his normal routine. *So many things,* he thought.

"Well," he said aloud again, "it's time to get things back to normal. This morning, it's a good jog around the Battery, a good breakfast followed by a good day's work. A little re- organization is all I need."

As he stepped from the shower, a loud clap of thunder made him jump and shudder. He turned on the radio in time to hear the announcer confirm that it was raining in Charleston. A tropical depression was offshore. It could turn into a hurricane at any moment. Unusually late in the season, but a fact, nonetheless.

The morning jog was out. He would jog in the lightest of mist but he wouldn't be seen jogging in the rain.

"At least I can have breakfast," he reasoned.

The kitchen was the only room on the main floor that he used for its original purpose. The third floor had a small one, but Garrett enjoyed the big kitchen on the second floor. It was, for the most part, as it had been when he was a child. New appliances were purchased when he remodeled the upstairs but 'the feel' was still there. To him, it was a room of aromas.

Occasionally he would sit in the room letting those aromas waft through his mind. The aromas he remembered were mostly from baking. He remembered chocolate chip and peanut butter cookies, homemade bread, and morning biscuits; aromas that recalled happy memories and the woman that had raised him — the housekeeper he knew as Queen Ester.

The old percolator was still there and would be called into service this morning. Although replaced by a Mr. Coffee, it still produced the same, fine coffee it had for so many years. It filled the house with its own special aroma. It was, however, an aroma that he associated with his father — it, the scent of Old Spice and Mixture 79 pipe tobacco. Today, it brought back the familiar bittersweet memories. Where was his father now? Why wasn't he here to see Garrett's success? Why had he not been allowed to prove to his father that he, too, could be successful?

It was the acrid odor of burning bread that jarred Garrett from his excursion in the past. He jumped to the oven and extracted the two pieces of charcoal that had once been English muffins. He said, aloud, the word that seemed to sum up his morning, so far, "Shit!"

Exercise was out.

Breakfast was out.

It seemed that organization was all Garrett had left. He took his cup of coffee upstairs. As he dressed, he began to organize his day in his mind. His only appointment was at 9:30 a.m. with Pegge Ravenel.

Pegge Ravenel, a friend and working associate of Ashley's, was to marry soon. She had bought a condominium in the converted Fort Sumter Hotel. She had a fascination with antiques. She would receive a number of family pieces, as was the custom, and she wanted to totally furnish her new home with older pieces. Ashley had told Pegge about Garrett and #13 Church Street, and she had filled Garrett in on Pegge and the situation.

Papa Ravenel, a very successful member of Charleston's elite as well as the owner of Charleston's oldest and largest newspaper where both Ashley and Pegge worked, was footing the decorating bill. So Pegge's whims would be satisfied. Sort of a wedding present.

He looked outside, again. He hoped the rain wouldn't cause the Ravenel appointment to be rescheduled. Business had been slow, partly due to few customers, partly due to reduced interest on Garrett's part since the Find. Deep inside, however, he knew that business wasn't the reason he wanted the appointment to be kept. Having someone at the shop, anyone, would help keep his mind off last night's nightmare.

The only other item on his list of things to do was to organize the treasures.

As Garrett waited, time seemed to slip into half-speed. As he watched the hands on the old grandfather clock they stopped moving.

It was a little after 10:00 a.m. before Pegge Ravenel and her mother arrived at #13 Church Street. The weather, they told him, had made them late and left them chilled and damp. Garrett suggested that coffee might warm them, or possibly a small glass of sherry. After all, it would give them a chance to discuss the decor of the condo and give Garrett a chance to see just how much of Papa Ravenel's money they were willing to spend. Mrs. Ravenel took the sherry, Pegge the coffee.

They moved into the main floor kitchen. The percolator was standing ready to provide its hot, tasty, aromatic coffee. The charred remnants of Garrett's earlier attempt at breakfast had been disposed of and its odor replaced by the friendly aroma of the coffee.

The threesome spent well over a half-hour around the kitchen table without even the slightest intrusion of Alexander Graham Bell's most annoying creation. Of course, there was some light conversation about Ashley, the newspaper and members of Charleston's social set. But soon the conversation turned to the matter at hand — Pegge's antique needs.

It was 12:45 p.m. before the Ravenels slipped back into the gray blanket that covered #13 Church Street, and all of Charleston for that matter. Garrett had contributed greatly to the furnishing of the parlor, one bedroom and the dining room. And the Ravenels had contributed greatly to Garrett. Other rooms would follow, he was assured, although Garrett had profited handsomely from the sale, he had provided the items selected at a much-reduced price. Part of the antique game.

Considering the walnut, Eastlake style pieces purchased for the bedroom, the mahogany parlor and dining room suites, the American oak accent pieces and an assortment of knick-knacks, Pegge and her mother had added some $24,000 of Papa Ravenel's fortune to Garrett's bottom line.

The morning conversation had yielded one extremely interesting piece of information. Pegge was looking for a special formal tea service. The one on display in the gallery was *nice* but she wanted a *very special* set. Garrett had also played down the one on display because he knew of the silver pieces in the Find. The ornate one by Revere. Very ornate, very formal and engraved with the Ravenel name on it. It even had 15 matching demitasse spoons. He had already formulated a plan. The Ravenel silver tea service would be one of the first pieces he would divert. And the purchaser, the elder Ravenel, would be ever grateful.

Not only would the sale be the talk of the town, it was very likely that a story would make the *Morning News*. The plan was well on it's way to formulation in Garrett's mind. A good story in the *News* would be good for his business and if it were picked up by the wires it could be the key to the national exposure he wanted so badly.

Trying to be vague, Garrett assured Pegge that he, personally, would accept the responsibility of finding the perfect tea service.

As he watched his customers blend into the gray blanket, he shuddered as the memory of his earlier dream softly crept across his mind's eye.

He returned to the kitchen for another cup of coffee. #13 Church Street was as silent as a tomb. Garrett walked to the door muttering aloud to himself. He looked through the window shears, half hoping someone would be there, half hoping for a day of isolation. There was a lot to do. No one was on the porch. No one was on the steps. No cars were parked out front. No one was there. A long sigh slipped from his lips.

"There's much to be done today, so I might as well get started," Garrett was talking aloud again, and he didn't even realize it.

He walked back to the desk in the entry hall. He reached for his pen and began to set the rest of his day in order. On the pad he wrote: 1) Mark the Ravenel items sold 2) Put the smaller items in the vault 3) Complete the cataloging of the Find 4) Call Ashley about tonight 5) Buy a book on the meaning of dreams.

He paused as he looked over the list he had just written. He hadn't consciously thought about the last item. Not consciously. It just happened.

"That's a good idea, Edward. Maybe you should ask Ashley about them as well."

CHAPTER 11

Monday dragged on. He had completed items 1 and 2 on his list. He had made some progress on cataloging the Find and he had called Ashley. She, however, was on assignment and wouldn't return to the paper until 8 p.m., or so he was told. Occasionally she was assigned a major news story that required her to be at the paper much later than normal. That didn't happen often but it was very annoying to Garrett when it did. The last time was his birthday. No big plans were ruined but it was important to him.

She called him at 7:00 p.m. Tonight would be one of those nights. It was a big story, page one likely and rewrites up until the final edition deadline.

"I wanted to be with you tonight. I've got a lot I wanted to tell you." Garrett's voice had drifted into an almost childish whine. It was always a battle inside him. He knew that it was impossible for Ashley to alter the situation. It was her job. And he knew how much a front-page by-line meant to her or any reporter. It was like an Oscar. He was happy for her but he wanted to have her with him and not at 1:00 a.m. which was what it looked like now.

"Just forget it, then," he tried to stop himself, but it didn't work. It spewed out, unable to be controlled by good, common sense. A hurt little boy trying to get even. "Go do your damned story. Don't you worry about me. I can get along quite well without you, thank you very much." They were words he didn't mean deep down inside but he wasn't dealing with these deeper feelings.

As he got ready to slam the cell phone into the wall a part of Garrett felt relieved. He had shown her.

"Screw her," he said aloud. "I'll have an evening on the town without her. After all, I'm not dependent on her. Let her crawl into bed with her page one story and see how warm it keeps her."

Before he could destroy the call by destroying the cell phone, his mind caught his hand in mid throw. He would have to replace the phone, then who would win?

Almost immediately the phone began to ring. Subconscious habit caused him to reach for the ringing telephone. Realizing it might be Ashley stopped him in mid air.

"Let her be the one to worry for a change. Tonight, I'm going to enjoy myself without her."

Garrett left the ringing phone as he walked, quite deliberately, upstairs to prepare for his evening on the town. He stopped at the third-floor liquor cabinet for some fortification on the way to the shower. The glass he carried was filled with vodka, nothing else.

Showered, shaved, dressed and warmed by a triple vodka, Garrett decided on dinner at Poogan's Porch.

"Good evening, Mr. Garrett."

"Good evening, Tom," Garrett greeted his friend, Tom Bass, "No reservations again. Think you can fit me in somewhere?"

"Certainly. As a matter of fact, I believe your regular table is free. Will Miss Barrineau be joining you?" The restaurant owner's comment caused anger and resentment to swell inside Garrett body.

"No! Just me tonight," Garrett snipped, more anger creeping into his voice than he had planned. "Sorry, Tom. Lee is working on a late assignment. So, I'm sort of on my own tonight."

"Dinner for one, it is then." Tom Bass' comment, no matter how innocent, served only to push Garrett deeper into his blue mood. Bass left the table. A number of friends and customers caught Garrett's eye, waved and went back to their meals and conversations.

"Mistah Garrett. It's a pleasure to see you here tonight. Miss Ashley joining you?" It was William.

"Damn it! Can't I go out by myself?" Garrett wanted to say. Instead, "No, William. Just one tonight," Garrett said with a measure of control. "And bring me a double vodka on ice."

The liquor helped Garrett enjoy his dinner and was the main

reason he decided to hit a couple of local bars before he returned home. He hadn't done that, alone, since he and Ashley had been dating. His first stop was the nearby Holiday Inn where a '60's folk group was playing. There, he found a few friends. They all asked about Ashley. He remained calm on the outside as he explained the reason he was a solo act that night, but inside was another matter.

Garrett made two more stops before the questions about Ashley's whereabouts finally got to him.

"I'm going to finish my evening in peace, where no one knows her," he said to himself. Garrett's decision to go to the Truck Stop would have repulsed him had he been more sober.

The Truck Stop was one of the seediest bars in North Charleston. The only topless and bottomless dance bar in town, it was rumored to have a back room for gambling, to be a hooker pick-up location, and to have direct ties to the Italian Family. Garrett stumbled slightly as he entered the smokey lounge, two steps down. It was the big, muscular bouncer who caught him. Cursing the darkness, Garrett pushed himself away from the hulk, hoping to appear more sober than he was.

He found his way to a table at the end of the runway stage. Red lights were focused on the stage and were the primary source of lighting in the place. Other lights were dimmed to the point of being a dull glow. Dancers, waiting their turn on stage, were sitting with some of the patrons. Some were topless, others had on their skimpy dance costumes. Some of the couples were talking, others were engaged in more intimate forms of communications. Under normal conditions, Garrett would not be caught dead in this place. But, tonight was different.

A blonde dancer appeared on stage. Her long, golden hair framed her face, fell over her shoulders and added an exciting additional movement to her large, heavy breasts. Garrett was mesmerized — by her breasts, by her body, by the entire situation. She continued to move her 20-year-old body from one side of the stage to the other, but, to Garrett, she was dancing for him and him alone.

All of the suggestive, sometimes vulgar, moves served only to keep Garrett's mind riveted on stage with his new-found blonde beauty. Two of the other dancers had asked Garrett if he wanted company. He told one, "No," and simply ignored the other's advances. His only interest was on stage.

Two more songs had reduced the blonde's costume to a pair of red, high-heeled shoes. She then moved a large wicker basket to the center of the stage. The lights lowered and the beat of the music changed to more of a jungle beat as she danced around the basket. With one fluid movement, she flipped off the top of the basket and stepped into it, as she continued her synchronized movements.

It was a few moments before Garrett realized the show had become a duet. The multicolored head of a large snake slowly slipped out from between her thighs. It continued to slither around her torso. Around her slim waist, once. Then twice. First its head, then its round, muscular body slipped between her breasts, its head finally nestled on her shoulder.

She took the head of the snake and held it to her cheek, as she continued to dance.

In his mind, Garrett was that snake. In the core of his being, it was he that was wrapped around this beautiful blonde. Wrapped tightly between her legs. Caressing her huge breasts. His long tongue touching her face. It was the most sexually arousing experience of Garrett's life. Beads of sweat sparkled like rubies on his forehead. It could have been from the liquor and the heat in the room, but the tightness in his groin could only have been the result of the lust of the moment and the blonde dancer on stage.

Too soon for Garrett, the song ended. The blonde's dancing partner had been deposited back in its basket. Another dancer was preparing to mount the stage.

As if she were reading his mind, the blonde walked slowly over to his table. She had slipped on the red bikini panties that matched her costume. Her form fitting dress was bunched at her shoulders, as if she had simply put it over her head. It lay in folds barely covering her breasts.

"Hi, I'm Penny, Penny Candy," she said as she slipped the dress into place. "Mind if I join you?" She looked into Garrett's eyes as she sat next to him.

"No. Yes, I mean ... sit down," Garrett stammered. A waitress had followed Penny to the table.

"Need a fresh drink, sir? How 'bout one for the lady?"

"Sure. All right, Oh, would you like a drink, Penny?" Garrett asked, showing his lack of experience with such situations.

"Sure, my usual, Rita," Penny answered the waitress, but she continued to look directly into Garrett's eyes. Never before had he commanded such undivided attention from such an unbelievably beautiful woman.

"One vodka on the rocks, one champagne cocktail," said the waitress to the unhearing couple as she left to place the order.

"What's your name?"

"Edward. Edward Garrett." The two made casual boy/girl talk until the waitress returned with their drinks.

"That'll be $14.41," she said as she set the drinks down in front of them.

"What?" Garrett demanded, a reflex action.

"$3.50 for yours, $10.50 for the lady's, plus tax, of course." Garrett's question was answered in such a practiced way that made it obvious, he wasn't the first to question.

Damn, the best champagne I know of wouldn't sell for $10.50 a glass, he thought. But, Penny's company made his objection a silent one. They talked for a couple of minutes. Garrett told her about his antique business. She appeared interested. He started to impress her by the story of the Find, but thought better of it.

It couldn't have been more than three or four minutes when the waitress was back. Penny's glass was empty, Garrett's almost full. Another drink was ordered for Penny and they returned to their conversation. She was from Los Angeles and had moved to Charleston with her former boyfriend who was in the Navy. She said she had little money, and supported herself with the money she made dancing and tips from appreciative customers. Her interest in snakes started when she was in high school. She decided to include Samson, her pet boa, in the act.

"He eats, so he has to work," she reasoned.

Her second drink was now dry.

"Why don't you order a bottle of champagne?" she suggested. "It's $90.00, but then we can spend some time together without the manager caring. Otherwise, I've have to move around the club. That's what I get paid to do." She paused as if waiting for his answer. "I'd much rather be with you." Penny's hand had slipped up from his knee to the inside of his upper thigh. Her voice was like the soft purr of a contented cat. His heart was beating like a drum on steroids.

Penny's suggestion presented Garrett with the ultimate dilemma, something he wanted to do that cost more than it should. The moments passed as he weighed the alternatives. Penny had turned to leave, taking his silence as a familiar, "No." He grabbed her hand to bring her back.

"What the hell," Garrett said. "It's got to be worth $90.00 to spend some time with you."

Penny called the waitress and ordered the champagne. Moments later it arrived. "How ironic," Garrett thought, "served with a touch of class." The bottle was presented in ice in a silver looking ice bucket, glasses were also in the ice, a white paper doily was on the tray and a single carnation.

"There's a place here in the back where we won't be disturbed," Penny was carrying the tray as she encouraged Garrett to follow her.

It didn't take much encouragement for Garrett to join her. He looked like a hungry little puppy following his master who was carrying a plate of food.

"Edward! Edward, wake up. It's me, Ashley." It was Ashley's voice, at least he thought it was.

"Are you all right, Edward?"

Garrett was trying to wake up. There was a jackhammer working on his head from the inside. His mouth felt like a World War One Army Brigade had marched across his tongue in their sock feet. His teeth were numb. Why was Ashley here? Was this another nightmare?

Ashley's efforts to wake Garrett continued as she began shaking him. Garrett was only aware of the pain in his head. He tried to stand up.

"Ashley, I ... uh ... I don't feel very good. I think I'd better ... get to the bathroom before ... before."

Ashley smiled at the sounds coming from the bathroom. *Serves him right, poor man,* she thought with a chuckle. *Little boy's big night out.*

Garrett grabbed an Alka Seltzer, ripped open the foil and dumped the tablets into a glass filled with water.

"Fizz, dammit," he ordered.

As he drank the result, he tried to organize his mind. He couldn't remember much about last night but he knew Ashley hadn't been with him. He had to get the events of last night straight in his mind. He saw his naked image in the bathroom mirror and it made him feel worse. His robe was on a hook behind the door. As he slipped it on, he once again tried to make some sense of what was going on.

He walked back across the bedroom. Ashley was seated on his still made bed. He had been sleeping across it. His clothes and shoes lay like a trail that began somewhere in the hall. All of this and his headache left him with only one conclusion — he had had too much to drink. But, how did he get home?

"Was my car parked out front?" His first question to Ashley presented his obvious memory loss about the evening.

"Yes, it's right where it always is."

"Is it all right?"

"It looked fine. Parked a little crooked, but fine." Ashley had pieced much of the puzzle together. "Out a bit late last night, were you?"

"I guess. I must have had one too many."

"Several too many, if you ask me." Ashley's attempts at humor were wasted on Garrett this morning.

Although more alert, there were still gaps in his memory. He remembered dinner at Poogan's and the Holiday Inn, but where had he gone after that? He simply couldn't remember. It was Ashley who suggested coffee.

The walk downstairs was a long one for Garrett. Each step on the carpeted stairs struck a gong in his head. Ashley started the coffee as Garrett sat at the table. Actually, the best Garrett could do was to slump over the table. The pleasant music of the percolator had begun when Ashley joined him at the table.

"Well?" she asked.

"Well, what?" was Garrett's reply.

"Don't answer a question with a question, Mr. Garrett. What happened?"

"What do you mean, what happened?"

"I said ..."

"I heard what you said. I'm not in the mood for this, Lee. My head hurts, my stomach is still weak and I don't remember very much about last night, at all," Garrett barely whispered.

"Convenient loss of memory, is it?"

"No, dammit. I just don't remember. Anyway, you're to blame for this. If you had come home at a normal time, I'd have been with you."

"And, if a frog had wings he wouldn't bump his ass when he jumps."

"That's stupid," Garrett snapped.

"No more stupid than me being blamed for your drunken escapade." In this verbal exchange, Ashley was clearly winning.

Garrett put his head in his hands. "I only wish I could remember what happened last night," he groaned.

Ashley began to feel sorry for her pathetic-looking lover. His eyes looked like two olives floating in a glass of strawberry milk mix. She laughed as she considered the imagery of this simile.

"It's not bad enough that I can't remember what happened to me, or that I'm sick, or that I'm lonely and cold, but now my lover sits there and laughs at me. That's one helluva note."

"I'm not laughing at you, dear Edward," Ashley managed a sincere and serious tone. "I was laughing at something that crossed my mind."

"Well I don't think anything's funny right now."

Ashley filled a coffee cup and brought it to the table.

"Here, drink this. It should make you feel some better, at least." She was setting the cup on the table when Garrett's stomach made a massive rumble. It echoed through his body and through the room, he was certain. He looked at the coffee, then for the closest sink.

"Let's go back upstairs, please?"

Ashley took the cup and walked, slowly, behind Garrett back up to his room. Once there, Garrett realized he hadn't asked her about her story. For a moment he considered not mentioning it, but, in the end he asked. Yes, the story had made the front page until the final edition when it was bumped to the second front by a national story. But a coup for her, regardless.

The coffee had helped to both warm and calm Garrett. He was

sitting in the middle of the bed with the covers wrapped all around him and tucked under his chin. *Sometimes he looks so much like a little boy,* Ashley thought.

She began to pick up some of the clothes that Garrett had spread from the hall through his room. Shirt, one sock, underwear, slacks. As she carried them to the clothes hamper, change and keys began to jingle.

"What do you want me to do with the stuff in your pockets?" she asked.

"Put it on the dresser."

"And your change?"

"In the jar." Garrett kept his change in a large, antique Mason jar. "Even the pennies?"

"The pennies go in the ... Oh, my God." Garrett almost retched again. In the pause that followed, hours of action passed through Garrett's mind's eye in seconds.

"My wallet. Is it in my pants?" he demanded.

"I don't know. Let me see. Yes, it's here," Ashley was beginning to get annoyed at Garrett's tone.

"Credit cards. They still there?"

Ashley threw the wallet on the bed.

"Look for yourself," she said.

Garrett grabbed the wallet.

"Thank God," Garrett found all of his credit cards in their exact places.

"Ohh! Shit!"

"Edward. Just what the hell are you doing?" Ashley's voice had lost any trace of humor.

"Damn her! $600. She took $600." Garrett wasn't speaking directly to anyone, but Ashley was.

"She?" Ashley was glaring at Garrett. "So, it's *she*, is it. Edward, this convenient loss of memory of yours has gone on long enough."

"I didn't remember, honey, honestly. Not until you mentioned pennies. Sit down, please. I'll tell you the whole story."

Garrett started at Poogan's and told Ashley everything that had happened — almost everything.

It was all Ashley could do to keep from laughing out loud. It had to be the oldest bar trick in the world. She almost didn't believe his story. How could Garrett be so naïve. But, the story was so preposterous, it had to be true.

"I'll sue the bastards. I'll get my money back. I'll see to it that bitch is put in jail. Her and her slimy snake. I'm going to call my lawyer, then the mayor and then the sheriff. I'll get something done. That bitch!" His headache forgotten, Garrett's voice was getting louder and he was talking faster. "I'll ..."

"Maybe you should calm down, first," Ashley's initial attempts to calm Garrett were futile.

"I'll make them pay. I will," Garrett repeated himself as if trying to convince someone, anyone. He had begun pacing his bedroom. The headache and his former condition forgotten.

"I'll get back my money and make them all pay. Just who the hell do they think I am? Some kind of idiot? Some dumb child ..."

Ashley stopped him. "Edward. Wait just a minute. You can't think for even a minute that you are the first to have this happen to you there. Do you?"

"Well I ..."

"It's a well-known fact that these things happen at the Truck Stop. Well known to the public and, I'm sure, well known to the police as well. I'm surprised you didn't know yourself." Garrett tried to interrupt with a denial but she went on, "The newspaper receives two or three complaints a month."

"Well, I am still going to talk to the mayor. I helped elect him. He'll do something. He owes me that much." Garrett didn't want to admit that Ashley was probably right. All he knew was his pride was hurt. He was made a fool of in front of Ashley. And, his $600 was gone. He felt like an idiot, and his head felt like it was inside a base drum at a Rolling Stones concert. If it had been someone else, he'd be laughing. But it wasn't someone else.

"Don't be surprised if you don't get anywhere. And don't go back there any more. I don't want you getting hurt."

Ashley began feeling sorry for Garrett. How naive he could be, sometimes.

"Lay back down," she consoled him. Let me rub your neck and shoulders. What you need is a good night's sleep. You'll laugh about this in the morning."

"Don't bet on it."

Garrett knew, down deep inside, he would do nothing about

the $600. The threat of violence was enough for that. But, he wasn't so sure about Ashley's warning not to return.

CHAPTER 12

It took only about 10 minutes of Ashley's rubbing. The measured rhythm of Garrett's breathing was Ashley's first indication that he had fallen asleep. Moments later the familiar rumbles started.

It was decision time. Garrett's bedside clock showed the time at 3:57a.m. She wasn't due at the newspaper until 1:00 p.m. Garrett would have to be up at 8:00 a.m. at the latest. She set his alarm, wrote him a note and taped it to bathroom mirror, turned out the lights and left for her home.

First it was a noise. A dull buzzing in the distance. It became louder and harsher. First, Garrett looked around the bedroom. It was a few seconds before he could see where the buzzing was coming from. A giant bee was buzzing around the outside of his house. It had the shape of a bumble bee but the size was what was remarkable. It must have been over a foot long.

Garrett stared at the bee for a few minutes before he noticed it had a face. As he looked at it, the features began to change. It grew eyebrows. The shape of a nose appeared and began to grow into a human nose. It was as if it had morphed into human face. A face that was familiar to him, although he couldn't exactly place it.

He wasn't afraid. He was inside his house. The bee, outside.

Garrett began moving from one room to another in the house. The bee followed.

As he moved from window to window.

The bee followed.

The buzzing was getting louder. Garrett moved back into his bedroom, to get away from the buzzing.

The bee followed.

He moved to the bathroom window.

The bee moved as well, the persistent buzzing getting louder. He moved to the French doors, looking out, praying the bee would not follow.

The bee was already there, and the buzzing grew louder.

As Garrett stared, the features on the bee's face began to change slowly. More human, and the expression changed from emotionless to a smile. Then, it became a smirk. The mouth began to move. The words unintelligible at first, but soon they cut through the din of the buzzing.

"Failure. Failure. Failure. That's what you'll be, Edward Garrett. A disgrace to the Garrett name. A failure. Never amount to anything, never a credit to the Garrett family. Never. Never. Never."

"No!" Garrett screamed at the bee. "No. You're wrong. Look at me. I'm a success. Damn you. Look, I'm a success."

"Failure! Failure!"

With the continued morphing of the face, Garrett finally began to recognize the face. It was the face of his father.

The bee began bumping into the window where Garrett was standing, screaming, *"Failure!"* as each bump added greater force.

"No! No!" Garrett screamed as he pushed against the window in an effort to prevent the bee from crashing through and entering the house.

"No! No!"

Crash!

The sound of breaking glass caused Garrett to sit upright in his bed.

"Where am I?" Garrett looked around his bedroom. The bedside clock was buzzing. A broken water glass was on the table and the floor. The covers were on the floor. No alien creature had invaded his room. No one was with him. Not his father. Not Ashley. He was alone.

"Another dream. God! When will it all stop?" Garrett paused, "Well, at least it wasn't like the others."

Garrett turned off his alarm. Taking care not to step on the broken glass, he went into the bathroom. There he found Ashley's note. As he began his morning toilet, he tried to piece his night together.

CHAPTER 13

His head still hurt. His eyes still hurt. Even his teeth still hurt. There must have been at least 35 cotton balls in his mouth. He even checked inside his mouth to see. The sounds that escaped from his throat were more like frog croaks than words. He slowly stepped into the shower. At first, he wouldn't close his eyes, fearful that elements of his dreams would return. Although soothing, the hot water did little to help the ache in his head.

Standing in front of his bathroom mirror, Garrett began to talk to himself as he took stock of his actions during the previous few hours.

"You were stupid last night. Why? Why?" Garrett's reflection made no attempt to answer. "You acted like a spoiled child when Ashley said she had to work late. You know how often that happens. And then that game with the blonde broad with the snake. Just what did you expect? Instant love in a place like that? I think you have lost your mind. You keep screwing around and Ashley'll find out what a loser she'd hooked up with and you'll make your father's predictions come true."

In the moments of silence that followed, Garrett considered what he had just said. The shaving lather in his hand looked like a piece of old meringue pie — dry and crusty. He rinsed his hands and began the process of shaving again. As he lathered his face, he realized how unsteady he really was. The way his hands were trembling was the most visible results of last night.

It was a shaky effort at shaving. All in all, however, Garrett did quite well. One nick on the chin and no major patches of unscraped skin.

Somewhat refreshed, Garrett dressed and went downstairs. He found Mr. Coffee standing ready to serve up hot and cheery cups of the elixir of life. Ashley had obliviously set the timer before she left. As he filled his cup, a twinge of guilt shot through him like a mild electric shock. He almost dropped the glass coffee pot.

Ashley.

The ringing telephone jarred him back to the present. It took a second for him to realize where he was and what was happening.

"#13 Church Street"

"How's your head?" Garrett recognized Ashley's voice.

"It's better."

"You were sleeping so peacefully last night, I decided not to disturb you." Ashley didn't want to tell Garrett that the real reason she had not stayed the night was her desire for a good night's sleep. *Sawing logs* was a kind expression to describe Garrett's snoring problem. He could literally rattle windows in his bedroom. Too, she didn't have to be at the paper until midday and she wanted to sleep later.

"I wish you had. Waking up with you in my arms is so much better than waking up with only a pillow for company," Garrett remembered his recent dreams. "Lee, do you know anything about dreams? You know, what they mean, and such."

"Not much, I'm afraid. I've read a little about interpreting dreams and dreams were a part of one of my psychology courses in college. Freud and his ideas about dreams. I wasn't interested in dreams then, unless he was willing to take me to a football game or out dancing."

"Ashley! Can't you be serious about anything." Garrett rarely called her by Ashley. Her given name was reserved for when he was either totally frustrated with her or trying to coax her into bed.

"Why this sudden interest in dreams, Edward?" A more compassionate Ashley asked.

"I don't know, Lee, or at least I don't understand. I've been having some disturbing dreams lately. More like nightmares. One strange dream about giant bees and my father — really weird. And the other night I dreamed I was being hung. I think I actually experienced what it was like to die."

Garrett said he didn't want to go into more specific details.

"Two things come to mind," she paused. Ashley knew she would have to begin getting ready for work soon and she had an early luncheon appointment, so she didn't want to have a protracted conversation concerning Garrett's dreams. "The shrink I saw, when I went to him, said to always keep a pen and paper next to your bed. When you wake after a dream, no matter how strange or insignificant it may seem, write down all you can remember. It will help keep track of important parts of it. Also, he said writing it down helps make the connection between the conscious and subconscious minds. He said dreams were the only way the subconscious mind can communicate with the conscious mind. Maybe you should try that for a while. I'll see if I can find a good book on dreams and bring it over tonight. That is, if you want me to come over tonight?"

"You know I want you here. I didn't want you to leave last night."

"You didn't even know I left last night."

"That's beside the point. I love you and I miss you when you're not here." Garrett was almost to his little boy whine.

What she was saying intrigued him. He hadn't known she had ever seen a psychiatrist. She had always seemed so thoroughly together. Maybe it would be a good idea to talk to her about the dreams later.

"I would appreciate a book, Lee, and maybe we could talk as well. These dreams are beginning to bug me. But, writing them down, I don't remember much about my dreams," Garrett heard himself saying something that had been true before, but not these last few dreams. He remembered them, every detail, with first person accuracy. "That seems, I don't know, somehow perverted or something."

Garrett wasn't sure he wanted anyone, much less Ashley, to read about what he was dreaming. At least, not until he understood what they might mean.

"Well, you can bet that's what a shrink will tell you to do, but there may be another way. Last year I did a story of a witch doctor from Beaufort named Doctor Bug. He was visiting out on Jim Island, as he calls it. You know it as James Island, just across the Wappoo Creek. He claimed that in addition to making roots, casting and removing spells, and doing hexes, he could expel evil spirits. He told me that you could tell if you were possessed through your dreams. You want me to see if I can get you an appointment with the doctor?"

It was Ashley's turn for a little tasteless humor and Garrett was quick to point it out.

"I don't believe you. My head hurts and I'm worried about my health and you taking cheap shots at me with this witch doctor bullshit. Be serious." Garrett tried to make light of Ashley's comments but he had heard the stories about the witchcraft on Jim Island as Storey even called it. *No,* he told himself, *this witchcraft is nothing but a bunch of mumbo jumbo.* "Don't forget the book, ok."

"I'll see you tonight, book in hand. By the way, Edward, you pissed off anyone on Jim Island, lately?"

"Lee!"

"Don't discount something you don't understand. See you tonight and I'll bring you a root, just in case."

Garrett almost threw the phone back on the desk. He could dish it out rather well when he started, but his insecurity could never take it very well.

As she hung up the phone, she was hooting. Never before had she dated someone so square, so conservative, so naïve, and so easy to *put on.*

"I wonder what keeps us together?" she said aloud.

"What?" It was the guy at the next desk that answered.

"Oh! Nothing. I guess I was just thinking out loud. Sorry," she said as she focused her attention on her computer terminal. She remembered she was on deadline.

Garrett spent the rest of the morning straightening the antiques in the store. Moving things from one place to another. Adjusting the look. Making it look new. He often found items would be sold in a short time after they were moved from one place to another, so he had made adjusting a way of life.

By the time he noticed the time, it was 1:00 in the afternoon.

Time to stop for lunch.

He returned to his desk with a sandwich. No customers had visited the store that morning. It was still raining with no sign of letting up.

He turned on the buzzer, which he could hear in the basement, placed a sign in the window that told prospective customers to press the button, and took his sandwich and a fresh cup of coffee down to the first floor.

He thought of Ashley as he went through the motions of cataloging. She was and had been the true bright spot in his life. She was the balance in his life. The Libra in his existence. He thought about what she had said. Maybe there was a simple answer to the terrible dreams of late. But, what could his subconscious mind be trying to tell him? Keeping a dream diary was a bit much, but if it might help ... He had almost decided that he would even see a shrink. He glanced at the treasures in this room of his house. Their untold value. Their untold stories.

"Bullshit!" he called out. "What a wuss you've become. All you need is a little sleep and to get this stuff cataloged. Then you'll be famous — and rich. Edward, you'll sleep better and you'll sleep richer when this is over — much richer." His laughter echoed around the room.

He took a long drink of the hot coffee. He felt better. And, with his newfound energy his imagination moved into overdrive. His head was filled with fantasies of his new-found importance. Surely he would be noticed by the people of Charleston, and the rest of the U.S., and the world, as well. He'd be on television. *Good Morning America*, *The Today Show*, maybe even Matt Lauer would want to interview him. Fate had truly shined a smiling face upon him; and it was about time.

He had already moved the silver, coins, swords, pistols and smaller items to the existing vault. They had already been photographed and cataloged. He had made a second set of pictures just for safety's sake.

He kept the larger pieces in the trove where he had found them. No one else needed to know about the Find. Too many people knew about it already. Could he trust everyone who knew already? Bob Storey was trustworthy and he kept to himself, most of the time. What about Lee? The love of his life. That's how he thought of her, but could he trust her to keep quiet about the Find?

After all, she works for a newspaper.

Paranoia had crept in the little room when Garrett wasn't

looking and was sitting there on his right shoulder, whispering in his ear. He continued to create scenario after scenario where his trusted employee or his lover breaks his confidence. Scenarios where they blew his big chance.

"I just don't know," he began talking aloud, again. "If I can't trust Bob Storey, who can I trust? He's worked here all of my life. Not even a hint of dishonestly. He's like family. And Lee — Lee loves me. But this room's worth millions. Many items are priceless."

As Garrett argued both sides of the dilemma with himself, he became aware that he was talking out loud and how ridiculous he sounded. He knew better. He grabbed one of the large trunks to move it so that it was in better light. Grunting, groaning and a maximum effort by Garrett had moved the trunk only a few inches. Like it or not, Bob Storey would be necessary to complete this project.

"I know he doesn't like it down here. Him and his *haints*. Well, in the past his love for extra money has overcome his fear of the haints; I'm sure it will again."

His call to Storey proved him correct. Garrett decided to quiz Storey, but the old man assured him that he had said "nothing to nobody," and he didn't intend to. Storey said he would be at the big house in about an hour, so Garrett decided to go back in the hole and work with some of the smaller trunks.

He knew some of the them were filled with odd assortments of trinkets. One had a variety of religious artifacts in it. A remarkable golden chalice encrusted in priceless gems, had the unmistakable symbol of the Knights Templar. There were golden crosses, gem stone beads and other pieces of altar dressing that bore many symbols he didn't recognize. He decided to move that trunk out to the center of the room where the light was better.

"This bare bulb doesn't give enough light, dammit. No bloody wonder Bob's afraid to be in here. The light makes every shadow look so ominous."

"Damn. Every time I turn around I meet some part of myself. Were all the people back then midgets?" The room had been cut from the rock on which the house sat. It was barely big enough for Garrett to stand.

Most of the spider webs that had originally draped the room

had been cleared away in earlier visits to the room. Occasionally, though, Garrett would run into the wispy artistry of one of these eight legged weavers. Clearly an effort to reestablish their domination over the hole.

There was a definite chill in the small room. "It's surprisingly water tight in here," Garrett said aloud, again. "There seems to be no water damage to any of the trunks or the other treasures. No mildew. No creatures, other than these annoying spiders. Amazing."

As he moved the trunk, he heard a loud thump. The hair on the back of his neck tingled. Goose bumps invaded his skin and his heartbeat quickened. He looked left, then right. The noise had echoed around the small room, giving no hint of its origin. To Garrett, an icy chill had filled the room, as if a crack had opened in the wall allowing the wet outside wind into the room. He stood as still as his nerves would allow him; as still as his shaking knees would allow. Sweat dampened his shirt and beaded on his forehead.

"What the hell was that noise?"

He was certain there wasn't anyone in the room with him. Certainly no one he could see. First, however, he looked around the room to assure himself. In his mind, he recalled the position of the things left in the room. Trying to superimpose that visual picture over the room as it is now. As best he could recall, everything was as it was.

"Could it have been my imagination? Am I losing my mind?" he asked aloud. The normal Garrett wouldn't have questioned his sanity in such a way, but ...

There were no additional noises and no additional movements from within the room. Garrett grabbed one of the smaller trunks and tried to make a pathway through the find. With its first movement, another thump echoed through the small room. Grabbing a nearby flashlight, Garrett moved to the source of the noise.

The only light in the small room was furnished by an automobile trouble light Bob Storey had found for him. Its single bulb provided light but in such a way as to create many shadows in the room. It was from one of the shadow areas that the noise appeared to have come.

"Dammit!" His voice, too, echoed through the room. "Something must have fallen. I hope nothing broke." His words, spoken aloud, were as much an effort to reassure himself as anything. He had never felt totally at ease in the room. He wasn't sure exactly why that was. Maybe it was Storey's talk about the *haints*. He didn't know, but whatever it was, Garrett knew he was uneasy about being in there.

His flashlight scanned the dark crannies of the room. Finally, the beam settled on a small chest, upside down and laying sort of cockeyed.

"That must have been what caused the sound," his said somewhat loudly. His words seemed to bounce around the walls. "I'm glad it wasn't anything important," he said in a whisper, as he picked up the small chest, inspecting it.

He remembered the chest from his early trips to the room. It had been empty, so it had been discarded. Forgotten in favor of the more exciting treasures of the Find. It was unusual, however. The chest was a little over a foot wide and three-quarters of a foot deep and about as high. It was carved, he presumed, from a stone like substance. Its gray-green color was intriguing. As he held the chest, the eerie chill of moments before returned to his bones. Fear gripped his chest making his breathing labored. He shook it off and moved to place the chest back where it had previously rested. Something made him pause.

Garrett's fingertips moved across the top of the chest. There was a number of depressions that his initial cursory inspection hadn't revealed. Irregularities in the carving was his first impression, however, his curiosity had begun to get the better of him. He held the chest closer to the light for a better look. Brushing off the layer of dust with his shirt sleeve, he was able to see that the depressions had a regularity about them.

"How about that?" The echo in the room re-asked the question.

The regularity of the depressions could not be wear or use marks. They had to have been placed there for a reason. Carved there.

"Could they be ciphers of some kind?" he asked the empty room.

They could be, but they were not letters he could recognize. In fact, he could barely make them out with his eyes. But, he could feel them and he knew something was there. He decided to solve that mystery a little later.

Garrett pushed the small gray-green chest through the hole and went back to his task of sliding the chests and boxes he wanted Storey to move, into the center of the room. He took a moment to catch his breath, leaning on one of the larger trunks.

Who was responsible for this cache of untold treasure? Who had encased it in this small room? When? Why? So many questions filled his head as he rested. He decided he would review the history of the house. Maybe it would contain a clue.

Aachoo! His sneeze was amplified as it bounced around the walls of the room. The 100+ years of dust had finally gotten to him. He crawled through the hole and walked up to the kitchen for coffee as he waited for Storey.

CHAPTER 14

Garrett had researched the history of his house a few years ago when it had been left out of a newspaper feature, "Glorious Houses of the Confederacy." He recalled he had found two major holes in the house's ownership. The first was right before the Civil War reached Charleston, the other right after it.

In the winter of 1863, Col. Jacob Heyward, the owner of Dessassauer House caught pneumonia and died three days after Christmas. In the fashion of that time, the house should have belonged to his eldest son. Col. Heyward had only daughters, five of them. The ensuing family squabble caused a great deal of conflict among the daughters, their husbands and Mrs. Heyward, who continued to live in the house. A duel resulted between two of the brothers-in-law leaving one dead and the other permanently crippled. Other spats between family members caused Mrs. Heyward to be hospitalized. Her absence resulted in a succession of occupants as daughter after daughter moved in and out of the house, each trying to convince her mother that she should have the house.

In her own way, Mrs. Heyward ended the argument when she sold the house for $15,000 in Confederate money that she gave to St. Michael's Episcopal Church. She sold the house and all its contents to Aaron Driggers, a prominent Charleston factor. Still hospitalized, Mrs. Heyward conducted the sale of the house without the knowledge of the daughters. When the family found out what she had done, she became the object of considerable anger and scorn. Two daughters refused to talk to her and it might have been better had the other three done the same.

The constant bickering and arguing and their efforts to have their mother declared legally insane, thereby negating the sale, caused Mrs. Heyward's death.

"Died of a broken heart," the family doctor was quoted by the local newspaper at the time.

Following the sale of the house to Aaron Driggers, the history of the house was uncertain for some five years. Whether the Aaron Driggers family ever lived in the house or not is not certain. Within a month of the sale, Aaron Driggers was killed when a buggy in which he was riding turned over after hitting a large rock. His driver, a family slave for many years, was thrown free, but Driggers and the buggy were dragged for four blocks before the horse could be brought under control by a passing cavalry officer.

The newspaper articles that provided the information about this part of the history of the house were limited, since Driggers was not viewed as a positive addition to that neighborhood. In fact, most of the story came from his obituary.

It is speculated that several members of the Driggers family lived in the house prior to the invasion of Federal troops during the Civil War. It probably stood vacant for some time as well.

In early 1865, Federal troops occupied the city. #13 Church Street was selected as the headquarters for the Yankee troops. Its unique design provided for offices on the main floor. The upstairs was used as quarters for the commanding officer and his aides. The downstairs housed his security troops. #13 Church was centrally located to the other homes that had been pressed into service during the conflict.

With the ending of the fighting in the area, Federal troops left the city.

Although not officially titled, the Dessassauer House was used by a number of Northern carpetbaggers following the war. Although few records exist concerning the day-to-day events of that period, an article in the Charleston Mercury, the white underground newspaper of the time, reported that the first Charleston County President took over the house during the first five days of his tenure in office. A black scalawag, he was shot in the back by his friend and sergeant-at-arms who was the only person allowed in his presence with a gun.

The executioner became County President until his untimely demise two days later.

Short terms of public service were common among the politicians of that time. The newspaper article recorded a long succession of political leaders with various titles, however, there was no mention of the Dessassauer House.

By 1872, a sense of stability had replaced the political chaos that followed the war. Stability in daily lifestyle and daily activities as well as politically. Charleston was a resilient town inhabited by resilient people. The carpetbaggers and scalawags had been ousted from governmental positions, and most had either left the city or been killed. Normality had begun to return to Charleston and to #13 Church Street. The house was pretty well intact, considering the string of recent occupants and that many other historic homes nearby had been destroyed in the war.

The true signal that normality had returned to #13 Church Street was in the person of Andrew Maybank and his young wife Sealla. When Maybank returned from the war, he was able to pick up with his cotton, rice and indigo plantation, thanks in no small part to the efforts of his wife and loyal former slaves. Its location on a sheltered peninsula northwest of the city made it impossible for the invading armies to see, and so it survived unscathed. With the revival of Charleston's social lifestyle, the young Mrs. Maybank wanted to be closer to the action. Maybank soon became a prominent fixture in the political landscape of the city and, as a result of his successful farming operation, a good reputation and a natural wit, he was soon elected to the state Senate.

The Dessessauer House remained in the Maybank family until Maybank's great, great grandson sold it to Garrett's father.

Even with all he knew about the house, Garrett could only speculate who could have sealed the treasure in the room under the basement. It could have happened long before the Civil War, but that wasn't likely even though most items easily dated many decades before.

He knew that many people had hidden their treasures before the federal troops occupied and looted the city. Could Col. Heyward have collected his neighbors' treasures, without his wife's knowledge, prior to his death? Could Aaron Driggers, the well-respected and trusted factor, have concealed the results of an illegal side business in this cellar room during his renovations prior to moving in? Was it a safekeeping place for treasure stolen by federal troops? Was it a treasure trove for political thieves during reconstruction? Or, could pirates have sealed one of the numerous tunnels in the area to protect their booty until it could be reclaimed?

The truth could lie in the answer of any one of the questions. Knowing the truth would be impossible for Garrett without a lot of luck. He preferred the story of the pirates. But what difference did it make anyway? He had the treasure now. That's all that really mattered.

CHAPTER 15

It was the sound of the buzzer that jarred him from his thoughts. He looked at his watch. Dust from the room and poor lighting obscured the face. He wiped it on his pant leg; forty-five minutes had passed. It was probably Bob Storey.

Storey began complaining as he entered the house.

"You should'a answered the door fast'a, Mista Garrett. I'm most near drenched to the bone. I'll probably catch ma' death. You know my rhumatis acts up when it's wet out." Storey's voice, however, was as strong as ever.

"Don't get me wrong, Mista Garrett. I'm glad you got some extra work for me. Can always use those extra bucks." Garrett always marveled at Storey. He was always well-paid, even now. Garrett provided him with a house. He paid no utilities. The senior Garrett, before his death, had arranged a trust fund for Storey, as he had done the other three employed servants. To the best of Garrett's knowledge, Storey had never touched any of that money. Judging from what he could find in his father's records, Storey's savings should be worth well over $800,000; with compounding interest, possibly much more.

Storey lived, however, like he paid his bills one step ahead of the re-possessor. Never married, his only living close relative was his mother. Storey made no extravagant purchases. He always bought used cars. And yet, he constantly *poor-mouthed* to Garrett.

"What's you got for me to do?" Storey asked as he dried off with the towel Garrett had given him. "I hope it ain't too strenus. You know, with all this rain, I ain't had no chance to stretch my muscles. I don't want to throw my back out."

Garrett studied Storey as he was complaining. He had to be over 60 years old. You couldn't tell it by looking at him. His gardening had kept him outside much of the time and his face was a walnut brown with the texture of expertly-tanned leather. Wrinkles cut deep furrows across his forehead, but they only added a look of rugged youngness, not age. Well-developed muscles rippled across his body when he moved, evidence of years of physical labor, and evoked the envy of men much younger, like Garrett.

Garrett had never met Storey's mother. He knew little about Storey's past except that he had grown up very poor. He had little education and exhibited a tendency to be introverted with everyone except Garrett.

He had told Garrett many times that working in the ground kept Mother Nature's fountain of youth flowing in his veins. Other people had often suggested some less holy origins for Storey's health.

He remembered, even when he was very young, none of the black servants would have anything to do with Storey. They said he had the *evil eye* and he could do *spells* on them. That was why Garrett's father had remodeled the carriage house for Storey — to keep him away from the house servants.

Garrett had been a visitor to Storey's four-room apartment many times when he was growing up. He saw nothing unusual there. Pictures of Storey when he was younger and a half dozen faded photos of a beautiful young woman. Garrett had asked who the woman was. Storey would always quietly answer, "Only a special friend." Storey had always seemed quite normal to Garrett.

But, when Storey entered the kitchen, Garrett remembered Queen Ester would scurry from the kitchen clutching her asafoetida bag. She had told him she wore it to *keep off the evil spirits.*

When Garrett was young, he never felt strange around Storey, no matter what the servants might have thought. Storey had always been a friend to the young Mister Garrett. Being an only child with no mother was a lonely way to grow up and Storey was Garrett's friend. After all, it was from Storey's magazines that Garrett received his first anatomy lessons.

Lately, as an adult and the head of the house, Garrett had begun to feel something odd when he was around Storey. Something that made him not trust Storey at all. The same aloofness that made Storey so unusually attractive when Garrett was a child made him suspicious as an adult.

Garrett had tried, unsuccessfully, to find out what Storey did when he wasn't working. He would often be gone all night. Always there for work the next morning. Garrett's subtle questions were met with evasive answers. So mistrust abounded, since the Find especially. Garrett had decided that first night that he didn't want Storey to know any more about the treasure than absolutely necessary.

"Well, Bob, what I wanted is to get some of those old trunks out of the hole in the first floor. I want to take a closer look at them. I've made some room for them in the room where we were working."

Garrett was speaking as he walked toward the stairs to the first floor. Storey hadn't move to follow him.

"Oh, Mista Garrett. Is you sure you want to mess around in that hole? There's some strong mojo working down there. I can feel it in ma' bones. Strong mojo, you can bet on that."

It was the first time that Garrett could remember having heard even a hint of uncertainty in Storey's voice.

"What's the matter, Bob?" Storey's hesitancy gave Garrett his first feelings of superiority over his gardener. "You think there's some of your haints down there?" Even though Storey worked for Garrett, there was always something about him — an air of self-assurance, superiority, something.

"Don't laugh, Mista Garrett. You may not be the last to laugh." Storey's voice had dropped to a whisper but Garrett heard it and it made his skin crawl. He paused for a few seconds on the landing.

"Enough of this shit, Bob. Haints or no haints, I want those trunks out of that hole. I've already moved the ones into the center of the room that need to be moved out. So, let's get with it, if you don't mind."

Garrett was pleased with his take charge attitude with Storey. He smiled as he made his way down the stairs with Storey following behind him.

"It won't take long, Bob, but a couple of the trunks are a little on the heavy side."

Garrett watched as Storey lowered himself into the small room through the hole. He landed with a grunt and began lifting the trunks out through the hole.

Six trunks, one large wooden crate and three recently sealed cardboard boxes, items Garrett had repacked to hide from prying eyes, were pushed up through the hole. They were followed by a perspiration-soaked Storey.

"I've had enough of this hole, Mista Garrett," Storey said as he climbed out of the hole.

"What do you think's in these here steamers?" As Garrett had presumed, Storey had begun to get nosey.

"Don't know yet, Bob," Garrett hoped his short answer would cut off Storey's questions.

"Here. I think I can get this one open for you." Storey moved to the largest of the trunks.

"No! Bob!" Garrett caught himself before he revealed too much of his desire to keep the contents secret from Storey. He didn't want Storey to see his anxiousness about the treasure. That would surely fuel his curiosity. "I don't want you to get hurt, Bob. You never know about these old trunks. Sometimes they were booby-trapped. I'll open them later, after I've had some time to investigate them."

"God Almighty, Mista Garrett. You mean these cursed old trunks could hurt a body? Well, I never. You said there ain't no haints in that hole. They're in them boxes, that's where they are. I ain't gon'a mess with those trunks, ever again. You want them moved, you move 'em. I ain't gon'a be in the same room as this God-forsaken junk. Something ain't right, Mista Garrett. Mark my words, something ain't right. I feel it. You want anymore of this stuff moved, you git yourself somebody else. You hear me. Git yourself somebody else." Storey's voice trailed off at the end, but the anger and fear were still apparent.

Garrett had seen Storey lose his temper before, so he knew he'd calm down in a day or so. Anyway, the heavy lifting was finished and the nosey Mr. Storey taken care of.

Why did he feel that Storey always pandered to his authority, his position, as if he were laughing to himself, somehow. No matter. Soon Storey wouldn't matter. No one would matter.

Another workweek had ended. Garrett had everything pretty well catalogued. It was truly an amazing find. As best he could determine, the treasure was worth between 50 and 100 million dollars. Some of the items were priceless, however, and could drive the value at auction upwards of 500 million, if it were a good day and the right people were bidding.

Outside the rain had stopped. The autumn sun had already begun its efforts to dry the drenched city. Garrett wanted to celebrate. The rain had stopped and he was a multi-millionaire.

Two good reasons for a celebration.

CHAPTER 16

There was a chill in Ashley's voice when she answered the phone.

"What's the matter?" Garrett knew he had to get to the bottom of Ashley's problem or they would have no fun tonight.

"Nothing, What's the news from the hole in the ground?"

"The *hole in the ground,* as you call it, is fine. Bob got the heavy trunks, the ones with the silver, coins and weapons out today. It's all cataloged, except for a couple of the unique pieces I need an outside opinion on. But, what's important to me is you. You sound so down, what's wrong?" Garrett wanted to be sincere and to sound sincere, but deep down he wanted this over as quickly as possible.

"Nothing," Ashley snapped back. "Nothing."

"Come on, Ashley. I know when you have a problem. I can tell it in your voice."

"I've had a hard day and I have a headache. You called, what do you want?" Ashley's abruptness indicated more than a hard day and a headache.

"Ashley, my love. I have no time for these games today." Garrett thought he was being funny, but too much of his deep feelings made their way into his comment.

"No time for games, is it Mr. Garrett? No time for me is more like it. Did you break your fingers working in your precious Find? Did one of those trunks fall on your head? Or, did you just forget where your telephone was? If I hadn't been so mad at you I'd have been worried that something bad had happened to you."

"Come on, Ashley. You know I've been working all my spare time," Garrett paused and lowered his voice, "on the Find." It was an odd feeling but he didn't want to say anymore about the treasure to Ashley. He trusted her but ...

"Working on the Find is one thing, and I know it's important to you — to us; but I'm important too. Don't you forget that or you just might not have me to worry about at all." The chill had begun to break in Ashley's voice.

"Well, it almost all done. Just a few more items to trace. But, I don't want to talk about it on the phone."

"I'm sorry, Edward. It's this weather. And work. Together I've been in such a bad mood for the past two days. And no calls from you. It's not your fault. At least, not all of it."

"Let's go to the beach. I have something I want to talk to you about."

"What a great idea. I need a break," Lee agreed.

"I'll pick you up in 10 minutes."

"Make it 20 and you have a deal."

Within an hour they were sitting at a picnic table near the Pavilion on Isle of Palms, each sipping a lemonade. Garrett started with his news.

"Well, it's almost done. Like I said, only about two dozen items to verify. Then I'll be done. But I already know it is easily worth 50 million dollars. A good auction and a little luck could jump it to 100 million, more if the right people are there." Garrett's voice had increased in pitch.

"I'm sure you're right, darling. But, let's not start counting our chickens before they hatch," Ashley interjected.

"Maybe you're right, but the thought of being a multi-millionaire has brought more than one smile to my lips over the past week. Now, I've got to plan the big announcement. There are so many things to display and so little room at #13 Church Street. I don't know how I'll be able to make room for everything and everyone," Garrett wasn't expecting Ashley to comment so what she said caught him off guard.

"I can't believe you still want to have the announcement at the store. Just as you said, it's too small. But there's a bigger problem — security. With a lot of people in the store, you won't be able to keep an eye on the things that will make you rich. I've been thinking about the announcement and I have some really great ideas." Garrett's look made Ashley question her timing. She knew how sensitive he was about losing control over things he considered *men's* decisions. Obviously, she had stepped into one of those, again.

"The house is too small. At least, you will agree with me on that, won't you?" Ashley began the familiar system of providing the questions for Garrett to come around to her opinion.

"Yes, I guess so. But, where else can I hold it and still get the credit and recognition for #13 Church Street?"

"That's what I've been thinking about, and I'm not sure right now. Give me until next week. I want to put the whole thing down on paper for you. But, I must have your promise. You must promise to read it completely, consider it just as I present it, and then talk about both the positives and the negatives with me before you make your decision. You will agree that I'm the one who knows how to get the publicity, right?" Ashley had already formulated the entire plan, but she wanted Garrett to have some time to mellow in his position of having the announcement at the store.

Garrett stopped and stared at Ashley in a quizzical manner searching for some hint. Why was she doing this? The Find was his. #13 Church Street was too small. Too small for him to get the right people to see the treasures. Too small to handle an auction of national importance. Too small, even, to get the people from Charleston that he wanted to know about his importance. Even with all the furniture removed, the main floor of the house could hold 200 people, tops. Not nearly enough to impress.

"OK, Lee. I'll consider your ideas, but don't think too *way out*. It is my intention to be the talk of the town, not the laughing stock." Garrett quietly appreciated Ashley's involvement. True, she could get the publicity he wanted. And, she could insure that many of the *right* people were in attendance. She could contribute greatly, but he didn't want her to take control. It was his, and he wanted the control and the credit.

There was a lull. They continued to look at each other. Measuring. Assessing.

"We can't leave this to chance, my love, we have to orchestrate it. You won't be the talk of the town; you'll be the talk of the antique world when I'm finished. You wait and see. If my idea works, you'll see. Two things, though. First, have you talked to anyone at Sotheby's or Christie's?" Ashley was talking faster, a sure sign that she was getting excited.

"No. I haven't talked to anyone about the Find, except you. Storey knows about the old trunks, but not what's in them. He's been very nosey, though. Why?"

"Well," Ashley paused. "Part of the real value for you here is surprise. I think it's best for you to keep the true listing of what will appear at the auction and show completely secret until the night of the announcement. Hints, innuendoes, assurances; but no listings. It'll make the crowd more excited on the night on the showing. Don't you agree?"

"I guess so. But if I don't have someone from Sotheby's or Christie's or one of the other respected houses verify my evaluations, then it's only my word. If I'm wrong ..."

"Edward Garrett, you don't need their verification on what you say. This Find and its value make you the authority. That's how you must be thinking. If you aren't, you'll never be totally successful. Never. Now's your chance. Your opportunity to grab for the brass ring, and the brass ring is within your grasp. It's your chance of a lifetime. Say you miss on one item or two. So what? I guarantee no one will have anything to say about it. Call the values high and everyone will be happy." Ashley was beginning to feel her frustration level rising.

"I just don't want anything to go wrong, Lee."

"Nothing will go wrong, *if* you just listen to me. I'm not going to let you blow this chance by not thinking big enough. The Senator's worst criticism of you is you think small. This is your chance to prove him wrong. I'm just not going to let you screw up this opportunity. Not for you, and not for me." Her voice trailed off as she completed her last sentence. She knew she was being dominating with Garrett on this, but it was that important.

"Leave Sotheby's and Christie's out of it for now. They'll be important when the time's right. Don't call them and don't talk to them if they call you. Not until we are ready for them."

Ashley knew she was right. Now she must either convince or coerce Garrett into agreement. Left to his own planning and execution, the announcement would surely be underplayed and probably poorly planned.

She would not have that happen. Not this time.

"You listen to me and Sotheby's will be calling you. So will Christie's and everyone else who counts. You'll be the talk of the antique world and all of Charleston and South Carolina, for that matter. Then I'll; *we'll* be able to shove those snide comments right up the noses of those stuck-up, pretentious society people I have to hang around. You'll have the recognition you deserve and I'll be there right by your side. I'll be so proud of you, baby."

Moments of awkwardness followed Ashley's animated expression. They continued to walk quietly along the beach, caught up in their own thoughts. Ashley broke their introspection.

"Something else has been bothering me, Edward. Are you aware of any laws covering the ownership of a treasure like this? I recall, it was a few years ago, there was a big legal battle over the ownership of a treasure found in a ship wreck off the coast of Georgetown. I'm not sure how it ended up, but I know the state claimed that the treasure contained historic artifacts over 100 years old, and therefore they belonged to the state of South Carolina. I started to look up the story in the newspaper's library, but I didn't have a spare moment."

"The treasure is mine, dammit. I found it. It's in my house. So it's mine. Mine, do you hear me? Mine!" Garrett was instantly frantic, then quietly insistent, then assured. "I found it. They won't take it away from me. I won't let them."

"Calm down, Edward. I only asked if you knew about the law. But it is something we must consider. I'll look into it further. I have an attorney friend who might be some help." Ashley tried to bring a calm into her voice.

"You can look into it all you want, but I can tell this one thing, that treasure's mine. It's on my property. I've spent untold hours with it and I'm not going to give it up, not without a fight. I'll destroy it first." Garrett's voice had calmed and dropped to a calculated whisper. "I'll destroy the whole damn thing, first."

Silence again consumed them as they continued their walk on the beach. Holding hands like a pair of junior high kids on an afternoon date, Ashley Cooper Barrineau and Thomas Edward Garrett, re-established some of the bond they had lost in the past few weeks of activity.

The beach was pleasant in the fall. The chill in the air kept the hoards of yelling, inconsiderate bathers away. No Frisbees careened pilotlessly through the air. No volleyballs strayed inadvertently from their rectangular fields of play. No remote-controlled cars played bully, spinning sand on unsuspecting sun worshipers. And, the more pleasant shrill cries of sea gulls caught in their effortless games of aerial tag replaced the piercing screams of diaper-dirty babies.

Edward and Ashley left the only footprints on the beach at this low tide. As it usually did, the beach had a calming effect on Garrett. They continued their walk, stopping only occasionally to pick up one of nature's mobile homes.

"You said something about your dreams, Edward." It was Ashley who broke the silence first.

Garrett hesitated for a moment, but finally told Ashley of his recent dreams. First the hanging, then the choking, and the one about his father.

Ashley listened, dutifully, and offered no comment and no conclusion.

For all who draw the sword will die by the sword.

Matthew 25:52

PROPHECY

Screams — from all sides. Ear-rending screams — cursing, crying, sobbing, yelling. Commands — military commands. "Don't let them get away! The infidels! Cut them down! Split the bodies in half! I want to see the streets red with their non-believing blood! I want their guts spread out for the others to see! For the glory of Almighty God!"

The command came from my right, from a horse-borne, metal-encased warrior. Reigning his horse to the right — a deft movement of his sword arm — I watch the action as the slow-motion sequence of a movie. The shiny blade stops at the apex of its deadly circle. Poised there for a fraction of a second as the target distance and movement are carefully measured.

Whoosh.

"No, no. Not my baby. Not my ba ... Aaagh!"

The young woman carrying the small infant was stopped in mid-sentence by the sword's swift action. An instantaneous spurt sends blood up the side of the white horse. Red spots dot the front of his armor like rust spots on a banished knight's mail. A sickening smell fills my nostrils. A sweet-sour smell followed by the stench of human excrement. The swift blow had sliced the baby in two and placed a long, gaping gash across the woman's body. A mixture of red and brown oozes from the gash. The smell had come from a now open bowel.

I watch with morbid interest — my eyes riveted to the scene even as my mind tells me to turn away. She lay there, under the stamping feet of the horse. Staring at her naked breast, the horror of the action blends with titillation at the sight of the unclothed body.

The blur of the hooves brings my attention back into sharp

reality as a sharp blow leaves a shapeless mass of flesh where the breast had been.

"Look out, you fool," the commanding voice yells at me. A sharp, well-trained move of my left hand shifts my shield into position. The sound was that of wood against metal. The shield had fended off the attacker's wooden spear. Then, it was a swift, effortless move of my right arm. My sword entered between the old man's ear and shoulder. He slumped to the ground on his back, a scream frozen in time on his lips.

"Good reflexes, my son. One less of those Allah-worshiping infidels to worry about. Keep up the good work. Glory be to God!"

On his shield was a cross. Across the top, an inscription, "Glory to God."

What kind of place is this? The sickening smell attached itself to my senses like dew on fall roses. The smell of death was everywhere. Screams and yells fill the air. Blood dyed the legs of our horses, caked on their bellies. Blood was everywhere. Splatters stained our armor, shields, swords, everything bore notice to the carnage. Even the village, in the streets, blood stands ankle deep.

A blood-curdling scream from my right sends a shiver over my skin. A pull on the reigns sends my horse in that direction. A lance meant for me grazes his right fore-shoulder, a lance meant for me. A moment's delay would have put the lance in an opening in my armor. Quick reflexes have saved my life, again. Reflexes trained and well learned.

The feeling of relief is quickly replaced by panic.

"Oh, my God!" I cry.

I feel I'm falling. But why? I'm soundly seated on my horse. Why am I falling? The lance must have entered my horse, hit a vital organ. I've got to maintain my balance, get to my feet. I've got to, I think. I must jump free of my horse.

"Help! Help!" I cry.

No one notices me as I fall. I look around. Everyone is fighting. No one notices.

"Oh, my God! Help me! Help me!" I cry again.

I jump, but the horse's momentum pushes me backwards. Balance, I tell myself. I must maintain my balance.

"Help me! Help me!" I cry again.

Thump!

I'm fighting to keep my breath. My helmet's gone. I struggle to regain my footing. The weight of the metal suit keeps pulling me down. What is the watery muck I'm in? Oh God. No! It's the blood and ooze from the bodies, that's filling my armor. Three faces come into view.

"Help me! For God's sake. Help me get up!" I scream.

The faces are unfamiliar, bearded and — foreign. No matter, help has come.

"Oh, no!"

Their eyes. In their eyes, the look. Hatred. Terror. Like the look on the face that my sword had separated from its body. Now I see six hands reaching for my face. Three ugly, twisted mouths scream their curses.

"Mercy! Show me mercy!" I plead as one pair of hands finds my throat.

I fight to fend him off, I break the grasp on my throat — gasp a breath of air. Another pair of hands is forcing my face into the muck.

"No!" I scream, but I hear no sound.

The smell is everywhere. That sickening smell. A rush of pressure forces my head under the bloody muck.

Close your mouth and eyes, I tell myself. *Stop breathing. Your comrades will help soon,* I assure myself.

I see the dark red color of the muck through clenched eyelids. The smell is ever-present even though I'm not breathing. Droplets of the muck push their way through my clenched lips. The taste causes waves of nausea to coarse through my body. Fighting not to retch. I'm limp now. Energy seems to have been sapped from every muscle.

"Hurry! Help me!" I want to call out.

I need air. The color of the muck is getting darker, much darker. The smell doesn't seem quite so bad as before. Help must be on the way.

I know what I must do. I must muster all the energy left within me. I must get their attention with one last scream. I pull together every ounce of strength from every corner of my being. At the very last instant I open my mouth and ...

CHAPTER 17

Aaaaahhhhhhh!"

"Edward, for God's sake. What's the matter? Wake up. Wake up!" Ashley's yelling blended with his nightmare.

His scream was like nothing she had ever heard. Like one from the other side of the grave.

Garrett was fighting her. She had never known him to be so strong. With one strong push, Garrett tossed Ashley out of the bed and onto the floor.

"Damn you, Edward Garrett!" Ashley called, as she grabbed the water glass Garrett kept on his bedside table and tossed its contents into his face.

"No! No!" Garrett screamed. "Not this way. Not this way!"

"Edward! Wake up, will you?" Ashley screamed again.

"Huh? What?" Garrett may have been on his way back to the present, but he was not yet totally awake, still fighting his unseen attackers with his hands.

"Edward! Wake up!" Ashley was shaking him now.

"What? Ashley? Is that you? Thank God you're here. Thank God you've saved me. That foul smell. Those ugly foreigners. You saved me, Lee. Saved my life."

"What are you talking about, Edward? It was only a dream. Another nightmare. I've been here beside you all night. There's been no one else in the room and no smell. Come on. Shake it off, all right? Here, I'll get a towel." Ashley went into the bathroom and returned with a towel.

"No! Not that towel. That's a new one, I don't want to wipe up this bloody mess with that. Get an old rag."

"Bloody mess? What the hell are you talking about, Edward.

It's only water. The water I threw on you to wake you up. Here, wipe your face and get up so I can change the bed linens." Ashley was pushing Garrett out of the bed as she talked to him.

Garrett walked, slowly and unsurely, into the nearby bathroom. He splashed more water on his face. By the time he had returned, Ashley had fixed the bed. They sat, together, cross-legged in the freshly made bed and Garrett described his most recent dream. Like the two others, he had experienced it through his own eyes. But this one was different. The growing erection during his description of the killing and mutilation of the young mother was his first indication. The slightly too large robe concealed his condition from Ashley for the moment. By the time he had finished the description he was fully aroused. It was both his aroused state and his embarrassment that caused Garrett to suggest they return to bed.

Lights out, Garrett slipped between the cold sheets. The coldness further titillated his sexually steaming body. Snuggling next to Ashley, desire overcame embarrassment.

What followed was over an hour of the wildest lovemaking that Garrett and Ashley had experienced. Thinking back on their unbridled passion, Ashley thought she could have easily been with another man. Garrett had never been so aggressive, so innovative, so inventive.

In the charcoal gray light of Sunday morning, sleep evaded her. She thought about the things that could have changed Garrett so completely in this part of their relationship. She decided that, for the moment, she didn't care what it was that changed him. In the satisfied glow that she felt, whatever it was that caused Garrett's new sexual aggressiveness was welcomed.

As for Garrett, sleep had returned, pushing exhaustion from his brain and muscles. Sex tonight had been reckless and wild. Uncharacteristic for Garrett, he had been the initiator. Their lovemaking had lasted well over an hour, much longer than normal. It had included three orgasms for Garrett, a first in his sex life. Garrett realized that during his lovemaking with Ashley, he had visualized the killing and mutilation of the woman of his dream. Over and over. But, what difference did that make? Fantasies were a normal part of Garrett's lovemaking ritual.

His youthful sexual fantasy came from an encounter that had

been an embarrassment to him. Francie Schwartz, revered as one of the best-looking girls in high school, as much for her large breasts as for her pretty face, had agreed to go out with him. It was a school dance and out for a bite afterward. She had a reputation, and he hoped to be one of her conquests. The night had progressed beautifully. Slow dances had allowed him to nestle between those sensual mounds that had made her so popular. She danced real close and as they swayed with the music, more time was spent rubbing than dancing. Burgers and shakes followed.

They had left the dance early, leaving time to cruise the areas where other teenagers went to be seen and appreciated. Garrett had talked his father into letting him use the new Cadillac. The one whose front seats would *lay back to make a bed,* or so the ads said.

Garrett was proud as he rode around Charleston with Francie snuggled there under his right arm. Occasionally, his hand accidentally glanced across the front of her sweater. What a thrill. Touching her breast. Something to talk about, brag about to the guys.

He stopped the car on an isolated part of Folly Beach. A real good parking place, the guys had said. A nice place to watch the submarine races. He and Francie played around in the front seat. Garrett had gotten his hand under her sweater. Feeling her breast through the heavy stitching of her bra. It was Garrett's elbow that hit the horn ring. It was Francie who suggested that he show her how the seats became a bed.

The added room made removing her sweater much easier. He fumbled with the catch on her bra. *Damn those catches.* Finally, success. His first gropes were a touch of heaven. He actually had his hands on Francie's breasts. No matter how many had been there before, it was his first and he was ecstatic. How much further would she go? That was his next question.

Having thoroughly explored the twin peaks, Garrett went in search of other territory. His hand slipped unimpeded up her leg. *Damn those panty girdles.* Off with the panty girdle, stockings, sweater, bra and with her skirt bunched around her waist, Francie had not been wasting time with Garrett. She had unbuttoned his shirt and unbuttoned and unzipped his blue jeans. Garrett was sure that night would be his night. He had slipped down his jeans and her panties when the blue and white car rolled quietly into the area with its lights off.

The flash light beam seemed bright enough to be a searchlight. Later, at the police station, old man Schwartz had blamed the whole thing on him. He made a big scene, and that big-titted slut didn't say anything. It offered Dr. Garrett another opportunity to berate his son's future. And by Monday everyone at school knew.

He endured the embarrassment and the snide comments from some of the girls and prudish boys at school, because he now enjoyed the admiration of the boys that counted. And some of the girls. Now he was included, where in the past, he had been left out. Acceptance, to a teenager, can be a most valuable thing.

That evening with Francie had provided Garrett with a source of many pleasant moments. Although she never knew it, Garrett finished that evening in his mind, literally hundreds of times, maybe more. Francie became Garrett's first conquest mentally, if not physically.

The exotic dancer, Penny, was the most recent source of his fantasies. In his mind, Garrett, had become the snake that had traveled around her body. First, touching her lips with the tip of his forked tongue. Licking her breast. Nuzzling his nose under the skimpy G-string of her costume. Slipping, very slowly, out of sight.

His fantasies never included Ashley, or any of the other girls who made up his list of conquests. Fantasies were made only of unsuccessful efforts. Francie Schwartz, Penny and a few others.

Garrett snuggled close to Ashley, moving in his dreams between those large breasts he knew so well.

"Francie, what a great body you have."

The saving grace for Garrett was that the way he mumbled, *Francie* sounded a lot like *Ashley*.

CHAPTER 18

Morning light had arrived and settled in comfortably before Ashley and Garrett began to awake. Garrett looked at the clock. Then he remembered that it was Sunday, no need to worry about the time.

"I'm glad you were here last night, Lee," Garrett said as he again yawned. Stretching, scratching he continued, "I would have never gotten any sleep after the dream. As it is, I feel great, the best rest I've had in weeks."

Garrett moved from under the covers. Still nude, he grabbed for his robe as he started to leave the bedroom. Ashley curled into a fetal position under the covers.

"A little breakfast will make us both feel better," he said to the ol' Mr. Coffee in the kitchen. He filled it with water and the proper amount of coffee, and plugged it in the socket. It didn't take long before the smell of the coffee was floating on the air as coffee maker was babbling away about its day, the weather and other things that concerned a Mr. Coffee. Garrett didn't seem to notice, possibly because he didn't understand Colombian.

The aroma of the Eggs Benedict and coffee had announced breakfast long before Garrett walked gingerly into the bedroom. The advance warning had given Ashley the opportunity to freshen up, brush her hair, re-straighten the bed, place last night's damp sheets in the dirty clothes pile and slip into her discarded nightgown. She was sitting in the bed drawing in a notebook when Garrett re-entered the bedroom.

"It smells wonderful, Edward."

Ashley put the notebook aside as Garrett set the large silver tray on the foot of the bed.

"Breakfast with Edward Garrett. What a wonderful way to spend a Sunday morning."

"It was good to be able to snuggle up next to you after we rolled and tumbled last night. I'm glad you didn't have to go home afterwards. I slept like a baby. No dreams."

Garrett was stretching the truth about no dreams. No nightmares would be closer to the truth. Francie had made an appearance in the dream that followed their lovemaking, but Garrett saw no need to bring that up.

"Good."

"The food or no dreams?" Garrett asked.

"Both," Ashley answered him with a mouth filled with food.

"What's that you're writing? Diagramming our activities of last evening for posterity?"

"No. Just some ideas on how to handle the announcement of the Find. Nothing set in stone. Just some ideas. But I think I'm on to something." Ashley answered him as she took another bite of English muffin soaked with freshly poached egg and home-made Hollandaise sauce.

"You plan to let me in on this scheme to announce my Find, or do I have to wait to see if I'm sent an invitation?" Garrett was trying to make light of the situation but enough of the bite got through for Ashley to know she had trod on Garrett's easily hurt feelings.

"I'll tell you when I'm good and ready, Mr. Garrett." Ashley paused long enough to fully capture Garrett's attention. "Just kidding, Edward. I'll tell you my idea, but first, will you answer some questions for me?" Ashley had finished her breakfast, Garrett was only half through.

"I guess so." Garrett had already been thinking about the announcement. Of course, it would be at #13 Church Street and he would preside over the event and make the necessary arrangements. After all, what could be better for business than to have all the important people in his store.

"How many people do you expect to have at the auction?" Ashley asked. Garrett paused.

"Well?" Ashley asked.

"Two thousand, maybe," he replied but there was a question in his voice.

"You still want the auction to be at #13 Church Street, don't you?" she asked.

"Well, yes. How did you know?"

"Just an educated guess," she said half aloud and half under her breath. "You realize there's no way to have two thousand people in here, don't you?"

"But having the auction here at #13 Church Street would be good for business. Good for me." Garrett hadn't been doing well in scoring points for logic, so he thought this one would be a winner for him.

"That's my point. The number of people you want at the auction is important." Ashley was using Garrett's answers to put him in a corner and he knew it. It always made him angry when she did this.

"Well, no. You know I want thousands of people at the auction. Important people. I had hoped I could arrange some way to rotate the people who I want there. Two shifts, maybe three." Garrett realized how ludicrous what he just said was, but he wanted to be right and he was grabbing at straws.

"What would you say if I could show you a way to have two thousand people at the auction, even three thousand at the same time? A way for you to sell as much of the Find as you want and get top dollar for each item. A way to make it the news event of the year. I bet I can even get the TV networks there." Ashley began to capture Garrett's interest. He abandoned what was left of his breakfast. He liked the idea of a way to sell. He liked the big crowd and he liked the idea of national media coverage. But deep in the back of his skull he resented being pushed around like this.

"All right, I'll listen; but remember antique people are very conservative. I know."

"Remember yesterday. We talked about you thinking too small. I didn't mean to be cruel — just truthful. This is your big opportunity — and, in a way, mine too, remember? An opportunity like this comes along once in a lifetime if that often. Think about all the problems of having the auction at #13 Church Street. It's simply too small. There's no parking. What will you do with the antiques that are already here? Move them to some place else? There's no room to put them here. It would cost you a fortune to store them somewhere else. Another thing, what about security? And insurance? No one in their right mind would insure the Find stored in your store."

All of Ashley's points made perfect sense, but the resentment still chewed at the recesses of his logic. Did she always have to be right?

"You raise some good points but where are you leading?" Garrett sounded far more formal than he intended. "All you've done is present questions."

"That's the real beauty of the idea; it answers all the questions I could come up with." The excitement was evident in Ashley's voice. "We'll rent a hall, like say the Hibernian Hall. It will easily hold three thousand people.

Garrett interrupted. "That's all well and good, but how will three thousand people be able to see, much less examine the items in the Find. And if they can't examine, they won't buy." Garrett was pleased with his display of control.

"Damn it, Edward. Can't you stop thinking small for one minute? It's the *event* that will make you the talk of the antique business and the talk of the town, not the sale of an item or two. Besides, what I'm thinking about is a massive multi-media treatment for the auction. Lots of pictures of each item projected big enough for everyone to see. Big enough so that everyone can examine without the item even being in the room. In addition to the excitement of the event, you'll get the excitement of the crowd working for you. Bidding on many or even all of the items could go on through the entire evening. It's the best of an open auction and the best of a priced sale. It'll be the first in Charleston and, I'll bet, a first in the antique business. And with the Internet's world-wide auction capabilities, bidders could be anywhere in the world where there's WiFi."

Ashley's idea began to take on a better shape in her mind.

"That still doesn't tell me how it would work." Edward, although still very skeptical, was beginning to catch her excitement and some of what she was proposing was lodging in his mind.

"Do you remember the show on Charleston's history that we saw at the Chamber of Commerce or that movie of China that we saw at Epcot?" Ashley asked.

"Sure, but what do they have to do with…?" Garrett was interrupted as Ashley began to answer his question before he finished asking them.

"The shows themselves have nothing to do with the auction, but *how* the shows were done, does." Ashley reached for her notebook. "I shouldn't be doing this until I'm ready but I'll show you some of the preliminaries. The Hibernian Hall is a square room. Using 12 screens positioned like this," Ashley drew a square and then started making lines that angled each corner with two lines between each angle.

"By placing a projector on each of these screens you will have a digital photo show, in the round, totally around the entire hall. Each photo change can be a new item shot from 12 different views. Some can be extra close-ups, others to accentuate markings, others could show the entire item. Everything that would be important for a potential buyer to see would be visible and many times bigger than life." She was pointing to the rather geometric pattern that looked more like it belonged in a high school mathematics book than a plan to announce the antique find of the century.

"What the hell is that?" Garrett asked.

"It's screen placement, Edward. I knew I shouldn't have started this until I was ready."

"Just give me a minute, Lee. So far, a lot of what you say makes some sense. But, I'm still not convinced that the auction should be away from the store. I'm sure that your idea about using digital images is a good one, but from what you've drawn, I simply can't tell."

"I told you I shouldn't have told you about the idea before I was ready. The only way to really show you what I mean is to make a small model of the room. I'll do that by the middle of the week. Then you can decide. Another thing we must be concerned about is security. I've already warned you about the state possibly claiming the treasure. But the security during the announcement, and before and after, is a major problem to consider. If you make the announcement with digital photos, you won't have a security problem. Then you can put the treasures in a mini-warehouse in Savannah, Charlotte or Jacksonville, out of the reach of the state and out of touch for any one trying to steal it."

"Now you've hit on a good reason, but I'm still not convinced." Garrett was trying to close this discussion. "It's your idea, so it's up to you to sell me on it and up to you to find someone who can pull it off. If I decide to do it, of course."

"You are on, as they say, Mr. Wise-ass," Ashley paused. "I'm going to make a national success out of you, if I have to drag you kicking and screaming all the way. And that looks like how it's going to be."

"What am I supposed to do?" Garrett sounded almost like a whiney kid.

"Your job, Mr. Garrett, is to keep your mouth shut. If you want this to be the talk of the international antique business, you must talk to no one before the auction. We will plan what to say when the time is right. That's very important. Talk to no one until we are ready, even if we leak the information. Oh, one other thing. Have your tux cleaned. You'll want to look your best to meet all your new-found best friends. Do you think you can handle your job, Edward?"

"I think it's time you stopped patronizing me. First Storey, now you, I'm not going to take it.

"I meant..."

Garrett stopped her. "I know what you meant. Believe me, I know what you meant. You don't seem to understand that I want this announcement to be a success as much as you do. Successful for me, for you, for us — but I feel like I'm losing control. I don't want to screw it up. Let's do it together. OK?"

"OK," Ashley replied, quietly. She was right, he was right, with right being on both sides, where could this argument go?

Long moments of silence followed.

"When is the Senator expected back?" Garrett asked, not really caring.

"Not until Tuesday. Most special sessions last two or three days. They are usually called by the Governor when he is being pressured by some group of people somewhere in the state. This one's from a do-gooder group in the Pee Dee trying to stop all industrial development on the coastal areas. One of the leaders of the group was a major contributor to the Governor's last campaign. The Senator thought he had killed the bill in committee. But the Governor called this special session. He's such a weak sister." Ashley had provided much more information than Garrett wanted, but not more than he needed. "I'm going home. Mom's by herself and there are things I can do there." She surprised Garrett by the announcement of her departure.

"Do you have to go? I don't want to be alone." It had slipped out before Garrett knew what he was saying.

"Yes, I think I should go. I want you to have some time to think about what we talked about. This is your decision now, Edward, your opportunity to be famous. I can only advise. I know I'm right, but it's your life, too. I love you." Ashley had closed the door before he had a chance to say anything else.

Why hadn't he stopped her? Why hadn't he said something? Why hadn't he convinced her to stay? He knew he could. Had he wanted her to leave? She was so competent, self-assured. Why did he feel so weak in comparison?

It's my Find, isn't it? Damn her.

CHAPTER 19

The rest of Sunday was basically undirected. He could have opened #13 Church Street for business, but there seemed to be no reason. He didn't really want to see or talk to anyone. He could spend time organizing the Find, but why? It would only remind him of his conflict with Ashley. He could go someplace, but where? If was during his deliberation that he realized just how much a part of his life Ashley had become. He hated himself for his weakness.

Why, at this stage of his life, had someone else become so important? Why had he become so dependant on someone when he prided himself on being so independent?

He plopped down on the sofa in his room and picked up the TV remote control. He switched it to the football game. Two teams were playing. He didn't care who because he wasn't really watching. The pictures were occupying his eyes, the sound his ears. Neither invaded his brain.

The day passed very slowly. Tiring of the football game, he walked around the Battery. Fall offered a plethora of beautiful pictures for his eyes that, today, were lost on him. As he walked, he thought. There seemed to be no answers. There weren't even any clear questions.

Garrett was restless throughout the rest of Sunday and it was well into the early morning hours of Monday before sleep came to him. Much too soon, the harsh sound of morning's raspy wake-up call echoed through the third floor of #13 Church Street and through the reaches of Garrett's head. He had forgotten to switch the clock radio from alarm to music. The grating noise prophesied about how his day would be.

He dragged himself out of bed and shut off the grating noise. In the bathroom, his look in the mirror on that Monday morning revealed the strain of recent weeks. At least what it had done to his face. Lack of sleep had left a vacant look in his eyes. There was a scarlet cast to the whites of his eyes. Furrows had been cut across his forehead. A pallor had begun to replace his customary tan.

For weeks now, Garrett had ignored his exercise regime and his visits to the tanning bed. The resulting lack of energy and listlessness had aggravated his nervousness. And the fading tan made him look even worse. He should have seen the signs of approaching exhaustion when he looked into the mirror, but he simply wouldn't accept the reality of the reflection.

Monday dragged on. No customers broke the monotony of the morning. Garrett replayed the events of the weekend over and over in his mind. Frustration was the result of the replay. He vacillated between being pissed off at Ashley's flippant attitude to being concerned at losing control, being afraid Ashley would leave him if he didn't follow her ideas, to being elated at the impending success the Find would bring him. To have characterized Garrett's emotional swings as a ride on the roller coaster of feelings would have been an understatement.

He expected to hear from Ashley during the lunch hour. It was two o'clock before he accepted the idea she might not call. The rest of the afternoon was a mental battle between his heart and his ego. Mondays are especially good days for egos, so the prideful Garrett resisted the temptation to dial the newspaper's telephone number. On Prideful Monday Garrett's ego refused to talk to Lee or even consider her idea for the auction.

A couple of just-lookers broke up the afternoon, but he continued to dwell on his weekend. A lot of what Ashley said made sense. So why did he hate the ideas so much? Why couldn't they have talked it out? Why did he resist her help so much?

Even the slow motion of the clock couldn't keep the big hand from finding the twelve. The small hand had already found the five. Garrett turned the "CLOSED" sign, locked the door and made his way to the upstairs kitchen.

The ice cubes made a friendly, tinkling sound as they filled the monogrammed glass he held. The Jack Daniels made a happy, sloshing noise as it mingled with the ice cubes. They snapped and crackled in a form of giddy, intoxicated laughter. The warm brown color smiled at him with a sense of accomplishment at the laughter of the cubes. It was a veritable sitcom, right there in Garrett's kitchen. Garrett was the only one in the room not in a jovial mood. Unfortunately, he missed it all. He swallowed the Jack Daniels with only one thought in his mind, to numb his overactive brain. The first was finished in two gulps. The second pouring wasn't nearly so fanciful an occasion.

Garrett walked into his bedroom, clicked on the TV and sat in his favorite, wingback chair to watch the news and wait for Ashley's call. He entered the middle of Family Feud. Steve Harvey was busy kissing the women and trying to be funny.

"100 members of a recent studio audience were asked to complete the following statement," Harvey said. If two-way television had been available to Harvey he would have been able to see that his efforts were wasted on Garrett. Although he was looking, he wasn't watching. It didn't seem to matter to Steve Harvey, however, as he continued his bright, effortless banter.

It was well into the news before Garrett returned to the conscious world. His mental and emotional trip had yielded little, if any, relief from his dilemma. It was a special segment of the local news. A montage of autumn scenes from around Charleston. Each brief scene was synchronized to a fast-paced musical selection.

It was a view of #13 Church Street that first caught his eye, but he soon realized it was an example of what Ashley suggested for the auction. Maybe there was something in what she said. The audio-visual display ended and was followed by a food store commercial utilizing almost the same technique. Garrett went into the kitchen for a refill. A fresh drink in hand, he went back to his chair and TV to wait for Ashley's call.

When Garrett awoke, the television was still on and some unrecognized person was trying to sell him a hair growing liquid. He wasn't interested.

His head hurt as a result of the libations. His neck hurt as a result of his awkward sleeping position, and something deep inside him hurt more as a result of the silent telephone. He stretched as he stood, trying to unknot some of his muscles. The chair, although quite comfortable, was less than an adequate bed. He moved to the bathroom, groped for the light switch and found the aspirin bottle. He took three, enough to handle his headache, he hoped, as he walked over to the bed to resume his sleep. He thought about Ashley.

Damn her, he thought, *why didn't she call?*

A voice deep from within him answered, *Damn you, Edward, why didn't you call?*

Garrett went right back to sleep. Dreams, if there were any, were unremembered. The music of his bedside alarm began at its accustomed time. Lucky for him it was programmed to sound at the same time each day. Last night, setting an alarm would certainly have been forgotten. The aspirins had done their job. Bed sleep had helped his cramped muscles and a fresh new day had removed most of the hurt inside.

But not totally.

Garrett's Tuesday dragged by much as his Monday had. Customers, in and out all day long, served only as interruptions. There had been numerous opportunities for him to call Ashley, but it wasn't until 4:00 that his concern replaced his ego.

"City News; Clark."

"Ashley Barrineau, please," Garrett tried to put a totally business sound to his voice.

"Miss Barrineau is out of the office. Can I leave a message?"

"Do you know how I might reach her? Is she at home?" Garrett persisted.

"No. I'm not sure of her itinerary or when she will return. Can I leave her a message?"

"I guess not. Just leave a note that Edward Garrett called." Dejection was evident in Garrett's voice.

"Oh! Mr. Garrett. Sorry I didn't recognize your voice. She said to tell you that she was in Washington and the she would return Friday. If you wish to call her, she's at the Embassy Row Hotel. I'm sure you can reach her there on her cell.

She didn't answer her cell. By the time Garrett had finished his call to the newspaper, D.C. phone information, the Embassy Row Hotel, Ashley's room and the Embassy Row message desk, it was 4:30.

For Garrett, it had been a very long day — a long week for

that matter, although it was only two days old. His mind ached; so did his body. A visit to the club might be the answer. A good work out, some time in the steam room and a massage. That was certain to make him feel better and occupy time, as well. He turned the sign early and went upstairs to gather his workout clothes.

The exercise made him realize how much his hiatus had done to his body. His muscles began to gripe about this invasion on his laxity. In his body, there was a sinuous meeting in progress. Biceps and triceps were present. The glutes sent a representative. The thigh muscles presided and the abs took the minutes. The question was called and a vote taken. It was unanimous. Garrett would pay for this unexpected liberty. Maybe not today or tomorrow, but it was agreed that each muscle group would find a way to make their individual displeasure known.

The warm, penetrating steam of the sauna, provided the key to unlocking Garrett's sweat glands. Slowly but surely, the poisons of the last few weeks began to ooze from his pores as if they were so many evil spirits being exorcised by the hot and misty holy man.

Seated in the steam room by himself, Garrett began again to think about the Find. It was a true stroke of luck, this time in his favor. He considered many of the pieces in his mind. Which ones did he want to keep? Which ones would be placed up for sale? It would be good for publicity to donate a piece or two to a couple of museums. His accountant would need to advise on that. Plenty of time.

The roughness of the oversized, terrycloth towel further sensitized Garrett's skin as he dried off following his steaming. The Club began to fill as other businessmen ended their day. Mike, the club's masseur, suggested he rest for a few minutes on one of the relaxation couches before his massage. Garrett unwrapped the towel he had tied in kilt-like fashion around his middle. Mike covered him with a sheet. He began to relax again. The quasi-public nudity practiced in this section of the club always made him uneasy.

He began to ponder Ashley's ideas. A large group was definitely a good idea. The audio-visual presentation could add greatly to it being a spectacular event. Selling through a bidding system could force the prices up, especially if the big boys from Sotheby and Christie's were there. Using the Internet would make the auction truly world-wide. He replayed the ideas, over and over. His thought was interrupted by Mike. It was his time on the table. Mike's educated fingers played soothing symphony on Garrett's disturbed muscles. It didn't take long for all thought to slip from Garrett's mind.

It was 7:30 before he returned home. He cursed himself for taking so long and for leaving his cell phone in his bedroom. Ashley could have called. He checked his phone and found no messages or missed calls.

For the next two hours, Garrett tried to occupy himself, waiting for Ashley's call. Television, reading, bookwork, nothing could capture his attention for long. He made and drank a pot of coffee. He finally wandered into the room where he had separated and cataloged the treasure.

Mine, all mine, he thought as he entered.

He moved slowly around the room, fondling this item, stroking another. He ran his fingers through a chest filled with gold coins. He had seen people in the movies do that, now it was him, and the coins were real, and they were his. He and gravity were creating a waterfall of shiny, gold metal. A shiver ran through his body as he picked up one of the old swords — flashes of his last dream went through his memory, so he quickly put it back. He continued through the stacks of the unique items he had carefully catalogued.

One thing attracted his eye. The little chest looked to be made of wood, but its green cast was unlike any of the others in the room. He moved closer and picked it up. Much heavier than it looked, it almost fell from his grasp. He remembered the empty chest from his earlier cataloging. It had been put aside in favor of the more valuable, the more interesting. It had a soft, silky, vibrating feel as he slid his hand across the top of the chest. No more than a foot across, about 8-inches deep and 8-inches high, it seemed to have some kind of power from within. He knew the chest was empty, but ...

He was aware of the power some people said existed in crystals. But he had never felt any power. This box, however, felt like it had mysterious power emanating from within. He moved his fingers back and forth across the top of the chest. It was his fingers that first saw what his eyes could not.

What are the depressions on the chest top?

They were regular, like letters, but he couldn't tell by the feel. Now, with his curiosity aroused, he looked for a better way to see. He tilted the chest this way and then that, to no avail. He tried to use the light to make shadows to outline the characters. Nothing seemed to work. Then he remembered something he had learned in grammar school. He found a piece of paper, but what could he use to shade with? A pencil wouldn't have a large enough flat surface. There were no crayons in the house. He found a china marking grease pencil. Maybe it would work.

Carefully, he passed the orange marker over the paper. The impressions began to become more legible. It brought a smile to his lips. He felt like a real detective, working on a case. They were obviously letters of some kind. Some cipher unknown to Garrett, maybe even a foreign language. This revelation sparked a whole new interest in this chest. What could the letters mean? Could they be the key to events of the past? Could they unlock some even greater treasure? Or could they be some perverted hoax? A joke by some ancient comedian. No matter, he had to know.

It was the ring of the house telephone that shook Garrett from his investigation. He ran up the stairs to the second floor to answer it. It had to be Ashley.

"Hello?"

"Hi Edward," it was the vivacious, happy voice of Ashley. "How's it going? I got your message, but couldn't use my phone. What's up?"

For some reason, it didn't occur to Garrett to be mad at her for not letting him know about her travel plans. Or, how she had acted when they were last together. For that matter, he only knew how happy he was to hear her voice. "I missed you, why didn't you tell me you were making a trip?"

She explained that she had told him about the trip. He remembered, but thought it was next week. She described Washington and a bit about what she was doing.

Then it was Garrett's turn. His news about the green chest was received with acceptable excitement. She said she was pleased to find Garrett in a better mood. If illegible letters on a small chest was all it took, she was pleased he had found them. In the three weeks since the Find, he had rushed from periods of elation to paranoia with unpredictable ease.

She hadn't told Garrett, but she had discussed him with the psychiatrist she had seen. Degrees of paranoid schizophrenia, he had said, was common among people who had experienced unexpected trauma. It was common among servicemen returning from war. Although not as common, similar erratic emotional responses had been observed among people whose life had changed radically and those who had unexpectedly inherited great wealth.

The Find had meant almost as much to Ashley as it had to Garrett, but in different ways. At times, however, she would like to have the old Garrett back, maybe not as exciting, but not as moody.

He babbled on about the chest and what he was doing for the next few minutes, how he would find out what the characters meant. She would be back Friday at noon and there would be no work on the Find over the weekend, but she should make no plans, because he had a surprise for her when she got home.

"I love you, too," Garrett held the phone for a long time after the disconnect click from the other end. He had missed her more than he had realized. He missed her happy, bubbling laughter. He missed her bright, inquiring mind. He missed her warm, cuddling body. His surprise trip to the mountains for the weekend would be good for both of them. A trip to their special place, Woodfields Inn.

CHAPTER 20

Garrett took the chest and his tracing paper upstairs. He sat at his roll-top desk and began trying to trace a better copy of the symbols. For the next two hours, he worked on the characters. The orange marker wasn't working anywhere nearly as well as Garrett wanted. He threw it across the office.

"Damn it to hell!" he cursed as he began a search for something that would give more definition to the shapes on the chest. Then he remembered the charcoal pieces he kept in the basement for restoring drawings. Running down the stairs from the third floor, he tripped on the last step, rolled across the floor, ending up against the wall in a ball, cursing a blue streak.

He carefully moved the various parts of his body to ascertain if the fall had done any damage. Apparently, all was well. He found the charcoal and hurried, a little more carefully, back upstairs.

The charcoal shading made the characters a little more defined, but not yet distinguishable. Staring at the pieces of paper that had now begun to inundate his desk, he began the task of reviewing what he had done and considering what he hadn't.

"Damn!" he exclaimed as he jumped from his chair. Why didn't I think of this before?"

Back to the basement, more carefully this time, he returned with a piece of picture frame glass. Moving his desk lamp to the floor, Garrett arranged the glass on his lap so that the light would shine up between his legs. This arrangement made the shading on the paper easier to see. He then began tracing the tracings. Overlapping the second and third generation tracings produced a fairly accurate representation of the characters.

The characters did resemble letters, but not letters that he recognized. Were the characters from an ancient language of just symbols that meant nothing? Was it real or a hoax? He preferred to think it was a language. But what language? He couldn't even hazard a guess. The characters looked Middle Eastern or at least had some of the flourishes of a Middle Eastern alphabet.

Garrett squinted at the harsh light. His fingers hurt from gripping the pencil and charcoal so tightly. Even his back had started hurting either from the unusual posture required for this work or the fall or both. The tracing had taken well over an hour to complete. Garrett paid particular attention to the details of each letter. He wanted the tracing to be perfect. The second generation of tracings worked better when he pressed harder.

Crash!

Darkness.

"Damn it all!" Garret cursed again, carefully sliding his desk chair backward. The desk lamp had been the only light in the room. It had been knocked out by a piece of the broken glass as it fell from Garrett's lap. He was careful to move as far from the broken glass as he could before he got up to turn on the overhead light.

The light revealed that the breaking glass had left cuts in each leg of his jeans. He looked at his hands. No blood and no obvious abrasions. Lucky, he thought. He could have been badly cut. He glanced down again. There was a reddish-brown spot at one of the cuts in his pants. He pulled off the jeans to see the damage. The blood had begun to run down his leg. Holding the cut with his hand, he moved quickly toward the bathroom. His quick movements and the jeans knotted around his ankles sent him sprawling to the floor, inspiring a string of profanities. Rolling on his back he jerked off the jeans and in one continuous motion, threw them across the room.

In the bathroom, with a wet washcloth he wiped the blood off his thigh and lower leg. A close inspection revealed a bloody, but superficial, cut on his right leg. More profanity followed.

A bit of alcohol and two large adhesive bandages stopped the bleeding. He slipped off the sweatshirt he had been wearing and slipped on his robe. He realized that the close work had given him a headache. Two aspirins and a large glass of water completed his personal doctoring and he returned to the bedroom to clean up the mess.

There were blood spots on the rug where he had fallen, Broken glass was all around his desk. He unplugged the desk lamp, picked up the big pieces of glass and pulled out the vacuum. The tracings he had been working on were torn. That was the last straw.

As tears welled up in his eyes, he yelled. "Damn it all to hell."

He didn't understand the tears. He never lost control of his emotions like this. But, they came in buckets. It was minutes before he regained his composure. He finished his cleaning. He decided his efforts at deciphering the letters were over for the evening. His head hurt, his back hurt and his fingers were cramped.

He turned off the top light and slipped into bed. The chill of the sheets sent a shock through his nervous system. He shuddered and, for an instant, considered wearing some warm pajamas. The idea was abandoned as his body heat quickly warmed his spot in the bed.

That night was filled with many dreams. In one he was chasing the well-endowed Francie across a crowded beach. He was totally clothed in a gray suit, she totally naked. He never caught her.

In another dream, he was at a costume party. It was at #13 Church Street. It was a group of family and friends, many of whom acted like they knew him. None he could place. At midnight, everyone unmasked. Garrett recognized the strangers as people from his recent nightmares. He woke up in a cold sweat.

His next dream found him in New York City but he was still in his house at #13 Church Street. Somehow it had been transported, intact, to an address on Central Park South. There, people were lined up to see him. They had a variety of antique items. He would look at each and announce a price. Each would thank him profusely and leave respectfully. Everyone who came thanked him over and over for taking time to see them. But he saw it in their eyes. No matter what they had said, it was there — hatred and envy. The line never stopped.

In his last dream of the morning, he was riding a bicycle, like the ones used by the high wire circus acts. A groove had replaced the tires. He was riding in a void, nothing was in front or back, nothing on either side and nothing above or below. Just a shimmery, white void. The bicycle's grooved wheels were riding smoothly on a large skinny, white rope. It disappeared into the void both front and back.

Pedaling was easy, almost like coasting. He had no problem keeping his balance. Although he could see nothing, he felt comfortable with his surroundings. He knew he had been riding for a long time, even though he wasn't tired or winded. He didn't know where he was going or why, but it didn't seem to matter either. Everything was progressing smoothly.

It was almost imperceptible, at first. An ever so slight vibration in the handlebars. Then he could see, off in the distance, the rope was moving. As it became more exaggerated, riding became more difficult. He fought the movements of the handle bars to keep control of the bicycle. He fought to keep pedaling. Soon he was hanging on to the bike for dear life, fighting with all his strength to keep upright.

It wasn't one big movement that finally did it. Suddenly, he realized he was falling. Falling into the white void. The bicycle had disappeared as had the rope. Spread out like a skydiver, he was falling, but he wasn't afraid. The white void enveloped him. It restrained his arms, his legs too. The restraint became tighter. He began to fight the void. Fighting to get free. Fear began to grip at his chest.

Breaths — more difficult. As he strained his eyes to see, he began to recognize the void that seemed to encase him. A soft, cotton-like material — a sheet.

He awakened to a room that was flooded with light. He pulled the sheet back. For a moment, the brightness was disorienting.

He hadn't heard his alarm. It was 9:15. He reached for the clock. The alarm had been turned off, just like any other morning.

Could he have turned the alarm off and gone back to sleep? He must have. It was the only explanation.

He jumped out of the bed, ran to the bathroom and hurried through his dressing routine. His exaggerated actions would prove to be unnecessary as it was another customerless day.

Garrett kept the store open until lunch. Actually, he closed for lunch a half-hour early. He wanted to get the necessary tools to unlock the secret of the small gray- green chest.

He knew the art supply store would have everything he needed. He selected a couple of lead pencils of different hardnesses. He added a selection of different papers. He would see which one would provide the most legible image. He also bought film for his camera, black and white Tri-X to copy the characters on the chest. He considered buying a digital camera, but opted to stick with his trusty old 35mm which gave him the ability to process the film himself. Black and white pictures would give him the higher contrast he wanted.

Art purchases made, Garrett stopped at Wendy's for a burger and fries for lunch. His lunchtime trip consumed an hour and a half.

Garrett unlocked the door, balancing his purchases precariously. Inside, he set up the kitchen table as he continued the search for the meaning of the mysterious characters. He set a new pot of coffee to brewing and locked the front door, placing the BUZZ TO ENTER sign in the window.

He carefully carried the chest from the upper floor down to the kitchen, pulled the blinds to darken the kitchen, and went to work.

No customers interrupted.

Using a single light, Garrett set it first at one angle, then another, each attempt was to get the best angle so that the shadows would intensify various parts of the letters on the box. Years of photographing his antiques were coming in handy. Not certain which angle would be best, he made two exposures of each new lighting pattern. He used various filters, even a few shots with a polarizing filter.

Photography completed, Garrett became entranced with the chest. The single flood light used in the photography made the chest glow. Its gray-green color was that of the Spanish moss that hung from most of the trees in Charleston and in the area for that matter. More of the gray on the surface, the green beneath. Under the intense light, however, the green became more dominant. It glowed, as if phosphorescent.

Garrett shot pictures into mid afternoon. Then he processed

the film. Dissatisfied with the results he repeated the process. Then he repeated the shooting again. It was midnight before he decided he needed to stop because he wasn't coming anywhere close to the results he expected.

He left the majority of his photography equipment in the kitchen and, with the little box under his arm, went upstairs to his bedroom. Placing the box on his desk, he stripped off his shirt and pants and slipped into his unmade bed and quickly drifted off to sleep.

His dreams that night were dominated by the mysterious little box.

It was mid morning on Thursday when Garrett awakened. He got up mad at himself. He hadn't had the success he had expected with his photography and he had slept way too long. He threw on the clothes from Wednesday and went downstairs to the kitchen. He put the OPEN sign on the front door and retreated to the kitchen where he put on a pot of coffee and made an egg and bacon sandwich for his breakfast.

He deposited his coffee and breakfast sandwich on his desk and returned to his bedroom to bring the little box so that he could ponder what importance this least valuable piece of the Find could actually have. He took a bite of the sandwich as he sat in his desk chair. He cleaned a space in the center of his desk and set the box there.

The small box held a mysterious magnetism for Garrett. He felt a desire to touch it. A gripping need to know more about this strange little box. It was not unlike the feelings he had when he was a child and he wanted to do something he knew he shouldn't. This, however, was a much stronger need and sinister in nature. It was a feeling deep inside his being. Inside his soul. A feeling of dichotomy.

He would later describe it to Ashley as a feeling of fascination and dread. Of fear and longing. Of love and hate. A feeling similar to what he experienced when he first saw the dead body of his father. He had wanted to embrace him, but he hated the thought of touching a dead body, even his father's.

That very same fear-fascination crept over Garrett's being as he slowly reached for the chest. At first, he moved only his finger tips over its surface, not quite touching it. He felt a vibration, the presence of an energy, or at least he thought he did. A feeling like the sound waves created by a stereo speaker slightly moving the air near its surface. A sensual feel. Almost like a soft down or a peach skin — like hair covering the surface of the chest.

The feeling was mesmerizing.

It could have been minutes. It could have been hours. Garrett couldn't tell. Hazy, undefined mental images began to form as the vibrations tingled his fingers. The feelings of fear gripped his heart.

Time — Stood — Still.

There were no customers to interrupt Garrett's contemplation. Sometime around lunch time, Garrett locked the front door, refilled his coffee cup and resumed his vigil, pondering the little box.

Transfixed, the hazy pictures danced across his mind's eye. Faces, unrecognizable distorted faces, with one thing in common. A look of death. Almost like death masks. Expressions frozen at the moment of death. Then they began to move — to speak. Silent words. Then whispers. They were calling his name.

"Edward? Edward Garrett? Edward?"

"Edward! What in hell are you doing?" Garrett hadn't responded to Ashley's voice. His mind was totally transfixed on the faces and the chest.

"Edward," Ashley softened her voice but it was her touch the broke Garrett's trance.

"Oh," he paused in confusion. "Lee. It's, it's you," Garrett stammered.

"Are you alright," Ashley's worried tone puzzled Garrett.

"Yeah! Sure. I'm alright." He had begun to recompose himself. "I was just concentrating on the letters here on this small chest. That's all. I didn't hear you. Why?" he asked.

"Well, I must have rung the bell a dozen times before I let myself in. Then I called you a number of times before I came in here."

The look in Garrett's eyes frightened Ashley to the point that she decided she wouldn't describe it to Garrett. It was a look she had seen many times during her newspaper career when she was on the police beat. The look of insanity created by meth, speed, or hallucinogenic drugs.

"When I came in here, you were staring at that chest. You looked like you were a — a thousand miles away. That's, that's all," she added.

"I guess I was. I didn't hear you at all." Garrett shook it off. He looked at Ashley and said, "No problem."

Garrett didn't understand what was happening or what had happened to him. He knew he felt strange. He felt he had had one of those out-of-body experiences he had read about. There were things he wasn't in control of and he knew it. But he didn't want to discuss it with Ashley now.

In an effort to change the subject, he hugged her and said, "Hey, what are you doing back from Washington so soon? You weren't supposed to be back until tomorrow. I'm only glad you didn't catch me with some girl instead of this chest."

"Edward Garrett," she said with half-hearted, playful anger as she cuffed him on the side of the head.

Ashley told Garrett about how her interviews had been switched around so that she finished early. She had found his excitement about the letters on the chest made her homesick so she arranged an early flight and here she was.

Garrett began to babble about the letters, the chest, the photographs and finally how much he had missed her. He was saving the best for last — the trip to the mountains.

"And, for this weekend, there's something very special. I've made reservations for us at Woodfields." Garrett knew that Woodfields was one of Ashley's most favorite places. The 150-year old inn was a former roadhouse and one of the oldest continuously operating inns in North Carolina. The 200-mile drive had often been fun as well.

"Oh, Edward, you sweetheart. You're a mindreader. I had already decided I would call them after I had had a chance to talk with you. I love you. When can we leave?"

"Well, let's see. I can close early tomorrow. I could ask Bob Storey to keep the store open but he's been acting quite strangely lately. Ever since the Find, I guess, he's stayed to himself, away from the house. I have to call him every time something needs to be done. And, when he's here, he looks at me in — well it's hard to describe. Like he's afraid of me. He's known me almost all my life. I guess everyone changes. Maybe he's losing his mind or just getting old and senile. There's no real need to be open Saturday. Hell, I'll just keep the store closed. We'll hit the road about 3 o'clock tomorrow, okay?"

"Whatever you say, Edward."

Ashley had noticed Bob Storey's absence and his strangeness. But strangeness was no stranger at #13 Church Street. Since the Find, Garrett was providing his share of strange as well.

"Oh, Lee. I'm so glad you're back. I didn't know how much I would miss you." He paused for a moment as he remembered the past two nights. "But now you're back and it's time to celebrate. How about drinks at the Pelican and dinner at Poogan's and after, well..." Garrett's voice had dropped to a most salacious tone, "I'll show you just how much I have missed you when we get back here."

"Just you wait a minute, my horny young man. It's me that's been on a fast track for the past week, not you. What I need is a good night's sleep, not a good night without sleep. That's especially true it you expect a cooperative companion over the weekend. Speaking of our weekend, I've got clothes to unpack and wash, so it's time for my departure." Ashley had already turned and was making her way to the door.

"Ah, come on Lee. Stop being a bitch." It was the recently evident Garrett whine. "You've only been gone three days, not even three nights. What's the matter? Out to all hours of the morning with those flashy young friends of the Senator?" Garrett's disappointment flared to the point of biting sarcasm.

"Stop being a whining bastard, Edward. I wasn't out to all hours of the night or morning enjoying myself. I had a rough schedule. I was up late in my room by myself preparing for my interviews. And, even though I don't owe you this, I wasn't out of the hotel one night, even for dinner."

"Dammit, Ashley, if I didn't love you so much, I wouldn't be like this." Garrett was still mad, only he wasn't certain at who. Probably more at himself than at Ashley. Lately it seemed like he couldn't win and he didn't know why. "I just don't know what's gotten into me lately."

He moved to her side and took her in his arms, "I'm sorry, Lee. I missed you more this time than ever before. When I saw you, I wanted to grab you and squeeze you so tight that I'd have permanent nipple marks on my chest. I wanted you to be pleased with the trip. And I wanted to take you right up to bed. I don't know — then I started acting like an asshole."

"I have some good advice for you Edward," she looked sternly as she finished her sentence. "Have a strong drink, take a hot bath, go to bed early, read a dull book and get a good night's sleep. If I can get Ruthie to wash my clothes, that's exactly what I'm going to do."

Ashley knew all she had to do was to suggest her plan to Ruthie, her mother's nurse and maid, and it would be done. But, she felt it was wrong to take advantage of a live-in maid, especially since she had finished college and was living out in the carriage house apartment. As it was, she would come home at least once a week to a freshly cleaned apartment, for which Ruthie would take no money.

"A good night's sleep will do us both a world of good and make the weekend a lot better." Ashley gave Garrett a peck on the lips and moved to break free from his grasp.

"I guess you're right, as usual, Lee."

They walked down the stairs to the door in silence, everything that needed to be said, had been. At the door they kissed again. One short, followed by two longs and a short.

"I'll see you tomorrow," Garrett whispered.

CHAPTER 21

Dawn brought with it a warm glow and the promise of a beautiful fall day. Even the harsh buzz of Garrett's clock radio couldn't chill the warmth that filled his bedroom. Whether it was Ashley's return or adhering to her advice, he didn't know. He did, however, have his first dreamless night in weeks from which he awoke rested and refreshed.

There were no customers to interrupt his preparations for his noon departure. A mid-morning call found Ashley equally refreshed, ready to be picked up at 1:00 and anxious for a good weekend.

The drive to Woodfields included only one annoyance. The uncrowded expressway allowed Garrett's attention to be drawn from his driving to cuddling and hand games with his loving cooperative passenger. It took the flashing blue light atop the highway patrol cruiser to return his full attention to his driving.

"Dammit! I was going almost 80," he said to Ashley but mostly to himself.

He pulled over to the side of the road ready for the obligatory lecture on the horrors of speeding. Only once did the idea of using the Senator's name tiptoe across his mind. But the trooper was young, courteous and other than an accusatory tone, he gave no lecture. Garrett paid the $95 fine to the officer and they were on their way.

Garrett made a couple of stops at some out of the way antique shops. He was looking for some real bargains. Finding none, they proceeded. It was almost seven that evening before they got to Woodfields. The familiar narrow, tree-lined corridor led to the entrance of the stately old inn. Set against the purple-orange striped sky of mountain dusk, there was a matronly look of patrician class about the entire place. A look of experience. A look of comfort and class. A look not unlike its owner.

The main building was showing its age in places, but it wore it well, much as the creases of character in the face of an elderly woman of the upper class. The sculptured gardens were a bit on the unkempt side, but they, too, fit the look of the inn more than if they had the neat, well-manicured presentation of previous years. The circular drive seemed to reach out like mothering arms ready to embrace a tired child after a busy day of play. The flowers with their pungent perfume welcomed all who came.

Garrett stopped at the entrance to the Inn for a moment. He glanced at Ashley before completing the drive. He could tell from the look in her eyes, she too, shared his love for this old Inn.

Garrett pulled the BMW into the mostly-vacant back parking lot. Not many people were there; strange for a Friday night. It meant a longer walk but he knew there were always available spaces. Their drive had been a pleasant one. Ashley had been playful, Garrett both happy and relaxed, more so than in a while. The *old* Garrett — the usual *off-work* Ashley.

As they walked across the gravel parking lot, Garrett playfully grabbed Ashley's behind. Her half-hearted efforts at scolding him only served to fuel his efforts to embarrass her. A finger in the ear followed, but it was a pinch on the breast that took Ashley from playful to serious. The rest of the walk to the front door was filled with his apologies.

As they reached the top of the circular stairs to the second-floor entrance they were met by Mrs. Moore. She had seen them drive up and since they were expected regulars, she was standing there beside the oversized entry doors.

"Miss Barrineau, Mr. Garrett. It's such a pleasure to see you here again." Mrs. Moore's voice had a hint of a British accent.

"It's our pleasure to be here, Mrs. Moore, and a pleasure to be greeted by such a lovely and gracious ..." Garrett caught himself as he almost said *madam*, "lady."

Although the pause was noticeable, he covered it by grasping her hand and kissing it during the silence.

"The honeymoon suite is prepared and waiting for you two," Mrs. Moore made no indication that she had noticed Garrett's indiscretion, but little escaped her sharp eyes or ears. Although she had discretely inquired concerning their current marital status, she again asked if this would be an official use of the special room.

In a somewhat motherly way she added, "Isn't it about time you children see a minister? If you ask me, you looked so much in love as you walked across the back lot. It reminded me of my younger years with Mr. Moore. Yes, it did."

Ashley blushed. She must have seen Garrett grabbing at her body. As for Garrett, he only laughed.

As they entered the foyer of Woodfields, Mrs. Moore offered them a glass of sherry and offered a toast to their health and wealth. Garrett looked at Ashley and smiled. The sherry probably was the source or Mrs. Moore's warm smile, since she religiously hoisted a glass with each guest upon checking in. It had become a tradition since she and Mr. Moore had purchased the Inn some 27 years before.

She rarely spoke of Mr. Moore since his death 12 years ago.

CHAPTER 22

After Mrs. Moore left, Garrett gave her enough time to get back to her office before calling to make reservations for dinner. That left enough time for them to unpack, enjoy a quick passionate time of love making, shower and change for dinner.

The food was excellent, as always, and the service slow, as always.

Following dinner, Ashley and Garrett retired to the library with Mrs. Moore. She had operated the Inn for the last 12 years by herself following the death of her husband. They had bought the Inn 27 ago. He had retired from the Royal Navy. They had been in India, a half-dozen countries in Africa whose names kept changing, and in the US, attached to the Pentagon as an advisor. When he decided they would leave Her Majesty's service, they had to decide where they would live.

Mrs. Moore was American. She had loved her time in England and India, but America was her home. Africa was his home, and always would be, even though his entire family had been killed during a native rebellion. Mrs. Moore would never be happy to retire to Africa. Everything considered, the Moores retired to the United States.

They traveled some and visited Woodfields. They both decided, here is where they wanted to live. Conversations with the then-owners revealed their desire to sell the Inn.

Changes to the Inn had been minor since that time. The furniture was different. The Moores had changed it to look more like an English Inn.

Based on comments of the guests, who weren't thrilled with the English Inn approach, they decided to change it back to a roadside inn, using a variety of antiques.

As they sat next to the fire in the library, Garrett looked appraisingly at Mrs. Moore. She was in excellent shape for her age, in her seventies. Some of her dark color hair fought to remain with the same tenacity that she exhibited in the way she maintained her Inn. Her attire was elegant, however slightly dated. She always dressed for every evening meal, even though she may be the only guest for dinner. She lived in a special suite in the Inn and took her meals with her guests. She looked like almost everyone's great aunt.

They had moved from the dining room to the library for sherry following dinner. She was especially talkative that night.

"I remember your first visit to the Inn, Mr. Garrett." Her years with Mr. Moore and their British friends and associates had left her with a lilt of an English accent. "You and your father were here for a week, I believe, that summer when we had all that rain. I remember you couldn't go outside. You were especially unhappy that visit. It had to be almost 30 years ago. Am I right?"

She looked to Garrett for confirmation. He nodded and she continued. "We tried everything we knew to do. Your father had come for a rest. It wasn't until I gave you a job helping in the kitchen that you were happy and he could rest."

Garrett smiled. He had forgotten his first job at Woodfields as a kitchen helper. The happy moments he now recalled made his smile widen. Mrs. Moore had brought a decanter of sherry and glasses with her to the library. She refilled their glasses and sat back down by the fire.

For another hour and a half, Mrs. Moore talked about the Garrett family, famous visitors to the Inn, her recollections of India and her horror stories of Africa. Ashley was fascinated. She would ask her editor if she could do a feature piece on Mrs. Moore as soon as she returned to Charleston.

Garrett had heard many of the stories before but he listened dutifully. He, however, was ready to adjourn to the honeymoon suite to finish what they had started earlier. He began to yawn more often, trying to give Ashley the hint. She was completely enthralled with the stories. Finally, Garrett decided to call an end to the evening.

"Well, Ashley. Its almost midnight. It's time we got started to bed if you want to get an early start tomorrow. And I'm sure we've kept Mrs. Moore well past her bedtime."

Ashley apologized to Mrs. Moore, who promptly told Garrett she rarely was in bed before midnight. But the break was enough to end the stories for the night and for Garrett to move Ashley toward the bedroom.

Their love making that evening was the best it had been since the Find. Garrett gave the credit for his prowess to the sherries after dinner. It was well after 2 a.m. before they went to sleep.

Garrett's sleep was quite heavy and short. He awakened at 5:30 and knew he would not go back to sleep. Although breakfast would not be served until 7:00, he knew there would be a pot of coffee in the kitchen. There always was.

He dressed quietly, careful not to wake Ashley, and made his way downstairs. Hot coffee in hand, Garrett moved out to the English garden. The moon had set and there was no light furnished by the Inn. Even though it was quite dark, Garrett had no problem finding the garden and his spot.

He liked this place. He had spent many hours there in the past. It was a wonderful place to think. His spot was on a massive wooden bench that had been worn smooth from years of use. Large Juniper bushes had been sculpted in shapes by the first gardener back when Mr. Moore was still alive. The years had turned these bushes into a large topiary art gallery.

During the spring, flowers would accent the garden and fill the air with their alluring sweet smells. This time of year, it was the Juniper's turn to dominate. To Garrett, the Juniper was the smell that represented the outdoors. He liked the garden in this season.

The sun was not yet peeking over the eastern hills when Garrett took his position on the bench. He was glad no one else was about the garden. So much had been happening in his life. So many wonderful things. He needed to put them in perspective and gain control of them.

As that thought floated through his mind, he realized that that was the problem. He didn't feel in control of his life. He knew he had to regain control, but how?

He felt the need to organize, to list the things that needed doing. His confusion stretched to almost every area of his life. This lack of control and confusion was new to him. His life, his day-to-day activities, his very existence was based on control, order, routine. That was one of the things he had promised himself at his father's funeral. He was now in control and he would be for the rest of his life.

The edge of the ridge he was facing began to turn from black to purple. Within minutes there was a deep red outlining to the ridge and the trees that gave the ridge its serration. The deep red became a crimson, giving greater definition to the tree-crowned ridge. Soon, he knew, he would not have the garden to himself.

His thoughts had tiptoed from one subject to another, much as a ballerina moves from toe to toe crossing a stage, before settling again on his nightmares.

A shudder racked his body as he thought of the dreams. All of them had ended in death. Deaths that were not only violent, but deaths that left him grasping for threads of his own life. Dreams so real they left him afraid to even open his eyes at their end for fear that they might be real. He didn't understand why he was having such violent dreams. Could they bear some portent of his own demise? And why now? Maybe it was time to consult someone who might be able to shed some light on their cause or their purpose, whichever was more appropriate. And he knew that it would have to be soon.

He had let his coffee get cold without taking the first drink. Back into the house for another hot cup, and no more thoughts about those horrible nightmares.

By the time he returned, the entire sky had changed color. The purple had worked its way all the way to the west and the first hints of yellow were making splashes through the branches to the trees on the ridge. Soon people were moving around in the Inn. Soon he would lose sole ownership to this part of his world.

His thoughts turned to Ashley. He recalled the animation of a few hours before. The titillating thoughts caused ripple-like little electric shocks to wash through his groin. She had been a welcomed addition to his life.

Maybe Mrs. Moore was right. Maybe they should be thinking about getting married. But now, with the Find, he would have his hands filled. Maybe he would have to discuss that with her.

His thoughts shifted to the Find. He was on the verge of becoming rich beyond his wildest dreams. Soon, very soon, the antique world would be speaking of Edward Garrett and the Garrett Find. He would soon be reading his name in antique journals, in the newspapers all around the world. He, Edward Garrett, would be called upon to deliver speeches. He would be looked up to by those Charlestonian snobs who, for so long, had looked down their noses at him. Anger began to well up inside him as he thought about Charleston.

It was Mrs. Moore that broke his train of thought.

"Thought you might want another hot cup of coffee. Chef told me you were out here with no coat. It's a might cold for no wrap this morning, don't you think?"

It wasn't until Mrs. Moore had mentioned the cold that he felt a chill.

"Thank you. It is a bit nippy, now that you mention it," he replied. As he took a long drink of the too hot coffee, she began talking to him, but not really *to* him.

"Mr. Moore used to love to sit right here where you are sitting. He said he did his good thinking right here. I'd find him here in the early morning, sometimes even late at night. He told me of his cancer here. It was because of it that I almost sold this place. Every time I see this garden I think about how much I miss him. But it's because of this garden that I could never sell."

Tears came into her eyes and they brought the story to an end.

PROPHECY

The room is dark. Torches provide the only light to illuminate it. The torches are stuck in holes carved into the walls of what looked like stone walls. Others are stuck in metal holders attached to wooden supports. Strains of classical music float faintly through the air. There's a slowness and deliberateness about the movement of the people who are there almost as if they are keeping time with the music. Mostly men, they are dressed in long flowing robes. Some are colorful but most are a dark color.

The torches illuminate a "U" shaped table in the center of the room. The room is large. The walls appear to be made of large rectangular shaped stones but it's hard to tell in the low light. The flickering light from the torches gives an eerie yet festive atmosphere to the room.

The next thing that becomes obvious is the odor. No single scent dominates, but the blend is one of sweets and sours, repulsive, yet enticing.

I close my eyes and lean back in my large chair as I inhale deeply in an effort to isolate each of the smells. Most obvious is the smell of burning tar that coats the torches. There are the sweet smells of incense burning masks less pleasant smells.

It takes concentration to isolate the other odors. The subtle appetizing smell of cooking food occasionally slips through the more powerful smells. But, through it all there's one powerful, overwhelming smell. A repulsive, strong, almost nauseating smell of decay.

As I open my eyes, I see that a large table has been placed in the center of the room. On the table is a massive, full grown roasted pig wearing a garland of fresh fruit.

Torches burn at the four corners of this table. A silence falls over the room as I stand. I look around the room. I feel a sense of approval, an acceptance that all is well.

I can hear myself saying, almost chanting, "En nomini del Patri et del Filio et del Spiritu Santo. Aaaaaamen. Mange."

With that the robed men I had seen earlier move to the table and begin ripping off pieces of the roasted pig.

My plate is filled first. Waiting for the others to be served food, I listen to the beautiful music that fills the room. I begin eating and the others follow.

The mood is a festive one. The room is buzzing with happy conversation. Wine is flowing freely, adding to the festiveness. Off in the shadows I see Francesca. The subdued lighting only adds to her beauty. Long, flowing brown hair frames her alabaster face. I would much rather be in my chambers touching and caressing her than here only looking at her from a distance.

The minutes that pass seem like hours. How long will it take before I can leave?

"Why should I concern myself with what they think," I say to myself in a mumble. "I am in charge here. They? They are but servants of one kind or another."

With a wave of the hand I call my most trusted acolyte, Georgio.

"Gather some food, plenty for your lord's appetite. Take it to my private chambers. Bring Francesca there and see that no one disturbs us. Not until morning. And then, only you."

With another wave of the hand I dismiss him and yawn in mock fatigue. Leaving this early will not go unnoticed but this is of little concern. However, pretenses must be upheld. They all know of my liaison with Francesca. Nothing is kept quiet here or elsewhere in the Vatican but, after all, it's the custom. Done before, many times. And who am I trying to convince?

I stand, pronounce an adequate blessing and leave the room. Climbing up the seemingly endless rows of steps, I finally reach the large wooden planked door that I know opens to my private chambers. It glides effortlessly open with a slight push.

The smell is of fresh air. Much more pleasant that the other room. Windows on two sides of the room are open wide and a breeze blows comfortably through. The food is already there on a table with lamps burning brightly on either end. Other lamps give the room a soft but warm glow.

There's the sweet smell of sandalwood. *God knows I love the smell of sandalwood.*

The opening of the door is an almost imperceptible sound. It jars me from my thoughts with an almost frightening urgency.

It's Georgio who stops instantly as he senses the fear he has caused at his entry. Head bowed, he waits to be recognized.

He inquires as to other special needs before the lady, who waits outside, enters. I assure him that everything is well and remind him of my desire for privacy. He leaves and within moments Francesca enters.

Slowly she walks across the room, tempting me with her moves. The breeze blows her hair and white gown as she moves. She is inches away when we embrace. She smells of rare oils, sandalwood and myrrh.

She backs away, just out of arm's reach and slips her arms from the straps that hold her gown in place. It falls into a small pile at her feet. Nude, she stands there smiling, ever the temptress. She pushes my hands away as she steps forward and begins removing my robes.

Soon we are on my bed, she, soothing my body with her hands. She is so lovely in the flickering lamp light. Moving the plate of food to the bedside, she begins feeding me the fruit. Each effort to touch and caress her body is rebuffed. I must eat first, she insists.

From the fruit, she moves to the meat. There is the pleasant taste of freshly roasted pig in my mouth. The taste of the herbs and smoke adds to the flavor, a flavor that I savor by chewing longer than usual.

The playful Francesca, suddenly impatient to finish my feeding, begins to gently stroke my ribs, which she knows is a sensitive spot.

As she tickles, I gasp for air. It is that gasp that pulls the half-chewed meat along with the air down my throat.

Choking for air as I try to dislodge the meat, I am able to hoarsely whisper, between gasps, "Get Georgio."

Francesca runs, still unclothed from the room in search of Georgio. I see a chalice of wine on the table near the bed. Still gasping for breath, I reach with an unsteady hand for the liquid. As I touch the chalice, gasps send my body into uncontrollable jerking that sends the wine spilling to the floor.

The chalice, too, bounces to the floor along with the green-colored wooden box I have started using for my personal seal and wax.

"Will help never come," I shout — or at least try to shout.

Still gasping I struggle on the bed. Crawling over to the edge of the bed I reach deep within me to gather strength to shift to my stomach. Laying there, looking at the floor I try desperately to cough and dislodge the meat.

"Where is that woman? Where is Georgio?"

The words form in my mind but I can't add voice to them. know I'm losing strength. Lack of air has taken most of the energy from my body. The edges of my vision are darkening. I can barely see the floor.

I can see the red stain of the wine like a pool of blood there on the floor. In it is the chalice, shining as the reflection of the lamps glisten on the shiny surface.

The wooden box is there too. It's haunting green color almost glowing as well.

"Help," I scream. But the only sound that slips from my lips is a hoarse gurgle. "Oh, please help me, God. Not like this. The Pope, naked, with his concubine. Oh God, No."

I feel hands turning me over on my back, fists pounding on my chest. But they are all very faint. I see faces. Francesca. Georgio. Others. But they, too, are faint and far away.

The sounds are sounds of crying, of frantic yelling, but they are growing softer.

"Oh God, no."

One sound is growing louder. A heartbeat. I feel warm like a blanket has been placed over me. Heartbeats.

The lights have been dimmed. Heartbeats.

I'm not gasping. Heartbeats.

I'm resting peacefully. Heartbeats. Heartbeats.

Silence.

"Oh God."

CHAPTER 23

The room was dark and silent. Garrett was sitting, upright in the bed. He wanted to scream, but he was afraid to find out if he could or not. His body was drenched with a cold sweat. Goosebumps made his skin feel like it was crawling off his bones. Waves of fear caused a nauseous feeling to grip his stomach. He was stone cold sober.

"Oh God, not again." It was his voice. He could hear it. *A dream? I'm sure,* he thought. "Oh God, help me," he screamed waking Ashley.

"Edward! Edward, what's wrong." It was Ashley's first attempt to get through to Garrett. Still shaking, Garrett didn't acknowledge or hear Ashley calling his name. Grabbing him and shaking, she tried again, "Edward! Edward!"

"Huh? What? What?"

"Edward. What's wrong?"

"Huh?" Garrett paused. "Ashley? Is that you? Thank God. I didn't know if I was alive or not."

"What are you talking about, Edward? Was it another one of those dreams?"

"God! Yes. What a hell of a dream it was. I was the Pope, I think. I was in bed with this girl. I was choking on some food. The smells were so real. The tastes. The feel of her touch."

"Calm down, Edward. Take a deep breath."

He did.

"Now another. And another. Now, are you more relaxed? Start at the beginning. Tell me everything you remember."

Garrett started with the room. He described everything he could remember. As with his other dreams, he was able to recall minute details about the rooms, the people, the smells, tastes and sensations. He was talking a mile a minute as he described the dream. Fear had opened the flood gates for his adrenaline, and the adrenaline that had opened the floodgate of his words had raised the register of his voice.

Ashley listened, patiently, unable to edge a comment, question or observation into even the largest of his small breaks for breaths. Her one question, "What of this dream was like the others?" brought another torrent of words. Finally, Ashley brought an end to Garrett's monologue with a number of consecutive yawns and a TV director's signal for cut.

"It's late, Edward. We can continue this in the morning — or later this morning would be more like it. But, I can tell you one thing, Monday I am going to take you to see my analyst, for sure. Maybe he can make something out of these dreams. Now, Edward, please try to go to sleep."

Ashley lay back down, a visual cue that the conversation was over.

Reluctantly, Garrett lay down, as well. He cuddled next to Ashley for security, as if holding on to her with a death grip could be called cuddling. It was some time before he returned to sleep. Listening to Ashley's rhythmic breathing helped, and he slept dreamlessly until morning.

Morning came long before either Ashley or Garrett was ready for it. Garrett was the first to wake up. He slipped out of bed, leaving Ashley undisturbed.

That's good, he thought. *I want a little time to myself. A little time to think.*

He dressed casually and went downstairs to the sweet smell of freshly perked coffee and croissants. The first swallow of the hot coffee sent a chill through his body. He quickly followed it with another, to warm himself up. He finished the first mug of coffee as he waited for a fresh plate of croissants and some of Mrs. Moore's homemade marmalade.

He jumped when Ashley touched his shoulder. He hadn't seen or heard her approaching.

"Ashley, dammit. You almost scared the life out of me." He didn't even realize he had called her Ashley instead of Lee. "We've got to talk and now's as good a time as any."

Garrett's face had become serious. They walked out to the garden, wordless, each with a mug of coffee and a plate of warm croissants and marmalade.

"OK, Edward, shoot."

"This is serious, Lee. I've been doing a lot of thinking this morning and I think I've come to some decisions. These dreams are beginning to get the best of me. I want to solve the problem. You said you thought your analyst could help. Well, I'm ready. I want to see him on Monday. I'll do almost anything to get them to stop. So, Monday it's to the doctor, okay?"

Garrett was on a roll.

"Now, about the Find. You said you would handle everything concerning the announcement of the Find and the auction. Well, I hope you meant what you said because I want you to do just that. I must be kept informed on what's happening but I want you to do it and I know you'll do it right. The way it should be. So, that's what I want you to do. I trust your judgment more than mine lately. You know the media. You know Charleston. You know me. I only know antiques. So, I want you to do it up right. I know you will.

"Another thing, I want to find out about the symbols on that box. What they mean. It's been on my mind a lot lately. I think I've got some good photos of it and possibly some good tracings. I want to find someone who can translate the symbols. I really want to find out what they mean. I know they mean something."

Garrett paused and almost turned white.

"Lee! The box was in my last dream. The one last night. The same box." Almost as if he were talking to himself Garrett continued, "Could the box be a link to my dreams? Could it be the reason for my nightmares? Some evil curse from the past come to visit death and suffering on me? It must be the key."

"No rash conclusions, Edward. You said you were thinking a lot this morning. Think about this. You said that the box had been on your mind a lot lately. That's probably why it was in your dream. Your subconscious mind put it there. Broad happenings, not specifics, have meanings in dreams. Specifics appear as a result of daily activities," Ashley paused.

"Are you sure?"

"Yes. Very."

"Maybe you're right. I don't know. I guess I'm grasping at any straw to answer the question, Why the dreams? I wish it were the box. At least then, it would be an easy answer. I've got to get out of this mood. I see the grim reaper hiding behind every bush. Let's pack up our stuff and get the hell out of here."

It was mid afternoon when Garrett dropped Ashley off at her parents' house. He really wanted some time to sort things out.

She said she understood, he really didn't care if she did or not at that moment.

She also said she wanted him to be totally sure about his decisions and she would honor them, no matter what they may be. He wondered if she really meant what she had said. It really didn't matter, it would give him some more time.

Time he did really need.

CHAPTER 24

Monday arrived for Garrett with a buzzing sound, a ringing headache, a gray sky and an all around dreadful feeling. It was the middle of his shower before it dawned on him the reason for the dread. The analyst. Today was the day to visit the analyst.

He had always hated the idea of psychologists. Their probing questions. A waste of time. A waste of money. Today, he was to see Ashley's analyst. He asked himself if this would be a waste.

He knew one thing, he didn't want the morning to start and he couldn't wait for the day to be over. If it weren't for those wretched dreams, he wouldn't be wasting any money on a shrink.

Ashley called at 11 o'clock. Dr. Williams would see him at 5:15 that afternoon. He didn't usually see patients that late, she had said, but because she had asked him to, and because Dr. Williams was intrigued by Garrett's dreams, he would make an exception.

That was all good, but it was Ashley's, *Be sure to be on time,* that had gotten to Garrett. He wasn't real sure he wanted to see the shrink today in the first place. But, one thing he was sure of, being treated like a child was one thing he didn't want. He did, however, close the store at 4:45 and at 5:05 he was opening the door to Dr. Alexander Williams' office, #7 Zigzag Alley.

The building was nestled at the back of an old ally in the heart of the historic district of Charleston, not far from the Old Slave Market and #13 Church Street. The house that doubled as an analyst's office looked like it could be the residence of any number of ghosts, apparitions, and spirits.

Small formal gardens flanked the house separating the three-story structure from the high brick walls topped with ugly iron barbs that isolated the house from its surroundings. The large, antique door opened into a small, sparsely furnished, but tastefully decorated, waiting room that had formerly been the foyer of the old house.

The circular stairway leading to the upper floor was at the back of this room. A small sign directed patients to be seated after signing a card and placing it in the wooden box on the desk. Garrett noticed the box was empty as he deposited his card. There were no other indications of any patients ever visiting that office. No magazines left in half read positions. Everything seemed to be in its perfect place.

At precisely 5:15 a young, old-looking man opened one of the three doors into the room and introduced himself to Garrett. He was casually dressed for a shrink. No herringbone jacket. No suit. Although Dr. Williams looked as if he would be at home in either — or jeans, for that matter. This day he was dressed in khaki slacks, dark blue sweater, Topsiders with no socks, and a light blue oxford shirt. Had he been at a Yale house party or on board a yacht or at a local *meet-market* he looked as if he would have been right in style. He was equally in his place here and now.

"Mr. Garrett. I'm Dr. Alex Williams, but please call me Alex." He was presenting his hand as he was talking. They shook hands. "Thank you for being prompt. Come into my office, please."

There was something about Alex Williams. A look, a presence that seemed to make Garrett feel more at ease. Maybe it was just his air of confidence. Whatever it was, Garrett felt it.

Dr. Williams began by having Garrett sit in a leather, over-stuffed recliner. "Push it back until it's comfortable, Edward." Then, with practiced awareness he began, "To begin with, I don't use a couch. It's old-fashioned. Although my theory and background may be old-fashioned, my techniques are not. The chair you're sitting in will allow you to be as comfortable as you wish. By the way, I am recording what we say but it's only to refresh my memory when I have to write up my daily reports. I will put them in your file unless you request otherwise. As with any doctor/patient relationship, everything we discuss is privileged — and I consider that highly confidential. No one, not even my secretary, has access to your tapes or your complete file.

"This is to allow you to be as open and truthful as you care to be. After all, it's only through a totally open dialogue that we can make progress. I want to caution you about one important thing. I don't do magic, perform miracles, create wonder cures or have all the answers. We find the answers together. Don't expect more out of this than you're willing to devote.

"And finally, I have only one major rule. I don't talk about you or your case to anyone. Not anyone. You may discuss our sessions with Miss Barraneau, if you wish. But I will not. Now, the tape's rolling, tell me about your dreams from the beginning."

Garrett was amazed at how fast the hour had passed. It wasn't until Dr. Williams had interrupted him that he realized he had talked for almost an hour. He had described two of the dreams but he had paid great attention to the details he remembered. He recalled far more than he thought he would.

"Thank you, Edward, you've been very thorough in your recollections of your dreams. However, our time for this session is up. Try to remember where you left off and I would like to see you again Wednesday if that's alright."

Garrett was thinking about how unusual it was for him to be so talkative as he listened to the doctor and to a stranger at that.

It must be knowing that Alex is an analyst. That must be it, he reasoned.

That night Garrett slept better than he had in weeks.

CHAPTER 25

In Charleston, on that particular Tuesday, dawn brought the sound of a distant rooster crowing, a ship's horn, birds chirping, traffic on Meeting Street, and Garrett's trusty old clock radio's alarm. Soon the raspy buzz of the clock radio alarm would be replaced by the equally raspy voice of the morning newscaster. A big yawn was followed by a big stretch as Garrett prepared to meet the day.

"I'd stretch a mile if I didn't have to walk back." He heard himself give voice to an old expression and it brought a smile to his face. It had been a long time since he had thought about that. It had been his father's favorite expression. Maybe that had been the reason he hadn't thought about it in such a long time.

Garrett had completed his morning routine and was on his way downstairs to open the business when he heard the sound of the front door closing. Fear formed as a lump in his throat, a bristling of the hairs on the back of his neck and arms and a slight tremor all over his body.

Could it be a thief — or worse? The fear clutched him and held him motionless there on the stairs. The moments passed like hours.

It was Ashley's cheery voice calling from the foyer that melted away the feelings of fear.

"Hey Edward, it's me. I used my keee ... eekh!" The word key blended with Ashley's scream and made a sound that started Garrett laughing.

"Damn you, Edward. You scared the hell out of me. Why didn't you say something to let me know you were here?"

"Where'd you expect me to be? I live here, remember?"

"You know what I mean."

"Well, you coming in like that startled me as well. It's just good I don't carry around a gun. So, I guess we're even. Ha, ha, ha." Garrett ended his sentence with a juvenile, sing-song effort to lighten up their first conversation of the morning.

"It's not funny, Mr. Garrett. Here I'm so concerned about you that now I'm having trouble sleeping and you playing kid games. You and your dreams, the Find, all this talk about curses, dammit, we've got to get things back to some semblance of order here."

Ashley wouldn't have admitted it but the whole situation had begun to get to her as well.

"OK, why don't we go back upstairs and we can play some adult games." Garrett started to pull her up the stairs by the arm.

"That does it. Either we sit and talk like civilized people or I'm leaving."

"OK, OK. I was just kidding. Lighten up. The coffee's on in the kitchen. Let's go in there, alright?"

Garrett sensed this was no time to continue playing with Ashley. In the half-hour that followed they talked about Garrett's appointment with the analyst. He explained why he hadn't called following it. She told him about her meeting with John James, owner of the audio-visual company, and the initial discussions on announcing the Find and the auction and, also, that she had located someone who might be of some help in deciphering the symbols on the box.

"A friend at the newspaper, you know Hal Ward, don't you? He's the religion editor and suggested you try Brother Andrew at Mepkin Plantation, the Abbey in Moncks Corner. According to Hal, he is a student of early biblical languages and has cooperated with the newspaper in the past on questions regarding that. He said that even if Brother Andrew couldn't recognize the symbols, at least he could rule out a number of possibilities, making the rest of your job a little easier. Hal said he's excellent to work with and, although he's a little strange, he's one of the best in the country. He does a lot of translating for Catholic churches and universities in North America, and even some work for the Vatican. I think we ought to give it a try. What about you?"

Ashley's enthusiasm wiped the annoyance from her voice.

"I know Mepkin," Garrett replied, "but I didn't know they have any contact with the public. They can't speak, can they? Vows of silence or something like that. And if they can't speak, how can this Brother Andrew look at the symbols if he can't leave Mepkin?"

"Sometimes you amaze me, Edward. All communications are in writing. And for that matter, they have taken vows of silence, not vows of *no contact*. There's even one monk who does have permission to talk. He does the shopping as well as all public contact. Anyway, I think it would be a good place to start. Could you get a copy of the symbols? Hal said if I could get it to him today, he would get it to Brother Andrew tomorrow."

"The enlargements of the pictures I made will be ready today. I can bring them to you this afternoon after lunch when I pick them up. But I can give you a copy of the tracings I made right now if that suits." Garrett stood up. "I'll get one now."

Garrett made the stairs to the third floor two at a time as he thought about finally knowing what the symbols meant. He picked out two of the clearer tracings and looked at them for a moment. He bounced back down the stairs as if springs were attached to his shoes.

As he brought the tracings to Ashley, she noticed, for the first time, the excitement that shown in Garrett's eyes. A new kind of sparkle was in his eyes. One she couldn't remember ever seeing there before.

As for Garrett, he was elated. Soon, he hoped, the mystery would be solved and he would be able to get the box off his mind. And with some good luck, the box just might be something else of value from the Find.

"Now let's talk about the announcement and the auction."

For the next 20 minutes Ashley talked about what she had done on the auction. The Hibernian Hall had been confirmed. Robert's Restaurant, Perdita's, Poogan's, The Abby and Henry's would all cater, something they never did, but *as a personal favor to Mr. Garrett ...*

The audio-visual had been discussed, John James would be over to talk to Garrett that afternoon. He understood how confidential the whole thing was. And the story — "Pegge will do the first story as part of the announcement. Edward. I trust her and she needs a big break. The first story's going to be tricky. We've discussed a part of it but she doesn't know the whole story. Her article will be mostly hearsay information about a historical art treasure find. No names, no places, yet. It will hit in Sunday's paper. A slide with a copy of the article will arrive at Christie's and Sotheby's on Friday morning. That should be enough to get them involved and get the ball rolling.

"Next Wednesday, Millie will do a follow up. It will include an interview with you. Next Sunday a major story with names, photos, everything. She'll even do interviews with Sotheby's and Christie's and anyone who will talk on the record to her.

"Next Friday the invitations will be hand-delivered. That should give us enough time to get them printed. Then we'll see just how many *friends* you have.

"James John wants to take pictures of the items as soon as possible. I suggest you rent a van today and load everything up tonight and take them over to his studio. He said he would need a day or two to photograph everything."

Garrett had been taking notes as Ashley talked. With the last suggestion, he stopped and interrupted her.

"Wait a minute, Lee. I don't think it's a good idea to move the stuff from downstairs. I know you know this guy and you trust him or you wouldn't have selected him. But I don't know him, and I don't want any of the items out of this house. If he must photograph them, he'll have to do it downstairs, and that's that."

"OK, Edward. I see what you mean. I'll take care of it. But there's another thing — once John's finished I think you should find a place to keep everything safe and away from here. Some place that won't cause a commotion. We've already talked about one of those mini storage warehouses. I've found one in Savannah. That way, the state of South Carolina can't get its hands on the treasure. And one more thing, I think you should hire a bodyguard. Someone who can give you protection. Once the word gets out, you never know what's likely to happen. I don't want anything to happen to you, my love."

Garrett sat quietly listening to what Ashley had said. Could she be right? Would it make that much of a change in his life? Could he really be in danger? Deep inside he knew she was right and he knew he would have to keep himself and the Find safe, but how? Ashley looked at her watch. She was an hour late for work. Quickly she grabbed her purse and briefcase and ran for the front door calling to Garrett as she left.

"We'll talk more this evening, Edward, but think about what I said. I love you."

With that, she was gone with the sound of the front door closing. For the rest of the morning, Garrett was alone.

A great deal of what Ashley had said made sense. But was all of the cloak and dagger stuff necessary? *A bodyguard? Moving the treasures out of state?* He pondered the situation, as well as his relationship with Ashley.

Where to from here?

Garrett sat at his desk in the foyer of #13 Church Street. Things had been moving so fast for him lately. He was happy for this time alone to think. For the next three hours Garrett had his thinking time. No customers interrupted him. No one called. Except for an occasional trip to the kitchen for coffee, Garrett had time to himself.

He tried to keep his thoughts centered on the Find, but his mind kept wandering. Thoughts of being rich, and what he would do with all that money. Thoughts of having even the biggest of the Charleston snobs calling him, asking his opinion, inviting him to their private functions.

Thoughts of the dreams.

Thoughts of the little box and the funny symbols.

No matter where his thoughts began, he found them coming back to Ashley. Did she love him as much as she said or did she have her reasons for wanting to be so involved with the Find? Each time he would shake the feeling, but each time it returned leaving a dull ache in the center of his being. He wasn't sure why he felt this way, but it wasn't a comfortable feeling.

His thinking took up most of the morning. It was the nagging feeling in his stomach that first told him he had let the majority of the morning slip away without doing anything constructive. It was approaching noon. Garrett picked up the phone and dialed Ashley's direct line.

"News, Barrineau." Ashley's work voice always sounded strange to Garrett. Sharp, businesslike, almost to the point of threatening.

"Hi Lee. How's your day?" Garrett tried to be light.

"Oh! Edward. It's you. It's been OK. But I've got some good news for you. Hal talked to the monastery. The representative of the monastery will stop by the paper this afternoon. Hal said Brother Andrew is interested in the symbols as well. Obviously, I didn't say anything about the Find. He just thinks it's some old box you came across. Just think what could happen if the box had some religious significance. We could donate it to the monastery. That way maybe some high church official could be at the auction. Wouldn't that be a stroke of luck. Did you get the pictures?"

"Slow down, Lee. You know I've been at the shop all morning. I'm just getting ready to leave, now. Do you want to have lunch?"

"I'd love to babe, but I can't. Between the announcement, the monks, and all, I've barely got time for work. I'll be here through lunch. Why don't you bring me something?"

"OK, but you're no fun anymore."

"Oh. What do you call the other night?"

"You know what I mean."

"No, I don't. You tell me."

"Tell me. If you're so busy, how come you've got the time to waste on this conversation?"

"You may have me there, smart man. Maybe you should get your ass over here with the pictures and my food."

"OK, Lee, OK. You get back to work. I'll see you in half an hour or so."

"And, talk about fun, Edward Garrett, you better be ready tonight." Ashley broke the conversation with Garrett abruptly.

"OK, OK, I've got two or three more graphs to finish and two cut lines to write. Then I'll shoot it down to composing. Tell copy to save me a good spot for it on the front page."

Back into the phone she hurriedly completed her conversation with Garrett.

"Got to go Edward. I'm on early deadline for this piece. See you soon."

The click ended the conversation before Garrett had a chance to get back at her. But wasn't that normal?

The first stop was the camera shop to pick up the photos he had made of the symbols. He tried to be nonchalant as he picked them up. He had been a customer for a number of years and the owners of the camera shop had clung to the business even though they were competing with all of the drug stores and large merchants.

"How'd they come out?" Garrett asked the guy who usually served him. He knew they looked at all the pictures they processed. And he often asked them for their appraisal of his work.

"Well, I don't know much about the subject, Mr. Garrett, but the exposures on most of them is right on."

Garrett's heart took a big jump and started pounding like a heavy metal rock drummer.

"What was that thing you were photographing? I said I thought is was some kind of stone."

Trying not to arouse any more interest than he could, Garrett decided the best answer was to tell the truth about the box, at least some of it.

"It's just an old box I found. Nothing important, but I wanted to see if these symbols would come up better."

It was normal for Garrett to photograph unusual things, so his answer caused no more conversation, at least not to his face. Garrett failed to hear the guy's comment as he left.

"It was one of Mr. Garrett's old boxes," he said to his companion in the store, "You never know what to expect from his film."

Garrett ripped open the envelope as soon as he got into his car. Sure enough, there before him was shot after shot of the green and white container top. In all but one of the photographs the symbols were clearly visible. Far more visible than he had expected. He quickly started the car, ready to rush over to the paper to show the photos to Ashley when he remembered her lunch.

The Spring Street Lunch and Deli was close by so he stopped in front and jumped out. Inside he ordered her favorite. "Give me a turkey on white, un-toasted, with lettuce and mustard, extra pickles and soupy coleslaw." *How could she eat that,* he thought. "And a corn beef on rye with hot mustard and potato salad."

"Lunch for Missy Ashley, Mr. Garrett?" The black man behind the counter had handled his requests before. "Sho don't see how

Miss Ashley can stand to eat turkey with mustard, do you, Mr. Garrett?"

"No, I don't, but she's the one who's got to eat it, and I've quit trying to change her."

Even though he was in a hurry, he waited and chatted patiently. Equipped with two sandwiches and more information and advice than he needed, Garrett left the Spring Street Lunch and Deli and headed for the newspaper office and Ashley.

He was aware of an uneasiness deep inside his gut as he entered the newsroom. He never admitted it to himself but this was her turf. He was the outsider and he felt it. He found her desk. Her computer terminal was on, a story in progress. He remembered how different it was from his expectations on his first visit.

There wasn't a typewriter in sight anywhere, not even on the secretaries' desks. Computers were at the writer's desk. Just like on TV. There, next to a coffee cup full of paper clips, was his picture. One she had taken on their first visit to Woodfields. He was sitting on the bench in the formal gardens. He had forgotten it. It was where he had sat for such a long time just a few days earlier. As his mind wandered, a voice broke the journey.

"Well, it's about time. I'm starved. I hope it's good." Ashley bounded to her desk, pushed the save key, turned off the computer, grabbed Garrett's hand and continued, "Let's eat outside."

It really was too cold for a picnic, but the sun was warming and, for different reasons, neither seemed bothered by the chill. Garrett showed Ashley the pictures as they ate. After their lunch, Garrett began what he thought would be a good conversation.

"Lee, I've been thinking."

"Not now, Edward. We've both got a lot to do. You've got to get things together for John to photograph. I've got to get these pictures to Hal for Brother Andrew. If he doesn't get them today it'll be a whole week before he's back. You and I can chat tonight."

"But ..."

"Finish your potato salad. I've got to get moving. Seriously, I've got things I've got to do. How about a long, leisurely dinner, a good back rub and all the talking your little heart desires?"

Garrett started to argue but decided that Ashley and his thoughts could wait until tonight. Back in the newsroom the pace had picked up. People were at their desks working on their terminals or busy on their phones. From across the room Garrett heard Ashley's name called. She acknowledged.

"I've got to go now, Edward. See you tonight." And, with a quick peck on his lips, she was gone.

Garrett left the newsroom slowly. He glanced over his shoulder as he approached the door. Ashley was busily finishing her story.

He took the long way back to #13 Church Street. He wanted some air and a change of scenery. He drove around the old sections, the SOB area of town. He had often told friends in other parts of the country that Charleston was the only place on earth where SOB was considered a compliment. Here, SOB stood for South of Broad, the area of restored, elite, grand old homes in the *IN* section of town.

The old houses had a special look today. Each showed off its own special personality. Architecture here was as varied as the people. Duplication, nonexistence. The drive did him some good. He even stopped at White Pointe Gardens and stood on the Battery for a few moments. Looking across the water was calming. The brisk, salt air may have smelled of the decaying marsh area, but to him, it was a smell that always brought with it thoughts of good times as a very young child.

He played here. He and his friends used White Pointe Gardens as their place to play pirates or war. It was appropriate since the real players had set the ground rules for both of these games many years before, but their play was for real.

As the wind blew, Garrett closed his eyes and allowed the kaleidoscope of mental pictures to play in his mind. The screech of tires erased his nostalgic journey through time. He turned just in time to see a car miss a young boy by inches, only a few feet from where he was standing. It sent a shiver through him. The youngster picked up the ball he had been chasing and ran back into the park untouched by the gravity of what had almost happened.

"Time to go," Garrett said, although he was the only one close enough to hear.

Back at #13 Church Street, there was one note on the front door. James John had stopped by, the note said he would call later. Inside he checked his answer machine for calls. Another message from John James, and there was one from an out-of-state customer.

He got a cup of coffee from the kitchen, sat at his desk and began dialing James John's telephone number.

"Creative Concepts," it was a friendly, female voice that answered the phone.

"John James, please. Edward Garrett calling." Garrett tried to be pleasant, but businesslike.

"One moment please, Mr. Garrett," Classical music entertained Garrett as he held for the photographer.

"Edward. It's John." It was an affable voice, one of friendship, even though they had met only once. "I called and stopped by earlier this morning. I wanted to get a look at where I would be working. Sorry I missed you. I do need to see the area and, if you don't mind, may I come over and take a look? Now?"

"Sure, I guess so. I don't have any specific plans and I don't have the items out yet, but ..." Garrett was trying to postpone this visit, but such a subtle hint was wasted on John James.

"No matter, Edward. I just want to see the room and make some preliminary plans, decide what extra equipment I'll need."

"OK, anytime you wish, come over." Garrett ended the conversation.

Two customers and three lookers later, John James arrived. Garrett showed him the room on the first floor that he would be using to photograph the treasures for the announcement. He asked for the use of a piece of the silver to use to verify the lighting and to check the color balance, lighting arrangement and backgrounds for his test shots. Garrett left him to set up his equipment and take his test shots. He had assured Garrett that shooting test shots today would make the actual shooting tonight go much faster.

Garrett wanted to be there during the test shooting but the ring of the customer entering the store changed his mind. Even though it had been a good sale, Garrett would have preferred to have been on the first floor with John James. The excitement of the impending announcement had begun to build inside Garrett.

He wanted the time to pass much faster, but there was so much that still needed to be done.

"I'll probably want to start with the photography tonight, after your hours." James statement as he reentered the second-floor office area took Garrett by surprise.

"Tonight? I have plans for tonight."

"Well, Lee asked me to clear my calendar for a shoot tonight and tomorrow night, so I assumed you and she had already cleared yours. I'm ready to shoot tonight, so just let me know, will you?" He sounded somewhat annoyed but his demeanor was still loose and friendly. "I'll wait for your call," he said as he closed the front door of #13 Church Street.

Garrett called Ashley. She confirmed that she wanted the photos shot tonight. She assured him that there would be time for the shoot and for them as well. She stressed the importance of getting these photos for the newspaper article and as proof for the people at Sotheby's and Christie's. She was persuasive and unyielding in her position and Garrett finally agreed. She suggested that he begin assembling the articles from the Find so that photography would proceed smoothly and ended the conversation with "I love you."

Garrett knew in his mind that the procedure outlined by Ashley was the best, but in his heart he wanted things to be more as they used to be between her and him. He put the CLOSED sign out, even though it was only 4:00, and went into the basement to organize the items to be photographed.

Ashley arrived at 6:30 with a bottle of wine and a bottle of champagne. She said that dinner was being catered and would arrive at 9:30. John James would arrive any minute and he would shoot until 9:00. The evening was all arranged.

The evening went like clockwork. Well over half of the Find was photographed. James John shot over 3,600 digital pictures. Garrett asked why he needed so many shots. Edward had argued the merits of film photography, but James John had prevailed with his argument that digital provided better quality images and the Find deserved the subtle quality only provided by High Def digital. Ashley said she would give him all the details later in the evening. Shooting stopped at 9:00 precisely. He left his equipment set up and was gone within minutes.

"Now to the bath," Ashley was pushing Garrett up the stairs as she continued her sentence, "We have just enough time to have a short shower before the food arrives."

The shower was soothing. They lathered each other up and Garrett started to feel around the body of his lover. She put a quick stop to it, saying there was plenty of time after a good meal. They completed their shower and dressing just in time.

Tom Bass was knocking at the door. The special meal was delivered by the owner of Poogan's Porch. William was left to serve it. The wine had been consumed during the photo shoot, but the champaign was still chilling in the refrigerator.

The meal had set the stage. The lovemaking had ended the evening on a perfect note. Ashley stayed the night and Garrett enjoyed the opportunity to be next to the one he loved all night long.

CHAPTER 26

Wednesday morning was somewhat rushed. Ashley had to leave early because she had to first go home before going to the paper. Garrett wanted to stay in bed. It was during shaving that he remembered that he had an appointment with Dr. Williams.

He had his coffee and English muffins and placed the OPEN sign in the window. Wednesday was a busy day at #13 Church Street. A number of tourist buses had disgorged hundreds of older ladies in the old section of Charleston. More bouffant hair-dos visited his shop that day than he had seen in the past year. Sales were what he expected from the group. They bought smaller, cheaper items but the sales were good for the shop, nonetheless.

He talked to Ashley in the afternoon. She agreed to come to the shop while he was at the analyst's office. She would get the photography started and then wait for him. He had to leave for his appointment before she arrived. He put the CLOSED sign in the window and locked up. She could use her key.

It was 5:15 when he opened the door to Dr. Williams' office. Almost simultaneously, Dr. Alex Williams opened the door to his office.

"Edward. Nice to see you. Come in."

Garrett again sat in the overstuffed chair.

"Tell me, Edward, have you had any more of these strange dreams?" Dr. Williams asked with no prelude.

"No, Dr. Williams. Not this week. The strange dreams have always happened on a Saturday night in the past. I've had dreams on other nights but they have been different. But, no dreams since I saw you Monday, at least none that I remember."

"Okay then, let's start where we left off last time."

"I'm not sure where I was."

"You had just started on the dream where you were a warrior of some kind. A knight in armor."

"Oh, yes. I remember."

Garrett recounted the dream. As he was telling Dr. Williams about the bloody murder of the young mother, he again found an erection growing. It embarrassed him and he shifted his legs to cover it. He became uncomfortable. He asked if he could use the bathroom.

When he returned, he asked Dr. Williams if he could end this session. That he had another appointment at the shop and he needed to be there in a very short time. Dr. Williams agreed, saying they could discuss his unexpected level of discomfort next time. Another appointment was made for Monday at the same time. And Garrett left.

Garrett had walked to Dr. Williams' office. He was happy he had to walk back to #13 Church Street. It would give him some time to think. Of all the strange dreams he had had to date, the third one was the most unusual. He recalled he was stimulated by the dream when he awoke from it. Every time his mind replayed the event, not the whole dream, only the slashing of the young woman and her bare breast and the horse crushing her body, he would have an erection. It embarrassed him every time it happened, but it happened nonetheless. He hoped he would have the courage to tell Dr. Williams about it on Monday, but he wasn't sure.

Garrett had barely crossed the street when the visual images of the dream played across the screen of his mind. There he was in the middle of Church Street sporting a full-blown erection. He looked around to see if anyone was looking. Everyone who was close enough to notice seemed self-absorbed. Everyone except one older man who was obviously staring at him.

Did he know? Had he seen? Or was it simply Garrett's paranoia?

He looked to be in his mid 60's, but what difference did that make? His clothing looked to be expensive and well-tailored but obviously worn and out of style. He had a face like a headache, wrinkles that seemed to have no beginning and no end. The problem was, he looked familiar.

Garrett quickened his pace and in the opposite direction from the old man. *Was he real?* That was Garrett's question. *Did I really see him? Or was he just an image in my mind?* Weeks ago he would have never thought that, but lately, he wasn't sure.

He had left Dr. Williams office at 6:00. It was almost 6:45 by the time he had walked off the erection and the feelings he had experienced. By the time he returned to the shop, John James was busy photographing and Ashley was involved with a cardboard model. She looked radiant when he walked into the basement.

"It will be wonderful," were the first words that came from her mouth as she ran to hug and kiss him. "Come here. You've got to see this."

She explained the model. There, made to scale, was the interior of the Hibernian Hall. Twelve large rear projection screens ringed the center of the room, suspended from the ceiling just over ten feet off the floor. A bank of projectors was positioned in the center of the circle. The projectors were some 18 feet above the floor, so as to not block the viewing from any place in the room. Audio speakers were a part of this projection pod.

Also in the center of the room was a circle of tables with an arrow pointing to them labeled *Catering Tables.* Bars were indicated in three of the corners of the room. In the fourth corner was a small stage and a podium. A note on the model indicated that the occupancy of the room with this configuration was 2,190 people standing.

It wasn't until Garrett saw the model that he began to understand what Ashley was talking about. A 360-degree projection screen would be projecting a dozen different images of each item that would be visible from any place in the room. A large projection screen on stage would project the list of all items in the sale, as well as the latest bid. As bids are placed they would be simultaneously recorded on the screen and online on the worldwide web. Following a particular item or a group of items would be much easier in this fashion.

Although he had been intrigued by this idea, he wasn't sure until now that it would work. He had already discussed the online auction process with Lee. Now he was able to enjoy Ashley's enthusiasm and see the possibilities of the worldwide exposure that would come from a web auction held simultaneously with a live auction.

John James photographed until 11:00 o'clock. Garrett and Ashley helped by carrying each item to be photographed to the backdrop and carrying them out once he had finished with them.

Garrett asked Ashley why he needed so many shots of each item. She reminded him that there would be twelve screens and that John was the professional and he wanted to be sure he had the right shots for the show.

Garrett was ready for this day to be over. He was happy when Ashley said she had to go home. He wanted some time to himself and he wanted a good night's sleep.

CHAPTER 27

Garrett closed the front door to #13 Church Street after he had bid farewell to James John and kissed Ashley good night. His body felt the rigors of the day. His muscles ached. Every one of them. He turned out the lights, set the alarm and walked up the stairs to the third floor.

The old home creaked as if it ached as much as he did. The hours spent in the basement with the dust covered relics left him feeling dirty. As he walked into his personal area, he decided he needed to shower before he went to bed. He stripped out of the dusty clothes in the hall way, leaving them in a pile outside the laundry room door.

He didn't realize just how cold the third floor was until the air flowing up from the stairwell assaulted his bare skin. Simultaneously, his skin turned into a sheet of goosebumps, whatever that was. His teeth started chattering, another questionable metaphor, and the family jewels sought a warmer place inside Garrett's body.

Rushing into the bathroom, Garrett slammed into the door jamb, causing one more issue for his body to deal with — a sharp pain and the inevitable bruise that would adorn his left shoulder.

Garrett grabbed for the hot water faucet and wrenched it on. The moments it took for the water to reach usable temperature seemed like an eternity in a frozen tundra. Taking only enough time to adjust the cold water to keep from adding a scalding to the growing list of maladies for the evening, Garrett quickly moved under the spray of the warming shower.

His body seemed to be in no hurry to warm. Not to mention that the side was being covered by the warm liquid left the other side exposed to the chilly air. Finally, the goosebumps receded and the family jewels reappeared and Garrett was well on the way to warming his body.

Stepping out of the hot, moist shower, Garrett grabbed the large terrycloth towel and began scrubbing his body, eliminating some of the stress that had been building in his body, along with the residual dampness. He walked to the bathroom mirror that was shrouded in a condensational mist. Wiping the reflective surface with the towel, he looked into the familiar face of the other Thomas Edward Garrett; the one who was quiet, with resolve. The one who thought he knew what he was doing, and why, or at least looked like he knew.

"Thomas Edward," Garrett said aloud realizing that this was the first time he had referred to himself by the name his father called him when he was caught doing something wrong. It had been a long time since he had heard the name.

"Thomas Edward," he repeated in a quieter tone. "You have the opportunity of a lifetime. Fame and money. And recognition. And acceptance. Your lifetime goals will be achieved. You've got to hang in there. You've got to keep it all together. Just a little bit longer. You can do it."

The pep-talk from the mirrored-image pseudo-psychologist made Garrett somewhat more at ease. The image in the mirror began to cloud at the edges. The result made it seem to float in a cloud, ethereal. The continued stress of the recent weeks was showing in Garrett's face. There were dark quarter moons hanging there under his eyes. The red network of lines that radiated from the pupils looked like a road map calling attention to his lack of sleep. It was time for a good night's sleep.

Garrett took a sleeping pill, turned and headed for the bedroom and the awaiting arms of Morpheus.

He quickly slipped between the sheets and willed his mind to sleep. For once his mind and his intentions were of the same accord, and the chemistry of the sleeping pill kicked in. Sleep came quickly.

Garrett's sleep was restless but there were no dreams.

CHAPTER 28

Thursday was one of *those* days. In his haste to get to sleep the night before, he hadn't set his alarm clock. So, when he finally awoke it was late or, more correctly stated, *he* was late.

He followed his normal routine, but it seemed every way he turned he would run into something. His routine was letting him down. He finally completed getting dressed and was able to make a pot of coffee and toast a bagel without major calamity.

When he arrived at the front door to put out his OPEN sign, A gaggle of sexagenarians was rounding one of the pineapple-capped pillars indicating the entrance to #13 Church Street. He was open, but not ready. *Gaggle* seemed an appropriate descriptor since, when they were all talking at once, it sounded like a group of geese honking together. It was all Garrett could do to keep from rushing inside and locking the door when he saw them.

The *quackers* actually turned out to be customers. One found something to add to her paperweight collection. Another collected perfume bottles and found three she couldn't live without. Another purchased a selection of vintage needlework, almost $5,000 total. A $100 deposit was placed by another of the group that would hold five other paperweights until the antique caravan deposited the customers back in North Carolina. They had agreed that she would go ahead and complete the sale and he could ship them to her at her home in North Carolina, not requiring her to pay South Carolina sales taxes.

Garrett slipped the CLOSED sign in the window at 2 pm. There was a reluctance to call an end to the day.

It had been the busiest and most profitable day in weeks. But he had promised to meet with Brother Andrew and the mysterious monk who knew so much about Biblical languages, and who just happened to be available on Thursday afternoon at 3 p.m. at Mepkin.

CHAPTER 29

Garrett had already provided the Abbey with the tracing and photos of the top of the box for this mysterious monk who held the key to the equally mysterious lettering on the little grey box. He was at a loss for to reason for the face-to-face visit. It should be easy to communicate through Brother Andrew and Hal at the newspaper. He certainly wasn't going to take the box to Mepkin.

With the way the Abbey was acting, it could be worth a lot of money and he wasn't going to take any chances. If it had religious significance, that would drive the price up and add to the importance and media coverage of the auction. He had read stories of how religious art collectors, churches and museums had gotten into bidding frenzies over seemingly unimportant antique pieces that turned out to have religious significance.

He remembered one particular article he had read about the international attention accorded a small stone Ossuary that was believed to have contained the bones of James, the brother of Jesus. It, also bore a carved inscription in Aramaic. Though it was ultimately proven to be a hoax, there had been a special documentary presented on The Discovery Channel. International media attention was generated by a press conference held jointly by The Discovery Channel and the Biblical Archeological Society. The Israeli Antiquities Authority and the Geological Survey of Israel supported the authenticity of the Ossuary and they were joined by the Royal Ontario Museum and Paris' famed Sorbonne University.

Regardless of the eventual outcome, the Ossuary was the talk of the worldwide religious, antiquities, collectors and historical communities for eight or more months. He made a mental note to add a comment concerning the possible religious significance of the box, as well as the interest shown by the Catholic Church, to the PR release and the information provided to the auction houses.

The beauty and diversity of the low country scenery shifted Garrett's attention from his thoughts about the box to the unfolding picture postcard that presented itself at every turn. Once he had left the interstate highway, the iconoclastic beauty of the rural low country of South Carolina was absolutely astounding.

He passed Spanish Moss-covered trees that lined avenues that could lead to an antebellum mansion or a dilapidated, unoccupied shack, each with its own charm, beauty and, either over-stated or under-stated grace. There were the ubiquitous handmade roadside sheds that displayed a selection of handmade sweet grass baskets, trays and assorted unique design pieces that were a testament to the creative soul of the Geechee crafts people of the low country. The fruit stands sold boiled peanuts and promoted their offering with hand-lettered signs that often contained unusual spellings of local fruits and vegetables.

There was a variety of rusting automobile carcasses and the under growth that struggled to engulf them. *A representation of the continual battle between nature and man-made,* Garrett thought. He smiled along with the thought that, in this place, it looked like nature was winning.

Turning off the main road and then off the side road, Garrett guided his BMW down a narrow ribbon of gravel and asphalt that connected the rest of the world to Mepkin Abbey. He passed a large stone entry marker that announced he was entering the Abbey grounds, but he knew that he had been driving on Abbey property for some time.

At one time, Mepkin Plantation was over 1,000 acres and well-known for its rice and indigo production. Its former owners, starting with Henry Laurens and including John and Clare Booth Luce, were leaders in politics and commerce. Garrett knew some of the history.

His attention was drawn from the manicured beauty of the Abbey grounds by a sign that announced, "Reception Center,

Please Check In." It was the illustration of a faceless monk on the sign pointing the way that caught Garrett's eye. He parked in front of a brown-stained frame structure that was the Reception Center and Gift Shop.

Inside, Garrett met Brother Andrew. He was dressed in a simple white muslin, thigh-length hooded robe over khaki slacks. It only differed from the oversize "hoodie" that Garrett wore when he jogged around White Pointe Garden on colder days in the material from which it was made.

Garrett and Brother Andrew exchanged greetings and pleasantries followed by Brother Andrew's suggestion that they should go. They walked along a gravel path lined by meticulously manicured gardens of greenery and flowering plants. There were the occasional sitting areas and meditation gardens. Another faceless monk sign suggested they were headed to the "Church/Library." It was not so dissimilar from the faceless monk on the sign that indicated the "Reception Center."

Garrett noticed that most of the monks he saw on the monastery campus wore a different attire than Brother Andrew. Their white robes extended to their ankles and were accompanied by a shoulder-wide brown overshirt with hood. Garrett asked Brother Andrew about the difference as they walked along the path.

"I am not yet a full member of the order. I wear the attire of an initiate. When I complete my training and take the vows, I will be allowed to wear the robes of a Monk," the emotionless explanation satisfied Garrett's curiosity and they continued to walk in silence.

Brother Andrew turned to his left abruptly changing direction to a side path, catching Garrett off guard. As Garrett caught up with Brother Andrew, he noticed another sign "Monastic Area" and the admonition, "No Visitors Please." The faceless monk on the sign was shown with an outstretched palm, a silent effort to halt the advance of the unwanted. Brother Andrew paid no attention to the sign or the intent of the faceless monk.

He ushered Garrett into a building called the refectory. He dipped his finger in the Holy Water receptacle, crossed himself and proceeded into the hallway. They stopped at the entrance of a small, private room across the entryway from the main room, which was clearly the dining room. The light level in the small room was much lower than the rest of the building which was flooded with natural sunlight.

In this private room sat a single person at the side of a table that would seat six people. His choice of seating location bespoke someone who was accustomed to being in the background. He still had his back protected by a plain wall, but the place he selected was not the position of power. He wore a woolen robe that was obviously hand spun, hand-woven and un-dyed. His hood was in place and completely covered his head. It shadowed his face and the attitude of his head did nothing to reveal his features.

Brother Andrew and Garrett sat across from the Monk as he and Brother Andrew exchanged words in Latin or maybe it was Italian. Garrett didn't understand what was said and didn't recognize the language.

"The Brother would like to know if you brought the box," Brother Andrew addressed Garrett. "He would like to examine the box as well as see the characters on the lid."

Garrett thought it strange that he was not introduced to the anonymous monk and equally strange that he was only referred to as, *The Brother*.

Garrett explained that he had the box in a safe place, outside the city and that it wasn't convenient for him to get it before he made the trip to Mepkin. Also, that he didn't understand why an examination of the box would help in the translation of the characters.

The Brother began speaking to Brother Andrew.

"Does he know the actual translation?"

Brother Andrew answered, "He has been told it meant beware." Both spoke in Latin or Italian. The quick question made it clear to Garrett that The Brother clearly understood what he had said and probably could communicate in English, should he care to.

"The Brother says the characters are loosely translated *Beware*, but it is an unusual choice of expression that has questionable connotations in its use. It is not a normal use for the word," Brother Andrew's cadence was slow and measured as if he were choosing his words very carefully. It was obvious he was concerned not to misstate the comments of the speaker and to be certain that he was conveying the intent of the speaker. There was clearly a fear of what misstatement might mean.

Regardless, Garrett looked at The Brother and said, "Communication is always difficult when one requires a translation. The particular nuances, the situation or the concerns of the individual can easily be lost in the translation. Is that not so?"

With his question, Garrett shifted his gaze to Brother Andrew.

Brother Andrew looked at Garrett and then at The Brother. He was in a quandary as to how to answer Garrett, and clearly concerned that he not anger the person he deferred to. It was The Brother who took control and broke the silence.

"I am sorry, Mr. Garrett. I should have shown you the respect of a direct answer. It is a simple case of curiosity on my part. The characters are not normally used for objects, and when used for objects, they generally have clerical importance. That's all. I would, however, like to see the box."

The voice was soft but with the touch of an edge. It was well-schooled in proper English. There was a lilt in certain words that carried forward the accent of the original language he had used with Brother Andrew. But it was clear to Garrett that there was a great deal left unsaid and he was more unsure of the intent behind the stranger's words than his explanation. And there was a chilled after-effect that served to raise Garrett's concern to a new level, as well as the hair on the back of his neck. The response continued to seem condescending to Garrett and it angered him.

"I will have to get back to you when I can revisit the Abbey. I have closed the store today to come here only to find information that could have been provided me by phone. I will have to see when I can spare the time."

Garrett realized that the anger he felt had begun to creep into the tone of his voice, so he paused a moment and asked for confirmation.

"Are you sure of the translation? *Beware.* That was it?" Garrett again directed his gaze to the strange monk.

"Yes. I am sure. *Beware.*"

"Well, that certainly raises questions, doesn't it?" Garrett's rhetorical question was left unanswered as he expected it would be, at least until he stood and turned to leave.

"Yes, it does." There was an ominous tone to The Brother's answer.

Garrett and Brother Andrew remained silent as they retraced their steps to Garrett's car. As they arrived at the car, Garrett turned to Brother Andrew, ending the visit with, "If there is more to be said, I would hope you would contact me at #13 Church Street."

Garrett added his thanks to Brother Andrew for his assistance to which Brother Andrew nodded his head as Garrett closed the car door. For his part, Brother Andrew stood, motionless, as Garrett backed out of his parking place and watched, dutifully, until the car was out of sight.

The faceless monk was the last vestige of Mepkin as Garrett drove past the stone marker. The sign stated, "Thank You for Visiting Mepkin. God Bless." It was the posture of the illustrated, faceless monk that caught his attention, both arms out, palms open. It was the same pose his minister used during the closing prayer on Sunday morning.

The visit to Mepkin had raised more questions than it had answered. Everything about the enigmatic monk presented questions. Could he even trust the monk's translation? Garrett was certain the Monk had not told him everything. What could he be hiding?

Garrett continued to play 20-Questions with himself on the way back to #13 Church Street. At the end of the game, he was no more certain than when he began. Knowing that the ciphers were translated with the admonition to *Beware* was a step in the right direction, but beware of what? Why was this nameless, faceless monk sent from the Vatican to see this empty box? Could his visit just be a coincidence? Why did he want to actually *see* the box? Could there be more to the translation? Garrett arrived at #13 Church Street in mid-question.

It was after closing time when Garrett returned to #13 Church Street. He went straight into the kitchen, poured a cup of the morning's coffee and popped it into the microwave. He sat at his desk, placed the cup of coffee on the coaster and noticed that there were messages on his voice mail. The first one was from

Ashley. She would be out of town that evening on assignment. Everything concerning the Find was being handled and she would speak to him tomorrow. Garrett decided the other calls didn't matter.

He returned to the kitchen, made a sandwich and watched the news as he ate. As he nestled into his easy chair and turned on the local news, he realized he was actually tired. When he awoke, the news was still on. It wasn't until he looked at the clock that he realized he had already slept five hours and was watching the late news.

He was still groggy so he turned the TV off, slipped out of his clothes and into the comfortable four poster bed.

Sleep came instantly.

CHAPTER 30

Garrett awoke at his normal time. For a change, he did his normal exercise routine, or at least some of it. He returned at the normal time, more winded than usual. There was a phone message from Ashley letting him know that she would return to Charleston early Saturday morning and that she would see him then. Also, that she would call before he closed the store since she was in an area where she couldn't take calls.

He stripped off his running clothes and turned the shower on. He stepped into the steamy shower and let the clouds of steam and the slow spray play over his body. Hot showers were a very relaxing time for Garrett. He tried the deep breathing like his trainer had told him about on his last time at the gym. But the hot moist air started him coughing and he quickly gave that idea up.

Once he had the coughing spree under control, he just stood there in the steam and the shower and let his mind float. Another idea suggested at the gym. Think of nothing, the trainer had said. Relax. Thinking of the trainer got Garrett thinking about the gym. The gym was on Bay Street. The newspaper was on Bay Street. He wondered what Ashley was doing. She hadn't said where she was, only that she would be there another night. She would be back tomorrow. Tomorrow is Saturday. Saturday follows Friday. Today is Friday. Friday was an appointment with the shrink. In an instant, Garrett had moved from relax and thinking of nothing to pissed off.

I must not be doing something the right way, he thought.

Garrett finished his *morning toilet,* as Queen Ester called it.

He dressed and then headed downstairs, started a fresh pot of coffee, and searched out and found a leftover croissant from yesterday's delivery. Garrett knew that a day-old Croissant can be cut, buttered and toasted and turn into nectar of the gods. At least the nectar of the fat little gods because of the butter and a dollop of specially selected jelly, this time from England.

"The English taste for jellies and jams is more varied and more complex than ours in the colonies," he said aloud.

Armed with coffee, the newspaper and his toasted, buttered croissant, he walked onto the back porch, sat in the old swing and opened the morning newspaper. Garrett's intent was to gather information about the events of international news as interpreted by the staff of the local newspaper, most of whom had the same set of inborn prejudices, educational preferences and cultured norms as did he.

The Charleston Paper was what's happening in the world but with a true Charlestonian twist on things. Garrett liked it. The news pages were Liberal but not too Liberal, and the editorial writers were Conservative, but not too Conservative. Politically, as with lots of things, Charleston liked the middle of the road, the means rather than the extremes. But they were genteel about it.

Thoroughly informed, Garrett returned to the kitchen, refilled his coffee, placed the cup on his desk and slipped the OPEN sign in the door. He made his circuit, straightening and turning on lights.

By the time he had returned to his desk, three customers were standing there for his directions. that was the start of his work day, and it was an indicator of what the rest of his work day would be like.

When he looked at grandfather, it was just before 5:00. Garrett was preparing to close the store. He was in no hurry. The ring of the telephone instantly reminded him that he had not heard from Ashley since early morning. It was her happy voice that greeted him, "Hi Babe. What's going on?"

"It's been a little rushed here," Garrett could tell from her upbeat voice that things concerning her story were going well. He started to complain about his day and the progress of the announcement but thought better of it. He knew that sometimes it's better to let your significant other enjoy her happiness even when you can't, so he let her babble on about her day.

When he looked at the clock it was already 5:15. He would have to hurry to make his appointment with Dr. Williams.

"Lee! Lee, I hate to interrupt but I have an appointment with Dr. Williams at 5:30. I need to hurry."

"That's right, Alex doesn't like his patients to be late.

Garrett left the store and slowly walked to the confrontation he expected and dreaded. He wasn't, intellectually, ready to answer the shrink's questions and he wasn't sure he was ready to deal with his response to his dream. It was 5:37 by the time Garrett opened the imposing door to the office of Dr. Alex Williams PhD, MD, FAAP an imposing psychologist.

"Mr. Garrett," Dr. Williams was using a parental tone that Garrett didn't like. It was the tone his father used when he was scolding Edward as a child.

They both took their places and the session started. "I sensed that you left our last session with a lot left to be said. It is important, if I am to help you, that you are honest and complete with me. If that isn't your commitment then you and I are both wasting our time. I don't like being so direct, but Miss Barrineau gave me the distinct impression that you were somewhat desperate to get to the source of your dreams. Is that correct?"

Garrett was taken off guard by the pointedness of the shrink's comment.

"Yes... I... er... Yes!" Garrett said with no little trepidation. "I do want to get to the source of the problem of my dream." What could he say? Could he tell the shrink that he was embarrassed by the dream? By the unbridled violence? But it was his physical response that was the real embarrassment. The erection.

"Mr. Garrett, I'm waiting and you're paying." Dr Williams paused. It was almost that he now sensed the source of Garrett's hesitancy.

"Edward," the doctor said in a softer, more caring tone, "the best way to discuss a difficult issue is to start with the facts. Why not describe the dream, then we can discuss the feelings, if you like."

Finally calmed, Garrett described the dream. He left out none of the details. Dr. Williams took some notes but remained silent and nonjudgmental through the entire description.

"Well, that's it. What could it mean?" Garrett looked plaintively at the shrink.

"We may never know its true meaning or what it symbolizes," Dr. Williams simply stated his comments. "We know the events of the dream," Dr. Williams paused, "but, what caused you such uneasiness at your last visit?" Silence followed.

"This isn't easy for me to say." Garrett squirmed in his chair alternating crossing his legs right over left, left over right, and again.

"Edward, it's just like the dream — just start talking."

"Doctor, I don't even understand this. Every time I describe the dream, I experience an erection," Garrett paused a moment, cleared his throat, looked uncomfortably around the room and began again. "Not the entire dream, but the specific part when the young woman's breast was exposed and mutilated." Again Garrett paused in the description. He looked around the room again as if he were looking to see if someone were listening.

"This is quite embarrassing. To the best of my memory I have never been so aroused by any masochistic or sadomasochistic feelings or images. The dream wasn't sexual. And, as I said, my response is both embarrassing and troubling," again Garrett paused. "What can this mean?"

"What do you think it means, Edward?"

Garrett looked at the shrink. In the seconds that passed as Garrett was forming his answer, the heat of his anger was building much like that of a pressure cooker.

That's just what I'd expect from a smartass shrink to do, ask me to analyze myself! That's what Garrett wanted to say and those were the first words that had formed in his head. But he stopped himself. Narrowing his eyes, Garrett focused his stare on Dr. William's eyes. In a measured pace and precise tone intended to show control, Garrett said, "The reason I am here is because I don't know what these dreams mean. If I am to analyze myself, I'll talk to my mirror."

"Let's not be hostile, Edward. The fact is that one's first thoughts in answer to a specific probing question often elicit the truest answer. Hostility, in your case, could reveal a deep-seated anger. The key to this anger may well have been prompted by the dream. The point in the dream that caused the physical response was a naked breast followed by mutilation. Since we are almost out of time, I don't want to go into this any further right now, but it could symbolize issues with your mother. Please consider this and let's pick up there on Monday."

With this, Garrett didn't know if he should be pleased that some progress had been made, or if he should be pissed off that the shrink wouldn't continue with a possible important breakthrough.

Garrett considered the possible conclusions and decided he was pissed off.

As he left Dr. Williams' office, he stepped into the dusk of a foggy evening. There was a chill in the air and he hadn't bothered to take a jacket with him to the appointment, even though he knew he would be leaving after the sun had set. The office visit presented Garrett with a bigger issue — a multi-faceted mental quandary. There was the sense of relief from telling the doctor about the effect the visuals of the dream had on him. Juxtaposed with that, the parental chiding he experienced at the beginning of the session.

How dare he presume to talk to Thomas Edward Garrett in that manner, Garrett thought, giving preference to the negative emotion rather than the positive. Then, issues with his mother. *How dare he!* His anger grew with each step away from the shrink's office. First, it was Ashley taking control of the announcement of the Find, then James John telling him where and how the pictures of the items of the Find should be taken and now this pipsqueak of a doctor, who couldn't be much older than Garrett, treating him like he was a child and accusing his mother of being the root of his problem.

"Damn him. Damn him to Hell," Garrett said out loud, the frustration and anger dripping from his words. His condemnation of the doctor echoed down the darkened alleyway that connected his route from Zigzag Alley to Church Street. He heard his words as they came back to him. A homeless man, huddled in a cardboard box in the doorway of an abandoned building, heard Garrett's words, but he was far too involved with a bottle of cheap wine to comment.

The fire hydrant militia standing at attention, festooned in their finest hand painted uniforms heard Garrett's words but, as we all know, when a military man is at attention he can not speak. So Garrett's words, spoken aloud, were both statement and answer. Frustration breeds frustration, and in frustration there is no solution.

Garrett kept on walking with only his anger and frustration to keep him warm.

CHAPTER 31

Garrett woke Saturday morning with no recollection of going to bed Friday night. Even without all of the strange things going on in his life, that wouldn't have been a good thing.

He remembered his anger at Dr. Alex Williams. That memory rekindled the fire in the anger furnace. He had never really wanted to go to this smartass shrink. The only reason he agreed to go was Ashley's insistence and the dreams. He had never liked the psychology students in college, walking around so smug. Like they didn't have any problems of their own. Like they had some kind of answer that no one else knew.

"It's her fault I feel like this," Garrett announced to no one in particular.

"Maybe I'll just stop going," he added.

The bedside clock heard him, but there was no time for a discussion. The calculator on the desk heard him, but wasn't able to convert his words into a mathematical calculation so it turned itself off in a state of confusion. Most of the other objects in his bedroom that heard his declaration responded with an apparent lack of concern. After all, they have seen Garrett's changeability in the past so, *go don't go*, what business was it of theirs anyway, not to mention he hadn't waited for their input in the past.

Since they were considered inanimate objects, their input would take years and Garrett couldn't and wouldn't wait. As he sat at his desk, Garrett continued his discussion with only the inanimate objects to hear. Only the wise grandfather in the corner knew the real answer, time would tell.

His morning shower had cleared his head a little but there was the nagging question of where he had been last night. Could he have gone to the Truck Stop again? No answer. Wouldn't he remember if he had come home and begun his drinking here? No answer. He put his thoughts aside, went to the kitchen, started the coffee, prepared some bacon, eggs and grits, even considered baking some biscuits but settled for toast. With the food properly positioned on a breakfast tray, he maneuvered back to his desk and started to do some paper work before the beginning of the business day.

Ring.

"Who could that be at this hour?" Garrett asked, looking at the phone. If the name of the person wasn't "Ring," the phone wasn't talking.

Ring.

"It's 8:00 a.m. for Christ sake," Garrett exclaimed, still looking at the phone. Still no additional information from the telephone.

Ring.

"OK, I'll answer it," Garrett again said in the direction of the phone. There was the inkling of what the phone thought right before his next pronouncement. *Just do it.*

Ring.

Then, Garrett picked up his cell phone.

"Hello, #13 Church Street."

"Is Mr. Garrett there, Mr. Edward Garrett?"

The voice had a very British accent. A refined, very British accent at that.

"This is Edward Garrett. May I help you?"

"Mr. Garrett, I am Sir Arthur Herbert. I represent Christie's in New York. You may have heard of us. I am in possession of some information concerning a collection of art objects that you are purported to possess. If this information is correct, I think Christie's and our clients may be very interested in what the collection may contain."

The question was pointed even if it was unasked. Garrett paused, not totally sure what he should say. The awkward silence communicated more to the alert Britisher than Garrett could have realized.

"Well, Ah ... I ... er" Garrett stammered into the phone. "There may be something to what you say."

He was unsure how much to say and how much to reveal.

"Come now, Mr. Garrett. I don't mean to be impertinent but we are professionals, you and I. Either you have the collection I heard about or you don't. A simple *Yes* or *No* will suffice."

The directness of Sir Arthur Herbert caught Garrett completely off guard.

"I ... Yes there is a collection, but I'm not sure now is the right time to discuss it."

Still unsure what he should say, Garrett was sure that he wanted to be better prepared for a conversation with a representative of Christie's, one of the two premier auction houses in the world.

"We are planning a formal presentation in a couple of weeks. You and your clients will be more than welcome. I'll be happy to include you on the invitation list."

It seemed like an excellent way to postpone further discussion.

"Mr. Garrett. One of the things Christie's provides its clients is the opportunity of anonymity. Another is the opportunity to get first choice at times when true art finds are made. We pride ourselves on this. Although we shall be happy to attend this formal presentation you are talking about, I would be less than candid if I didn't express our interest in an advance showing, time to allow for verification of the objects and first selection. I'm sure you know what I mean. Surely you haven't made this known to others."

There seemed to be a softening in the demanding demeanor of the representative of Christie's. In fact, Garrett thought he detected an even plaintive tone developing in Sir Arthur Herbert's voice. Over the next few minutes Garrett explained how the purchases of the objects would be carried out. The conversation ended on a different note than Sir Herbert had expected.

Garrett was surprised. First, at the attitude the well-known antique auction gallery's representative had taken and then at how quickly he had regained control of the situation. Christie's coming to him and asking for preferential treatment from him.

He remembered his last trip to England. There at Christie's main showroom he had been just another American buying

English antiques. He remembered the cold, almost impersonal handling of the auction. Little time to inspect the items, even the very expensive ones. There, he was a number and a checkbook. It was almost the same at Sotheby's. One unknown antique dealer from Charleston, South Carolina. Now, being called with a request for special treatment by Christie's. Ironically, it made him feel as good as he had in many months. He decided he would call Ashley to tell her the good news when he heard the telephone ringing again.

"Hello, #13 Church."

"Mr. Edward Garrett, please."

The voice was unfamiliar but a soft pleasant one with no apparent accent.

"This is Edward Garrett. Can I help you?"

"Yes, at least I hope so. I am Doctor Cynthia Morgenstern PhD. I'm with the New York office of Sotheby's. I have been asked to check on a group of art treasures that have been reported to be in your possession. We received a note from a Charleston newspaper with a slide that is most interesting to us. Can you give me some more information about the item in the slide and what other items there may be available?"

The representative of Sotheby's put Garrett at ease with her subtle, undemanding tone.

"Well," Garrett hesitated but decided to be more open than he had been in his conversation with Sir Arthur Herbert. "Yes, there are a number of items that may be of interest to you, but they will not be available for viewing for a couple weeks yet. We will have an open showing, in a rather unique manner I might add, and you will certainly be invited."

As Garrett paused to catch his breath, the voice on the other end of the phone interrupted.

"Pardon me for interrupting, but I was hoping I could get more information on the phone — today."

She was courteous yet very persuasive in her effort to gain an advantage.

"I wish I could help, Ms Morgenstern, I mean Dr. Morgenstern, but I don't want to do anything to take away from the showing. I can tell you that there are a number of items in the collection that are museum quality, one of a kind finds."

Garrett hoped his vagueness would stop the questions.

"Yes, it is *Doctor*, but my friends call me Cindy. I can appreciate your interest in keeping information about your discovery quiet, Mr. Garrett, but you must understand my position. My superiors have asked me to find out what I can about the pieces you have. If I come back to them with vague generalities, they will think I haven't done my best. Could you be more specific? What period are the items from? What is their country of origin, in your opinion? What types of other items are there? These are the questions to which I have been asked to find answers."

The woman on the phone was very professional in her efforts to get more information from Garrett.

"I'm sorry, Dr. Morgenstern. All I can say is that there are items in the collection that are worth a great deal of money. Some are even priceless, in my opinion. At this moment, I'm not sure which items will be made available for sale, but everyone will have an equal opportunity to bid on them on the night of the showing. And, to your other questions, the items cover a large time span and vary in type from weapons to coinage. I don't mean to be short or to place you in a bad light with your superiors, but that is all I can tell you. In fact, it is more than I told the representative from Christie's who called just before you."

Now Garrett was beginning to get somewhat annoyed with the persistence.

"You were contacted by Christie's? I thought we were the only company to receive the information. If I may ask, who from Christie's contacted you?"

"A Sir Arthur Herbert called only a few minutes before you. And I told him less than I told you."

"Oh, that phony *lord* with his phony English accent. Mr. Garrett, Sir Arthur Herbert, as he calls himself, is a product of a Queens neighborhood and a good New York acting school. The closest he's been to royalty was when he played Henry VIII in *Anne of a Thousand Days*. He didn't even give a good performance at that."

Sounding much more cynical and much less soft, Cindy Morgenstern was sounding more New York and less pleasant.

"We want to represent you in the sale of these art items, Mr. Garrett. We are the best in this area, and I believe you'll not be happy with anyone else. I don't want to get in a bidding contest with our friends across town, but I can assure you we will meet any offer they made you and I know we will be better able to communicate on this matter, just you and me."

"I..." Garrett couldn't even start his sentence before she interrupted again.

"My private phone number in New York is 212-555-1672. You can call me anytime day or night." Dr. Morgenstern said more with the intonation of her voice than with her words. "Don't forget 212-555-1672. Call me," she paused and very sexually continued, "Edward, isn't it? I'll be awaiting your call."

Her voice trailed off. There was a click before Garrett could say anything. Garrett sat for moment holding the phone and staring at the number he had just written. Calls to him from the two top auction galleries in the world. To him! Maybe the Find was a bigger discovery than he realized. But the tone of Dr. Cynthia Morgenstern's voice was unmistakable.

"If you wish to make a call, hang up and try the number again."

The tinny sound of the computer-generated telephone voice made him realize he was still holding the phone. He replaced the phone on the desk. It was with more than a little feeling of guilt he called Ashley. He wanted to tell her about the conversations with the representatives of the two most important antique companies in the world and to find out which pictures the newspaper had selected to run with the story.

Ashley seemed preoccupied. She didn't sound like she appreciated his accomplishment. She should have understood what the calls of a representative from Christie's or Sotheby's meant. She talked about a Pulitzer. She was trivializing his accomplishment by her attitude. All she could do was question him about moving the treasure to Georgia. All she wanted to know was if he had gotten the mini-warehouse rented yet? Was the truck taken care of? Would Storey be willing to help? Did they need other people to help carry the heavy items? Questions that were none of her damn business. He would take care of everything.

Garrett wanted to just hang up on her, but as he was doing more and more lately, he sat quietly, stuffing his anger, compacting it into every cell of his body, cramming more and more anger into every muscle, every connective tissue, every bone, every nerve until it was turned into a genuine rage.

He couldn't sit still. And she continued asking those inane questions. He paced as he continued the conversation. He wanted to scream at her. He wanted to — in the midst of his fit he realized, what he really wanted was her recognition. But that realization didn't cool his phosphoric, white-hot anger.

She didn't understand. That Cindy Morgenstern understood. *She* implied sexual favors to get access to his treasure. *She* knew how important this was ... *he* was.

Ashley Cooper Barrineau was so engrossed with her story and her newspaper and her plan to announce his Find that *she* didn't have time for him. Soon *she* would see — just like the rest of these self-involved people in this place they call the *Holy City*.

"Huh," Garrett was extracted from his personal world of self-importance by Ashley's repeated question.

"Edward, are you still there?"

"Yes, sure, I'm right here. I'm working on it, all of it. I just called to let you know that I got a call from Christie's and Sotheby's, but I guess we can talk about that later," Garrett acquiesced to Ashley one more time. He knew how single-minded she could be when working on a story.

She told him that she would be back in Charleston mid-morning Sunday and that she was saving Sunday dinner for the two of them.

"Let's go someplace special," she had said. Garrett started to ask where, but he knew it would devolve into their favorite pointless discussion of, "Where do you want to go?" "I don't care, where do you want to go?" "I don't care, what kind of food do you want?" "I don't care, what kind of food to you want?" until someone got angry.

To save time, energy and not add fuel to this discussion fire, Garrett said, "Alright, I'll let you know when you get here."

That seemed to satisfy Ashley even though he had no idea where they would be going. But, there was lots of time before he would have to actually make a decision.

Garrett decided to put on his College of Charleston sweat pants and shirt and walk down to the *slave market*. He would not open the shop until later, if at all. He wanted some espresso, some kind of pastry, maybe a scone, and absolutely no one making the slightest suggestion what he should be doing. A short five-block walk up Church Street would place him right in the center of the old market.

Almost two centuries earlier, slave traders would have been selling young black men and women from elevated stands throughout the long open-air stone block building. Glistening, oiled naked bodies would catch the sun rays in a brilliant burst of reflected light much like the facets of a shinny diamond. Sunlight sparkled off the soft rounded bodies of the teenage girls, their modesty stripped from them in the same way as their clothes.

Some cowered in a futile effort to cover their nakedness while others stood erect and proud, refusing to accept the ignominy of their situation. Garrett stopped to stare and was jostled by the crowd intent only on the objective du jour.

There were many local artisans that displayed finely crafted baskets made from coastal sweet grass. In some cases, constructed in the same way and same design as they had been for well over a hundred years.

Occupying many of the same elevated stands as the slave merchants had, a cadre of middle-aged to older mammy-like black women would weave their baskets from the bunches of grass brought to them by their children or husbands.

There was a small number of stalls that sold selections of local, home-made jams and jellies. The prized red pepper jelly was proudly displayed, each claiming a unique family recipe.

An occasional stall would offer home-baked goods, usually featuring Charleston Bennie Seed Cookies. African slaves brought the benne seeds, now known as sesame seeds, with them from their native country. The sweet, chewy, crunchy cookies were the result of combining the seeds with a little flour, brown sugar, molasses and a few other ingredients that made each a unique creation.

Restaurants, bakeries, and coffee shops dotted the edges of the market now. Decorum, gentility and equal rights laws had caused the dropping of the word, *slave*.

Now, it was just the *market* or the *old market.*

Garrett's favorite coffee shop, The Bean, was at the corner of North Market and Anson Street, in the half-basement of an old cotton warehouse. The Bean drew an unusual mix of clientele. It wasn't like one of those trendy, new coffee shoppes, as if adding the "e" makes them more "in." It had been there for 30 years. Each of the major hurricanes to hit the South Carolina low lands would result in The Bean flooding. The owner would simply pump the water out, bring in industrial dryers, and quickly resume business as usual. He had even installed the wiring with most of the electrical plugs near the ceiling, so electrical wires were a part of the interior design.

The ambiance of The Bean had nothing to do with the décor. They were never able to get 100% of the odor of a flooded building out of The Bean, but the customers didn't seem to mind.

Garrett arrived about 10:00 a.m. The room was still very crowded as it had been all morning — actually every morning. Bill Everett, the owner, saw Garrett waiting in queue out front. He always kept his eye out for local regulars and sent a waitress out to bring Garrett inside and provide him the next available table. Everett knew that tourists come and tourists go, but guys like Garrett would spend their money in their favorite place all year round.

The violin of pride in Garrett was singing like a classic Stradivarius. Seated before all of those people standing out there at curb side. He really did feel important. He made a mental note to come here more often.

The Saturday morning copy of the *News and Courier* featured at the top of the page, above the masthead, a two-line teaser to the Sunday paper feature story, "Local Man finds Multi-Million Dollar Treasure. Details page 1B tomorrow." He knew who that was and what the treasure was. No one in the restaurant knew, just him. That guy over there sipping his coffee, that girl putting on lipstick, the older couple having cappuccino, the students who used The Bean as an extension of their study hall, none of them knew. They were in the presence of a major news maker and they didn't even know.

Uncharacteristically, Garrett ordered a triple espresso from their Jamaican Blue Mountain coffee beans and a cinnamon scone. The total would be tripled what he normally spent at breakfast and with the order received, Everett smiled. The *pull them in when the place is crowded* is the best technique to raise the ticket average.

Garrett finished his espresso, ate his scone and read the newspaper with a frequent glance around the room. Other than Everett and two of the waitresses, Garrett didn't recognize a single soul in the room. That is until a black woman who had been sitting by the door with her back to him stood to leave. She turned and looked directly at him. Her expression was one of recognition, but he knew he had never seen her before.

Why is she staring at me? Garrett thought. A moment later she was gone. Could it be true, or was his mind playing tricks on him? Tourists were everywhere on the weekends in Charleston. She could have been a tourist that just looked familiar. He couldn't be sure but it troubled him enough for him to spill some of his coffee.

Garrett left The Bean after dropping an unusually large tip. Everett smiled again.

He looked at his watch only to find that he hadn't put it on. It was strange that he would have neglected that part of his dressing routine. In that fleeting moment, Garrett recalled a number of small changes in his routine that had begun to concern him. He had always been a creature of habit and it had served him well.

He was distracted by the tower chime from St Michael's church. Following the chimed intro, the bell rang only once. Since he was certain that it wasn't 1:00 o'clock, the time must be half past something. It must be half past 11:00. As he moved into the flow of people in the Old Slave Market, he saw a clock in one of the stalls that confirmed his suspicion, 11:32.

Garrett sat at his desk with a smile on his face. It had been there since he started thinking about the Find. The newspaper article would hit the street Sunday morning. With it, everybody in Charleston's antique world would know how important Edward Garrett was. Garrett sat, basking in the warmth of the recognition the newspaper would bring.

At some point an element of the happiness of that recognition started to turn to dread. All of those people sticking their nose in his business. The more he thought the more the negative side of notoriety began to be winning. It was somewhere between notoriety and dread that reason slipped its foot.

The treasure is right here, in your basement.

No security system exists that will keep thieves away from *his* treasure. He decided then and there that he had to move the treasure, and it had to be moved before too many people read that article. He immediately called Storey and told him to rent a moving truck and meet him early Sunday morning. He checked the Internet and found there was a number of secure personal storage places in Georgia before you get to Savannah. He made a call and reserved a large storage unit.

Garrett closed the shop.

His first stop was a hardware store where he found a padlock that could not be cut. With the lock, a bundle of bungee cords, three rolls of duct tape and a Snicker bar, he left the store and returned to #13 Church.

A call to Storey found a griping, grumbling Storey. His day off, his plans, always something, there was a litany of reasons why Storey didn't want to make the move. Garrett's offer of $250 put an end to the negative Storey and signaled the beginning of the cooperative Storey. He would be ready at sun-up on Sunday morning.

With all of the necessary plans made, Garrett ate an early dinner at home, leftover steak and salad and a glass of wine, and got ready for bed. He had felt extremely tired since leaving the market. Not as tired as he felt when he had worked many hours, more like when he was carrying a heavy load. He slipped into bed with the intention of reading, but went to sleep with the book folded over his chest.

PROPHECY

In the early moments of wakening, it was the sound of the wind that I noticed first, playing a soft, rhythmic tattoo with the sail rigging. The lapping of the waves on the hull added to the rhythm. Add the gentle to-and-fro tossing of the old ship, and you have the music that had lulled me to sleep for almost 5 weeks now.

Happily, we are only days from our destination. In the inky blackness, I am increasingly aware of the smell. More than a smell — smells would be more accurate. Intermingled. Not quite a stench but almost.

I struggle to separate the smells in my mind. Some are much stronger. Fermented apples; like mead.

No! Not fermenting — spoiled.

As I grapple to identify more of the smells, more become clear — spoiled fruit, old wood, dried meat. All with an overriding scent of salt.

Occasionally, the little scent buds that cover the lining of my nose sort out the acrid smells of human vomit mixed with urine. My innards lurch. I clinch my eyelids in an effort to shut out the stench by blinding my vision.

Nothing helps.

My insides lurch again! But it's more than just my insides, it's a different movement of the ship. It's an unmistakable movement other than a ship on an agitated ocean.

I am praying with all my might. My petitions to our Lord Jesus Christ, Mother Mary, the Holy Spirit and every saint whose name I can remember. My prayers, along with a sip of the medicinal brewing capabilities of Brother Caddish, whose potion had allowed me to slip the bonds of the reality of the cursed journey, give me peace. But the reality of impending danger has invaded my cramped little room through the same portals as those wretched smells.

New sounds, almost indistinguishable, almost unreal. It has a different tempo and there was an echo. Or is it my dreams? Focusing is difficult, but I am able to start making them out. They're footfalls. People are moving around on the deck. Moving with haste. One thing is certain, something is wrong.

"Our Father, who art in heaven,
Hallowed be thy Name. Thy kingdom come.
Thy will be done, On earth as it is in heaven.
Give us this day our daily bread. And forgive us our trespasses,
As we forgive those who trespass against us.
And lead us not into temptation,
But deliver us from evil.
For thine is the kingdom, and the power, and the glory,
for ever and ever.
Amen."

Awake! I check the safety of the box. The box and its precious contents are safe. The box has become the symbol of my assignment — the future of The Church in the new world.

Again I evoke God's blessing and oversight, "God grant that I can complete my mission." If it's God's will that I build the church in the new world, build it I shall, to the glory of God and the Holy Catholic Church.

A momentary silence with no special thoughts allowed me to listen. The silence is reassuring. The only sounds are those of the wind in the rigging and the waves playing counterpoint to the creaking of the wooden hull.

The report and reverberation of a cannon shot is unmistakable. Seconds later the scurrying of feet was quickly followed by the crunching of splitting wood as the cannon ball tore through the wooden mast, and the better part of the severed mast crashed into the main deck.

I grasp for my Rosary and whisper additional prayers.

"Hail Mary, full of grace, the Lord is with thee; blessed art thou among women, and blessed is the fruit of thy womb, Jesus. Holy Mary, Mother of God, pray for us sinners, now and at the hour of our death."

I can hear the disorganized conflicting commands on deck, screamed by the officers directing the response. More cannon fire. The screams of the injured now echoing through every recess of the ship. A sudden lurch. I crash to the floor. My candle is pulled from its hanging place. The hot wax burns patterns in my arm.

I know we've been rammed. More yelling, more screams, more crying. And more prayers. I'm able to crawl under my bunk. I know my chance is concealment.

More whispered prayers.

"Glory be to the Father and to the Son and to the Holy Spirit; as in the beginning, is now and ever shall be, world without end. Amen. Amen."

Heavy foot falls echo through the corridor that leads to my room. Slamming doors. More yelling, more crying, more screams. I grab for the box. Its gray-green surface is almost calming. I must protect the treasure. I must protect the Church.

"O my Jesus, forgive us of our sins, save us from the fires of hell, lead all souls to Heaven, especially those in need of Thy mercy. Amen."

The door to my room crashes open. The intruder must have a lantern, I can see light dancing all over the walls and floor. I can see his ankles. I can smell him. I dare not move lest I give away my hiding place. I continue my prayers, a whisper even in my mind.

"Hail, holy Queen Mother of Mercy, our life, our sweetness and our hope. To thee do we cry, poor banished children of Eve; to thee do we send up our sighs, mourning and weeping in this valley of tears. Turn then, most gracious advocate, thine eyes of mercy toward us; and after this our exile, show unto us the blessed fruit of thy womb, Jesus. O clement, O loving, O sweet Virgin Mary."

The silence is deafening. Holding my breath may help, but it makes my throat burn. I see his foot fractions of a second before I hear the blood curdling yell and the crushing that virtually disseminates my hiding place.

Rough hands grab my neck. These heathen hands press my collar into my neck cutting into my throat like a knife. The Church's treasure is ripped from my grasp. I am jerked to my feet. The stench of this unwashed body and rum-drenched mouth serve only to punctuate the vileness of this unthinkable act. I am dragged through the corridor, up the stairs and across the deck. The pain increases with every stumble as every movement is accented with their profanity.

"Why? Why now, God?" I ask.

"Shut your mouth!"

The command was accented with his left fist as it shattered my nose and jaw. I heard the soft clicking of my teeth as they bounce along the wooden deck. I feel the warmth of the blood as it trickles down my neck.

"Leave him live."

The voice was soft, demanding, commanding and with the rounded tones brought by culture and learning.

"What do we have in the box?"

"Gold and jewels, cap'n and him a priest."

With that statement, the heathen loosed my neck and pushed me, roughly to the deck.

"I said, let him be."

It was a growl of displeasure that dribbled from the erudite heathen's mouth.

"Well, what would a man of the cloth, who had taken a vow of poverty, be doing carrying such a large amount of gold and jewels?"

"I am an emissary of his holiness, the Pope," I slurred since speaking clearly was impossible with my broken jaw and missing teeth, "on a mission to establish a church in the new world islands."

Maybe God had sent this soft-spoken, cultured man as my means of escape.

"Well, well. A new church, is it father? Are you Jesuit?"

"No. I am a brother of the Franciscan Order. Why?"

"Just curious."

As we are carrying on this almost civilized conversation, all manner of atrocities are going on around us. Bodies are being hacked into pieces and tossed over board. Schools of sharks and barracudas are feasting to the screams of other travelers who have been thrown overboard alive.

"I'm Episcopal myself," he said, "St Luke's. It's a fine church. It's in Charleston."

He stopped and pointed to his left, but not particularly suggesting that anyone look. Three of his men moved swiftly. With the utmost accuracy and minimized motion, the two heathen swordsmen caught two of the crew in mid air as they jumped to engage the pirates. The now headless crewmen fell to the passageway floor, well short of their mark. Two heads rolled from their shoulders, one stopping right next to my foot. The clean cuts attested to the trained accuracy of the pirate crew. A look of surprise now frozen on their faces.

This is a curious situation. This is the closest I have ever been to violent death. I have seen the dead, old and young, but never at the instant of death.

"Sorry we can not continue our discourse. I have pirating to do and you have a church to start."

My heart soared. I was to be saved. I would be able to complete my mission. The church will replace the gold and jewels. And, I will live.

"And, I must apologize in advance," he continued, "I will be fulfilling my mission, but you, my dear Franciscan Brother, will not."

The motion of his hand flowed with the same civilized softness of his words as he gestured that I should follow his crewmen out of the safety of his presence onto the deck.

I have a feeling of lightness, floating as I am lifted and thrown like a stone in an ancient Olympic game. I'm sure my face must have mimicked the look of surprise on the head that had rolled past my foot. The last thing I saw as my line of sight passed the ship's edge was his hand, scooping up the jewels and the gold pieces from my treasure box. My beautiful grey/green stone box.

The water is cold, so cold that I am immobilized by the shock. I try to struggle with all my might to return to the top of the water. Every muscle in my body is drawn up in knots due to the frigid water, so I might as well be encased in a block of glass.

With my eyes open, all I can see is blackness. The salty water burns my eyes so I close them. The missing teeth allow amounts of the briny water to slip past my lips and burn my throat. I sense that I can smell the salt in the water but there is more, spoiled, rotting life just like onboard the ship. I am flailing my arms in an effort to reach the surface.

Actually, I am doing that in my mind, since the chill of the water has immobilized my body. At first, there is a bump on my leg. Then I feel a bump on my arm. I can see a bright light. I must be close to the surface now. There is another bump on my leg. The light is brighter now and the water is warmer.

I will my eyes to open. The burning brings with it the realization that I am no closer to the surface of the water than when I closed them. I must be losing consciousness because I see shapes moving in the water as if silhouetted by the moon light. Some moving fast, some moving slowly.

I know I'm losing consciousness. I want to be alert until the end to give myself the last rites. But I know I have little air left to sustain my body. There's more bumping as if someone is trying to shake me back to consciousness. Then, there's the smell — the single thing I can concentrate on. The smell of death. Now I can see an eye. A single round, black unmoving eye and a row of teeth. I scream in the soundless deep.

CHAPTER 32

The scream is a sound from another world. It emanated from deep in some unknown recess of his soul. An evil connection to another world. A stranger wailing from inside his body.

As he regained touch with reality, he found himself in a tight ball in the center of his bed, clutching his belly. The smell of death is in his nostrils, in his brain, in his being.

The retching starts. Violent spasms. Gut wrenching contractions. Welcoming them, the opportunity to expel the evil that he was feeling from the core of his being. He wanted to see some demon, any demon, actually sent flying across the room by the retching, followed by a black and green trail of the decaying mass of underworld creatures that have possessed his body. The heavy retching released all other bodily functions. It was like his body was seeking every possible exit to expel the unmistakable evil that has built up within him.

All that was expelled was the wine, steak and salad from dinner – the portions that have been processed by his body and the portions that hadn't. And the urine and excrement.

"I believe I am dying. If not, I wish I were," he said aloud in a weak voice.

It took time to reconnect his brain, his body and his self to the reality of now. He must have been lying in a vomit, urine and excrement pool for at least half an hour. It caused him to start a new round of retching. Nothing was left inside his body to expel, but that information hasn't reached the source of his need to retch. In a humorous moment he thought, *I expect to see my toenails flying out my mouth and across the room.*

Slowly, he was able to sit, then stand, then move, with the help of the furniture, to the bathroom. He started with a cold shower, but it caused him to recall the images of the dream. He quickly switched to hot water and slowly watched the residue of his dream slide from his body and into the waste water drain.

He lost count of the number of times he covered his body with soap. He still didn't feel clean. He repeated the actions. Once the last of the warm water was dispensed from the shower head, he left the shower and stopped to visit the mirror. He had no idea what he would see, but he knew he must find out what the man in the mirror looked like tonight.

There, captured inside the world where left is right, was a haggard, yet human, Edward Garrett, not an unrecognizable demonic creature. Not the reflected image of the Dr. Edward Garrett who had been dispensing telepathic, psychological advice that he had last seen in *mirrorland*. Not the quirky grinning Edward Garrett that looked back at him from his driver's license. Just a tired, drawn, pallid Edward Garrett, the visage of a clueless middle-aged man cursed with this *dream albatross.*

But for what transgression?

"What guilt do I bear? What sin am I guilty of to deserve this torture?" Tears welled up in Garrett's eyes, released and signaled the beginning of a grand parade of tears to the antique, porcelain sink below.

"Am I cursed with these vile dreams like the ancient mariner who must wear the dead albatross until his lesson is learned? What is my lesson? Oh, God, what is my lesson? Of what am I guilty? What? God? What?" With his last rhetorical question, Garrett released all control, slumped into a naked pile on the bathroom floor and sobbed uncontrollably.

Exactly how long Garrett remained on the floor was unimportant to anyone, including himself. It seemed that the reservoir at the end of his tear ducts ran dry about the same time as his nerve endings began to register how cold it was there on the tile floor. With his left hand grasping the basin and his right the door handle, Garrett was able to focus his remaining strength sufficiently to stand. Willing each of his aching joints to regain a vertical position was accompanied by a painful groan.

Garrett washed his face, slapped his face vigorously to bring back the circulation and with it a semblance of flesh color. He stood there gazing at his reflection and recalled his troubled mind's comparison of his situation to that of the old seaman's in the classic poem by Samuel Taylor Coldridge. He recalled a single line from the poem:

"Instead of a cross, an albatross About my neck was hung."

Again he asked the questions in his mind, "Of what am I guilty? What is my lesson?"

It took the better part of an hour for Garrett to clean the mess he had made in his bedroom. With the soiled sheet and other bed dressings in a plastic bag in the laundry area, mattress scrubbed and almost dry, fresh sheets and blanket in place and nearly a full can of air disinfectant still hovering around the room like an apple-cinnamon fog, Garrett extinguished the light in the bathroom and slipped between the fresh sheets to, hopefully, re-enter sleep in a no-dream zone.

CHAPTER 33

The rooster crowed. Dawn came and went. The rooster crowed again. The sun tipped his hat hello to the people already swimming in the Atlantic Ocean. The rooster crowed yet one more time. And the denizens of the *Holy City* began to yawn, shuffle, scratch various body parts, acknowledge their bed mates and start their Sabbath morning in the manner of their choosing.

All save Edward Garrett and Storey, who had been up for hours. Garrett had called Storey at 4:00 but it was 4:30 before either of them wanted to start loading the treasures of the Find on the truck that would carry them to the safe confines of the StoreAll in Savannah. Just off West Bay Street and just inside the state of Georgia, Garrett reasoned that the Find would be much safer than in his house. If the stories he had heard were true, the state of South Carolina would likely confiscate the entire Find since many of the items were over 100 years old and would be considered of historic value.

It was shortly after 7 a.m. when the rental truck pulled up in front of the StoreAll office. Garrett had to awaken the manager who wasn't very happy about his early customer. Garrett's decision to rent the largest unit he had available put the manager in a little better mood but it was Garrett's offer to pay six months rent in advance, unload the truck, and lock the security fence so that the manager could go back to bed that wiped the frown from his face.

It took 45 minutes to unload. Garrett and Storey were both exhausted. By 8:15 they were driving through the sensor that would close and lock the gate in the perimeter security fence.

The Find was safely locked and protected in Georgia, away from the grabbing hands of the South Carolina government.

They stopped for breakfast at Waffle House. Both were silent. Just before they were getting ready to leave their breakfast table, Garrett, in a low voice, said, "No one, do you hear me, Storey, no one is to know about what we have just done. Is that completely clear?"

Storey nodded.

"I want to hear you say it, Storey, and I want you to swear on the Bible and on your mother's life that you will tell no one where we put the antiques this morning."

Garrett was being melodramatic in Storey's opinion but he said, "I swear."

"Say the whole thing, Storey. I want to hear you say that you swear on the Bible and on your mother's life that you will never reveal the location."

Story looked at Garrett. It was the look on Garrett's face that frightened Storey. He looked like a man possessed.

"OK Mista. Garrett, I's swear, on da Bible and da life of my mother, I's ain't gona tell noone where we's bin this morning. Is that better?"

"Alright, lets go."

Garrett paid the bill, joined Storey in the truck, and they proceeded back to #13 Church in absolute silence.

Garrett slipped into the bed he had left earlier that morning as soon as he arrived back at home. He didn't intend to sleep only nap, rest, relax. When he awoke, it was mid afternoon.

He looked at the clock.

"Is it really 3:35 p.m.?" Garrett asked out loud, looking straight at the clock.

The clock started to say, *No idiot, it's 7:00 a.m. I'm just screwing with your mind, you know, like everyone else is.* But the clock decided to just look its silent answer. No need to further distress his already questionable sanity.

Garrett yawned, stretched, looked around the room and remembered a strange dream.

He was looking at himself in a painting that hung in the vestibule at the church. He was Christ sitting on a stone that looked like a throne. Angels were all around him. Each would sit in his lap, kiss him on his lips and say, *Don't get up.*

"Why would angels be attracted to me? What could the hidden message be?"

He was trying to remember if he was dressed in fine clothes of if he had the appearance of wealth. The picture wouldn't return to him.

There was a call from Lee. She wanted him to call as soon as he got her message. She wanted to go over the arrangements for the auction. He looked at the phone and finally, Garrett spoke to the empty room, "She is getting into too much of my business. She doesn't have a need to know. That's it."

There were 25 missed calls on his cell phone, which he continued to ignore. Garrett started his Sunday morning in mid-afternoon. He made what was possibly the worst pot of coffee in his entire life. He took one sip and tossed the entire contents in the sink. He decided to make some toast. He burned the bread. He took some bacon out of the refrigerator but replaced it in a moment of clarity. He could easily start a fire in his condition.

He could not seem to process an entire thought or carry an idea to conclusion. Garrett roamed from one room to another, much as his thoughts roamed from one subject to another. Nothing was being accomplished. Afternoon merged into evening and Garrett didn't even notice. He was in a fog of space and time.

At 7:00 p.m. Ashley called. His conversation was without clarity, so she suggested that he return to bed and she would talk to him in the morning.

He did and quickly fell into a deep sleep.

CHAPTER 34

It was Monday morning before Garrett looked at his Sunday newspaper. He had already visited with Mr. Coffee who had provided a warming cup of coffee and the toaster offered a hot bagel. Armed with all the necessities of a good morning, Garrett settled into the comfortable chair that accompanied his office desk.

There, on the front page, in a little block at the top for everyone to see was the announcement — "Charleston Antique Dealer Makes Sensational Find. Details on 1B."

He pulled out the B section and found that he and the Find were the subject of the entire front-page feature articles. Pegge had used six of the pictures they were going to use at the auction. He reread the article and reread it again. After the third time through he smiled.

"Pegge has done an excellent job," he said out loud.

Grandfather almost chimed at the wrong time. It was the first time he could remember Garrett giving someone a compliment. But remember, Grandfather was old and his memory wasn't what it used to be.

"So, this was the reason for all those telephone calls," he thought.

Garrett walked to the front door to get the Monday morning paper. There was a dozen or more business cards stuck in the door. *What could all of this be about?* he wondered. Garrett gathered the cards and the newspaper and returned to his desk. Before sitting, he refreshed his coffee.

There was another article about the Find in Monday's paper. Not very long, but it provided information about the auction and featured a couple of different items that would be sold.

Garrett put the newspaper aside and began to look at the business cards that were on the door. Business cards from people who wouldn't give him the time of day just last week, but who were now wanting to have dinner, lunch, breakfast even just coffee — anything he would agree to. He put them all aside and retrieved his calendar that was covered by all of the mess.

Garrett reconfirmed he was to meet the infamous Doctor Bug. He created and then slipped a hand lettered sign on the front door, "Visitors by appointment only." Then he added his cell phone number even though it had reached the maximum number of voice messages it could hold.

Garrett called the sheriff's office. He asked the clerk that answered what he needed to do to get a concealed carry permit for the Glock revolver he had recently purchased. It was obvious he wasn't the first to ask that question because she quickly responded that he would need to fill out an application, pay the $50 fee and, if his record was clear, he would receive official notification in 90 days.

"90 days?" Not what Garrett wanted to hear. "Isn't there a faster way?" he asked.

She assured him that state law required the waiting period.

"Tell the sheriff to give me a call. I need his help to speed this up."

He then returned to his living quarters to complete his morning toilet and prepare mentally and physically for his meeting. Selecting what he considered appropriate attire to meet one's witch doctor was easy. Garrett's typical uniform was khaki slacks, a blue button-down collar shirt and docksiders.

He looked at his image in the closet door mirror and said to the mirrored image, "If this isn't satisfactory for the good Doctor, that's just too bad."

He shivered at the thought of meeting an actual witch doctor. The image in the closet door mirror had nothing to say to Garrett. He wasn't nearly as talkative as the bathroom mirror.

Garrett was not a believer in the occult. He had, even on occasion, scoffed at the entire idea of VooDoo. But only in front of longtime friends would he admit that he had some questions. After all, in the low country of South Carolina, where stories of witch doctors and their activities abound and where residue of painting the thresholds with indigo was a style on many houses, was it really a good idea to take a chance on tempting the spirits?

In fact, Garrett's knowledge of VooDoo was vicarious at best. He had heard of Doctor Eagle, the best known of low country witch doctors. And he had read about Doctor Buzzard from the movie, *Midnight in the Garden of Good and Evil.* When Storey told him that he was to meet Doctor Bug, it was all Garrett could do to keep from laughing out loud.

That Storey had convinced Garrett to make the hour and a half drive to Saint Helena Island to see Doctor Bug was even a surprise to Garrett. It was only when Storey reminded him that everything of a normal and natural nature he had tried had failed. So, wasn't it worth the time to try his version of the supernatural?

Garrett gave in. Maybe it was desperation, maybe sleep depravation, maybe it was simply a weak moment. Or did he simply acquiesce to the persistence that he knew would follow Storey when he set his mind to something.

Regardless, it was Monday afternoon and Garrett found himself in his delivery truck speeding south on US Highway 17, headed for Beaufort and the nearby island that was home, office and domain of Doctor Bug. There was no way he would show up on Saint Helena Island in his BMW. He figured that the BMW would give the wrong image to the witch doctor, and he didn't want to be overcharged because of the perception of wealth it might give this black man who lived in what was described as a shack.

A careful search of birth records in Beaufort County wouldn't reveal even one person with the surname, *Bug.* But there, for everyone to see, was recorded, in 1940, the birth of Wilber Walters. In the Walters' family Bible, if you were lucky enough to look at the genealogy it contained, you would be able to easily see that Wilber Walters was indeed the seventh son of a seventh son of a seventh son.

Why is this important?

In English folklore and in this country, the seventh son is said to be both lucky and gifted. This tradition may have had its origin in the Bible. Jacob's seventh son was named *Gad,* the

Hebrew word for *luck*. Tradition further stated that double that — the seventh son of a seventh son — was said to have the power of healing. Treble that — seventh son of a seventh son of a seventh son —Who knows?

For the record, young Wilber and his entire family for many generations, were well-known and accepted on Saint Helena Island and in much of the South Carolina lowlands for the powers they possessed. If you had a pain, Doctor Bug could mix up a salve or ointment. If you had a stomach problem, he could mix up a tonic that would settle a worried stomach and make you sleep. He could help get the attention of someone who had wronged one of his patients, place or remove a spell, ward off evil spirits or put together the exact blend of powerful herbs in what the locals called an asafedity bag.

Usually worn on a silk cord around the neck, an asafetida (as it was properly spelled) bag was designed for the purpose of warding off evil spirits — and all but the best of friends, due to the smell.

Newspaper articles documented that Doctor Bug had been responsible for preparing a tonic that kept dozens of Low Country Blacks from being drafted. His tonic caused potential draftees to have fast and irregular heart beat. When it was discovered, Doctor Bug was arrested and a judge said he would have to pay a large fine or go to jail. Doctor asked if he could pay the fine in cash. The judge said yes. He asked for his valise. It was brought to him. He opened it in the courtroom and counted out his fine in crumpled dirty fives and ones.

But by far, the Doctor was called on much more often to help with one's love life. Doctor Bug was well-versed in the arcane practices he needed to perform the functions of his craft. There was a story told of Doctor Bug and a nationally known photo journalist who visited the Doctor while illustrating a story about the *black arts*. In the midst of having his photograph made over and over, Doctor Bug stopped his concocting and looked straight at his visitor.

"You're a professional, aren't you?" Doctor Bug asked.

The journalist replied, "Yes, I am."

"What are you going to charge me for taking my picture?" asked the doctor.

Explaining that no charges would be made because the photos would be used to illustrate a story, the journalist added, "In fact, I will be sending you copies of the best pictures."

However, Doctor Bug's world was simple, a service required a payment. The journalist was asked a simple question.

"How's your love life?"

"No complaints," was the answer after an uncomfortable pause.

"No matter," Doctor Bug said, "I's make you a general potency root. It'll help in a lotsa ways. Now," Doctor Bug added, "Never, never throws dis root away. Such isa lack of respect for da spirits and, well da spirits jus don't like dat and they'll reverse the spell. Lets me illustrates da point, let's say that you got things that normally points up at times. Well ifn you disrespect the spirits those things you got'll always points down."

Doctor Bug turned his head facing the journalist who was ready to laugh with Doctor Bug. As the story goes, the emotion on Doctor Bug's face literally cut in half. His left side was smiling like it was a joke. The right side was as serious as an image could be. There was no laughter.

This is the way the story was told. The unusual object, stored in a plastic bag, was carried by the photographer in his pocket. It required a time-consuming explanation on more than one occasion, particularly by airport security check points, or when visiting a new lady friend's place. That's how the actual story developed among his friends, but it was real enough.

The story was factual. It happened in the presence of the county sheriff who collaborated that it actually happened, but it still drew more than its share of comments and the storyteller more than his share of strange looks.

Finding Doctor Bug's home/office/laboratory was easy enough. There was only one road between Beaufort, South Carolina and Saint Helena Island. Take that road to Frogmore and turn right beside the General Store. Drive past Old Penn School and proceed to the end of the road. There you will find a hand-lettered sign, on a piece of natural wood planking nailed to a tree. It simply read, "Bug's" and there was an arrow.

What looked like the entrance to a path was actually a well-traveled but overgrown road from which you could see the tidal marsh of Saint Helena Island. It was high tide when they arrived, so ocean water filled the marsh as far as the eye could see. In three or so hours, the water would begin its retreat back to the ocean, leaving a variety of dead and decaying organisms and a marsh smell not too dissimilar from the smell of one of Doctor Bug's asafetida bag. To Doctor Bug, it was the smell of home.

Garrett and Storey reached the open area that held Doctor Bug's house and all of his minions. It could easily be the location of a "B" horror movie — the unpainted wooden plank house at the end of a meandering dirt road at the edge of a nameless marsh. But there they were.

A flock of scrawny chickens pecked aimlessly around the yard. Near a 10-year-old pickup truck, a one-legged rooster stood carefully eyeing the visitors. Garrett had to stop his imagination before he considered the story of the red-feathered monopod. At that instant, the rooster elected to crow. The sound caused a shiver to rise from the core of Garrett's being, rise along his spine to the base of his skull causing the hair on the back of his neck to stick straight out and vibrate with the tingle of fear.

The screened door was the only protection for those on the inside from those on the outside. On this day, the 98° temperature was matched by the 98% humidity. It was a typical low country summer day. The building that served as home/office/laboratory for Doctor Bug did not have the benefit of air-conditioning. But as Garrett and Storey ascended the wooden steps, Garrett shivered again, this time from the coolness that emanated from inside the structure.

Garrett stopped a few steps from the door. Could his mind be playing tricks on him or was the air coming out from the house actually cooler? Shouldn't the temperature be nearly the same inside the house as it was outside, especially since all the doors and windows were wide open?

The appearance of a bright-eyed black man at the door stopped Garrett in his mental tracks. Doctor Bug, in appearance, could have been 50 years old, maybe younger. His appearance, his attire and his adept walk provided no hints to clock his actual age — approaching 70 — nor did the amount of mostly black hair that crowned his head. His grinning face revealed a complete set of mostly brown teeth.

Doctor Bug welcomed Garrett and Storey in the *Gullah* dialect, a version of Middle English mostly spoken by the multi-generational dwellers of St. Helena Island, regardless of race. He was dressed in a pair of worn but cleaned and pressed dress pants that were held perfectly in place by a pair of suspenders.

Garrett was intrigued by the repeated image of an eagle head that traversed the suspenders. A starched and ironed plaid, long-sleeved shirt complete with tie, and a light-weight sports jacket completed the ensemble. The amazing thing was that, while nothing matched, when taken as a complete picture, the attire was as appropriate and complementing to Doctor Bug as Garrett's khaki slacks, blue button-down shirt and Docksiders were to him.

Following Doctor Bug into the old house, Garrett led Storey into the sitting room. Although visibly worn, the furnishings were of much the same quality that Garrett would have expected of many of his antique-loving customers. His trained eye scanned the room and found a number of items he would have welcomed at #13 Church Street. It was all he could do to keep from offering to buy a beautiful end table on the spot. Worth over $1,000, he would have gladly paid $500 right then and there.

Better keep this visit on a professional level, Garrett thought. *Doctor Bug's profession that is.*

Garrett and Storey followed Doctor Bug through the house to a large room off the kitchen. Garrett whispered to Storey that the house inside had to be at least 20° cooler than the outside. Storey's expression told Garrett that now wasn't the time to explore the source of Doctor Bug's HVAC.

Doctor Bug settled into an antique leather high back executive desk chair that fitted him like a well-worn leather glove. Garrett and Storey sat in matching leather arm chairs in front of a magnificent claw-footed library table that served as Doctor Bug's desk. Neat piles of papers, boxes of bottles and vials, stacks of magazines and file folders covered all but a 2 by 2-foot square in front of where the doctor sat.

The 20' by 20' room was lined with antique Eastlake buffets that were neatly filled with boxes, tins and wide-mouthed jars obviously containing the raw material for the roots, potions, salves, tonics and assorted treatments that Doctor Bug prepared for his patients. The work areas on each of the buffets contained a variety of equipment. Garrett recognized a number of different scales, some lab bottles and flasks, and a mortar and pestle. There was a number of other apparatus whose purpose Garrett could only guess.

There were three book shelves with glass sliding doors like you would expect to see in an old attorney's office. Two were packed with very old-looking volumes. The third was stacked with catalogues. The room was clean, dust-free and neatly appointed, as were all of the rooms Garrett had entered on his way to the doctor's office.

Garrett's mental inventory of the room was interrupted by the entry of a young black woman who quietly asked Garrett and Storey if they wanted a glass of iced tea. She was carrying a tray with two glasses filled with ice and a cut-glass pitcher containing a royal purple liquid. That created a silent dilemma for Garrett. Did he say, *Yes,* and take a chance on what he might be drinking; or did he say *No* and take the chance of offending a bona fide witch doctor?

Common sense won out and Garrett took the first sip of what he would tell people was the best tasting sweet tea he had ever tasted. He started to calm down, a bit.

"Now, Mista Garrett, wats yo problem?" Doctor Bug took occasional notes on a legal pad as Garrett described his dreams. At first, he was hesitant. But, within minutes, he was openly describing his dreams, in detail, even the resulting erections caused by the pregnant peasant girl.

"Your dreams?" Doctor Bug's dialectic accent seemed to have disappeared. "Do you see things through your eyes in the dreams or do you see as if someone watching?"

Garrett's answer, through his eyes, caused Doctor Bug to suspend all conversation as he moved to one of the book shelves to extract a well-worn volume. Flipping through a few pages, the doctor paused to read a particular passage and placed the open volume on the side of his desk atop a stack of folders and told Garrett to continue.

Doctor Bug's only other question was when Garrett had the dreams? What day? What time?

There was an awkward moment of silence as Garrett finished

the description of his dreams and before Doctor Bug began to speak. The next sound came from the direction of Doctor Bug, but the sound was unworldly. If the guttural sound actually came from Doctor Bug, the expression did not require him to open his mouth. It sounded like a single word question.

"So?"

But the voice bore no resemblance to that of the good doctor.

Doctor Bug promptly stood. Storey quickly sprang to his feet. Garrett followed more slowly.

"Sit yourselves down." It was a gentle command. "I's got a bunch of work to do fore you folks leave."

The instant that Garrett and Storey reseated themselves, the young woman returned with the pitcher as if she had been summoned. She quickly filled Garrett and Storey's glasses, placed a piping hot cup of something at Doctor Bug's place and left quietly.

Doctor Bug moved adeptly about the room looking occasionally at the book he had opened during Garrett's description of his dreams. The assemblage of powders, herbs, twigs, leaves, and other unidentifiable items ended up in the large stone mortar. As the last ingredient was added to the mixture, Doctor Bug stopped still, collected himself, took a deep breath, held it, touched his forehead, his lower left side near his hip joint, the upper right side of his chest, the left side of his chest over his heart, his right hip and finally, his forehead again, forming the symbol of a five-pointed star. Then he folded the fingers of one hand into the palm of the other, as if in prayer or contemplation.

Haunting strains of a single instrument began the very instant he folded his hands. The music sounded like it came from a harpsichord — but not quite. The music continued as Doctor Bug picked up the stone pestle and began chanting in a low mumble as he carefully ground the contents of the mortar into a powder.

The chanting blended so well with the music that the exact words were unintelligible. Garrett intently listened to hear what Doctor Bug was saying, but he couldn't tell if it was English, Gullah, a foreign language or some form of VooDoo gibberish. The music and the incantation stopped simultaneously.

Mixing the amalgamation with some sort of jelly substance,

Doctor Bug carefully sandwiched the concoction between two pieces of a 5-inch-long root that he had split for this purpose.

Another short meditation was followed by a repeat of the five-point star crossing symbolism. Doctor Bug came back to the desk and slipped into his leather chair. He set the *root* in the middle of the clear space and looked intently at Garrett.

After a few minutes of silence, Doctor Bug cleared his throat and began his explanation.

"Mista Garrett, what we got here is a serious spirit. In fact, it may be a complex spirit that has taken control of yo mind."

Doctor Bug again folded his hands fingers to palms and continued looking at or through Garrett's eyes.

"There are some things I needs that I don't got. I will order them s'afternoon and UPS will be bringing them day after tomorrow. So you gots to come back. Do you understand? Complex spirits are unusual. I don't know what you's done or to who, but this is a mighty powerful evil and since all of yo dreams have ended in death, I ain't sure this spirit is from the netherworld or this'en. I will look into it some mo and if I was you, I don't think I would be making no body mad at me.

"You take this 'root'," Doctor Bug offered the object to Garrett, "and be shor you has it with you all the time. It's got some protection in it till I got the stuff I be ordering.

"Now, today's 'root' will be $100 and the table in the front room will be another $100, if you's still wants it."

It was the emotional directness of the statement that took Garrett completely off guard. How did he know that Garrett was interested in the table? Storey didn't know, so he couldn't have told him. The reasoning part of Garrett's brain was running laps around the inside of his skull. There was no way.

"Sure," Garrett hesitated before he finished the sentence. He didn't want to ask how he knew but he certainly wanted to know.

"Yes, I would like to purchase the table, assuming that it is alright with you. I wouldn't want you to part with it if it is a family heirloom."

"No. No family piece. It was given as a part of payment. I'd sooner have the money."

Garrett paid the witch doctor with two crisp $100 bills.

Carrying the table out to the truck, he and Storey wrapped it in the blankets from the cab of the pick-up truck and secured it in the truck bed. Garrett walked over to Doctor Bug and again thanked him for the table.

Garrett extended his hand to shake in a farewell. Doctor Bug acknowledged his thanks but did not meet the hand gesture. He looked Garrett in the eyes again.

"Mista Garrett, this ain't nothing to take lightly. Spirits ain't nothing to play with. Making fun of the *haints* ain't no way to fix the mess you's in. I will see you on Friday?"

The questioning inflection of Doctor Bug's statement required an answer from Garrett. An affirmative answer seemed to satisfy the doctor who turned at the end of his comment and walked quickly back into the house.

Sweat in a few short minutes, had totally drenched his shirt and left wet stripes down Garrett's slacks. He couldn't tell if it was the heat and humidity, or if his body was reacting to this unusual visit with the supernatural. He wanted to ask so many questions but there was no one there to answer.

In the silence, Garrett again noticed the scrawny chickens grazing on the hard sand front yard. Again, his gaze fell on the one-legged rooster maintaining its surveillance. A shiver coursed through his body as if a blast of ice cold air had blown by him.

Shaking himself, Garrett approached the passenger's door of the truck. As he opened it, he noticed that the ocean had beaten a retreat from Doctor Bug's island place. The signature scent of the low country, Eau de Marsh would have been a good name, snuggled right up next to Garrett, Storey, the one-legged rooster, the scrawny chickens, the truck. In fact, it snuggled up to everything within reach like a long-lost lover.

Garrett rode home in silence. Storey, for once, respected Garrett's privacy. So much had happened in such a short time that Garrett needed his space to sort it all out. He didn't know what he believed and what he didn't. Time would certainly tell.

Garrett's mind replayed the events of the past few hours as rode home. Doctor Bug's apparent knowledge of Garrett's thoughts troubled him and he vacillated from amazement to total disbelief. Could he actually know or had Garrett telegraphed the information to a very observant fraud?

Could he actually read Garrett's mind or was he the charlatan that one part of his mind so totally believed?

Regardless, Garrett had a *root*, a second appointment and a table that, when sold, would make the entire trip worth the time.

As Storey maneuvered the pickup truck over the Ashley River Bridge approaching the peninsula that is Charleston, he spoke the only words to leave his lips since the truck and its occupants left the marsh-side home on Saint Helena Islands.

"Please Mista Garrett, please, don't disrespect the spirits. I know you don't believe and maybe you don't care either, but I's seen what the spirits can do. I's seen it." Storey's voice trailed off as he reiterated the request. It sounded more like a plea, "Please don't disrespect the spirits."

Garrett could tell that Storey's request didn't require, nor need an answer. Silence from both followed. As Storey pulled the pickup into the drive space in the back of the building at #13 Church Street, he quickly moved to unpack and remove the table. He didn't wait to be told what to do and he didn't wait for Garrett to help him. Garrett couldn't remember that ever happening.

There was something on Storey's mind and it appeared to have him in a highly agitated state. Storey said good night and quickly retired to his quarters. When Garrett climbed to the second floor and began checking the windows, he noticed candles burning in every room of Storey's carriage house. Garrett didn't know what Storey was doing and he really didn't care.

He knew that he was very tired and sleepy; he knew that the short trip to Saint Helena Island had taken a lot more body energy than he expected, and he knew he would be going to bed very soon.

Windows and doors checked. He looked at his office phone, 40 voice mails. He was pleased. He opened the front door and there he found dozens more business cards left by his *friends* and other well wishers.

What a change that represented. People coming to him. He collected the cards and closed and locked the door.

Back inside, he glanced through the collection of cards. There was one from the Sheriff with a note on the back. The note informed Garrett that state law requires a 90-day waiting period before issuing a carry permit, but he would look into it for his friend.

Garrett climbed the stairs and retired to his sleeping room. He glanced out of the window in his bedroom to see that the candles were still burning in the carriage house. Storey could practice anything he wanted to, Garrett just didn't care. Right now, the only thing he cared about was the bed and how quickly he could go to sleep.

His sleep was fitful, filled with dreams that were complex, intertwined and not remembered by Garrett in the morning. The only thing that he was able to remember was that the one-legged rooster was a main character.

It seemed like only minutes before he was awake again. He reached for the bedside lamp and something in his mind clicked. He jumped out of bed and quickly retrieved a plastic pouch from his top dresser drawer. Slipping his root under his pillow, he resumed his re-entry into the no-dream sleep zone.

VooDoo or no VooDoo, with the vividness for his latest dreams, he was taking no chances. He would sleep with Doctor Bug's root under his pillow and he would carry it in his pocket. It was the crowing of the one-legged rooster, in his last dream of the night, that woke Garrett from his sleep. The illusionary cock's wake-up call arrived only moments before the annoying *buzzzzz* of his bedside clock radio.

The morning routine went smoothly. The Garrett in the mirror had nothing to say. His shower was refreshing. Descending the stairs to the second floor, he was welcomed by the aroma of freshly perked coffee from the preset coffee maker. Mr. Coffee was doing his best to start off Garrett's morning in the right way.

The weather was warm and clear. Customers started knocking on the door early and kept him busy through lunch time. Storey had cleaned and oiled the end table from Doctor Bug's house and brought it upstairs. Garrett placed a price of $1,100 on the table and it was sold within 45 minutes of its display. He silently chided himself for under-pricing the table, but that thought was quickly followed by the warming feeling that he had made $1,000 on a $100 investment.

That was the first time that Doctor Bug's and his visit had worked its way into his thoughts since he had put the root, covered in plastic wrap, into his pocket early that morning.

He decided he would spend his lunch hour at the Old Market. The lower half of the market's stalls was rented to local sellers of curios. The city made every effort to keep this area from looking like a flea market, and it did have a higher quality of merchandise, but he had occasionally found items in the area that interested him.

He was on his trip through these stalls when he noticed what looked like a Hummel figure on one of the small tables in an open area of the market. He didn't want to seem too anxious. If it was a signed Hummel, it could be worth three or four hundred dollars at the shop, much more if it was rare. He picked up four or five items as he attempted to appear casual and finally picked up the porcelain child figure. A quick glance at the base confirmed his initial evaluation. He held it and picked up a valueless vase that was sitting on the table.

"What is your very best price on these items?" Again it was his best, practiced manner to give the impression of only casual interest.

"Thirty dolla for the two," was the reply from the older black woman sitting behind the table. He had not looked at her prior to this interchange.

"Thirty is your very best price now?" Garrett using his utmost to control the child-like glee he was experiencing at finding such a bargain.

"Why, yes'sa Mistuh Garrett, I couldn't let 'um go fuh a penny less than thirty dolla." Garrett looked again at the woman. He didn't recognize her, although she did look slightly familiar.

Maybe she has been in the shop? No.

"Ok," Garrett said. "Thirty it is. Do you have change for a fifty?" Garrett knew he had thirty dollars in his change pocket but he continued his game.

"Yes'sa. I sho do. By the way, was you able to sell that table?"

Garrett froze. In that instant, he recognized the older woman that was in the kitchen of Doctor Bug's house. He didn't recall ever seeing her even look in his direction, but he knew that he had seen her in the kitchen.

Her question had caught Garrett totally off guard.

"Yes, I did."

"Well, we hope you make as much off this lil Hummel," her smile let Garrett know that she, too, knew what he was buying as she and the witch doctor had known what the table was worth. A shiver coursed through Garrett's body. A chill that wasn't pleasurable.

Garrett took his change, crammed the crumpled bills into his pocket, thanked the woman and clutched his treasure tightly in his hand as he moved away from the table, not looking back and not looking at any more tables.

He wandered aimlessly through the streets around the Battery, occasionally stopping to look at the water, Ft Sumter, Ft Johnson, a ship, but seeing nothing. The events of the morning had him genuinely distressed. The visit to Doctor Bug's was not what he expected. There were many unexplainable things that happened there. Then the young woman in the coffee shop and now this. Garrett struggled to get these things sorted out. He had to make some semblance or order of the things that were increasingly getting out of order.

Garrett arrived at #13 Church Street at 2:00, exactly. The church bells rang out two loud gongs. That afternoon he had one customer. She was a very prim and proper lady smelling of lavender. Wearing white dress gloves, she carried her purse in a very proper manner. She casually looked at everything on the main floor. When Garrett asked if she had found what she was looking for. She asked about only one thing.

"Do you have any Hummels?"

Garrett felt the same shiver as at the market earlier that morning. She paid $6,000 for the figure without any haggling. He had placed a high price with the hope that someone wouldn't know the real value and wanted to haggle. It was not that rare.

She thanked him graciously and departed. The scent of lavender hung in the air for the rest of the day, a reminder of the strange events of the day. The sale of the Hummel and the table provided Garrett with significant profit and was no coincidence.

Both included Doctor Bug. *Could this VooDoo stuff actually be working?* A genuine smile crept across his face.

The Garrett in the bathroom mirror wouldn't recognize him.

CHAPTER 35

Garrett opened his calendar/sales tracking chart and realized the he had an appointment at the end of the day with the shrink. He also noted that Ashley was out of town. He hadn't thought about contacting her, and she was obviously busy or she would have called.

He pondered the idea of telling the shrink about Doctor Bug. After considering the pros and cons of full disclosure, he decided that he would, for the moment, keep these divergent forms of medical assistance operating independently.

There were calls; they were unanswered. There were knocks on his front door; they were ignored. There were more cards hanging on the door; also ignored. The afternoon went happily off to play hide-n-seek with the morning. Garrett double-locked the front door, set the alarm and exited through the back.

He had just enough time to walk over to Dr. Williams' office before his appointment. Remnants of the perfect day were everywhere he looked. The warm sunlight had brought the most out in the remaining blooming flowers and the muted color in the early evening pallet. The canvas of grey and green, ocher and brown that were the anchor hues of this late fall day.

Garrett was noticing evidence of approaching winter. Although the brown leaves heralded the end of fall, the bright pastels and the strong primary colors of the remnants of spring and summer flowers fought hard to keep their place in this masterwork. It was the best of what you could call God's day.

Exactly on the minute, Garrett opened the front door to Dr. Williams' office. He filled out the card and placed it in the tray provided by the shrink. Having to do that always pissed him off.

He knows who I am. He knows that I have an appointment this afternoon. This is another one of those shrink tricks to maintain control. Another way to get inside your head — using the lunacy of filling out this small card to maintain the upper hand. He may be hiding his little tricks from some of his crazy patients, but I had figured it out during my first visit.

His butt hadn't hit the seat of the waiting room chair when the door at the other side of the room silently opened and Dr. Williams appeared in the door way. Garrett stood and closed the distance between him and the shrink. It was Dr. Williams who spoke first.

"Edward, you missed your appointment on Monday and I didn't get a call. You know I will have to charge you for that appointment."

It was like Dr. Williams was standing in the doorway and wouldn't allow Garrett into his office until Garrett agreed to the billing.

"Sure, whatever."

Garrett was nonchalant in his reply but he said the right words and the doctor preceded him into the office. An hour later, exactly an hour later, the Shrink closed his notebook, stood up and said, "Thank you, Edward. I will see you next week."

With the abrupt closure, Garrett gathered up all of his mental dirty laundry and headed for the door out. As he walked through the empty waiting room he thought it strange that he never saw any other patients waiting to sit and talk.

It was a good appointment in Garrett's view, even with his concerns. He had talked about how good business had been. He talked about the priest and the pirates dream. And, like a kid with a new toy that he can't keep quiet about it, he talked about his visit to Doctor Bug. It was the first time Dr. Alex Williams had interrupted Garrett during a session.

"Edward, I suggest that you be very careful in how far you take this witch doctor stuff. I have no personal experience, but a couple of my patients have had. Real or imagined, there can be a lot of power exercised by some of these witch doctors. Please be very careful."

Those were the words he used. With that, Dr. Williams closed the session. He thanked Garrett for being prompt and reminded

Garrett of his concerns about the witch doctors of the low country. As was the general practice, Garrett left Dr. Williams office with many more questions than when he had entered.

He stood on the corner of the doctor's alley and Church Street. He rewound his mind's video of the day. He was basking in the warmth of the memory of the profit he had made on the Hummel and table sold earlier in the week when he heard the crowing of a rooster.

It sent a shiver that rippled across his skin and brought back the memory of his visit to Doctor Bug and the strange happenings on St. Helena's Island. But especially the memory of the one-legged rooster. That image quickly faded into the last warning of Dr. Williams. His visual memories left him shaking far more than the chilly weather called for. The chill in the air and the fact that he hadn't thought to wear a jacket caused him to quicken his steps.

What was that? It sounds like footfalls on the cobble stone street.

Garrett stopped. *Silence.* Starting toward #13 Church again, he was certain he heard someone following him. It could have been an echo of his own steps but he was certain someone was following him. He stopped again and looked around. North. South. He was the lone pedestrian on the street that evening. It was only 7:00 but it was already quite dark.

There was no moon so the only illumination of Church Street was the old-timey street lamps that were made to look like gas lights which provided a great deal of ambiance but not much illumination. It was the ideal setting for Garrett to revisit his week so far. The sky was crystal clear. Any heat that had built up during the day had long since dissipated.

There was a building fear from his experience visiting with Doctor Bug and the uncertainly of the next visit on Friday. His thoughts of Doctor Bug served to magnify the chill of the night air.

What had Storey gotten him into? What had he gotten himself into? Why had he even listened to Storey in the first place? And then, there was the warning from Dr. Williams. What did he know?

Garrett's walk back to #13 Church Street was peppered with questions and self-doubt and the fear that he was being followed.

Grandfather was striking the half hour as Garrett turned the lock on the front door and entered his home/office. The sound resonated through the empty house, bouncing from one antique to another. Garrett quickly crossed the room to the security pad to key in the numbers that would keep the police from making another false alarm visit. He picked up the cell phone that he had left on his desk. He was surprised that he had completely forgotten he didn't have it with him at the shrink's office. He saw there were 20 messages waiting to be dealt with.

"Not now," he said out loud as if the electronic object could understand.

On to the kitchen for his evening meal. He made a pot of coffee and then moved to the refrigerator to see what choices he had to consider for dinner. At the open refrigerator, he perused the array of left-overs that smiled at him through their clear containers. A couple were frowning, the result of the extended time they had occupied their place on the shelves. A few were green — with envy, possibly — but green none-the-less.

Honeyed ham, sliced smoked turkey and Genoa Salami were selected. Rye bred festooned with mayonnaise, mustard, tomato, pickles and lettuce. The tastes of the unusual meat selection blended, contrasted, melded, combined, separated, mixed, mingled, infused, amalgamated and segregated. It was a masterful performance at the theater of the mouth. Garrett chewed his sandwich in a manner not fit for public exhibition.

Grandfather called it *obscene*. He added, *no one should have such pleasure in the simple act of eating.* But, Grandfather was old, and a clock to boot.

Garrett looked at the front door of #13 Church. It was the feeling that someone was watching him that jarred his attention from his dinner time culinary adventure. It was accompanied by a chill that sent shivers throughout his body and a chill in his bones as well. He looked all around him. No one. Only the sound created by Grandfather counting off the seconds.

He stood and looked around.

Nothing.

He returned to his desk. He opened the top draw and withdrew a 9mm Glock17, *the most widely used law enforcement pistol worldwide*, the gun salesman had told Garrett.

Yes, it was loaded, all 17 rounds, and ready for action.

Garrett, with his confidence bolstered by his powerful friend and with the endorsements of those law enforcement officers, opened the door and stepped out on the front porch. He was ready for any poacher or Peeping Tom. The street lights cast ominous shadows on the street in front of #13 Church Street but there was no one in Garrett's view. He looked in every direction, his pistol at the ready.

No one was there. No one.

Could his mind be playing tricks on him? With that, he quickly closed the door, secured the lock and returned to his desk and the culinary extravaganza awaiting him. But every so often he glanced at the door. The Glock sat right there on the desk, ready if called upon.

As he returned to eating, Garrett's attention was refocused as the first message appeared on his phone. It was from Ashley Cooper Barrineau. She was indeed out of town and not expected back for a couple of days. It wasn't until Garrett sighed, either in relief or aggravation, that he realized how much the relationship between Lee and him had been strained as of late. He continued to resent her involvement in the impending announcement and the auction of the Find.

The second message was from Brother Andrew at Mepkin Abbey. The Brother that Garrett had met with previously would appreciate another face-to-face tomorrow at 3 pm.

"Please be prompt," was Brother Andrew's last request.

"What?" was the only word that would come from his mouth, along with a few crumbs of bread and meat.

He quickly finished off the last bite of sandwich and started a rant that lasted for some time. It started off with, "Just who the hell does he think he is?" and ended with "Screw him!"

It seemed like none of the words that Garrett was able to string together would have benefited from punctuation, nor would they have added to the meaning of the rant. Garrett was, to say the least, exceedingly unhappy with the manner in which he was being treated by this anonymous visitor, purported to be an emissary of the Pope.

The third call was a personal call from the Sheriff. He assured Garrett, as he had in the note he had left on his card, that it was a

90-day process to clear someone to receive a concealed carry permit. But because the request came from Mr. Garrett, he would personally call the head of the SC Law Enforcement Division, the state agency in South Carolina that issued carry permits, and that he would put all the pressure he could to speed that process.

"Screw them and all of their Red Tape," Garrett said aloud. "I own the gun and I'll carry it wherever and whenever I feel like I need protection. That's my Second Amendment right. And I deserve the special attention."

With that, Garrett took a sleeping pill and went to bed. He turned off the bedside light. He quickly fell asleep, but, throughout his dreams, he was being taken advantage of.

CHAPTER 36

Although he couldn't remember setting the alarm, the raspy buzzer of his bedside clock radio successfully penetrated the cobwebs of his medicated sleep and managed to pry open his eyes to start the new day. The soporific drug provided the sleep he so desperately needed, but not the desired rest. It was all Garrett could do to stand and haltingly walk the short distance from the bed to the bathroom.

With a click, the room was awash in light and Garrett's good friend and counselor appeared in *mirror-world*. Garrett decided not to have a protracted discussion with his reverse counterpart, and was able to complete his toilet and get reasonably dressed with no interruptions. By the time he got to the kitchen, the coffee was brewed and hot.

He took a minute to open the front door to see if the morning paper was on time. There it was, right there on the door mat — not in the shrubbery, not in the front yard, not on the roof. All were locations where he had found the latest news in days past.

As he stood looking at the front page of the newspaper, he glanced up and down the street, remembering last evenings feelings of being watched. Again, the same chill permeated his body. He shook it off. Only his mind playing with him.

With one grasp, he collected everything he needed to know about happenings in Charleston, South Carolina. He headed back to the familiarity of his kitchen and the comfort of his cup of coffee.

Good coffee is such a magical drug. First, there is the anticipatory effect. Just thinking about a hot cup of coffee fires off neurons in the brain that crank up the memories of those wonderful feelings of the special cups of coffee in the past, creating a slightly euphoric state.

Garrett started thinking about coffee even before he started down the stairs to the kitchen. Then there's the aroma. Wafting up the stairs was a special combination of scents that titillate the olfactory receptors, situated like row after row of little *smell* soldiers stationed throughout the lining of the nose. These sensitive *smell* soldiers are directly connected to the body's limbic system. The limbic system is a group of sub cortical glands (the hypothalamus, the hippocampus and the amygdale) the little glands control emotions.

The brain's usual reaction when detecting a stimulus is to first process the information delivered to the senses by cortical identification which will trigger an emotional response. But the devious sense of smell has a unique way of doing it. Smell sensations are relayed to the cerebral cortex only after the deepest parts of the brain, those sub-cortical glands, have been stimulated. In other words, incoming aromas first trigger an emotional response, which is then followed by cognitive recognition.

This was especially true for Garrett this morning. Deep in the recesses of that complex body part that rests between Garrett's ears, is a gland that releases minute amounts of oxytocin, creating a desire. It could be said that coffee is a sexual stimulate.

This morning, Garrett *wanted* that cup of coffee, and his brain was telling him that he *needed* that cup of coffee as well. Then there's that reassuring warmth of the cup cradled in his hands. The comforting feeling that further accentuates the bonding affect that oxytocin naturally creates. Sitting at the kitchen table, Garrett's body was alive with sensations he couldn't have understood even if he wanted to. Sensations not unlike sexual gratification.

That first sip. Always a new experience, each and every time.

Nothing is like that first sip of coffee each morning. Then the rush begins. Xanthine Alkaloid, an effective psychoactive stimulant found in the coffee, is instantly released as soon as coffee reaches the stomach. Xanthine Alkaloid affects virtually every bodily function. It increases heart rate, stimulates the central nervous system and metabolic rate, causes the eyes to dilate, induces anxiety, causes ringing of the ears, is responsible for rapid breathing and hypoglycemia and is highly addictive. More commonly called caffeine, Xanthine Alkaloid requires no FDA packaging notification, isn't found on any governmental list of illegal substances, does not require a surreptitious visit to the XA drug dealer in a back alley and is available in large supply at almost every corner coffee shop.

Garrett was no stranger to the affects of Xanthine Alkaloid and he could easily be classified as a XA addict.

Think of it — XAA chapters meeting in mornings, all over the world. Just discussing how much they miss their morning coffee.

"I had a six-cup a day habit", "Mine was eight", "I was seriously considering mainlining, but I liked the taste too much."

Not this morning, not for Garrett. He had his cup of coffee and an almost-full pot in reserve and he had his newspaper. So, on this particular Wednesday morning, everything was in its proper place.

Garrett placed the CALL FOR AN APPOINTMENT sign on the door of #13 Church Street at the proper time. His XA habit was satisfied, at least for the moment. He was in the middle of his customary walk through the store. He used this time to make certain that everything was in the most advantageous position.

The front door bell jingled.

Customers already? Why no call? he thought to himself.

It turned out not to be a customer, but James John there to discuss the presentation for the auction. Standing just inside the front door, he reported that everything concerning the presentation of the Find was on schedule and that he was very happy with the results. He was happy with the visuals. The projection equipment was ordered and would be on site five days prior to the big event for rehearsals and adjustments.

Standing in the foyer, James John was reading from a check list that he and Lee had created. Garrett interrupted him.

"John, wait a minute. I don't know what to say about my manners. Come in and let's continue this report over some coffee. It's fresh brewed."

John James didn't expect manners or anything else from Garrett. He was a paid supplier and he had long since had no expectations from his clients, especially Edward Garrett.

"Thank you," John replied. "Certainly, if you are sure it wouldn't be too much trouble."

Garrett assured him it would be no trouble and it would be warmer for both of them. Coffee in hand, sitting at Garrett's desk, John continued his list. The internet supplier had arranged for the largest number of connections ever in South Carolina. A bank of 300 servers had been leased to assure speedy response to bids, and they were being installed in a meeting room in the Mills House.

Fiber optic lines connecting the Mills House and the Hibernian Hall were already installed and verified. Ebay had been contacted and was online already; all they needed was a go. Catering provided by the Mills House was on schedule, even though that was not John's responsibility, as was a room-block reserved for Garrett to handle any rooms he required for his personal use.

The Presidential Suite was set for Lee and him. The Mills House had guaranteed that one entire level of the parking garage would be cleared two days prior to the event. There would also be sufficient electrical capacity ordered to specifically accommodate the restaurant's catering needs so they could prepare their menus and keep everything hot as Garrett had required.

"All is at readiness, Mr. Garrett," John assured him.

"Thank you, John," Garrett offered his hand, "I had my doubts, but you seem to have a good handle on everything and I appreciate that. Report your progress only to me. I don't think I need to impress the importance of secrecy in this situation. It is worth money to me and to you."

The ringing door bell interrupted the conversation. Garrett excused himself and left the kitchen for the front door. It was two ladies that looked to be in their 40's and a mid 20's young woman. As Garrett expected it was a mother, an aunt and a bride to be — looking. Garrett welcomed them, suggested where they should start their look.

He was interrupted by the bell, again, this time by a young couple entered asking about oak kitchen furniture. He sent them to the lower level and returned to finish his talk with John.

"Customers," Garrett said, almost with disdain. "But that's

what pays the bills." *For now*, he added in his thoughts.

John gathered his papers, finished the last swallow of the coffee and excused himself. As the door closed behind John, Garrett checked on the young couple who were down stairs sitting in the various kitchen chairs checking on the comfort. He then returned to the main level and caught up with the wedding party. Happily, they were up to their ear lobes in silver.

It took the young couple two hours to decide on a kitchen table and four chairs. But it was an $1,100 sale. The bride-to-be was going all out. The selected silver pieces were for the rehearsal dinner, showers and various pre-wedding functions and couldn't be used at more than one function, for appearance sake.

We wouldn't want the family to look cheap, would we?

It was always amazing to Garrett how much money would be spent on these nuptial socializing events. The final sale was $6,400. It was barely lunch time and Garrett had already sold over $7,500.

Garrett decided that he deserved a celebratory lunch. Today he would be lunching at Henry's Restaurant. After all, he loved their She Crab Soup and that was one of the places that you could always find a selection of Charleston's *Blue Blood*s everyday at lunchtime.

He decided to walk the six blocks that separated Henry's from #13 Church. Garrett had missed many of his normal morning exercise routines since the Find, so this would do him good. He added his cell number to the OUT TO LUNCH sign, just in case.

Garrett stopped on the welcome mat on the first step at #13 Church. He looked North and South. He saw cars parked next to the fire plug garrison. He stretched and yawned. The midday sun found his shoulders. The sun had heard about Garrett's stress. Word travels fast on the street. The sun had decided it was going to give Garrett's shoulders some relief. So with every movement, every turn, every stretch, Garrett felt the warmth of the sun's rays.

The warmth of the sun's massage made Garrett feel better. He stretched again. Garrett yawned again. And continued releasing the stress and strain that had built up in his body. He was actually beginning to de-stress as he walked to Henry's and was beginning to feel alive. His view of the gardens along his walk revealed the effort on the part of autumn to take over Charleston. But the stronghold the evergreens had assured that the dominant color would be green.

Had the Confederate army had the same resolve as the towering evergreens, the outcome of the battle of Charleston would likely have been different.

Garrett turned north on Church and headed for Henry's, now only a few blocks away. Henry's had been a fixture in Charleston since the early 1920's. Located on Market Street facing the Old Slave Market, it was safe to say, if this building could talk, books could be written, reputations made and reputations destroyed.

The non-descript, white, cinder-block building provided no suggestion of the quality of the food served inside. There was an out-of-place old wooden cutout crab sign above the nameplate commemorating the fact the Charleston's She Crab Soup was invented here. At least 15 other restaurants claimed the same accolade, but when you walked in this place you could easily agree with the sign.

Outside, the pealing paint, faded colors and general unkempt exterior made you question if you were even going to enter the establishment. In fact, the pealing paint on the crab gave it a hairy appearance from a distance. Inside, however, you knew you were in a place with a lot of great history. There were signed pictures everywhere. Hollywood stars, baseball stars, football stars, political stars, musical stars and lots of people who thought they were stars.

Framed newspaper articles chronicled the history of Henry's, the good and the bad. There was the Mayor's wall — signed pictures of every Charleston Mayor since Henry's opened. The Governor's wall was much the same. Newspaper reviews of the great food hung beside the accounts of prohibition and the raids on Henry's for selling illegal liquor.

There were lots of pictures, but the one that the original Henry honored with the place behind the main desk was Congressman L. Mendel Rivers. He would often say that Rivers was the last and maybe only great South Carolina statesman. The manager interrupted Garrett's musings and even called him by name.

"Greetings Mr. Garrett. Will you be dining with us this noon?"

Garrett wanted to say, "No, I'm here to buy a car," but he understood the question and he understood the game. His actual answer was that he would be a party of one.

"I saw the article in the paper, Mr. Garrett. That must have been quite a find."

Garrett smiled. With that he was passed off to the head waiter and was well received by him as well. He also commented on the newspaper article. Garrett was escorted to a corner booth. The corner booths were reserved for recognized important people.

It was late in the lunch hour so there weren't many people left in the restaurant, but being seated in a corner booth was another boost to Garrett's ego. He would be sitting in a place of honor.

Two people who were also dining stopped at the table and commented on the auction. One said he looked forward to attending.

Lunch was unrememberable. When finished, he quickly paid his check. The game of see and be seen hadn't produced the excitement he had expected. He left the restaurant and decided he would walk through the market.

Garrett had barely turned into the market when to saw the woman from Doctor Bug's. The market was a wide-open shed-like structure with vendor areas mostly delineated by the tables that were used to display the vendor's wares. Garrett moved from vendor area to vendor area; any time he looked in her direction, she was watching him. It was so disconcerting that Garrett left the market far sooner than he had planned.

On the way back to #13 Church he couldn't help looking behind him to see if she were following him. When Garrett opened the gate to #13 Church he noticed the strip of Spanish Moss that was on the bottom step. He looked around to see if he could tell from where the moss had blown. Finding no answer, he kicked it off the step.

Back inside, Garrett sat at his desk. It was then that he remembered his appointment at Mepkin Abbey and the admonition that he was to be prompt. Again, it aggravated him.

Where did the mysterious monk get off trying to tell him what to do? Garrett closed the door and aimed the BMW toward Monks Corner and the campus of Mepkin Abbey.

He was preparing for this next meeting with The Brother. Even with the windows closed and the heater on, Garrett couldn't shake the chill he felt deep in the core of his body when he remembered the last meting with the faceless monk. He arrived at Mepkin 15 minutes early.

Self-talk throughout the short trip served only to further the aggravation he felt as he sat outside the Gift Shop/Visitor's Center. Garrett had thought of getting coffee in Summerville when he realized he would arrive at Mepkin early, but he didn't. As usual in his life, rationality won out. So he arrived 15 minutes early with no coffee, adding slightly to his aggravation level.

He parked where the sign with the faceless monk said to park. He locked the car out of habit and went inside. There was one clerk, probably a volunteer, inside the center. She was the only person other than Garrett in the place.

He announced his appearance and the purpose of his visit. A short telephone conversation followed and she reported that Brother Andrew would be there to escort him very soon. Garrett roamed around the gift shop area. He was looking but not seeing anything. He was totally lost in that land of the mind called *thought.*

Brother Andrew appeared at the door and called to Garrett. He was different. He actually looked different. His face was different — drawn, stressed, almost haggard. And his demeanor was abrupt. As they walked to the refectory, Garrett thought he might not even recognize him if he passed Brother Andrew on the street. He really looked that different.

They retraced their steps to the refectory, only this time, without conversation. They arrived at the room of Garrett's previous visit. The mysterious Brother was standing in the darkest corner of the room. Garrett waited to be recognized before speaking.

He wasn't.

The Brother began talking, "I have been asked to express to you, quite forcefully, that The Church may be interested in that unusual box you have. We believe it may be our property, but we will not know until I have the opportunity to examine it. I need for you to bring the box to me here and soon."

Garrett felt his aggravation turning into resentment. Now the faceless monk had become rude. This representative of The Catholic Church presumed to give him orders?

Unacceptable.

The words, *When hell freezes over,* stuck in his throat.

Who the hell does he think he is?

Garrett took a moment to compose himself and then he spoke with measured meter.

"My dear sir. I assume you do represent The Catholic Church, as you say you do, since we are meeting here, but I have no proof of that. Also, I believe I was quite clear at out last meeting. My position hasn't changed and isn't likely to change no matter how many times you summon me here." Garrett's intent was to leave the impression that he was working quite hard to remain in control of his anger.

"It is my job to convince you otherwise."

"Not much chance of that. And what makes you think it is property of the Church?"

"I think it is, and you are being difficult, Mr. Garrett. Is it your plan to make big money at that little auction you are having? Do you really think you can intimidate The Church?"

"I will be exceedingly clear, my mysterious friend, about my plan, as you call it and your ownership of the box. If your job here is as you say, then you can notify your superiors that you have failed. And failed quite miserably. This is our final discussion concerning the box. Do you understand me clearly?"

Garrett's voice was slowly gaining volume and intensity.

"Our *final* discussion." As punctuation, Garrett turned and left the room and the building. It took Brother Andrew half the distance to the Gift Shop to catch up with Garrett.

"I don't think that was wise, Mr. Garrett. The Brother was rude, but he is used to getting his way. He is Opus Dei, you know."

Garrett looked at Brother Andrew who, at that moment, was trying to reclaim the words he had just spoken. There was a look of pure terror on Brother Andrew's face. It was obvious that he had over-stepped his bounds, that he had said something he shouldn't have. Garrett didn't know what *Opus Dei* was, but it was certain that Brother Andrew did, and feared the repercussions he expected for revealing the identity of the monk from the Vatican. Brother Andrew said nothing else on the walk escorting Garrett out of the restricted area.

Garrett got into his car and maneuvered it to the exit of the Mepkin campus. As he looked in the rearview mirror he saw Brother Andrew with his hands in a praying position. Garrett gave the finger to the faceless monk sign that admonished him to drive safely as he exited.

On the ride back to Charleston, Garrett realized that something wasn't as it seemed. There had to be more to that little box that met the eye. He chose to take the long way home.

The drive through Summerville was always relaxing. The trees and their cover of Spanish moss made a living tunnel for Garrett to drive through. The sun was retreating by the time Garrett reached Middleton Place and Magnolia Plantation. When he reached the old Ashley River Bridge, he was having a hard time keeping his eyes open.

Traffic was still congested as he reached Meeting Street, but he was only a dozen blocks from #13 Church Street. He rolled down the driver's side window to allow the chilled air to keep him awake until he reached the house.

Garrett realized he was totally exhausted. All of the excitement of the Find, the aggravation of the visitor from the Vatican, the details of the presentation and running the business. He parked the BMW, entered through the back door and headed up the stairs to his residence.

As he lay down for the night, his thoughts returned to his idea that there was more about the little box than he had initially realized.

Solving that problem would be a project for Thursday.

CHAPTER 37

Thursday morning started with the raspy buzz of the clock radio. Garrett reached over and flipped the switch that changes the noise to music — a much more pleasant way to start the day.

He had released most of the aggravation that had built up on Wednesday. Today was a new day, and today he would find out what attraction the little box had for the Vatican and for the rude monk at Mepkin.

He was up and finished with his morning routine in record time. With his morning coffee in hand, he settled at his desk with the little box.

Step one, visual inspection. It looked like wood but had the feel of stone. Other than the carving on the top, it was a simple box. *Stone that looked like wood could be petrified wood,* he thought. But that didn't explain the feeling of energy Garrett got when he felt the box. But other than the feel and the carved letters, there was no visual clue to suggest the importance of the box.

At that moment, the bell rang announcing a potential customer was standing outside. Possibly a customer who couldn't read the sign that said, VISTORS BY APPOINTMENT ONLY. That presented a quandary for Garrett — continue with the box or open the door for the customer. He covered the box and made his way to the front door. Old habits won out.

The customer at the front door asked Garrett if he had a particular piece that he collected, which Garrett would never have placed in his store. So, with Garrett's negative answer, the customer retreated to Church Street. He chided himself for even answering the door.

The sign clearly said, "Visitors by Appointment ONLY," he mumbled under his breath.

Garrett returned to his desk. With his visual inspection complete, he located his ruler and began to take measurements of the box. The exterior measurements were 12 inches wide, by 8 inches deep, by 8 inches high. Nothing out of the ordinary. The top was a sung fit, but did lift off the rest of the box. Again, nothing out of the ordinary. There was nothing that suggested its purpose.

Had it not been for the gold coins it contained when Garrett uncovered the Find, there was no reason why it should be in the trove at all. The top — 12" X 8" X 1". Again, nothing unusual. The inside measurements — 10" X 6" X 4".

Nothing unusual, except, wait a minute, Garrett reasoned. If the top was 1" thick and if the bottom was 1" thick, then the inside measurements should be 10" X 6" X 6." Definitely a clue. There could be a false bottom. Could something important be contained in a space between the bottom of the inside of the box and the bottom of the box?

Garrett collected the tools he thought he would need to find an answer. Armed with a couple of magnifying glasses, a razor blade, a utility knife, and a sharp-pointed probe, he began the further investigation. For the next three hours, he searched, probed, scraped, felt, magnified, looked and felt some more. If there was a secret way to open the box, it was as big a secret when Garrett finished as it was when he started.

It was mid-afternoon. The little box sat in the middle of Garrett's desk. If it had a face, it would be smiling. Like a flash of light, Garrett had a brain storm. Well, not so much a storm, more like a fall rain shower with a little lightning, and one or two claps of thunder.

X-ray the box. Maybe if there is anything hidden in the box, maybe it will show up in an X-ray.

So, Garrett collected the little box, put it in a shoulder bag, slipped the Glock in his belt under his shirt and headed for his family doctor's office. He was amazed at the surge of confidence he had from the feel of the *cold steel* as it touched his skin. The weight was reassuring, and just carrying it gave him a boost of adrenaline. He felt more like a man.

It was near closing time and Garrett knew the nurse had no sense of humor. He explained he wanted an X-ray of the box because he was shipping it to a dealer in Holland, and the Dutch dealer didn't want to have any problems with their customs people, so he wanted an X-ray included with the International Documentations.

Amazingly enough the nurse accepted Garrett's story without even a raised eyebrow. She took the X-rays but said it would be Friday afternoon before she would have them ready for him. That didn't make Garrett very happy but what alternative did he have? His appointment with Doctor Bug was Friday morning so Friday afternoon suited his schedule.

Garrett packed the little box in the shoulder bag and returned to #13 Church Street. He parked the BMW in the back yard, entered the backdoor. He secured the box in a lockable draw in his desk and went to open the front door. There he found, attached to the inside of the screen door, a small note.

"We need to talk about the box. I will return at 4:00 this afternoon. Please allow me an opportunity to explain."

It was written on Mepkin note paper. Garrett was surprised by the conciliatory nature of the note.

"Please allow me an opportunity to explain."

He knew it had to be from the rude monk from the Vatican. Garrett saw that Grandfather was saying that it was 3:45 but Grandfather was 12 minutes fast.

With a fresh cup of Mr. Coffee's finest in hand, Garrett shifted the guest chair so that the light would fully illuminate the mysterious Brother's face. He then settled in his desk chair — two could play head games. He smiled as he sipped his coffee and considered what he would say and what the Brother might say.

As 4:00 approached, Garrett decided he would let the Brother direct the discussion. Precisely at 4:00 the mysterious monk appeared at the front door of #13 Church. Garrett opened the door, invited him in and asked if he would like some fresh coffee.

The Brother entered, accepted the coffee and asked where he should sit. Garrett showed the Brother to the chair with the most visibility. The Brother moved the chair over a couple of feet, which defeated Garrett's purpose.

Today's score Monk — 1, Garrett — 0.

Garrett asked the Brother how he wanted his coffee.

"Black."

Garrett delivered the coffee and sat in his chair to wait for the beginning of the conversation. There was a moment of silence. Garrett moved his hand to touch the gun still in his belt. Having the pistol in his belt seemed to level the playing field with the monk.

Without warning, the mysterious monk pushed back the cowl of his robe revealing his face in a manner that made it appear that he had evaluated the situation and decided he needed to at least appear to be open.

Garrett almost pulled the gun when the monk made his move. But he caught himself before the Glock was in plain view. The brother appeared as a clean-shaven, 30-something with closely cropped sandy colored hair. He bore no ethnic characteristics. The only unusual physical characteristic was that the Brother had one brown eye and one blue eye.

"Mr. Garrett. First of all, I owe you an apology. Where I live, representatives of The Church are rarely questioned. I should have been more courteous. There is some indication, however slight, that the little box you have may belong to The Church. The only way we will know is to examine it. That is why we are interested. Is it possible that I can see and examine the box?"

Garrett was a little taken aback by the apologetic attitude of the monk. Brother Andrew had accidentally dropped the little tidbit that the monk was Opus Dei, and then appeared to have been extremely unhappy that he had provided that information. There was a look of intense fear on his face.

Garrett researched Opus Dei and found that it did actually exist and, as a prelature of the Pope, answering only to the Pope, with authority world wide. Although officially founded in 1928, there was a suggestion that the organization, loosely structured, had existed many years before with no specific name.

As a member of Opus Dei, the monk answered directly to the Pope, would be entrusted Church projects with extreme importance, and operate anywhere in the world without the need of approval of the local Church officials. In recent years, thanks to a couple of best-selling books and movies. Opus Dei had been considered by some as the militant arm of The Church. Even with consistent denials, there were many who believed that Opus Dei operated on the edge of laws and occasionally over stepped their bounds. Armed with the information Garrett found in his research, he felt more comfortable talking to the monk.

"I don't think my position has changed, Father," Garrett said actually baiting the monk, since not all Opus Dei were priests. The monk did not take the bait.

"I can assure you that the box will be completely safe and we will only need it for a few hours."

He ignored Garrett's effort to get more information about who and what he was.

"I am quite certain, sir, or do I call you, *Father,* that I am not willing to turn the box over to you, regardless."

With that, Garrett started closing books on his desk to indicate the conversation was over.

"You can call me either," the monk replied, "but I do hope you are willing to listen to reason. I am sorry I insulted you in our initial conversation, and also sorry I was so demanding in our second meeting. However, this is extremely important to the Church and the Pope."

This was the first time the monk had invoked his association with the Pope.

"The Pope has taken a personal interest in the box and would be willing to have a Papal plane pick you up here in Charleston and fly you to the Vatican for him to see the box. Would that make your decision easier?"

A personal meeting with the Pope in the Vatican? Could I be dreaming? Was that a bona fide offer? A trip to the Vatican just to let the Pope see the box?

Then common sense took over. If the Pope was that serious, there must be some truth in the importance of the box.

"Sir, *Father,* I do appreciate the Church's interest in my little box, and I appreciate your kind offer, but The box will be shown, for the first time, to the people who are registered to bid. I would be happy to provide you, or any representative of the Pope, accommodations for the auction — but that will be the only way you can verify that the box is what you think it may be."

With that statement, Garrett stood signaling the end of the conversation.

The monk made another effort to persuade Garrett.

"Mr. Garrett. Would you be willing to put a price on the box?"

"We have discussed this long enough." Garrett said as he moved around his desk and toward the door. "The box will be in the auction and you can show your interest in the same way as the others who are there to bid. May I escort you to the door?"

With that, Garrett moved one step closer to the monk

As the monk stood he said, "His Eminence will not be happy with this."

With a somewhat threatening tone of his last statement, the monk left #13 Church. Garrett's dreams that night were filled with men dressed in monk's clothes.

Right before he woke there was a troubling dream about a man with a beard — and one brown eye and one blue eye.

<h1 align="center">CHAPTER 38</h1>

The sun rose on Friday with very little fanfare. It was chilly in Charleston. There were enough clouds to allow the sun to play hide and seek. Traffic was normal. Garrett's coffee pot had been programmed to provide its eye-opening elixir and it performed normally. The newspaper was in the normal place. Garrett awakened at his normal time. And, he got ready for a normal day. The day, however, had anything but normality planned for Edward Garrett.

At his desk, Garrett had his morning coffee and bagel in the normal manner. He knew he had to travel to Saint Helena Island for his *follow-up* appointment with Doctor Bug. He had left Storey a note that he wanted to leave at 9:30. The plan was for an 11:00 appointment with the witch doctor. Lunch at the Beaufort Inn and be back at #13 Church by 2:00 to get the report concerning the X-rays of the box.

Storey had only been inside #13 Church one time since he threw his keys on the table and left. Garrett thought he should call Storey to make sure about the appointment with Doctor Bug. He went to the back door, looked to see if there was any movement at Storey's house and found that Storey had already moved the truck to the place he always parked it when he was joining Garrett on a trip.

It wasn't yet 8:00 and Garrett was almost ready. He located the initial root that Doctor Bug had given him. He didn't want to show up for his appointment without the root that was his treatment. Garrett couldn't see where the root had helped, but, he reasoned with himself that it had been a pretty good week. His sales were up. The meeting with The Opus Dei monk was good.

Even his visit to the shrink had been good. Could there be something to this VooDoo stuff?

He put the BY APPOINTMENT sign out and included his cell number, fixed a cup of coffee to go, stuffed the root in his pocket, slipped the Glock in his belt and locked the front door and set the alarm. He then walked out the back door, locking it.

They started toward Saint Helena Island 10 minutes early. They were well on the road to Beaufort before either of them said anything. Storey was the first to speak.

"I's sorry for bein' rude. There's a lot going on. I's got some family problems and I's need to go to Columbia for a few days to take care of the problems."

Garrett didn't answer right away. A number of thoughts ran through his mind like little feet wearing soft houseshoes.

Just like Storey to leave me with no one to help get ready for the auction, Garrent sulked. Who is going to handle the heavy work? I wonder what kind of family problem Storey is having? That's good, he's been acting strange lately, I don't want him here. But, I am going to need help.

Finally, Garrett said, "I'm sorry, too. There has been a lot going on. I didn't know about your family problem, but you need to take care of that. I'll hire some people to help with the auction."

In a moment of caring, Garrett added, "Is there anything I can do to help?"

For the first time, Storey began to talk about his family. Yet he seemed to try to catch himself in mid-thought. Like he had said too much. It was like he was trying to catch the words and stuff them back in his mouth.

After a moment of silence, he said, "No, nothing I can think of. I's just need to be there, at home."

Then Storey fell silent. Garrett considered starting the conversation again but decided to sit quietly.

They got to Gardens Corner and turned left on US 21 headed to Beaufort. Storey started talking again but this time, about today's visit to Doctor Bug.

"Please be respectful of Doctor Bug. You's may not believe in what he does but there's a lot'a people who swear by his advice."

"Storey, I have been thinking. Since the witch doctor gave me the root I have been having some good days. There just may be something to this VooDoo."

He was talking to Storey, but what he was saying was as much for himself as it was for Storey.

"Yes, some pretty good days, indeed."

Garrett was answered by silence from the driver's seat. They turned right at Frogmore General Store and headed to the world of Doctor Bug and the one-legged rooster. It was close to low tide when Storey pulled the pickup to a stop in front of Doctor Bug's place.

The smell of the marsh, the decaying material that showed its head when the water retreated, was especially strong on this day. The rooster was there on the porch

Garrett thought, *I wonder how a one-legged rooster could get up the half dozen steps to the porch.*

With that thought, the rooster took flight right in his direction, almost as if the rooster had read his mind. Shivers coursed through Garrett. The rooster redirected his flight path and landed on the roof of the old pickup that was in the exact place it was when they last visited the good doctor.

Doctor Bug again greeted them as they approached the door of his home/office/laboratory. He ushered them into his office and gestured for them to sit where they had sat earlier in the week. The young black girl brought out what Garrett had begun calling Doctor Bug's Fabulous Iced Tea for Garrett and Storey. Doctor Bug started the conversation.

"As I's told ya, Mista Garrett, you'se involved with some mighty strong magic here, yes sir you is. I had'ta order some pretty expensive tools so yo visit and yo root is gonna cost more this time."

Garrett started to say something but Storey cleared his throat reminding Garrett about the respect.

"This here root gonna cost you two hundred dolla. But you gonna be happy you got it when all dees evil spirits stays away from you," Doctor Bug was looking directly at Garrett the entire time he was talking. "Now I's done gone and made the root and I's got it right here but you'se got to understand that it's gonna take a day or so to start working for you. You's understand dat?"

Garrett said, "Yes, sure," more to keep the Doctor from

launching into another long diatribe. With that thought, Garrett added his only concern. "So, tomorrow is Saturday. If my dreams follow the same sequence as in previous weeks, I will have another dream. This $200 root isn't going to keep it away?"

"Mista Garrett, I's a doctor. I's don't see the future. I's got a friend cross the marsh who does. You wanta talk to her?"

"No. No. Doctor Bug. If I dream tomorrow night and that's the last one. I will be one happy patient."

With that, Doctor Bug handed Garrett a neatly packaged root and Garrett handed him two crisp $100 bills. Doctor Bug held each of the bills up to the light to see the watermarked images and put both bills in the top draw of his desk.

The Doctor may use the ancient arts in his medicinal, work but his business skills were up to the minute, Garrett thought.

The tide had turned and was coming in to Doctor Bug's house as Garrett and Storey were leaving. The one-legged rooster was standing on the roof of the old truck in exactly the same place as when they had entered. He gave Garrett and Storey one last throaty crow, "Cock-a-doodle-do," as the truck left the parking area.

CHAPTER 39

Garrett was lost in his thoughts as they made their way back to Charleston. He considered the meeting with Doctor Bug and the new root.

"If it stops those horrid dreams, it would certainly be worth $200." That was the angel on his right shoulder that said that.

"But if it doesn't, you have been totally taken and you wasted $200. Doesn't that make you feel like you just bought a bottle of champagne?" That was the devil on his left shoulder.

"Get thee behind me, Satan." Garrett actually said that out loud.

It caught Storey by surprise and he slammed on the brakes. If Garrett hadn't had his seat belt on, he would have cleared the front windshield and probably been the truck's new hood ornament.

"What the Hell!" Garrett was looking at and talking to Storey.

"You said, 'Get thee behind me Satan'. Were you talking to me? You shocked me."

Storey could barely whisper the comment. It not only shocked him it; troubled him as well. Now Garrett felt stupid.

"No, Storey. I wasn't talking to you. I didn't even mean to say it out loud. Just, let it go. I'm glad we are on Frogmore Road and not on the highway. You would have caused one more hell of a wreck."

The pair were silent on the way back to #13 Church. Storey thinking that Garrett had lost his mind and the problems he had at home. Garrett thinking about the auction and trying to imagine what could be in the box. It was 11:30 when Storey maneuvered the truck behind #13 Church.

Storey looked at Garrett, "Thank you for being respectful."

"Thank you for driving. It gave me some time to think."

With those terse comments, the two separated. Storey moved quickly to his house and Garrett to the back porch of #13 Church. As he was placing his key into the lock, he realized it was close to lunch time and, since he had skipped breakfast, he was hungry. In their haste to leave Doctor Bug's, the plan to lunch at the Beaufort Inn had been totally forgotten. Garrett got into the BMW and headed for The Bean.

He ordered a house coffee, unlike his usual long list of *how* he wanted his coffee, and a chicken salad sandwich. As the word *chicken* slipped from his lips, he thought about the one-legged rooster and shivered.

It was unusual that there were so few people in the popular coffee shop — maybe it was too early. Garrett had taken only one bite of his sandwich when he noticed the woman from the Old Market and Doctor Bug's. She worked at the Old Market, just across the street from The Bean. Could it be a coincidence or could she be watching him?

He quickly finished the sandwich and left The Bean before she did. There were too many things happening surrounding Doctor Bug for it to be a coincidence, but there really wasn't a connection. Certainly not one that he knew. He shook it off and headed over to pick up the X-rays.

He arrived at the office to find a large envelope waiting for him. He waited until he got to the car before opening it. The X-ray showed that there was, indeed, something in the box; something metal. It looked like coins, but the shapes were irregular. If they were coins, they would have to be old and most likely hand struck.

He slipped the X-ray back into the envelope and placed it in the floor-board of the passenger's seat. He was excited. A chill came over his body. It gave him shivers. He said to the empty passenger's seat, "It's just excitement. Nothing else."

The empty seat smiled. *Time will tell.*

Garrett parked the BMW at the back of #13 Church. Taking the Xrays from the car he approached the back door. There on the back step was another strip of Spanish Moss. Garrett made a mental note to ask Storey if Spanish Moss had a meaning in the

VooDoo rituals. He would also look it up on the Internet if he remembered.

Entering through the back in #13 Church, Garrett disabled the alarm system, collected the box from its safe place and slipped the X-rays under his arm as he went to the basement and his work area.

Again, he carefully analyzed the negative picture. There were definitely a number of metal objects. They were circular but as he originally noticed, they were slightly irregular. Other than the fact that there were 30 of them, the X-ray told him nothing more. He could see some indication of markings, but nothing he could identify. Garrett sat the box under the light on his work table and laid the X-ray beside it. He wanted to consider what to do next.

Why would someone place coins in a sealed compartment in a little box and then scratch something on the top that means *Beware?*

Beware! That's what they said it meant. He had no idea. He seemed to go into suspended animation as he stared at the box. He tried to concentrate but that just didn't work. Nothing made sense to him. His only conclusion was that he would have to destroy the box to see what was inside.

He found a hammer and set about breaking the box into pieces. It was stone, probably petrified wood. It must have been a dense wood because breaking the box into pieces without damaging its contents was no easy process.

Finally, he had setting before him, what appeared to be 30 very old silver coins, but he did not recognize their origin. They were a little less than an inch in diameter. Each coin had some sort of bird on one side and a profile of a person on the other side.

For the next two hours Garrett searched for a match in his research library. There were open books covering most of his work area. He had no idea where to start, but he knew he had to find out what these coins were. And maybe why they were sealed in the little box. It was well after 5 o'clock before he took a break.

His cell phone showed he had a number of messages. He stopped long enough to return Lee's call. He had to tell her about the discovery.

When she answered, "Lee I'm so excited. That little box that was in the Find had a false bottom and you wouldn't believe what it contained. Guess what I found."

"Edward, I have a busy day and I don't have time for your guessing games. What did you find?"

"There were 30 old, possibly silver, coins in the box."

"What are they worth."

"I don't know. I am researching that right now."

"Well, when you find out what they're worth, let me know. We will need pictures so we can add them to the auction."

It amazed him that Lee wasn't more excited. Sure, she was focused on her work, but this was what made the antique business interesting for Garrett. Finding something of value when you didn't expect it.

"OK. When will you be back in Charleston, Lee?"

"I'll be back Sunday afternoon. I'm flying into Columbia. Could you pick me up at the airport? I'm supposed to arrive at 3."

"Sure, my love. I should know more about these coins by then."

"Don't forget. 3 pm. Write it down on your calendar."

Damn her. She is more interested in being picked up than what I have uncovered. Damn her.

"I'll be there."

"I have to go. See you Sunday."

There was a click signaling the end of the call before he could answer.

She could at least have been a little more excited. She has been different since the Find. And she is acting like it's hers. She's different, Storey's different. Am I the only person that is sane here? he thought.

It was early evening. Garrett's head was hurting. His shoulders were sore from sitting in an awkward position as he searched the books for the coins. He grabbed some leftovers from the kitchen, a bottle of Ibuprofen and a ginger ale and headed to the basement to get back to work.

It was 4 a.m. when he awoke. He had finished the food. He knew that, because there was an empty plate on the side of the work table. The ginger ale can was more than half empty and the top was off the Ibuprofen bottle, so he must have taken the pills. But the ache in his head was all he needed to know that the initial dose hadn't had the desired result.

Three more pills, the rest of the ginger ale and he decided it was time to try to sleep in a more comfortable position. As he climbed into his bed there was a smile on his face.

Sleep came quickly.

CHAPTER 40

It was a golden glow that surrounded his bed when he opened his eyes. He was awash in a warming light. It took a couple of minutes to clear the Ibuprofen cob webs from his head. The pain was gone, but he was waking from a hard, deep sleep.

When he was *back in his body*, he noticed that sunlight was streaming in his bedroom window and completely encircled his bed and much of the bedroom. The sun's warming light brought with it a comforting feeling. It wasn't his first choice, but Garrett decided he should get up to begin the morning.

But it wasn't morning.

Could the clock be right? Could it really be a little after 2:00 in the afternoon.

Confirming his initial observation, Garrett climbed out of his comfortable cotton womb and made his way to the bathroom. His normal morning toilet took almost an hour this day. He was moving in slow motion and joints and muscles were taking longer to react, but he finished, dressed himself, and went downstairs.

The kitchen was the first stop. Mr. Coffee was right there on the counter but greeted him with cold coffee. It was almost like the coffee pot was saying, *If you had been here on time, it would have been hot, but since you weren't considerate of my time you get cold coffee.*

He empted the pot and started over. As the new pot of coffee was making, he went to the front door to get the morning paper. It was just inside the gate, dozens of feet from where it should have been. Cursing the paper deliverer, he grabbed the paper and walked back to the front steps.

Then he noticed the strip of Spanish Moss in the same place it was two days ago. He had intended to ask Doctor Bug if it had some VooDoo meaning but in the pressure of what was going on with Storey it was forgotten. He remembered that Storey had said that Spanish Moss had importance to the witch doctors but he didn't elaborate.

Ridiculous!

Again, he kicked it off the step and reentered the house. It was almost 5:00 before he sat at the work table in the basement. It was an unusual Saturday; sleeping so late was unusual, having no customers was unusual, not having Lee here was unusual. That was the day — unusual. Ensconced at his work table, in front of his computer, he decided to see what the Internet had to say about the mystical qualities for Spanish Moss.

He found that because of its strong jinxing qualities, it was used by many workers in the black arts as the stuffing for VooDoo dolls considered to be the most magical and most ominous. There were no references for the specific uses of strips of Spanish Moss in hexes or evil spells, but Garrett focused on the use of the word *jinxing* in one article.

There was information that the use of Spanish Moss as a magical talisman preceded the witch doctors and that it was used for many reasons by Native Americans, especially in the south, and that it represented the Aztec goddess Xochiquetzal in rituals involving virgin sacrifice and other activities that represented death.

He found enough information to start his skin crawling. Regardless of whether he believed it or not, Garrett was happy he had a bona fide root from a bona fide root doctor for protection.

Garrett settled back in his work area and picked up one of the coins and a powerful magnifying glass. There was clearly a bird on one side but the writing wasn't legible. There was a male profile on the other side. For the first time, he could clearly see the obvious Romanesque shape of the nose. The bird was clearer so he hadn't spent much time looking at the profile.

OK. Roman.

It was two hours later when all of the little pieces of the puzzle finally slipped into place. Comparing the coin to examples from an authoritative numismatic tome, he had discovered that the coins were silver shekels. He put the book up and moved to his computer. He found the there was a long history of silver shekels.

In addition to the Romans, silver shekels were used by Greeks and Phoenicians. They were minted, usually by hand, from 124 BC to 60 AD. The bird was the symbol of the Greek God Heracles, the son of Zues.

Garrett found the stories about Heracles to be legendary. His image represented strength and the name meant, *Glorious Gift of Hera.* Hera was Zues' wife. But that was another story.

He was able to make out the initials KAP which the Internet revealed represented Kratos Romaion which translated means, *Power of the Romans.* The shekels were used by the Romans during the time when Herod the Great was king the Jews, and were also called the Herodian shekel. They were initially minted at the Tyre Mint, and the early coins had the Mint's symbolic club on the eagles left leg.

Tyre is still a city located in southern Lebanon near the Mediterranean Sea. At the time the coins were minted, Tyre was an independent city-state and kept much of its independence even during the Roman occupation. The articles indicated that Jesus had visited Tyre and healed the demon-possessed daughter of a Canaanite woman as reported in the Gospels of Matthew and Mark.

It was then that a small article caught Garrett's eye: *Coins of the Bible: Shekel of Tyre.* He opened the article and found a list that made shivers course through his body.

Temple Tax — Shekels of Tyre were the approved Temple Tax payment. Exodus 30:13

Money Changers — Shekels of Tyre were the currency that the money changers would have been using when Jesus overturned their tables in the Temple in Jerusalem. Matthew 21:12 and John 2:15.

Peter's Fish — The shekel that Peter found in the mouth of the fish, as Jesus had directed him, was a Shekel of Tyre. Matthew 17:27

Judas' Coins — As were the 30 pieces of silver given Judas for betraying Jesus. Matthew 26:15.

Garrett was looking at the historic account, but not seeing the significance of what he was reading. When it sank in, he almost cried. Everything began to fit together to reveal a finished puzzle — 30 Shekels of Tyre, the box with *Beware* (if that was really what it said) on it, the interest shown by The Catholic Church and the persistence of the visiting Monk and his demand that it was Church property.

But even then, he couldn't believe what was becoming obvious. He started to call Lee to share his excitement. He picked up the phone and replaced it on the desk. He didn't want to go through all of her demands. He wasn't sure if he wanted to put the coins up for auction or not. He wasn't sure if he even wanted to sell them or not. He wanted some time to think about this.

This certainly was an unusual Saturday.

Garrett had a soft leather pouch in his desk. The pouch would be the ideal place to keep the coins out of sight. He put all 30 shekels in the pouch and tucked it in his pocket. He would put them in a place in his bedroom where no one would be able to find them.

With that, Garrett turned off the computer, closed the books he was using and turned off the lights in the basement before climbing the stairs to the main floor. He double-locked the front door. Then went to the kitchen. He needed food and time to think.

He made a sandwich out of the limited offering in the refrigerator and made a mental note to go shopping on Sunday. He took the sandwich and grabbed a ginger ale in preparation for heading to the upper floor. He stopped and paused a moment. *This is a time to celebrate.* He replaced the ginger ale and grabbed a long neck. A little beer would make him sleep better and make the meager dinner seem more like a celebration.

Armed with the coins, the much less than gourmet invention of the Earl of Sandwich, the celebratory creation of Anheuser Busch and the protection made by Gaston Glock in his belt, Garrett started to climb the stairs to his bedroom. Stopping at the control pad for his security system, he made a commitment to himself to set the alarm every night, something he had become quite lax in doing for the past few years.

In his recliner, he placed the sandwich plate on his lap and his beer and the Glock on the side table next to his reading light, and sighed with relief. The auction was going well, the business was going well and his most recent find would certainly give him the recognition he so wanted.

With that thought, the image of his new root floated through his mind. He quickly got up, went to the dresser and retrieved the magical root stuffing it in his robe pocket.

No point taking any chances.

He ate his sandwich as scenario after scenario played on the stage of his mind. How would he announce the find of the coins? Who could he get to manage the information? What were the best ways that he could get the credit for finding them?

Idea after idea continued to unfold in his mind. With only crumbs left as evidence that a sandwich had previously sat on the small plate, Garrett took a healthy swig of the half-empty beer bottle and, as he reclined the chair, his arm touched the grip of the reassuring 9mm pistol.

Now, he could continue his assignment to be in thought as his eyelids began to get heavy.

PROPHESY

You!"
"Bastard!"
"You! You!"
"Scum of the earth!"
"Killer!"
"Bastard! Stinking, thieving, Bastard!"
"May you rot in hell for what you have done, Gentleman Pirate Steed Bonnet!"
"Who's a Gentleman now?"
"Bastard! Hanging's too good for you. They should tie you to that gallows. Let the gulls pick at your flesh until the tide brings the crabs to gnaw your toes off and other sea creatures feast on your flesh until you drown. The sea should finish you off just as you did to so many, you thieving, killing pirate!"

The angry mob — cursing, spewing obscenities as I am pushed through them. The ropes are cutting into my wrists. The pain in my chest, it's almost unbearable. Someone else punches me. The pain takes my breath. The gasping for breath causes more pain.

I'm being pushed to a place, but where? All I can see is a sea of anger. Faces blur, only the anger is clear. People spitting at me. They want me dead. But why? I start to scream, why? Why? Why?

I can't continue. I fall to my knees. The stones dig holes in my flesh. I fall forward. I feel sharp pointed rocks pierce my cheeks, the instant I hear the crack echo through my head and feel the ground. Moments pass. I can hear them. Then, I feel like I'm flying. I see the arms of two men picking me up, forcing me to stand. My legs don't want to hold up the weight. My muscles stretch like rubber bands that have lost their elastic.

They could kill me, but no. It's clear, they want to disgrace me.

They can take my life but they won't have my dignity. I struggle to stand. The surface gives, not like the rocky street. The surface oozes between my toes, lick at my ankles. The smell is unmistakable — the stench of rotting plants and animals — the marsh. Are they are pushing me into the marsh? I can see the wooden arm stretching over the heads of the crowd, like half of a forgiving crucifix.

Now, it's all too clear. That is the gallows. They are going to hang me. A shiver courses through my body. There are people pushing me, hitting me, spitting on me. They drag me up three steps to a platform. All I can see is a sea of fists. All I can hear is a choir, chanting obscenities. All I can feel is the pricking pain from the horse hair rope on my neck. The sea of fists is now obscured by a big, burley, hairy giant standing in front of me. As I look up to see his face; the hair on his chest blends with his thick beard. It is almost humorous. I know that face — the blacksmith. I hear his voice, but his lips are barely visible.

"You and your fellow pirates have killed men, women and children. You have burned and destroyed people's property. You have stolen. You have committed all manner of crimes here in Charles Town and seaports throughout this part of the world. Do you have anything to say for yourself."

I struggle to form words but none are able to escape my mouth. I have never killed women. I have never killed children. But I am unable to come to my own defense. Then I hear that voice again, over the cursing of the crowd.

"Since you have nothing to say for yourself, I declare you guilty and sentence you to hang by the neck until dead."

I can see the town that has been my home. Familiar buildings. I look out across the crowd of screaming facing and I see people I know — my *friends*. People who owe me money. Why won't they come to my aid, speak in my defense.

With that thought ringing in my head I feel my legs being kicked from behind. I struggle to regain my footing as the rope around my neck tightens instantly. At the same time, people around me are punching me, kicking me. I feel the tight tug on my neck and I can't breathe. There is no way out.

I remember words I had heard as a child in church — *He that lives by the sword, shall die by the sword.*

My body is still swinging, still being punched, still being kicked, but I can't feel any pain. All I can feel is a comfortable numbness. I can't see.

Darkness.

CHAPTER 41

Garrett awakened into a world of numbness. He tried to move with little success. He finally regained feeling in his arms and legs and looked around to see if the crowd was still there. The surroundings were familiar and, with that, he realized he was in his bedroom and in his recliner.

Another dream.

"The root is no damn good and neither is that damned witch doctor."

He was speaking aloud as he had been doing a lot lately. Who was he informing? No one. No one was there to hear him. Garrett moved to his bed. He carried the root, the pistol and the coins. Now, he wanted the protection and the assurance that they would be easily within his reach. All three were safely placed under his pillow. He glanced around his room, clicked off the light and tried to continue his sleep.

The rest of his night was fitfull sleep. There were no dreams but he woke every hour or two. Every time he awoke he checked under his pillow for the coins, the loaded Glock and the root.

He awoke to the sound of bells ringing from atop Saint Michael's church. It was Sunday. He thought for a moment about getting dressed and attending the late church service. But there was too much to do — this was the week and everything had to be perfect.

He slipped into his robe and headed to the kitchen. He reached the landing of the third-floor stairs before he remembered the coins under his pillow. He retrieved them, stuffed them in a pocket of his robe, in the other pocket he carefully stuffed the Glock.

He paused for a moment and decided to add the root to the pocket with the coins and then headed to the kitchen.

Mr. Coffee, un-programmed and waiting for instructions, silently sat there on the kitchen counter. Garrett hadn't set the timer nor had he filled it with water and coffee.

No problem.

Water tank filled and coffee in its proper place, with a simple click of the start button, Mr. Coffee came to life and began processing the perfect cup of coffee. He put the bagel in the toaster, the pistol and the coins on the table and headed to the front door to collect the morning paper.

The question of his personal security halted him before he opened the door. Almost everywhere he went lately it appeared that people were watching him. For the moment, he put that thought in a pigeon hole to be dealt with later. As he opened the front door he found the paper missing but there was a strip of Spanish moss there on the step where the others had been.

Across the street, there was a guy standing, smoking a cigarette. Was he watching for Garrett? Could he be waiting for Garrett to leave the house?

Garrett quickly retreated into the safety of his house. Double locking the door, he peered out the window. He was still there. Garrett moved from the door to the front window. The guy was gone.

Where did he go?

Could he be his neighbor who had finished his cigarette and returned inside or could he be a stranger watching Garrett, his movements? He couldn't remember seeing him before but maybe it was just a coincidence.

Yes. That's it.

But was the moss a coincidence? Too strange. Collecting the previous thought about people watching him from the pigeon library, he decided he needed to deal with that consideration. Should he carry protection or not? Should he hire a body guard? Garrett decided that protection was the better choice, so he decided to keep the Glock with him, even if he were in his bed clothes and robe. The reassuring feel of the weight in his robe pocket eased his mind as he returned to his breakfast.

Garrett piddled around in the basement. There was a number

of occasions when he heard the front door bell ringing.

It is amazing how many friends you have when you achieve notoriety, he thought.

Some time, mid-morning, Garrett showered, shaved, quaffed and after-shaved himself. Garrett returned to the business level of #13 Church and to his desk. He looked at his phone and recognized two repeated numbers from area code 212. New York could only be the representatives from Christie's and Sotheby's. He didn't want to deal with them before he left for Columbia to pick up Lee.

There were two calls from area code 202. When he cross-referenced the numbers on the Internet he found that the numbers were for the IRS and the FBI. Something else to deal with later.

It was noon. Garrett was ready to pick Lee up at the airport. He decided he had enough time to go the back way, through Summerville. He collected a cup of coffee to go, the Glock, the root and his sun glasses. He decided that putting the coins in the freezer section of his refrigerator was the safest place he could find in a short time.

Who in their right mind would look in the freezer?

He looked at Storey's carriage house and saw no evidence of anyone moving. He backed the BMW out of its parking place and aimed it toward Columbia — well toward Summerville; and then Columbia.

Garrett made the drive to Columbia a leisurely one. Lee's plane was scheduled to arrive at 3:00 p.m. Garrett arrived at the airport at 2:30 only to find out that her plane had been delayed. It was now expected at 4:00 p.m. This seemed like it was happening more and more often. Her work was more important than his. Her schedule was more important than his. Her friends were more important than his. She wasn't like that when they first started dating. He decided he could wait in the lounge.

He walked in and sat at the bar and ordered; "Black Jack and branch."

It always sounded fake when he said it. That was the way the actor in the commercial ordered it. He sounded so cool so with it, but, most of all, so masculine. There were a half-dozen travelers in the lounge. Two couples were talking animatedly.

Both couples were drinking *island* drinks. A good sign they were preparing for a vacation. There were two middle-aged men, obviously businessmen, each nursing a drink. There was one other person in the lounge other than Garrett. He really looked strange. He was wearing a black suit and a white shirt. He had on a non-descript rep tie. His haircut was clearly military — a flat top with white sidewalls. Even in Columbia it was odd. There were many military people in Columbia, thanks to Fort Jackson, and many retired soldiers kept the signature hairstyle. But in Garrett's opinion, he wasn't old enough to be retired and he was clearly no recruit.

Garrett continued to drink his drink. But he continued to watch Garrett, and Garrett continued to watch the guy.

The guy got two calls while he was sitting there. Normally that wouldn't be anything special but it was his mannerisms. The conversations were short; one or two words. He turned his ear away when he spoke. And he wrote something in a small notebook kept in his inside coat pocket. Also, the guy looked muscular and the suit coat didn't fit him very well.

Garrett looked straight at the guy, who never turned away, and thought of the DC telephone numbers. Could the FBI be following him?

With that thought, the airlines announced the arrival of Lee's flight. Garrett headed to baggage claim to meet her. He didn't see the guy in the black suit.

He saw Lee headed to the baggage claim belt. She didn't look happy. His greeting was met with a perfunctory kiss and a statement of what her face had already communicated. The plane was an hour late. She couldn't get first-class. Every seat was sold. The people on either side of her were both overweight. She was unable to use her laptop.

And, she was *not* happy, a fact that he had already surmised.

"Let's get your luggage and get back to Charleston. You'll be in a better mood and we can enjoy being together."

Garrett was trying to soothe Lee's ruffled feathers. As he analyzed that thought, he shivered when the one-legged rooster again hopped through his mind. He hadn't told Lee about his visits to Doctor Bug. What would she think? What would she say? A subject to bring up on the way back to Charleston.

"What suitcase did you take?" Garrett asked as they both continued to look at the parade of bags that marched by them on the rolling beltway.

"The purple one," Lee's terse answer put a period on their conversation.

Round and round marched the bags like good little soldiers. Of course, the suitcases weren't marching, but they were in a line, except when one of the owners extracted his bags from the parade. The number of soldiers dwindled till there were none. Garrett and Lee were standing beside an empty, stopped baggage carousel.

"Damn!" was all Lee said. She could have said a lot more, but the word with its inflection was all she needed to say.

Garrett told her that he would fetch the car while she dealt with the Lost Baggage attendant and he would pick her up just outside the baggage area door.

Garrett was waiting patiently in the car while Lee argued with the one person who could help her get her lost baggage. She got in the car and slammed the door.

"They sent the bag to Cleveland. Some idiot couldn't read. Cleveland is CLE and Columbia is CAE. I hope they fire the dumb S.O.B."

"It's ok, Lee. We can come back up here tomorrow." That was Garrett's answer to the problem.

"They will send the bag in a limo tomorrow to the house. That's not the point. If people just did their job, I would be on my way to Charleston with my luggage and in a good mood. As it is, I'm in a bad mood. I'm on my way to Charleston and my luggage is on it way to Cleveland."

Crossing her arms, Lee sat fuming, in the passenger's seat.

"I've had an exciting week, Lee. You wouldn't believe what I found out about the little box and the coins that were in it."

"Give me a minute to relax. This has been a trying day for me."

With that, Garrett's story about the 30 pieces of silver, the Pope, the invitation to the Vatican, Doctor Bug and all of the other important stuff he was going to tell her about was put on hold while she tried to relax. Now it was Garrett who was fuming.

When he heard her rhythmic breathing and the occasional

snort, he realized Lee was sleeping and he was driving.

The only word that came to mind was, "Damn!"

As he entered the Interstate, he started a discussion with himself. No mirror to talk to, it was just in his head. The only question under discussion was, *Do I take Lee to her house or do I take her to #13 Church?* Had Grandfather been in the car with him, he would have said something like — *You idiot. She's asleep. She couldn't give a rat's ass about your Find. Don't you get it? I think you are an idiot.* Grandfather always cut through the BS and got right to the point. *I'd put her out right now and let her walk back to Charleston. That's what I'd do.*

Garrett remained quiet for the rest of the trip, and Lee snored for the rest of the trip. He pulled the BMW to a stop in Lee's drive way. She was still asleep. He nudged her with his elbow, a little harder that he needed have.

"What the Hell!" Lee looked at him and continued, "What do you want?"

"We're here, at your house, Lee."

"Good!" was the answer he got. "We'll talk tomorrow. I need a good night's rest. I love you."

The last part of that sentence was all but drowned out by the slamming of the car door. Now it was Garrett who was fully pissed off by the way Lee had treated him at the airport, during the ride home and now as she dismissed him. He's the one that would need to relax.

It was beginning to prey on Garrett's mind. The closer he got to the big day, the grand unveiling of the Find, the more difficult his relationship with Ashley seemed to get. Every time he had an idea, she had a better one.

He was glad to be alone tonight. He didn't need all of Lee's BS and questions. He didn't need her control drama.

Most of all, he didn't need her incessant demanding attitude.

CHAPTER 42

It was Monday morning and Garrett woke with a headache. *This is no way to start the most important week of my life,* he thought. With that, Garrett slipped his hand under his pillow where he found the Glock and his root.

Where are the coins?

He jerked up the pillow looking for the coins. He pulled back the covers and jerked the bed from against the wall.

Where are they? Who could have gotten into the house? The door was locked and the alarm set.

If someone had triggered the alarm, Garrett would have gotten a call. Did Storey have the alarm code? Garrett was certain that he had never given Storey the code. He sat in his favorite chair, looking at the pile of cloth that had previously been a properly made bed. As he searched the recesses of his mind, he recalled he took Lee to her house. He remembered that he was unhappy with her for not wanting to be with him. He remembered being happy that he was going to have some free time to himself.

Then he remembered. He had put the coins in the freezer. He went downstairs to get them. With the coins safely in his pocket, he sat at his desk and made a new sign.

We will be closed for the rest of the week.

It continued,

Hope to see you at the auction — 8:00 Saturday.

He had hoped the sign would dissuade people from calling and ringing the bell and knocking on the door.

Mr. Coffee had responded to the program Garrett set before he went to pick up Lee at the Columbia airport. As he looked at the coffee pot, he thought about heading to The Bean. That thought caused him to pause.

He had been thinking a lot lately that it probably wasn't wise to be out in public with all of the notoriety that he had been getting. So, The Bean was not the choice for breakfast. He thought about toasting a bagel in the toaster.

"No," he almost shouted.

He knew it would take a little longer, but he had no particular place he needed to be until his shrink appointment late that afternoon. So, he would cook one of his special meals, even if it were only a meal for one. He gathered all of the essentials from the refrigerator. He would have sausage and sausage gravy, buttery course-ground yellow grits, scrambled eggs with Italian spices and an oven-toasted cheese bagel along with his hot, sweet *Special Garrett's Blend* coffee.

Forty-five minutes later, Garrett was settling down to enjoy his breakfast.

With a refilled coffee cup, he moved to his desk. Periodically, the front door bell rang and, occasionally, there was a pounding on the door from someone who obviously couldn't read. Garrett ignored all efforts to gain entrance.

He was looking at the check list that John James had left him. It seemed like a very comprehensive check list. There was a time table. He noticed that he was expected to check into the Presidential suite on Wednesday afternoon and check out on Sunday. That seemed like a good schedule. He wanted to be near the Hibernian Hall during the setup and not be bothered by the press of people who were trying to get to him. Being closeted at the Mills House was certainly the best way to drop out of sight.

He noted that the check list indicated that four security guards would meet with Garrett and James at noon today. Garrett hadn't realized that he would be required to be at that meeting which would be at The Mills House. He glanced over at Grandfather, the silent sentinel and keeper of time. It was almost 11:00, so he knew he had to make his way to his quarters upstairs.

It was exactly noon when the BMW rolled to a stop at the valet station at The Mills House. Garrett had the Glock carefully stuffed in his belt. John James was just inside the entry door and escorted Garrett to the Board Room for their meeting. The four men stood when Garrett entered the room. He had never seen four people together that were so big. They looked like the front four for the Atlanta Falcons football team.

God, what giants, he thought. "So, these men are my security team," he said to no one in particular. "I expect these guys can handle any problem," he said to John James.

The lead giant briefed them on the the plan: from the time he checked into the Mills House, two of the team would be at his side. The four will rotate, 12-on 12-off, until the auction is over. They will be with him when he is not in his room, and they will be outside his door when he is in his room.

The lead giant handed Garrett a fob, not unlike the remote key to his BMW. Amazingly, the giant spoke English in a soft and educated voice.

"You will keep this with you at all times. At the slightest hint of a problem, press the button. One of us will be there immediately. He will decide if he needs help. We will be in constant radio connection through the miniature radio transceivers that fit in our ears. All four of us will be as close as a radio transmission from the time you move to The Mills House until the auction is over and we are dismissed."

Garrett looked at John James. They exchanged thumbs up. After a few more housekeeping points, Garrett returned to the valet, reclaimed his car and headed back to #13 Church.

He drove by the front of his house. There were at least a dozen people sitting, lounging or standing on his front porch. Three television remote trucks were parked along the curb. It looked like he would have to find a better way to deal with friends and the media than to just ignore them.

He parked the BMW behind #13 Church. As he opened the car door, a young man carrying a TV camera ran to intercept him. He was followed closely by a young woman holding a microphone. The young woman started talking before she stopped walking. She linked three questions together without stopping for a breath.

Garrett put his hand in front of the camera lens and pushed it back into the young man's face, evoking an expression of pain followed by a few swear words including S.O.B. — and that didn't mean South of Broad. He then turned his attention to the young woman who had, by then, stuck the microphone in Garrett's face. He pushed it out of the way and in no uncertain terms insisted that she and her companion were on private property, and that they were to leave or he would have the Sheriff evict them, and he would press charges for their trespassing.

The young woman yelled something about public's right to know and he had lost his rights as a private citizen while the cameraman again called him an S.O.B.

Garrett quickly slammed the car door. He reached into his pocket as he ran to the back door of #13 Church. Unlocking the door, he was able to get inside before the two could marshal their wits and start chasing him. He locked the door as the security system began barking orders that he was trespassing and he should leave the premises immediately or the police would be summoned.

Garrett looked at the talking key pad for a long second and then started laughing. Irony is a strange comedian. The timing of the demanded threat from the electronic voice to call the police as he was threatening to call the Sheriff finally sank in. Garrett started screaming at the alarm key pad.

"Call them. Call the police. Call them, damn it!"

Could their slow response be the result of the times they had been sent a false alarm? He grabbed his cell phone and punched in 911. On the third ring, he began cursing the phone and the police who were supposed to be on the other end.

Before the 911 operator could answer, there was a pounding on the front door and an amplified voice that announced "Open the door. This is the police. Open the door or we will break it in."

With the second pronouncement Garrett came to his senses. The door was expensive and the security it provided was more essential now that ever before. Garrett ran to the door as the electronic voice chimed in again and the voice outside announced once more, "Open the door. This is your last warning. Open the door or we will break it in."

Garrett fumbled with the lock as he yelled "Wait a minute, Wait a minute!"

Garrett opened the door to reveal three Police officers with their service revolvers ready and aimed at his midsection. Then there was knocking at the back door and another threat that he had to open the door or they would break it in. A momentary thought flashed through his mind that there wasn't much creativity in the writing of the police department's pronouncements. The Police at the back door parroted the officers at the front. He quickly invited the officers at the front door in as he raced to the back door before the officers made kindling out of his back door.

One more time the electronic voice demanded the intruders to leave the premises. Garrett threw up his hands in exasperation. At that moment, his belt released its hold on the Glock and it came tumbling out of his pant leg, renewing the attention of the Police. With his hands still in the air, Garrett called to the ranking member of the Police squad to stop their actions because he was the owner of the property.

The command to, "Hold where you are," was given by the lead policeman as he verified that it was actually Thomas Edward Garrett that was speaking. With Garrett's identity assured, the policeman in charge ordered the squad to secure the premises, since many of the gathered friends and media people had rushed inside to witness the unfolding drama at #13 Church.

With normalcy returning, Garrett sat at his desk and offered a chair to the officer who had his gun. Garrett's outward demeanor had settled down even though, inside, he was a jangle of nerves. He thanked the officer for coming and apologized for the call from the alarm company. He did ask how he could keep the unwanted visitors from accosting him on his own property. The officer provided Garrett with some suggestions, things he needed to do, so the situation didn't escalate into a reenactment of today's situation. Garrett said he would, then the officer turned his attention to Garrett's Glock.

The officer picked up the weapon, looked at it, turned it over in his hand and then looked straight at Garrett.

"Do you have a permit to carry this weapon concealed, Mr. Garrett?"

Garrett stammered as he told the officer, "No."

But then he said something about his First Amendment rights and this being his property.

The officer courteously allowed Garrett to complete his defense of having the gun and where he was carrying it.

"You see just how easy it is for a situation to escalate and get out of control. You could have easily been shot by one of my officers, or you could have easily become a murderer. All it takes is seconds. That is the reason we don't want every Tom, Dick and Edward carrying guns."

He placed the Glock on the desk in front of Garrett.

"This Glock is a great gun. You do have the constitutional right to carry it here on your property, but I believe you had it with you before you came home today. I probably could make a case for ticketing you and confiscating the gun, but I'm not. Put your gun up. Don't carry it outside your property. And we will clear out some of the mob that is camping out on your property."

With that the officer stood and waved his hand to the assembled officers in #13 Church.

Some headed out the front, and some headed out the back.

CHAPTER 43

Garrett was sitting at his desk. He looked at Grandfather and announced, "This is no way to start the most important week of my life."

Grandfather didn't say anything because he was a clock.

There were still people at the front door. They were ringing the bell. They were knocking on the door. Now the TV team that accosted him was knocking at his back door. Garrett picked up his cell phone and pushed the quick dial number for John James.

"Hello."

Garrett started his conversation without any pleasantries.

"When can those security guards start working?"

"Any time you want them."

"Get two of them over here as soon as you can. I've got people on my front porch, people in my yard, and people at my back door. I can't even leave my house."

"They are still in my office, Mr. Garrett. I will send all four over right away. I am certain they can solve your problem. They will call on your cell when they are at your doors."

"They better get here soon, I'm paying for their protection."

Apparently Garrett was talking to Grandfather because no one else was there. Grandfather was still smiling inside again. His only answer to Garrett was, *Tick, Tock, Tick, Tock, Tick...*

It wasn't five minutes before Garrett's cell phone rang.

"Hello."

"Mr. Garrett?"

"Yes."

"Everything is under control. We do need to talk about our working schedule."

When Garrett opened the door a few of the people who were still waiting on the sidewalk started to move toward Garrett. One of the guards stepped out between the group and Garrett. He was 6'8" if he was an inch and Garrett estimated his weight at 280. He was a giant to the gathering. In addition to his imposing frame, he had taken a 9mm Glock from a concealed holster. It wasn't dissimilar to Garrett's pistol.

The group stopped, almost as one person. This armed giant said to the assembled people, Garrett's friends and some who wanted to be Garrett's friends, in the softest command voice Garrett had ever heard, "Mr. Garrett will not be receiving guests this day. I would suggest that you call before you return. Visitors are welcome only with an appointment."

Garrett was amazed at how quickly this guy had taken complete control of the crowd.

The leader turned to Garrett and said, "Let's go inside and discuss the schedule you will need for us, prior to your move to The Mills House."

He, too, had a most soft but commanding voice.

They sat at Garrett's desk. The security guy started first.

"I realized that I have not introduced myself. I am Grant, actually Bob Grant, but we go by our last names. I already know you are Edward Garrett. Now, Mister Garrett, about your schedule for the rest of the time you will be at home. We do not believe the people who were here today meant you harm, but you are now a very public figure, and, as a result, may be the target for some wacko who wants to get his name in the media. We need to accompany you everywhere you go."

Garrett paused before replying to Grant. Was he really a public figure? He couldn't hide the smile.

"Mister Garrett, this is no laughing matter. You could be in danger and you are paying us to make sure nothing happens to you."

Garrett stammered, "This afternoon, I'm supposed to be at the office of a shrink I've been seeing lately. That's the only appointment I have until I go to The Mills House."

"Doctor Williams," Grant interrupted Garrett. "I'd cancel that if I were you."

"Sure. He's pretty much a shyster anyway."

Grant closed that conversation with a quick answer. "A shyster is a lawyer. A shrink is slang way to say a psychologist. By the way, I am a lawyer."

Again, Garrett stammered, this time a weak apology to Grant.

"No matter," Grant replied. "I would not leave #13 Church until we take you to The Mills House. We can arrange to have your meals brought in."

Grant's plan brought to the surface the old feeling in Garrett. This was his program, his Find, his auction. First, it was Lee telling him what to do, now this guy Grant is telling him what to do. It was that old feeling of insecurity that started talking.

"If I am a public figure, as you say, shouldn't I be seen in the public?" Garrett smiled again at how quickly he regained the control of the conversation.

"That's fine if you want to get yourself killed." Grant looked him straight in the eyes again, and added, "I thought you hired us to keep that from happening." His tone made Garrett cower inside.

Garrett sucked it up and said in his most commanding voice. "You're right. I will stay inside here."

Garrett agreed, but that old feeling of insecurity was there inside, and he could not shake it. The schedule was agreed upon, Garrett would be responsible for his own breakfast, the security team would handle lunch and dinner.

Garrett's cell phone ring got his attention. He looked and saw Lee's number appear. He looked at Grant and said, "It's my girlfriend."

He was getting ready to punch the connect button when Grant added, "Tell Miss Ashley I said hello. Oh! By the way, the FBI and the IRS are trying to get in touch with you. The FBI wants to know where you got the items that will be in the auction. That's really none of their business, but I would get in touch with the IRS if I were you."

With that Grant turned and headed for the door. It took a minute for Grant's closing comment to sink in. When he looked at his phone, Lee's call had gone to voice mail. He called her back, but got her voice mail. He cursed the phone. He pushed redial and again got her voice mail. She was leaving him a message. The third time was the charm, the call went through and Ashley answered. Garrett told her of his morning. She said she was planning to bring dinner over, his favorite from Poogan's Porch.

She would see him around 6:30.

CHAPTER 44

Garrett walked idly around the store. He picked up an item looked at it and put it back in its place. Again and again and again. It was barely 5:00 and Lee wouldn't be here for an hour and a half.

At 5:15, he sat back at his desk and pushed the *on* button on the TV remote. He couldn't remember the last time he watched television. The TV came to life almost instantly and it was in the middle of a coffee commercial. That started Garrett's desire for a good cup of coffee. A smile of satisfaction crept across his face. Regardless of what Lee has said, or John James, or Pegge, or Grant or anyone else, he could always count on Mr. Coffee to give him a magnificent cup of coffee. He walked into the kitchen, prepared the coffee pot and pressed the start button.

He leaned on the kitchen counter, preparing for the spiritual moments of the first aroma of brewing coffee. That was his comfort food and his drug of choice. Mr. Coffee didn't fail him — the wafting aromas played with Garrett's olfactory senses. Little coffee fairies flitted about from smell sensor to smell sensor. They were such a tease.

Garrett filled his cup and sat back at his desk. Grandfather's rhythmic *Tick, Tock* was the only sound Garrett could hear. *Tick, Tock, Tick, Tock.* It became hypnotic and it wasn't long before he was sleeping in his desk chair. It was the incessant pounding on his front door that pulled him out of the dream-free coma he was enjoying. He woke with a start, looked around and as lucidity connected him to the present, his first question was,

"Where are those security guards who were supposed to keep people away from my door?"

A glance at grandfather brought him to the realization that it was 6:30, and the pounding was probably Lee with their dinner.

Opening the door, he had already started the explanation of falling asleep. Lee was unexpectedly compassionate.

She brought the bags of food in and placed them on the kitchen table. Garrett had utilized the house's dining room to display more antiques. So, even though it wasn't very elegant, the surroundings didn't take away from the wonderful meal.

Garrett began telling Lee about his day. The police story brought laughter from Lee, something she shared with Garrett now that it was over and he could see the humor in what was a difficult situation as it was happening. She told him that she had met with John James after his meeting with him earlier that day. She expressed that she was pleased with the way things were going.

Garrett almost challenged her on the role she was taking in his project, but said nothing. He began talking about Bob Grant and the giants that were his security. He mentioned Grant's message to say, "Hello to Miss Ashley."

Ashley interrupted the story by saying she had met Bob Grant a year or so ago when he had worked for her father by leading a local security detail when the President had come to Charleston to visit the Senator.

Her comment, "He is a gentle giant" plucked the jealous string in Garrett's heart.

Had they dated? What were her feelings for Grant? Were they more than friends? Lee, anticipating Garrett's jealous streak, quickly told Garrett that Grant was happily married with children and he was an elder in his church. Garrett wasn't sure that made any difference but, again, didn't say anything.

With the meal completed and the post dining conversation completed, Lee suggested that Garrett take a hot bath while she cleaned up the kitchen. She would join him for a passionate evening of love-making which they had missed, since so much was happening in their lives.

"With the security team outside, you can cut your phone off and there will be no one to interrupt us. I want to show you just how much I love you."

Lee kissed him on the forehead, squeezed his crotch and sent him off to his third-floor quarters. Garrett filled the garden tub with hot water, stripped and slipped into the warm refreshing water. There was room for Lee. When she arrived, she almost jumped into the tub. They played, splashed each other a little, cuddled and spent some time kissing. It was almost child-like. Both were having fun.

It wasn't competitive the way the Find had been getting. Lee was the old Lee, and Garrett was the old Garrett. By the time the water cooled, they were ready to adjourn to the bedroom. Lee had lit candles before goimg into the bathroom, so the room had the romantic lighting of a dozen or so candles. The aroma was of sandalwood, a scent they both liked.

Each slipped under the soft, enticing sheets. Cuddling, kissing and tender foreplay was followed by an urgency of two lovers who had been separated for some time. Finally, everything was ready. Everything was ready except Garrett. He had never before experienced any kind of dysfunction. One could say he was always ready — occasionally too ready for Lee's taste. This night, nothing.

Their conversation started with Lee asking, "What's the matter?"

Garrett, feeling challenged said, "I don't know. Maybe it's what you're doing."

To which Lee replied, "Like, what do you mean?"

The conversation escalated from there. Soon, Lee was crying. Garrett was frustrated. No one knew what to do, and worse, each was blaming the other.

Lee expressed her frustration by getting out of the bed, picking up her clothes, putting them on.

"Where are you going?" demanded Garrett.

That was the wrong thing to say.

"We haven't been together intimately in weeks. Are you thinking about some other woman?"

That didn't help and all Garrett could say was, "Damn you."

Which also was the wrong thing to say.

Lee stomped out of the room heading for her car.

That left Garrett in the bed, by himself. He couldn't believe that this perfect evening was ending like this. He still believed it was her fault, and she believed it was his fault. Garrett slammed his fist on the pillow next to him. There was a hard spot in the middle, so Garrett picked up the pillow to reveal the root Doctor

Bug had given him. The words spoken by Doctor Bug echoed in Garrett's head — *Keep this with you at all times. If you don't, things that usually point up will always point down.*

"It can't be. I don't believe that witch doctor mojo. It's not real." Garrett must have been talking to hear himself. But even as he said those words, a shiver coursed through his body.

"Damn," was all he could say. He cut off the light, pulled the covers over the bed now made for one and cursed again, "Damn."

It took him almost an hour before he could successfully move into dreamland, but not before he had sipped and then guzzled two old-fashion glasses of the cognac he had in his bedroom. Right before he fell into a deep sleep, one word was heard from the bedroom; "Damn!"

His dreams were filled with metaphors. Faucets that wouldn't work. Fountains that sputtered.

All sorts of things that had to be erect or they wouldn't work.

CHAPTER 45

It was 10:00 when Garrett's eyes opened as slits. There was a pain just above his left eye. His stomach was queasy, not to the point of a vomit, but uncomfortable, especially when coupled with the headache.

The cognac that was his friend last night was no friend the morning after. Garrett struggled to sit up in the bed. In a moment of lucidity, he reached under his pillow. There he found the three items that would be his constant companions, certainly until the auction was over — the Glock, the root and the bag with the coins in it. It was then he decided, with or without Lee, he was going on a vacation as soon as the auction was over. Somewhere where they didn't know his name. He had experienced notoriety, and now wanted it only when he wanted it, not all the time.

His movements to and in the bathroom were slow and deliberate. He took a long, hot shower. It was while sitting on the toilet that he realized he hadn't even looked at his phone. He wondered if Lee had called. He stopped before he had wiped, shuffled with his pajama bottoms bunched around his feet, to his bedside table, picked up his cell phone and shuffled back to the toilet. He sat and looked at the phone's display, looking for Lee's number. It wasn't there. There were calls from Pegge and John James. There was a call from a 202 number he didn't recognize and a call from Bob Grant.

Garrett finished his toilet. He put his phone aside and looked at the Garrett that lived in the world on the other side of the mirror. Looked wasn't the appropriate word — it was more like stared.

His mind took a short side trip, like down a rabbit trail. He wondered what it would be like, living in his world. Seeing everything backward, seeing each minor flaw as well as the major ones. Unable to speak, unable to make changes.

With that thought, his phone began to ring. As he looked from the mirror image to the phone, the thought of how sublime it would be in a world with no sound passed fleetingly through his mind.

The call was from John James. Garrett had to verify a number of details concerning the auction. Yes, he would be moving into the Presidential Suite Wednesday evening. Yes, he would be there until Sunday sometime. *Yes, Yes, Yes.* All of the details confirmed.

Garrett went back to the mirror. Considering his life for the past few weeks, he would gladly exchange places with the reverse image of himself.

"Damn you!" he yelled. With that he realized he was talking to a mirror. Was he loosing his mind? He didn't have an answer. Neither did the mirror.

Garrett shaved while trying not to look at himself. After the second nick and the toilet paper patches to stop the bleeding, he started paying attention to the job at hand; scraping the facial hair that somehow appeared each morning. Rationality walked in the bathroom, took Garrett by the shoulders and shook him rigorously.

He spoke again to the mirror image, "This is ridiculous. You are only an image of me."

He stepped back into the real world, finished his shave and completed his morning ritual. He called Bob Grant, as much as a way of checking to see if his security team was working as it was to let him know that he needed to go to the Hibernian Hall and The Mills House before lunch. He told Grant he wanted to leave in 30 minutes. Grant said he would meet Garrett at the backdoor. Garrett finished dressing and went to the kitchen for a cup of coffee. Since he had not programmed Mr. Coffee, it was a 10-minute wait. He should have time to enjoy the cup before he needed to meet Grant.

Regardless, he thought. *He works for me now. He can just wait for me.*

Garrett took his time with his coffee. Just as he was finishing his first cup, there was a knock at the backdoor. Garrett looked out the curtained window in the door to see Bob Grant standing there. Garrett opened the door.

"Good morning, Bob. Hope you have had a good day."

"Actually, my day would have been better if you had been on time. I work for you, but please be more considerate of both my time and yours."

Grant's soft commanding voice was the same as it had been the day before. It was a voice that grabbed you by the shirt collar and pulled you eye-to-eye with the speaker. It put Garrett on his heels.

Stumbling for the right words, he said, "Well. well, I'm sorry I wanted a cup of coffee, and the Mr. Coffee took longer than I thought but I'm finished now."

It was pathetic effort at an apology, but it allowed Garrett to close the door, put the cup in the sink and shake his head.

"Who does he think he is? He is going to have to start treating me as the boss here."

With that pronouncement Garrett opened the back door. It was the first thing he noticed when his feet hit the back porch. There, on the top step, was a strip of Spanish Moss. He kicked the moss off the step but a shiver went through him as he briskly walked to the waiting car.

Garrett met John James in the lobby of The Mills House. He was accompanied by Bob Grant and one of his associates. He was ushered into the Board Room to meet with the General Manager and the President of the company that owned The Mills House. They thanked Garrett for selecting The Mills House for his event. The President added that he recognized that many people who select to stay in the Presidential Suite need extra security.

The Suite was on a special floor which it shared with only four upscale, individual rooms. The entire floor had been reserved for Garrett, and access to the floor was by a special elevator operated by a key card and a security code. Garrett, alone would have control regarding who had access to that floor. He or his representative would select the number sequence that would operate the elevator. That was for his security and the protection of the hotel. There were more discussions but they were mostly between Grant and the representatives of the hotel.

Garrett looked around the room. There was a number of antiques in the room. He recognized some priceless paintings that hung on the mahogany walls. He noticed a silver tea set on one counter. There were a few expensive glass pieces. There were three carvings by local artist, Grainger McKoy. They were not in keeping with the classic décor, but fit the space and would be recognized by important local people.

Nice touch, he thought. There were a couple of what looked to be classic jade vases and, in the middle of that thought, the president addressed him.

"Mr. Garrett. This suite has been reserved for you for your stay. In addition to being a suitable office for you," and with that he picked up a small remote panel, pushed a couple of buttons, prompting three of the mahogany walls to slide out of sight and reveal a wall of video screens. A very large television screen occupied the second wall with a variety of controllers with readout screens. A third wall held an equipment setup he didn't recognize and had no idea what it was for.

The President continued, "we have customized a unique surveillance system based on the requirements of your security team. From where you are sitting, you can see the entire auction area, the images that will be shown on the screens in Hibernian Hall, your suite and the Presidential floors, including both entrances of your elevator. This will serve as your command center. It will allow your security team to have a constant observation point for visual contact with you when you are in the hotel and the Hibernian Hall and every step you make between the two. During the auction, it will be converted to an observation center to utilize two-way teleconferencing for your worldwide customers to have a secure way to bid and a way for you to have a recorded copy of their bids. Mr. Grant has been extremely thorough."

There was a lapse in his conversation as if he expected Garrett to comment.

"Very nice," was the best Garrett could come up with.

Additional conversations concerning the Board Room/command center were between the President and Bob Grant.

As he was returning to #13 Church, Lee called his cell phone. He answered and she apologized for being so emotional. His reaction was to also apologize for being so insensitive, but he added that he still didn't know what the problem was. The image of the root passed through his mind and he touched his pant pocket to make certain it was still there. He would never admit to the possible affect VooDoo had on him, his actions and the situation. They agreed to meet later for dinner at #13 Church.

"I'll take care of ordering for us," she added. It caused a twinge of that old feeling that she was intentionally taking over.

The car pulled in the back parking lot of #13 Church. Two TV news teams were on the street waiting for his arrival. Grant said something into the mouthpiece of the small microphone that made him look like the lead singer for the new vocal group, "The Giants." The other two members of the team appeared almost like magic and moved quickly to the parking entrance to block the news teams from entering the property.

Both of the news girls were yelling questions as he entered the building. One part of Garrett wanted to be interviewed like a famous person but he remembered that someone may be willing to shoot or stab him just to get their name in the media. So, he quickly moved into the building.

Grant ushered Garrett to his desk and joined him. Grandfather casually glanced over at the pair showing a modest amount of interest. These were exciting times at #13 Church, yes they were.

Grant debriefed Garrett on the morning meetings. He was satisfied that The Mills House had followed his specific directions. Garrett would be safe and secure throughout the auction. Grant said he understood that Miss Ashley, as he referred to Lee, was taking the responsibility for the evening meal. He again reminded Garrett that he was as close as his alert button which he asked to see. Garrett felt of his slacks and remembered he had put it in his desk drawer. He retrieved it to which Grant again admonished him to keep it with him at all time.

"Keep it in your pocket or under your pillow," he suggested, "good places so it is close when you need it."

Garrett was taken aback by Grant's mention of the pillow

hiding place. Does he know about his hiding place for the coins or the root? Could he be a double agent working for him but also working for that weird Brother from Mepkin? Or with Lee, if she were trying to get control of his treasure? Or with Storey? Right now, no one of those suspicions seemed more likely than another. He decided he would talk to Lee about Grant and her relationship with him at the evening meal.

Grant left and Garrett prepared a pot of coffee. The amazing aroma wafted through the kitchen of #13 Church. Garrett realized it was quiet. No one was banging on the doors. The phone wasn't ringing. It was just him and his treasure and his coffee. With the reassuring hot cup cradled in his hands, he sat at his desk. He was asleep before the second sip.

Garrett was awakened by Lee pulling on his shoulder and telling him to wake up. Still half in the world of sleep and half in the here and now, he looked at her not certain of what he was seeing.

"Lee?" he questioned. "Is that you?"

"Yes, Edward. I am me." She thought his question was dumb. He knew who it was.

"I was asleep. Have you been here long?" Garrett was having difficulty connecting with the present.

"I have been here long enough to know you were sleeping. Has anyone ever told you that you make horrible noises when you are sleeping?"

Garrett did realize it was a rhetorical question and didn't even try to answer.

Lee added, "I've got the table set and placed the food. Are you ready to eat?" That was another rhetorical question.

Lee stayed the night. It was the first time they had been intimate in weeks, discounting the debacle of the previous night. Garrett checked to make sure the root was under his pillow along with the emergency remote button, the Glock and the coins. Garrett smiled as he thought, *before long I am going to have to get a larger pillow.*

Love making was tender, demanding at times, but considered successful by both. As he was putting out the bedside light, Garrett remembered he had not discussed Grant with Lee. Maybe tomorrow.

Today was a day of satisfaction, certainly the evening was.

Darkness and the rhythmic breathing of a beautiful woman sleeping beside him helped Garrett go to sleep. His dreams were filled with a variety of situations but one thing was constant.

He was alone in each.

CHAPTER 46

When Garrett awoke on Wednesday morning, Lee had already left for work. He was disappointed. He had wanted to pick up where the evening left off.

Garrett slipped on his robe. He put the root and the coins in one pocket and the emergency call button and the Glock in the other. That didn't work. He tried the emergency button, the root and the coins in the other. Still didn't work. The Glock is just too heavy. He finally decided that if he left the Glock in the bedroom, at least while he was in #13 Church, it made no difference how he divided the other items. So, armed with Grant's emergency remote button, Doctor Bug's root and his coins, Garrett retired to the kitchen where Lee had started Mr. Coffee before she left for work.

He poured himself a cup of coffee to start and decided he wanted a good breakfast. He made his famous shrimp omelet, grits, bagels, a slice of ripe tomato, some orange juice and another cup of coffee. Sitting at his kitchen table, he savored his favorite breakfast. As he was putting the dishes in the dish washer, his cell phone rang. Grant's number that appeared on the caller ID.

"Yes?"

"Mr. Garrett. There's a gentleman here to see you. He doesn't have an appointment but you may want to see him."

"See who? I'm not dressed, I'm in my robe. Besides I've got to pack to move to The Mills House."

"You may want to slip on some casual clothes and meet me at your desk. Cardinal Guscipi Vassilli, curator of the Vatican Musea is here to see you."

There was a pause.

"Yeah, you're right. Give me five minutes and escort him into the foyer. I'll be down in a few minutes when I'm presentable."

This is an honor he didn't expect. Grant escorted the Cardinal into the foyer of Garrett's home and his office. Grant offered him a chair but he was told that the Cardinal would stand until Mr. Garrett returned. Grandfather looked askance at the Cardinal. He had never seen a real live Cardinal before, but what did he care? He was Episcopal.

Only a few minutes had elapsed when Garrett appeared at the top of the stairs and descended to the foyer. He greeted the Cardinal with a slight bow. The Cardinal extended his hand exposing a beautiful ornate ring with a large red stone, probably a ruby, held in place by 4 crosses, and Garrett shook his hand.

After all, he was Episcopal.

He offered a seat to the Cardinal. The Cardinal complimented Garrett on the store and specifically mentioned two items that were very valuable, so Garrett would have an appreciation for the Cardinal's experience and training.

Garrett thanked him.

"Mr. Garrett, what is the marvelous aroma here in your home?" The Cardinal spoke perfect English with not even the hint of an accent.

"Well, Sir, I have just finished my morning meal, and you could say the menu was one of my own concoctions."

"Could that be a shrimp omelet I smell?"

"Why, you are correct. It was a shrimp, western omelet."

"I miss not being here in Charleston. I spent a couple of years at Mepkin as an initiate in the order. I was sort of like Brother Andrew, whom you met. I, too, have ties to Opus Dei organization. I developed a great appreciation for fresh shrimp. Fond memories of Charleston."

With that, the Cardinal shifted from a conversational tone to a more formal one.

"I am told that you may have in your possession a small box that may have some interest to The Church. The Holy Father has asked me to return to Charleston to investigate this matter."

"Sir, Father, I don't know the proper way to address you. I met with the Brother and I thought I was very clear to him. In all due respect to you, sir, the Holy Father and the Brother, as I told him, the box would likely be placed on sale at the auction on Saturday. Pardon my shortness, but I thought I was exceedingly clear to the Brother."

"Well, Mr. Garrett, we think the box contains some items that are valuable to The Church, items that are actually property of The Church, and would have little value to collectors."

Garrett couldn't believe how naive the Cardinal thought he was.

"Sir, you are welcome at the auction. All of the items that are to be auctioned are in a safe place and nowhere near here. That is a precaution I was advised to put in place, since some of the auction items are of extreme value. I'm sure you understand, as I understand there are significant precautions taken with the extremely valuable items in the Vatican archives. Your treasures, Sir."

The Cardinal changed his demeanor with Garrett's comment.

"Mr. Garrett, if we are correct and the coins are in the box, I must warn you that they could have a curse on them. I will be at the auction. Please allow us the final bid on the box."

"We'll see." Garrett closed the conversation by standing. The Cardinal followed, shook Garrett's hand and turned for the door. When he reached the door, he turned back to face Garrett.

"Dio la Benedica," he said as he made the sign of the cross. He left and closed the door behind him.

"For future reference, Mr. Garrett, when a principal leader of The Church offers his hand to you and he is wearing an ornate ring, it is proper to kiss the ring."

Grant was trying to help Garrett in his dealings with The Church.

"When a person offers his hand here in America, it is an offer for a hand shake," Garrett said back to Grant, and closed the conversation by saying, "When in Rome ..."

Garrett walked up the stairs. At the landing, he turned and said he was going to pack for the five days at The Mills House.

CHAPTER 47

Garrett packed for four days, but to look at the luggage, you would have thought he was staying at The Mills House for four weeks. He started moving the luggage onto the third-floor landing. Two of the security team appeared at his quarters without a call and took all the bags from Garrett, leaving him nothing to do except to walk down the stairs with his shoulder bag containing his root, the coins, the emergency button and his Glock.

He, his luggage and the security were loaded in two cars for the trip to The Mills House. They were greeted at a special private entrance by the General Manager, the butlers who would handle all of Garrett's needs while he was a guest in the hotel and a beautiful young woman whom he had not met.

Grant handled everything. Garrett was sent to his suite along with a member of the security team and the young woman. Garrett was ushered into the living room while the security man searched the other rooms in the suite. The young woman made small talk while she verified the contents of the bar and the kitchen. She asked Garrett if he had any special requirements for beer, wine or snacks.

Garrett suggested a couple of brands of beer and wine and some snack names. She verified that they were all stocked in the refrigerator, the wine cooler and the pantry. She carried a couple of bowls of cashews which she placed around the living room.

Garrett was amazed that all of his favorites were already available for him. The young woman told him that she was available at number 7 on his house phone. The butlers were on number 5. The manager on number 3. If he wanted any of the guest rooms, press O and the operator would connect him. The young woman told him that she would act as his executive assistant/secretary during his stay in the hotel. She would screen his calls and make calls for him. She also would handle any correspondence for him and be his liaison with hotel staff — housekeeping, room service etc.

As she turned to leave the room, Garrett noticed, for the first time, she was wearing a silver cross. He thanked her and she again reminded Garrett she was as close as number 7 on his house phone.

As the elevator doors closed, Garrett started wondering, could she be here to watch him? Could she be an operative of The Church? Could she be working for the Opus Dei Brother? Could she *be* Opus Dei? Could she be placed there by Lee to see if he was true to her? There could be dozens of people she could be working for. Or she could be working for herself. Lots of people knew about the Find and its probable worth. He touched the shoulder bag, making a vow to keep it near.

With that thought, the elevator doors opened again to a flurry of action resulting in his bags being moved into his sleeping room, hanging clothes in his closet, computer on his desk, toilet articles placed in his bathroom. It was so organized it looked like a ballet. As most of the dancers collected at the elevator door, Grant brought Garrett a glass of wine and sat in a chair near him and took out a notebook, which he handed to Garrett.

"This, Mr. Garrett, is your handbook. It contains the minute-by-minute …"

Garrett interrupted Grant's monologue. "My what? What is a minute by minute?"

Grant picked up right where he had stopped. "Your schedule for the next three and a half days. Everyone involved with the auction has a copy of what is in here that relates to them. They have been instructed that we will be following this to the letter. That means we will be following it to the letter, as will you. There will be times when you will not be needed, so during those times, you are free to do what you want. Those times are in blue in the book. But when you are expected to be somewhere, those times are in red. Please be courteous to the people who are working with you and for you. Be prompt. Otherwise, one of the security team will be sent to find you. The emergency call button is also a GPS, so we will know your whereabouts at all times."

Again Garrett interrupted, "Why is that important?"

Grant gave Garrett with an incredulous look.

"Mr. Garrett, you have hired us, or we have been hired by your organization, to make certain that you are protected, but an additional part of our assignment is to make certain that everything goes off without a hitch. We will do both jobs. This notebook is the way we will make certain we do the best job possible. This book tells everyone, and that includes you, Mr. Garrett, where they are supposed to be, doing the things they are supposed to be doing throughout the assignment. There are many people utilizing the book to do their jobs. That is why we are on page 25 right now."

Grant flipped to page 25 in his book. There was a big bookmark there.

"You see that we are in the middle of your orientation. In 15 minutes you are expected to be in Hibernian Hall to view the progress. Your baggage is in place and we are in orientation. So all you have to do for the next few days is refer to this schedule and you will know where you need to be and what you need to be doing. Do you understand?"

Garrett's old insecurity began to surface.

"What if I want to do something else? After all, this is *my* auction of *my* Find."

"That may be true, Mr. Garrett, but, it is *my* job to make you happy with the results of this auction; and I am very good at that. Very Good. So please be where the book says for you to be when the book says to be there."

With that Grant closed his book and told Garrett he had to be doing his job and he was expected in Hibernian Hall in 12 minutes.

Garrett got up from his chair and moved to the window. He could see Hibernian Hall and flocks of people scurrying around — all working for him. He felt completely inadequate for that responsibility. So it was Grant's job.

"Well, we'll see, Mr. Grant," Garrett said out loud. "We'll see just how well you do your job."

Grant added, "Time to be heading to Hibernian Hall."

Garrett picked up his shoulder bag and his book and boarded his elevator with his destination in mind. He was intercepted by one of the members of his security team who was to escort him to the auction hall. He was told that he could recognized each member of the security team by the special colored daily lapel button.

"That would be easy with or without the button." he reasoned. Just look for the tallest people in the place.

They walked over to the hall. Garrett passed a dozen people and none seemed to know it was his project. His bodyguard opened the side door, the one closest to The Mills House. Before he allowed Garrett to enter, he looked inside.

He then told Garrett, "Whenever you need to move around this place, please make sure one of us is with you. One of us will be at the bottom of the elevator. Later tonight one of our team will be at the entrance of the elevator as well as at the bottom. It's ok inside, so we can enter."

Garrett was absolutely shocked when he entered the hall. The video pod was hung from the ceiling in the middle of the hall. The video team was centering and synchronizing video material. He could see the pictures of one of the swords. It was magnificent. There were detail pictures flanking the primary picture. The image was perfect, even though it was tilted to be seen better, there was no perceptible key stoning. It looked very professional. The sound team was setting speakers to provide an even sound signature over the entire room. A single tone was being amplified and a dozen people were running around with db meters taking readings as they talked into headsets.

Other teams were setting up the beverage bars and the refreshment tables. Bob Grant was talking to a group of uniformed police officers and a few other people who looked like body builders, probably additional security. The moment he saw Garrett, he motioned for him of come to where he was standing. He then signaled to one of the sound guys and he immediately brought him a wireless microphone.

When Garrett arrived, Grant whispered in his ear, "Mr. Garrett, these people are working very hard for you. They need some encouragement from you."

With that Grant pushed the *on* button on the microphone and announced for all to hear; "Attention everyone." All work stopped. "I would like to introduce you to the person who is making all this possible. This is Mr. Edward Garrett."

Garrett was surprised at the applause he received. It was remarkable. Grant handed the mic to Garrett.

"First of all, I would like to thank each and every one of you for helping to make this event possible." More applause. "Without each of you and your contribution, one of the most important events in the antique world would not happen." More applause. "So thank you, from the bottom of my heart." More applause. Garrett couldn't believe what he had said — neither could Grant. Grant smiled at Garrett.

"I didn't think you had that in you, Mr. Garrett. Good job."

Garrett wasn't sure if that was a compliment or an insult.

"Now you have another place to be," Grant said as he pointed to the book. Garrett checked the book and saw he was scheduled to be on the parking deck to meet with the caterers.

That was repeated the rest of Wednesday afternoon. Visit a work site, be impressed, make some comments which were pretty much the same in each location. Nowhere was the reception as reassuring as the groups in Hibernian Hall. Garrett was beginning to feel important.

It was precisely 6 p.m. when he returned to The Mills House. He was ushered into the hotel conference room that doubled as his office. The beautiful young woman was there with a stack of messages. The room was filled with flowers and gifts. Per Grant, gifts were to be checked by the security checking point at the airport. Grant must have some influential friends. Garrett's cell was at the head of the table along with an executive writing set up.

Just like a first-class executive office., Garrett thought.

Grant entered the room as soon as Garrett was seated.

"We have reviewed your messages and prioritized them for you. There were a few threats, but we don't consider any of them to be credible. Mostly wackos. There was a call from the director of the local office of the IRS. I suggest you contact him tomorrow.

"There were a few calls from the local FBI office. The head of the local office is a friend of mine and I let him know that you were on the up and up and would contact him after the auction was over. He seemed satisfied.

There was one message — well, I just don't know what to do with it. Do you know a Doctor Bug?"

Garrett confirmed that he knew the witch doctor from Saint Helena's Island.

"Why?"

"Well, a nice African-American lady left a package at the front desk and said to tell you that it was for protection from Doctor Bug."

Garrett said he had known Doctor Bug for some time and he was certain it was safe. He added, "And from what I am seeing in this office and from what you say, I'm going to need all of the protection I can get."

The package was given to Garrett and he slipped it into his shoulder bag.

"There was also a message from Cardinal Vissilli, who is also a guest here in the hotel, saying he hoped you had changed your mind and that he is here if you want to talk to him. Dinner will be at 8 p.m., and I have taken the liberty of inviting Miss Ashley to join you. I hope that is alright with you."

Garrett glanced at the beautiful young woman and saw no change in her demeanor or expression. He looked at Grant and said, "Sure, no problem. I look forward to seeing Lee."

Grant escorted Garrett to his suite and immediately left. Garrett walked around the suite before he sat in the recliner in front of the TV. He found the remote and turned on the local news on Channel 5 to see what else was happening in The Holy City, local slang for Charleston.

There was a picture of #13 Church and the announcer was beginning the story. "This is the location of what is becoming the focal point of the biggest news event in Charleston this year. What is being described as the biggest antique and historical find in recent history is unfolding as we are speaking.

"We are live from #13 Church Street, the home and Antique Store of Edward Garrett, prominent local antique dealer, who will be hosting the auction that has brought celebrities, the elite of the antique world and even a personal representative of His Imminence the Pope.

"Sally Williams, what is going on here in Charleston?"

With that introduction, the girl started talking. "We have been here since early morning. Here is video of Cardinal Guscipi Vassilli, who we understand, is the curator of the Vatican's art collection and head of the famed Vatican museum and library. He was unwilling to comment on what in the auction would interest the Vatican or His Holiness. The Cardinal was inside #13 Church Street for 20 minutes and had nothing to say to the media gathered here. Not long after the Cardinal left, two cars left the back of the building. That is the latest from #13 Church Street. Sally Williams reporting live."

The local anchor continued, "We have been receiving reports that we haven't been able to confirm, that Edward Garrett is currently sequestered at The Mills House. We will interrupt programming when we have more information. Now to Meteorologist Ben Moore for the latest weather."

With that, Garrett pressed the power button on the remote.

Silence.

Garrett sat in the recliner looking at the blank screen. The local anchor called him prominent. After all these years, he was being noticed. And the television station would interrupt programming when they had more information about his auction. A part of him couldn't believe his eyes and ears.

Grant knocked on the door, entered and announced that Miss Ashley was here. Garrett stood when Lee entered the room. After an awkward moment, they embraced and kissed.

"Are you excited?" she asked.

All Garrett could say was "Yes."

Food was being carried into the dining room as Garrett told Lee about the news report. His descriptions lasted until the butler on duty came to the sitting area and announced that dinner was served. Garrett and Lee continued to talk through dinner. Lee reminded him that he had promised Pegge an exclusive interview. He said he remembered, and asked when that would be appropriate. She suggested Thursday morning. She could meet him over breakfast here in the suite.

"Will you let her know, Lee?" Garrett asked.

"Sure," was her reply.

"Is everything ok between us?" Garrett asked.

"Edward, this is a high-pressure time for you. The Find will change your life. I believe you are already seeing that. Because I am the Senator's daughter, I have lived with notoriety all my life. It is a hard thing to deal with. You are beginning to see what I mean. It has its benefits, but there are definitely drawbacks. I really don't think anything has changed between us, but we need to get through this weekend, and then talk about where we go from there."

"You sound like you are ending our relationship."

"No, I am not. And I hope nothing changes. But you need to concentrate on the auction." Garrett looked like a wounded puppy. Lee got up out of her chair and sat in Garrett's lap.

"I'm going to be just down the hall until the auction is over. I will be here to do everything I need to do to make the auction a success. Actually, most of the responsibility is Bob Grant's."

"How do you know him, Lee?"

"I told you before, he was the senior member of a detail that Washington suggested to the Senator when the President visited here a few years ago. That's where I met him. He and his wife and kids were our guests at our Hilton Head compound."

"He is very demanding."

"He is very good. He is a retired Special Forces colonel and was hired by a Saudi Prince to head his security detail. He was working for Blackwater when we hired him. He is in great demand and is here as a favor to my family."

"Are you sure there is nothing between you and him?"

"Edward, shame on you. He is 20 years older than me. He's married and has three children. And he's a Christian, for God's sake."

"OK. He just seems very protective of you."

At that moment there was a knock on the door and in walked Bob Grant. Following him was a giant Baked Alaska, carried by two of the hotel's hospitality wait staff.

"Time for dessert," Grant announced.

Lee continued to sit on Garrett's lap.

"Bob, Edward thinks there is something between you and me."

"Thank you, Mr. Garrett. Miss Ashley is one of the sweetest, smartest and best-looking young women I know. However, the only woman more desirable to me than Miss Ashley is a short,

Irish spitfire named Mrs. Grant. She owns my heart and always will." It was the first time Garrett had seen the man smile. Maybe that was true.

The wait staff served the pair their Baked Alaska and everyone exited the room, leaving the couple alone.

"Let's go to the bedroom," Garrett looked at Lee with a big boyish smile.

Lee responded, "Edward, I'm going ..." she paused. "I'm going to leave you alone here in your suite, and I am going down the hall to mine. You need your sleep tonight and so do I. I have a big day tomorrow. You have a big morning with Pegge and you have a big weekend ahead of you." She kissed him, "Edward, I love you." Lee left him sitting at the dinning room table.

Garrett looked at his watch. 9:00. What could he do? There was a knock at his door and in walked the maid, the butler, the bus boy and the beautiful young woman who was assigned as his secretary.

"How was dinner, Mr. Garrett?" the butler asked. Garrett replied it was outstanding.

"I am going in to prepare your bed for the evening," the maid told Garrett as she moved smartly from the dining room to the master suite. The bus boy cleared the remaining silver and plates from the table and wiped it thoroughly and left the room.

The butler stood to the side and the beautiful young woman said, "I have reviewed tomorrow's schedule with Mr. Grant. Everything in your office is ready for you."

"Pegge Ravenal will be here tomorrow morning for an interview. Can you make arrangements for her to be escorted here?"

"Certainly, Mr. Garrett."

Garrett turned to the butler.

"Will you make arrangements for coffee and pastries here in the suite at 8:00? Unless I let you know otherwise, there will be two."

"Certainly, Mr. Garrett."

"Your room is ready, Mr. Garrett."

"Thank you."

The maid and the butler left the room and the beautiful young woman asked, "Is there anything else I can do, Mr. Garrett?"

The question seemed to hang there in the air.

"No. Thank you."

With that, she turned and left the room. Had there been a pin hanging in the air somewhere and it hit the floor, you would have heard it drop.

Garrett roamed around the Presidential suite, not knowing what to do. He walked back into the kitchen to get another beer. Then he changed his mind. He was a special guest in a special suite. He would drink something special. He looked in the liquor cabinet and found an impressive Cognac. He filled a large snifter half full and started looking for a warming candle. One wasn't obvious so he carried the glass over to the recliner.

A push of one button on the remote converted the large black screen into a virtual entertainment cornucopia. Garrett sat in the recliner, cupping his hands around the snifter to warm the golden liquor and release the pungent aroma of the fine Cognac.

He was tempted to leave it on the local news channel so he could see the stories about him again. He decided that he wanted some mindless television, so he started changing the channel. NASCAR racing,

No.

Professional football.

No.

International Soccer league. No. International Soccer league in Spanish. No. International Soccer league in French. No. No. No. Old movie. No. Shopping Channel. No. Infomercial. No.

There were more channels on this TV than he had at home. He kept it up for another few minutes and decided to leave it on a channel that played old international movies with English sub titles. The visuals were mind-numbing. He muted the sound so that he had silent movies with the dialogue in English sub titles. He sat in a visual stupor as he sipped the marvelous liquor, allowing it to titillate his taste buds. The aroma brought his smell sensors to life.

The last thought he remembered was that this was indeed civilized.

CHAPTER 48

At 7:00 a.m. Grant knocked on the door and entered the Presidential Suite. He found Garrett in the recliner exactly where he was the night before. The empty snifter was cradled in his right hand and his left hand was on the remote. As Grant looked at the man he was responsible for, his thought was; *if the sculpture of David exemplified Renaissance Man, then a sculpture of Garrett in this position would exemplify modern man.*

Grant awakened Garrett with the suggestion that he shower because Pegge Ravenel would be there in 60 minutes. It took Garrett a couple of minutes to re-enter the world he left only hours before. He dropped the snifter which broke precisely where the bowl was attached to the stem.

"Damn," he said.

Grant said, "Go shower, I'll take care of the mess."

Garrett was showered, shaved and dressed in 45 minutes, leaving time for a cup of coffee. He went into the kitchen to look for the Mr. Coffee he was accustomed to. The only thing in the kitchen that looked like a coffee maker had water in it and cups next to it but there was also a wire carousel that held little plastic cups with various names of coffee on them. He grabbed the telephone and pressed the number of the butler.

"Good Morning, Mr. Garrett. How can I help you?"

"I don't know how to make coffee in this kitchen. Where's the Mr. Coffee?"

"I'll be right there."

"Would you like Italian Roast, or maybe Mocha Java, or a nice African Arabica or a blend of mild beans."

"Just give me a damn cup of coffee. Italian Roast, I guess."

Garrett watched as the butler slipped the small cup into the front of the machine, pressed words on the touch screen and pressed the *start* button. Within seconds the dark brown liquid was filling the cup as the wonderful aroma was filling the room.

Garrett said to the butler, "Well, that new-fangled contraption looks like it has merit. I may have to retire my Mr. Coffee."

As Garrett took his first sip of modern brewed coffee, there was a knock on the door to the suite and Grant ushered Pegge Ravenel and a photographer into the sitting room. Garrett walked in from the kitchen at the same time. The butler asked Pegge if she would like coffee. She said she would like an Arabica if he had one. The photographer accepted one too.

Garrett spent an hour with Pegge. He provided many of the specifics that she had already received from John James. Occasionally, he prattleed on about an item, Pegge courteously listened like she was interested. She finally got to the point.

"Tell me, Edward, what one item is the mind-blower of the collection."

Garrett wanted to tell her about the coins but couldn't bring himself to because he still wasn't sure he would sell them. Pegge coaxed Garrett and begged him but Garrett wouldn't budge.

"OK," Pegge finally said, "I'll just be as vague as you are. And we will see." Her article would run on Friday morning.

Grant reappeared indicating that Garrett had a call he needed to take. Pegge thanked Garrett for his time and she said that the photographer had taken pictures of Garrett during the interview and she would get the necessary pictures of the items she would include in her article. And she and the photographer left.

Garrett was more than a little miffed. Now Grant was deciding whose calls he should take?

"Who is on the phone?" Garrett asked.

"The local IRS director would like to talk with you. He can stop the auction if you don't meet with him, so ...?" Garrett answered the IRS director's questions and, ultimately invited him and his representative to be his guest at the auction.

"He just wanted to make sure he got the government's share of the proceeds," he said to Grant who already knew the reason for the call.

Grant invited Garrett back to the dining room table.

"Now, Mr. Garrett, today is Thursday. There is only one thing that you need to do today. We need for you to review the images and the announcer's script to make sure the right words are with the right images. Is that alright with you?"

Garrett asked if he would be doing that at Hibernian Hall and Grant said, No, security concerns required him to remain in the suite.

"I'm getting tired of this suite," Garrett told Grant.

"Tired of this opulence?" Grant asked.

"Well," Garrett tried to explain, "When I am here by myself, it's sort of lonely."

"I'll send someone up to keep you company."

There was a tone in Grant's voice that Garrett didn't like. And for his part, Grant didn't understand Garrett.

"Would you like brunch?"

"Yes, I guess I would."

"I'll send the butler up. He'll take care of that." Grant left the room and Garrett was alone again.

Fifteen minutes later, John James knocked on the door and waited for Garrett to open it. He carried a laptop into the room. The beautiful young woman followed him. Garrett was directed to sit at the dining room table. The butler and a member of the wait staff entered. The waiter asked if he could bring a brunch buffet to the room so Garrett could make his own selections. Garrett agreed and asked John James to join him for brunch.

John James declined the invitation and began to show Garrett how to use the computer so that he could check the images and descriptions for the auction. Garrett confirmed that he understood and John James left the room.

"Where would you like me to go," the beautiful young woman asked Garrett.

"I'm sorry," Garrett said. "What do you mean?"

"Well, Mr. Grant said I was to keep you company."

"I'm sorry, my dear," Garrett was almost laughing, "Mr. Grant misunderstood what I said. I don't need you here. You can go back to the office." Garrett couldn't believe he was sending the beautiful young woman away — but he was.

Garrett began working on the script that would be the basis

for the presentation on Saturday. He looked at the images and at what the announcer would say before he turned it over to the auctioneer. There would be 350 lots auctioned. Garrett had gotten through the first 17 lots when the knock on the door distracted him.

In walked the butler, followed by the waiter pushing a hot and cold rolling buffet cart. Garrett had started getting hungry, and the presence of the cart made the feeling even stronger. He restrained himself until the waiter had positioned the cart, made final adjustments to the food offerings and motioned to Garrett that it was ready. Garrett thanked him, walked over and picked up a plate. While he was making his selections, the waiter prepared his coffee and water, and his mango juice. Garrett made his selection.

"Do you have any bagels?" he asked the waiter.

The waiter indicated they did and left the room to fetch bagels for him. Garrett carried his plate to the table where he was working.

"Will you be needing anything else, Mr. Garrett?" asked the butler. Garrett said "No," and the butler said he would wait for the waiter and escort him downstairs when he returned with Garrett's bagel.

Garrett worked diligently on his assignment. Having the proper information and comments would allow the auctioneer to get top dollar for each item. Five hours later, he was still at the computer. Trips to the bathroom and back to the buffet were his only breaks. His back was beginning to hurt.

Based on his calculations, he was nearly finished. He stood, stretched, walked to the window to check on progress in the parking deck. He could see that many of the vendors were already setting up.

This should be an event that will set a new standard, even here in Charleston.

Garrett called the butler.

"Yes Mr. Garrett. What can I do for you?"

"Does the hotel have a massage therapist for in room service?"

"Why, yes we do? Would you like a massage?"

Garrett almost said, "No. I was just curious." Instead of being a smart ass, he just said, "Yes, please."

"Male or female?"

"Female, please."

"One will be here in 15 minutes."

Should he finish the computer work, or take a hot bath? The bath won. Garrett had just walked into the sitting room wearing the hotel robe when there was a knock on the front door. The butler entered followed by a healthy woman near Garrett's age, carrying a massage table and wearing a backpack. The butler directed the therapist where to set-up and walked to where Garrett was standing.

"The massage is complements of the hotel, sir."

Garrett fell dead asleep some time during the massage. He woke with a start, not knowing where he was. He reached for his pillow. It was gone. He sat up.

"Where's my pillow," he yelled. It certainly sounded childish. It shocked the therapist. The security team member stationed just outside the door ran into the room with his pistol drawn. It took a couple of minutes for things to get sorted out. Garrett was embarrassed. He apologized to the therapist and the guard. He blamed the hours working on the computer. Everyone left the room except the therapist who was waiting for her table.

It was then that Garrett realized he was naked. He grabbed the sheet on the table and his robe and retreated to the bedroom suite. He returned to the sitting room and again apologized to the therapist. He handed her a $100 bill. She said she was already paid, but he insisted since he had put her to extra trouble. She finished packing the table, picked up her back pack and left the room.

Garrett walked across the room to the liquor cabinet and poured a generous cognac. He returned to the computer to finish his assigned task.

It was almost 6:00 o'clock when he finished. His cell phone had rung once, but he ignored it. This time he looked at the readout. It was Lee.

"Hi. Where are you?"

"I'm just leaving the paper. Want company?"

"Sure."

"See you in a few."

Garrett decided to stay in the robe. "Maybe Lee will stay the night. A little company is just what I need." Garrett was speaking aloud. His phone rang again, this time it was Grant.

"Do you want your evening meal for two?"

"What?"

"You said the Miss Ashley may spend the night. Would you like dinner for two?"

"How did you know?"

"The room is wired. I can hear everything that goes on. It is a security precaution."

"Understand me, Mr. Grant. When Lee is here with me, you are to turn off the sound. Do you hear me?"

"Certainly, Mr. Garrett. Certainly."

Lee did spend the night. The dinner was excellent but the company wasn't. They disagreed about almost everything. Even their lovemaking was unfulfilling.

Finally, around 10:30, in frustration, Lee said she was going to sleep in her suite. She was mad and disappointed. He was mad and disappointed. Those were the only things that they had agreed on all evening. Lee went to her bedroom. Garrett spread out in the recliner with a large snifter of Cognac.

By 11:00, he was repeating the night before.

CHAPTER 49

Lee left her suite at sun up. She checked on Garrett and saw him asleep in the recliner, totally naked.

That should be embarrassing enough for him, she thought. *Serves him right.*

The chasm between Lee and Garrett had been widening for some time. Garrett, who had always been a little weird, had gotten worse. He had always been a little insecure about some things; now it was a lot and about everything. He wouldn't let anyone who had been hired to handle parts of the auction do what they had been hired to do. He wanted them to explain what they were doing. People cringed when they saw him coming.

Lee left The Mills House through a private exit, found her car and headed for the paper. It was Friday morning. Dress rehearsal day. Any necessary final touches or changes had to be made by noon Friday. Garrett was expected at 10:30 for a final inspection, so that slight changes could be accomplished. A full dress run through was to start at 1:30. It would be over at 4:00. The entire crew would be released at 4:00 except the security detail who would be in charge of the hall until Saturday morning.

At 9:00 sharp, the butler knocked on Garrett's door — again — again. No answer. The Security Team member on duty alerted Grant. Grant was staying in one of the rooms on that floor. He used his key card to enter the room. Garrett was in essentially the same position as he was when Lee had checked on him before leaving for work. Grant approached Garrett, checked for a pulse and yelled, "Mr. Garrett, wake up! And put on some clothes."

Garrett jumped up and realized he was naked. He tried to cover himself as best he could with the brandy snifter. It didn't cover much and even though there wasn't much to cover, he did the best he could. He was running to the bedroom when he caught his foot on the edge of a rug. He stumbled, tossing the snifter against the wall. He fell, sprawling, bruising both his knees and his pride. He stood, apologized, covering himself with his hands and walked, haltingly, thanks to the bruised knees to the bedroom. It was all Grant could do to keep from bursting out in laughter. He maintained control but couldn't keep the smile from appearing on his face.

When Garrett returned to the sitting room he was shaved, dressed and, from all outward indications, without any residual effects from the Cognac of the previous evening. It was 9:45 and time for breakfast before the technical run-through that started at 10:30. Garrett told the Security Guard that he wanted to eat breakfast in the hotel dining room. The Security Team member said he didn't think that would be a good idea and suggested he call Grant. Garrett blew up. He didn't need Grant's permission to go have breakfast. He was tired of being treated like a child. He was having breakfast in the restaurant of The Mills House. *Period!*

Garrett opened the door, called the elevator, entered it when it arrived and headed for the restaurant. He hadn't taken 10 steps before being surrounded by media people asking questions, well-wishers wishing him well, and a variety of people asking for money. He quickly got behind the Security Team member who backed him into the elevator.

"Damn," was all Garrett could say.

Back in the Presidential suite, Garrett sat in the recliner. He was amazed by the press of people.

Grant opened the door and addressed Garrett. "What the hell were you thinking? There are reasons why you are sequestered in this room. Your security has been entrusted to me and to us. No more trips to the lobby without the entire Security Team, and only then when the coast has been cleared. I don't want your blood on my hands." Grant turned on his heels and left the room.

Garrett called room service and almost immediately the butler entered the room.

"How can I assist you, Mr. Garrett?"

Garrett said he wanted some breakfast; eggs and bacon, biscuits and coffee. He sat in his recliner and shook his head.

"Wow. Unbelievable." That was all he could say.

Grant told Garrett when it was time to go to Hibernian Hall.

The technical check went perfectly. Craft Services wheeled a buffet cart into the hall for Garrett, the crew and the security team assembled there. Grant asked Garrett if steamed oysters by Bowen's Island was to his liking for lunch. It was Garrett's favorite, or at least one of his favorites. The oysters were the centerpiece of a sumptuous buffet for all the workers.

Once lunch was finished, the dress rehearsal started, promptly at 1:30. There were stops when something didn't go exactly right. There were at lease a dozen production assistants. making notes. There was little for Garrett to do, so he decided he would just watch. He was happily surprised at how impressive the production was. Regardless of Garrett's opinion of him, Bob Grant knew his business. By 4:30, Grant called a wrap and everyone started heading for the exits. The first opened door caused a rush of people wanting to get inside and get to Garrett.

Grant yelled, "Stop!" Everyone stopped, crew, technicians, even the people from outside.

"Everyone back to their places. Security get these other people out of here." Grant found a microphone and when the entrances had been secured, Grant talked into the mic.

"This was the first breach of our security. There will not be a second. If I catch someone violating the rules we have in place to maintain the security of this building, you will be fired on the spot and blackballed from our company events forever. Any questions?"

Silence.

"OK. Security Team, get the doors ready for our people to leave."

The two front doors of Hibernian Hall were opened with two Security Team members at each door. Crew and technicians were allowed to leave. The public wasn't allowed to enter.

"Now, Mr. Garrett, what do you think of your production?" Grant asked Garrett in a totally civilized voice.

"I must say I am impressed, Mr. Grant. Very impressed."

"Functions like this one are our real business. I am glad you are pleased," Grant added.

"Now, Mr. Garrett, let's go back to the Presidential Suite for a cocktail or two before dinner and an early bed time. Miss Ashley will be staying in her suite at the hotel. You two do what you want, but I need you up and ready for a long day at 9:00 o'clock tomorrow morning. Final Dress Rehearsal will start at 11:00. We will run through the entire show. Final Technical Rehearsal will start promptly at 3:00 pm. Food will be sent in for you when you get hungry. Let's get the rest of the Security Team and get you back to The Mills House."

Grant waved to the Team members, doors between the Hibernian Hall and the Mills House were unlocked and the team formed a ring around Garrett. As they headed out of the door to the walkway between the Hibernian Hall and The Mills House, the mass or people who were gathered outside pressed into the team and Garrett.

"Just keep moving," Grant said to Garrett. "As long as you are with us, you will be safe."

They got to the hotel and to the private elevator. Garrett immediately went to the bathroom for a shower. The hot water cascading over his body washed some of the stress from him. It seemed like each of the shower heads was aimed at a place on Garrett's body that was hurting. Friday was coming to a close.

Tomorrow is the big day.

His shower complete, Garrett found a towel, dried, and started looking for the Presidential Suite robe. It was soft and lush and felt like piles of soft cotton when he slipped it on. He started to walk back to the sitting room, wearing only the robe but thought better of and before opening the door between the bedroom and the sitting room he slipped on the bottoms of his PJs. It was a good thing because Grant, Lee, John James and two of the Security Team were having drinks at the dining room table. The topic of discussion was how well everything had gone today. As Garrett entered the room, Grant was announcing the Saturday schedule.

"The final dress rehearsal is at 11:00, the final tech rehearsal is at 3:00, call is at 4:30, the event doors open at 6:45 and the big show starts at 8:00. That is a little early for our customers on the west coast, but if they are serious, they will be happy to be able to bid on line, or they will already be here to bid in person. I'm going to bed early and I suggest you all do the same. We do owe thanks to Edward Garrett for making all of this possible. Thank you, Edward."

Garrett realized that this was the first time Bob Grant had acknowledged him. There was applause. Garrett smiled and accepted the accolade with a casual but appreciative, almost shy, gesture.

"I was thinking that we should all have a drink to celebrate a successful auction and an event to remember for all of Charleston." Garrett walked over to the bar as he was talking and filled a snifter with cognac. He offered the bottle to the others. With everyone holding a glass, he said, "To success. I am pleased to host this fantastic event. It will surpass even my wildest expectations."

He should have stopped with, "To success." But as was normal for Garrett, he pressed for everyone to recognize him. Everyone in the room already knew that the success of the event would rest with everyone except Garrett.

As the room began to empty, Garrett walked over to Lee.

"Are you going to have dinner with me?"

"I've already committed to eat with Bob and his wife. She has come to town for the event. Besides, you need your rest. Tomorrow is your big day. You need to be able to take advantage of it. Sleep well. I'll see you in the morning."

Lee walked past Garrett and out of the door. She was the last to leave. There he was — Thomas Edward Garrett, standing on the edge of the biggest day of his life with no one beside him. An old song played in his mind; *Alone again, naturally.* He reached for the cognac bottle and his snifter as he walked over to the recliner. There he was again, snifter in one hand remote in the other, just as he was last night — with one difference; he had clothes on.

The aroma from the cognac was calming. The mind-numbing television selections were mind numbing. About 30 minutes after the Presidential Suite had cleared, Garrett stood on his way to the bathroom. His eyes were drawn to the box that was left for him by Doctor Bug. It had been sitting on the side of the bar. He was surprised he hadn't seen it before.

He crossed to the bar and picked up the box. It was about 4" X 6" X 2" wrapped in white paper and tied with heavy duty hemp string. Garrett turned it over and over in his hands. Nothing to identify that it was from Doctor Bug and nothing that gave a hint of its contents. Garrett carried it to the dining room table. He collected a knife from the buffet and began the process of opening the box, thinking how thoughtful Doctor Bug was for sending him a gift.

String cut and wrapping paper discarded, Garrett slipped the top of the box off to reveal a human shape made of Spanish Moss. Garrett was a kaleidoscope of emotions; surprised, curious, happy, fearful, angry — but he decided to end his emotional merry-go-round at friendship.

It was so kind of Doctor Bug to send a humorous gift. He knew how Garrett had been concerned about even visiting the root doctor so he sent a joke gift. Had Storey been anywhere near he would have assured Garrett that Doctor Bug had no sense of humor. Garrett put the doll back into the box and replaced the top. He continued his trip to the bathroom and returned to his recliner.

At some point in the evening, certainly after midnight, he made his way back to the bedroom. Sleep came and went. Dreams were varied but one thing was constant, there was Spanish Moss and Garrett was alone in each one.

He awoke at 7:00 to what he was certain was the call of the one-legged rooster.

CHAPTER 50

The day of the big auction had finally arrived.

Garrett sat up in bed looking around his bedroom for the one-legged rooster from Doctor Bug's compound. Just the thought brought a shiver to his body. A chill to the core of his bones.

He walked to the room safe to see if his shoulder bag was still there. It was, as were the coins, both roots and the Glock. He closed the safe door and checked the handle to make certain that the door was locked. The treasure was intact; no rooster was in the room, neither one-legged nor two; and the roots there too, regardless whether they worked or not.

Everything was right with Garrett's world with one exception; Lee wasn't there.

"Well, damn her. She has been more interested in her newspaper and her Bob Grant than with me. Just damn her. I don't need that kind of loyalty and I don't need that kind of love. Damn …" His last statement trailed off even as he said it.

He called the butler and asked for breakfast — bacon, eggs, toasted bagel, butter and pepper jelly. He opened the door and told the Security Team member that he would be ready to go to Hibernian Hall at 10:45 for the 11 o'clock final dress rehearsal. He also said he didn't want to be disturbed, and only Lee or Grant would be welcomed.

The elevator door opened to reveal the butler, the waiter and his breakfast. The dining room table was set, coffee poured and the silver dome that covered his breakfast selection and kept it warm removed. A folded copy of the morning *News and Courier* was beside the plate.

Garrett sat and said, "No," when the butler asked if Garrett needed anything else. He and the waiter were dismissed.

There it was, right there on page one, the whole page — his story. Pegge had done a marvelous job. In addition to the story about the auction, there were pictures of #13 Church Street, pictures of some of the more spectacular items in the Find, current pictures of Garrett from their files and ones that Pegge's photographer had taken at the interview as well as other pictures from Garrett's life. The story was continued on the inside of section A.

Section C, the society news, was filled with pictures of the celebrities who were attending the auction. In the center of the front page there was a picture of Cardinal Vassilli leaving #13 Church Street. What better advertisement for his business? There was a smile on Garrett's face.

Garrett finished his breakfast. He took his time in the shower. He shaved and he looked for the Edward Garrett he had been talking to at #13 Church Street. Apparently, he hadn't been sent an invitation because it was a different Edward Garrett in the bathroom mirror at the Mill's House. Garrett completed his toilet and walked to the window overlooking the courtyard separating the hotel from Hibernian Hall. He didn't even consider the fact that he was naked. No one could see him, anyway. The courtyard was a beehive.

Garrett dressed, sporty casual it would be. At exactly 10:45, Grant and the assigned security team member knocked on his suite door. Grant opened it to find Garrett completely ready with his book and his shoulder bag. Grant was pleasantly surprised.

The trio made their way to meet the rest of the security team augmented by the senior members of the Charleston Police Department. The entourage made it through the throng in the courtyard.

Everyone was at Hibernian Hall for the final Dress Rehearsal and the final Technical Rehearsal. All of the logistical people seemed to be handling their responsibilities.

The properly functioning electronics would be the key to the success of the auction. It would handle the bidding, the payment and the arrangement for the shipping. A triple system of encryptions for the computers had been developed by Grant and

John James. Every indication was that it was operating smoothly with no glitches. The informational system had also been developed by Grant. Everyone, whether live in the hall, on line through a dozen web sites, on ebay worldwide or on twitter, would be able to see live time information as they were bidding. This was the auction to end all auctions.

Garrett walked into his private suite in the hall. The technology in his area in the hall was a duplicate of the technology in his office conference room in The Mills House. He sat for a moment and looked at the screens. He had to admit that Grant had done a great job with the technology.

As 6:30 approached, Garrett went back to The Mills House Presidential Suite accompanied by the Security Team. He got dressed. Lee was in her suite, he guessed. This isn't the way he had imagined the evening would be. He tried to call but got no answer.

It was 7:00 when he finished dressing. He needed to be seen. The Security Team, all four of them, was there to accompany him to Hibernian Hall. So was the Police team. Bob Grant was probably already at the hall. Garrett guessed Lee was already there as well.

"Damn them. Damn all of them," Garrett said aloud. Only the Security Team heard him.

Garrett entered the hall. Applause started and soon was the only thing you could hear. Edward Garrett was the Toast of the Town so to speak. Lee, looking more beautiful that ever, walked to his side. An announcer from somewhere in the hall spoke into a microphone, "Mr. Edward Garrett and Miss Ashley Baraneau." More applause. Even with the Security Team, people were grabbing at him. Trying to shake his hand. Garrett made his way on stage. He was handed a mic.

"Thank you all for being here tonight. I hope you leave with the items you came to buy."

The Hibernian Hall had been transformed into a grand reception hall. Garrett had wanted to make sure no one entered the presentation room until it was ready. The line of people who wanted to get in had begun to form three days before the auction. Garrett had left a few openings for people who hadn't received an invitation. He had taken 100% credit for this idea even though it was Pegge Ravenel who suggested it to Ashley, as a way to draw additional media attention to the event.

"Nothing will make it look more like an event than a long line of people waiting to get in, especially if they have camped out," she had said.

Well, she was right. The auction had been the lead story on every news show in Charleston, and most of the state, as well as the front page of the newspaper, for three days. Word on the street was that certain people had paid line sitters up to $2,000 to assure that they were able to get in.

The visuals of the Find were fantastic. There was a continuous showing of visuals on the screens that started at 6:30 and played until 8:00 The giant screens projected each item in a larger-than-life majesty. The lighting had accented the best features. John James had certainly earned his money. From anywhere in the hall you could see at least three of the imposing screens. In addition to the slides he had meticulously made to show off the pieces in all of their glory, there were short video clips, and a dynamic audio track with an announcer giving the authentication information of each piece along with a perfectly orchestrated music track. With the slight echo, the big room and the speaker setup, he told Ashley he was certain that if there was a God, that is exactly how he would sound.

The overall effect of the visuals, decorations and settings was that of a stage production. The visual pod suspended over the center of the room drew everyone's attention the instant they walked into the room. The visuals from the pod were emulated on the towers of screens in each corner. Garrett was always surrounded by the security team. Only special guests were able to speak to Garrett. He looked like the President with his Secret Service team.

Cardinal Vassilli approach the group.

Garrett said, "Let him in."

The Cardinal congratulated Garrett, they posed for pictures, then the Cardinal whispered something in Garrett's ear. "The actual quote on the little box was, *Woe unto the man who betrays the Son of Man.* I believe you have the coins, I believe they are the legendary 30 pieces of silver. I believe they are cursed. That's why the Church is interested in your little box."

The Cardinal quickly left. If the Cardinal's pronouncement was disconcerting, Garrett pushed it from his mind. He had too many other things to think about. He would think about the Cardinal and his cursed box later.

As previously decided, the auction bidding would be divided into three sections; the first handled by Sotheby's, the middle section by Ruttenburg and Cohn, the South's best known antique auctioneers, and the last section by Christie's. Neither Sotheby's nor Christie's was happy with the arrangement, but the magnitude of the Find in the antique community made it a necessity for each to have a part of the auction. And neither wanted to take the chance of being left out. In addition to the bidding on the internet, two hundred telephone lines had been installed by various auction houses to place bids live for their clients around the world.

Garrett had decided to have a catalogue available at the beginning of the reception. Lee had taken control of the production of the catalogue. It rivaled many of the soft back, coffee table books Garrett would see when he visited the homes of his SOB clientele. Most were never opened. But it was the appearance, and that was the important thing. The appraisers who had authenticated the Find each had published their findings in books that they were selling to collectors.

Garrett had insisted on a Charleston menu for the reception. That meant that he had overridden Lee, who wanted an English high tea since most of the antiques in the Find were English or, at least, from a time when high tea would have been regularly celebrated in Charleston. Pegge Ravenel had insisted upon having a hip-New-York scene menu. Garrett put his foot down. If he was to be respected by the local blue bloods, he had to show them that he knew how to put on a Charlestonian celebration that would rival anything any of them could do. So, for this one night, he would be a Charlestonian's Charlestonian.

Media had collected from all over the world. Lee and Pegge had put together a superb media kit. There were photos of most of the Find items, comments from various experts who had examined one or more of the pieces, authentications and evaluations on many of the items, and letters from the Mayor, the Senator and other special people in Charleston.

Over one hundred media outlets had requested media kits and credentials to attend. The auction itself was reserved for bidders and invited guests. A convention hall in the Mills House next door had been reserved for media by Lee. Pegge was the media's contact. She had already broken the story and her articles were the talk of the town.

The Times of London and the BBC were among the ten media outlets that were issued an invitation to the auction. The three major television networks, three antique trade magazines, the *News and Courier* from Charleston. *The Huffington Post* was the sole internet news provider, and *USA Today* completed the invited media. There were five media pool reporters, three photographers and two writers who fed the rest of the print media, and two video crews that fed all of the television stations attending. Radio coverage was reserved for the opening and closing media gatherings.

The city of Charleston had assigned 200 policemen to assure protection for the people coming to the auction and control of the thousands that were expected to be observing the comings and goings of the special people who were invited. Garrett had been assigned three senior officers to assure his protection. Grant had graciously accepted the officers provided by the Mayor, but asked that they be secondary to his Security Team. The Mayor had insisted that this was one of the biggest things to happen in Charleston and that nothing was too good for Charleston's number one citizen, Edward Garrett. The officers didn't see it that way.

Limousines had started to bring special people to The Mills House, the Hilton and many of the exclusive Bed and Breakfast Inns on Friday. Some of the guests stayed with friends on the Battery and other private SOB addresses. Many of the SOB houses were quietly available to be rented.

Garrett expressed surprise at the number of celebrities that had flown in from the West coast. When he found out that Lee had arranged with The William Morris agency for many of the people they represented to be at the function and to assure the coverage they would receive, he was pissed. One more way she was controlling and manipulating his event.

He was happy that these household names were here to

celebrate his Find, but he was still pissed at Ashley. He had always thought that being a celebrity would be fun. Being recognized at restaurants, in the supermarket. Being stopped by people he had gone to grammar school with or who attended the same church for years but had never recognized him or acknowledged him.

Now it seemed that people who barely knew him or didn't know him wanted to talk to him. Everyone seemed to want a piece of him, and now he resented it. Recognition was what he had craved from his early childhood. Now he had it, in spades, and it just wasn't what it was cracked up to be.

The auction started. Everyone had a place to be and something to do. Everyone except Garrett. He walked into the control room and watched as the auctioneer called out the items, recited the paragraphs that Garrett and written or rewritten for him. He would announce the item and opening bid. He would read the paragraph. Winning bidders would be notified by email and payment arrangements and deliveries made. Garrett was amazed at the size of the bids.

He noticed Lee was standing next to Grant. She had a handheld computer screen. He walked over to her and asked what she was doing.

"Tracking bids — that's my job Edward. Don't you have something to do or someplace to be."

Garrett looked like an abused puppy. He was an outsider at his own event.

Lee was tracking bids, Bob Grant was directing the event, John James was overseeing the audio visual, all of his new friends were focused on the audio visuals and the tote boards that showed the current high bids and who had them, and he had three security guards watching every move he made. This was his event and he wasn't in charge of anything.

It was pretty much a replay of his entire life. Except now he was a celebrity — and nobody cared; he was prominent — and nobody cared. He was standing at the side of the stage watching Lee and Grant manage and direct *his* Find.

He turned to one of the Security Team.

"What's your name."

"Steve"

"Well Steve, there's nothing for me to do here, we're going to the control room at the Mills House."

"Grant told us to stay with you here,"

"Well, Steve, I'm going to the control room in the Mills House. If you guys want to protect me, then we will be going to the Mills House. Or you can stay here by yourselves." Garrett's resolve was obvious so, after a little discussion among the three security guards, the quartet made their way to the door and the path that led to the Mills House. Very few people even noticed the group move.

Garrett and his security team arrived at the control room. It, too, was a bee hive of activity. He looked around and the only person he recognized was the beautiful young woman. He walked up to her and asked what she was doing.

"Right now I am talking to Grant, relaying directions to the group here in the control room."

She was the one person hired to keep him company and she had been redirected by Grant.

"Ok guys, we are going to observe the auction from the Presidential suite."

Garrett led the trio to the private elevator that took them to the floor that housed the Presidential Suite. When they reached the door, Garrett spoke to Steve.

"Who has the key card, Steve?"

"Grant."

"Who else?"

"You."

"I don't have a key card; never have."

"Let's find the General Manager or the President of this place."

The group reboarded the elevator and headed back to the control room. Garrett found the beautiful young woman who doubled as his secretary. He asked her, "The suite is locked; where can I find the General Manager?"

"He was here a minute ago, wait a minute and let me finish this for Grant."

Garrett was fuming. *Grant again.* It was his event. His! He was interrupted in mid-thought by the arrival of the General Manager.

"How can I help you, Mr. Garrett?"

"I need a key card for my room."

"Who has the one you were issued?"

"Grant."

"You will have to get it from him. There is only one card and the person who it was issued to selected the entry code. So, you need to contact Grant."

That was not what Garrett wanted to heat. He looked at Steve.

"Either go get the card from Grant or take me home to #13 Church Street."

It was a dilemma for Steve. The team had been directed not to leave Garrett's side. Ethical or not, the only logical thing was to take Garrett to #13 Church. The group moved to the curb and entered their private limousine.

"#13 Church."

Storey was unpacking his truck when the limo pulled into the back of #13 Church.

"How's your mother?" Garrett asked.

"What? My mother! Oh, she's fine." Storey quickly closed the door to the carriage house.

Garrett didn't really care anyway.

"Steve. You and the guys are welcome to stay out here, but I'm going inside, having a stiff drink and going the bed."

He went inside, locked the door and walked to the kitchen. He picked up a bottle of Cognac and went to his bedroom on the third floor. He grabbed a glass and sat in his recliner. He took the remote and turned on the television. The TV came on instantly in the middle of a local news bulletin talking about the thousands of people trying to get into the "biggest event in Charleston's history." He quickly changed channels, settling on a mindless movie. He poured a glass full and began drinking.

It didn't take long for him to doze off.

It was 11:00 when he awakened. He took another drink of the cognac and stumbled to his bed, where he fell into a deep sleep.

It is blood money.

Matthew 27:6

PROPHESY

The softened glow from the far away light allows only enough illumination to focus on the apparitions moving about my room. The *shape-shifters*, moving to and fro across my view. It takes all of my concentration to focus on these ghost-like figures.

Where are they coming from? Where are they going? Why my room? And then there's that odor. Does it accompany the apparitions? It's an earthy, yet, somewhat familiar odor. What is that odor?

My concentration is divided between focusing on the shapes and defining that odor. It's an ominous, permeating odor. As consciousness slides in, replacing the shroud of sleep, the odor places itself clearly in my mind. It's smoke! Wood is burning someplace, and someplace nearby.

The ghost-like images begin to merge into a layer of smoke hanging like a wispy gauze draped from the ceiling of my bedroom. Something is on fire and I need to find out what.

As my feet hit the floor, the smoke begins to invade my nostrils, affecting my ability to breathe. Stumbling to the door, I grab for the knob. It's hot to my touch. Opening the door is like having a giant dragon exhale a full puff of smoke and fire directly into my face.

I can't breathe. I struggle to regain control as I slam the door shut. It's my house that is on fire. Everything that I have accumulated. All of my antiques. All of my treasures. Even my life — all is in jeopardy.

Panic sets in. What do I do? Where to go first? The smoke seemed to be clouding my thoughts just as it has clouded my ability to see the room clearly. I stumbled over a chair.

Cursing it I stumble over the table. A lamp and picture frames hit the floor and crash into hundreds of shards. The reality of the situation sets in. Tears well up in my eyes, then roll effortless down my cheeks. They hang motionless for seconds as if gathering the courage. Then free-fall only to splash on the shards of glass on the floor.

This is no time to feel sorry for yourself, Garrett.

Deep down inside my gut, it's like a switch is thrown. A calming knowingness takes over. I crouch close to the floor, and there I'm able to breathe better. I know that the third-floor balcony is the only way out.

The coins are the key to everything I've every wanted. Everyone in Charleston knows Edward Garrett. Everyone in the antique world knows Edward Garrctt. Everyone that matters in the whole world now knows Edward Garrett.

I make my way to the hiding place. The coins are safe. They are right where I have hidden them. The leather bag that holds the world's most famous coins is right here, safely within *my* fingers.

Glancing back at the bedroom door I can see the flickering light sneaking under the door as the fire makes its way up the stairs, ever closer to me and my well-being. I have to escape. The window is the way out.

The thickening smoke is making breathing even more difficult. Crawling toward the window is harder. I must make it. I must survive. Success within my grasp. I reach the window. I summon all of my strength and push.

Oh, no! The window is stuck. I've got to open it. One more push. The old sash moves an inch, and stops cold.

The smoke is so thick I can't see the bedroom door; only a bright glow at it bottom. The fire is right outside the door. I know it. I've got only one more chance. I move so that I can get a quick breath of fresh air from the cracked window. Standing, reaching deep inside me, I place as much leverage as I can. The window holds fast for a moment then breaks free and slides open. I scramble out of the window, onto the upstairs balcony.

Coughing; gasping for fresh air I fall on the cold balcony floor in a ball, grasping my chest, breaths coming in heaving shallow gasps. I'm able to look back into the bedroom. Fire has breached the door. Flames are lapping up the door and spreading across the walls. My well-being rests on being able to get from the third-floor balcony to the ground.

There. The branches of the old pecan tree. For months I had been after Storey to cut those branches. They were way too close to the balcony. I can climb down the tree. *Who would have believed that I would owe my life to the laziness of that damned Storey?*

I clinch the coin bag in my teeth as I grab for the stoutest of the branches. Testing momentarily to see if it will hold my weight, I jump. The giving of the branch makes me think the branch would snap; but no. The branch holds my weight and I am able to climb down to the bottom limb, only about ten feet from the ground. Swinging down, I allow my body to stretch to it total length. The pull on my muscles feels great. There's a burning in my arms that lets me know that I am indeed, alive. I decide to hang there and savor the feeling.

Moments later I shout, "Alive! Do you hear me? I am Alive!"

I'm still some three or three and a half feet from the ground. I release my grip and, as I'm in free fall, time slows. The seconds it takes me to hit the ground turn into minutes. I can't believe it. I've made it. My landing left a great deal to be desired. It wasn't a sharp, two-point landing. It was more like five or six points.

When I hit the ground, my left leg gave way. I tried to compensate, but the resulting torque on my body, the majority of my weight went to my right leg and it gave way. The ground united with my back, right knee and — at that point I lost count.

As I moved, preparing to stand, I surveyed the damage. First to me. There was a pain in my left leg and a burning in my chest. My right wrist might be broken. But other than that, I seemed none-the-worse-for-wear. Even as I tried to stand, my left leg gives way. I again find myself rolling in the leaves.

Stopping to gain my composure, I hear the sirens. The fire trucks are on their way. I discover that I am able to crawl. On my knees, I make my way out the back gate to a small grassy area next to the carriage house.

Storey? I think. *Where's Storey when you need him?*

Then I remember, *He is away with his family.*

No matter. As I sit in the grass I continue to gather my thoughts. Everything I have spent my entire life gathering is going up in smoke. *What will I do now?* I ask as I start to cry.

In the moments of silence broken only by the wail of the siren and my occasional sobs, I hear a soft, controlled voice from deep inside me; *Garrett. You're a fool. Nothing you have gathered until now matters. Nothing you've done until now matters. You have the coins. They're the real treasure. #13 Church street is significantly over insured just in case of a moment like this. You've just had the most successful, self-satisfying evening of your life. You are ready to start your life anew.*

A new feeling began filling my being. A feeling of assurance. Of confidence. These were new feelings to me.

"You're right," I said aloud with only the trees and the leaves to hear. "Now I am *Somebody*." Steve Martin's character in *The Jerk* flashed into my mind and a smile flashed on my face.

The sound of the fire trucks had grown.

CHAPTER 51

T hank God," Garrett whispered as he opened his eyes. It took some moments before he was able to focus on his surroundings and a few additional moments before he realized that the, "Thank God," was premature.

The softened glow of the faraway light allowed only enough illumination to focus on the apparitions moving about the bedroom. The *shape-shifters* seemed to be moving to and fro across his vision. It took all of his concentration to focus on these ghost-like figures.

Where are they coming from? Where are they going? What's that smell? The thoughts flitted through Garrett's mind like a recent memory.

He tried to divide his attention between the shapes and the familiar odor; the ominous, permeating odor. As consciousness replaced the shroud of sleep, the odor identified itself clearly in Garrett's mind.

Smoke. Wood smolke. Something's burning. Something is burning, and it's someplace nearby.

Ghost-like images drifted across the ceiling, merging, dancing, hanging like a wispy gauze draped from the ceiling over the entire bedroom.

It's the dream, Garrett thought. *Just the dream.*

This is not dream! The thought hammered Garrett's mind like a thunderbolt. He leapt out of bed, unsteady on his feet as the smoke invaded my nostrils, affecting his ability to breathe. He stumbled to the door and grabbed the knob, only to jerk back in agony. It was scalding hot.

He stripped off his shirt and used it as buffer to turn the door knob, and opened the door to an inferno. It was as if a giant dragon exhaled smoke and fire directly into his face.

Garrett had the presence of mind to slam the door shut.

Everything that I have accumulated is represented by this house. All of my antiques. All of my treasures. I'm going to lose them all. The thought flashes through Garrett's brain, replaced immediately by. *Idiot! If you don't do something, and quick, you're going to lose your life!*

Garrett fought panic as the thickening smoke clouded his thoughts. He turned and stumbled into chair and fell into a side table, knocking over a lamp and picture frame that shattered on the floor into hundreds of pieces.

Suddenly, Garrett is wrapped in a comforting calm. He's already seen this event. He knows how it ends. Recalling his dream, he crouches close to the floor where he can breathe better.

The third-flood balcony, he thinks. *That's the way out.* He can see clearly from his dream.

The coins! They are the key to everything I have ever wanted. Everyone in Charleston will know Edward Garrett. Everyone in the antique world will know Edward Garrett. And, for that matter, everyone that counts in the world will know Edward Garrett.

"Be calm, Edward," he told himself out loud. "You know how this will end. You've seen it in your dream. You know the way out. All you have to do is be calm and follow the dream. Just don't panic."

Trying to avoid the wicked shards of broken glass, Garrett managed to retrieve the bag of coins from their hiding place. Despite his dire circumstances, he can't resist taking pouring them out of the pouch, into his hands. He gazed at them, mesmerized, before a racking, smoke-induced cough brought him back to his senses.

The flickering light sneaking under the door urged him forward. Garrett dropped the coins back into the leather bag and worked his way toward the window.

He was calm, confident. He has already lived through this once. He crawled on his hands and knees, but at last reached the window. Standing was an effort, be he had made it. He would survive.

Garrett summoning all of the strength he possessed, placed his hands on the middle sash and pushed!

To no avail.

I remember, Garrett thought. In my dream. *The sash only gave a little on the first push.*

He redoubled his efforts and pushed again. The old sash failed to budge.

Anxiety began to run its fingers up his spine and doubt clouded his thoughts. *I know this is the push that will open the window and I will be free,* he encouraged himself.

No movement.

I've got one more chance and I know that the window will open this time.

Garrett clenched the leather pouch in his teeth, freeing both hands to exert as much leverage as possible on the window sash.

The window held firm.

Garrett's face was a mask of amazed consternation.

This can't be happening. I saw my escape in my dream. I have the coins. I get out. I'm famous.

A memory floated through his mind, just moments before panic took over. He recalled ordering Storey to nail his window shut as added security against a break-in. Storey had protested, saying it wasn't safe. Garrett had laughed and told the old man, "Just do it."

Garrett dropped to the floor, desparate to get one more breath, perhaps summon enough strength to break the window and crawl out.

He sensed a movement in the room. Was someone there? A fireman to rescue him?

He tried to call out, to gain the fireman's attention. The figure in the smoke saw him, and approached. Garrett, smiled, relieved. The figure bent over and pressed its knee into Garrett's chest. It pried the leather bag containing 30 pieces of silver from his hand, then stood, and walked away.

The last thing Thomas Edward Garrett III saw was a cloaked apparition going out the door.

EPILOGUE

Sunday

An article that appeared on the front page of the *News and Courier* told the story of Edward Garrett's fame and fortune.

Prominent Charleston Antique Dealer Dies in Fire.

Edward Garrett, 43, died in the fire that engulfed his antique business and residence at #13 Church Street last night. The cause of the fire is as yet unknown, but is considered suspicious by the Charleston Fire Department. Arson detectives are investigating.

Fire Department Captain, William Driggers, first on the scene, reported seeing a figure dressed in what appeared to be a "hooded cloak" leaving the area as he arrived. Police are attempting to verify this and other leads and have asked the public to call if anyone living in the area has seen anyone resembling the description.

A life-long resident of Charleston, Garrett had gained international attention on the day of the fire. At the center of a major antique controversy, Garrett had offered, at auction, a large and important collection of museum quality antiques. The auction was held at the Hibernian Hall and resulted in a gathering of the social elite of Charleston, the politically positioned in the state and region, and the *who's who* of the antique and museum world.

The auction drew the attention of wealthy private collectors from all over the world, anonymously represented by Christie's and Sotheby's, over 100 of the nation's premier museums, and what was estimated as thousands of important world-wide collectors. The auction was as much a media event as an art and antique auction.

A surprise visitor was Cardinal Guscipi Vassilli, Curator of Musea for the Vatican.

Estimates of the total value of the sale ranged from $400 to $500 million, because some sales were kept confidential as were the buyers. See a complete story on the auction on page 3A.

Circumstances concerning Garrett's acquisition of the collection are a matter of speculation. According to Ms Cindy Morganstern, a spokesperson for Sotheby's, it is extremely unusual for so many museum quality items to appear at one place, at one time, without someone at Sotheby's knowing of their existence.

"When I asked Mr. Garrett where he had gotten the collection, he was so vague that I detected what I believe to be a man with a lot to hide. But the items were truly a once in a lifetime collection and he did receive top dollar at the auction," added Sir Arthur Herbert, Acquisitions Director for Christie's in New York.

Garrett had no living relatives and funeral arrangements are incomplete.

EPILOGUE II

That afternoon a Gulf Stream IV bearing the insignia of Vatican City soared skyward from the Charleston Metropolitan airport. The passenger manifest listed Cardinal Guscipi Vassilli and entourage by name. There was one additional passenger — un-named.

Ashley Cooper Barrineau grieved, even though the relationship between her and Garrett had become strained over the past few weeks. He had changed. She accompanied the Senator to the funeral home to make arrangements in the absence of any known relatives.

At first light, Robert Storey hooked up a 20' trailer to the old pickup truck. Turning it south, he drove toward Savannah, Georgia.

APPENDIX 1

Time line showing the movement of the 30 pieces of silver

Jerusalem - 33AD — Judas throws coins into the synagogue.

Jerusalem - 33AD — Owner of Potter's Field seals coins in box.

Jerusalem - c. 1350 — A Knight finds box filled with jewels and sends it with other treasure to the Pope.

Rome - c. 1452 — Pope Alexander likes the box and keeps it in his chamber.

Somewhere near Hispanoila - c. 1700 — A young priest is traveling by ship to the new world with the box filled with money to start a parish.

Charleston - 12/10/1718 — Stede Bonnet, aka _The Gentleman Pirate_, is hung at low waters mark at White Point garden, now the Battery in Charleston.

Thomas Edward Garrett III – current —

APPENDIX 2

List of Characters (in order of appearance)

Judas Iscariot – Historical Character - Hanged
According to the New Testament, one of the twelve original disciples of Jesus Christ. He is known for the kiss and betrayal of Jesus to the Sanhedrin for thirty silver coins.

Thomas Edward Garrett III - Fictional Character – Died in a House Fire
The protagonist, age 43, antique dealer, the only child of Thomas Edward Garrett II, a surgeon from Boston who moved to Charleston with his new wife 10 years before Garrett's birth. Although Dr. Garrett was a prominent surgeon, his son grew up an outsider to the children his age since, in Charleston, it takes three generations to be accepted as a Charlestonian, something he desperately wanted.

Charleston – Historical Location
Charleston appears as a character because many of its idiosyncrasies. The city itself made the plot of the story possible. It is as unique as it is beautiful.

Queen Ester Legare - Fictional Character
The maid, housekeeper and nanny to Edward Garrett. A religious black woman who could trace her family back to slave times in Charleston. The name Legare is common in Charleston aristocracy. Since slaves, when freed, usually took the sir name of their masters, her family probably belonged to one of the Legare plantation owners. She taught Edward Garrett all things good.

Robert Storey - Fictional Character

The 65+ year old gardener, handy man, helper in the store. Storey had lived in the carriage house at #13 Church Street for as long as the Garrett family had owned the house.

Ashley Cooper Barrineau - Fictional Character

The love interest. Preferred to be called *Lee,* she was a newspaper woman and the only child of Senator Bradley Cooper Barrineau. She was named as somewhat of a joke because the Ashley and the Cooper rivers create the peninsula that is Charleston.

Tom Bass - Historical Character

Owner of Poogan's Porch and manager of Perditas Restaurants. A convivial person with a great sense of humor and a marvelous ability to make a customer feel at home.

William, Andre and others - Fictional Characters

Patterned after many of the great wait people in Charleston restaurants.

Bradley Cooper Barrineau - Fictional Character

Patterned after many influential southern politicians. Preferred to be called *the Senator.* Probably the most powerful person in the South Carolina government at that time. A partner in a famed Charleston law firm that bore his name. Father of Ashley Cooper Barrineau.

#13 Church Street - Fictional Location

A house with a history and a secret. The house, its history and its secret are all instrumental to the story, hence the listing as a character.

Owner of Potters Field - Fictional Character – Strangled

Patterned after the individual in the New Testament from whom the Jewish leaders bought the property used to bury stangers and paupers. Necessary to begin the journey of the coins from Jerusalem to Charleston.

Pegge Ravenel - Fictional Character

Friend of Ashley's at the newspaper. She broke the story of the Find and helped with promotion and public relations.

Penny Candy - Fictional Character

Patterned after many such dancers and con artists. Dancer and "B" girl at The Truck Stop, a bar that used to be in North Charleston.

14th Century Knight - Fictional Character – Drowned

Patterned after classical knights that fought in the Crusades. His story was drawn from a quote I remember from school which recorded that, *the streets of the city were ankle deep in the blood of the infidels for the Glory of God.* Source unknown.

Francie Schwartz - Fictional Character

Patterned after the owner of every man's first encounter with a set of real breasts. Francie was a classmate of Garrett's who had a reputation. It was said that she was easy.

Mrs. Moore - Historical Character

The owner of Woodfield's Inn, the oldest continually operating Inn in North Carolina. Mrs. Moore existed, though maybe not in Garrett's life as indicated. She operated Woodfield's Inn in Flat Rock, North Carolina. She was a marvelous woman, who I suspect has passed on.

Pope Alexander IV - Historical Character – Choked to Death on Food

AKA Rodrigo de Borja, gave the Papacy an utterly depraved reputation. Rodrigo was also known as the father of Cesare and Lucrezia Borgia, who were worse than he was. His demise helped complete the journey of the coins.

Francesca - Fictional Character

Patterned after the young courtesans favored by Popes during the Middle Ages and the Renaissance. Prostitutes were regularly entertained by the Popes in Church headquarters.

Dr. Alexander Williams - Fictional Character

A psychiatrist recommended to Garrett by Lee. He was added to keep Garrett's psychological side occupied until we could make room for Doctor Bug.

James John - Fictional Character

Patterned after a good friend, the guy with two first names was an audio visual expert.

Brother Andrew - Fictional Character

A Trappist initiate at Mepkin Abby Monastery (an actual place in, where else, Monks Corner, South Carolina).

The Brother - Fictional Character

The Church's contact person for Garrett. He is Opus Dei, a Prelature of the Pope himself, and therefore he took direction directly from the Holy See. His visit was as strange as he was.

Grandfather - Fictional Character

A clock. For the benefit of this story he is provided anthropomorphic ability to observe, think and reason, but not talk.

Sir Arthur Herbert & Dr. Cynthia Morgenstern PhD - Fictional Characters

Representatives of the two major auction companies, each trying to impress Garrett. Each thought Garrett to be as small-minded as his small town antique store. Each tried to use their position to gain the upper hand.

Young Priest - Fictional Character – Drowned While Being Eaten by Sharks

On his way to open a new Parish in the new world, this young priest is given the box filled with gold coins to establish a Parish in the new world. As they are approaching the Island of Hispanoila, the ship he is on is attacked by Pirates. Everything of value is taken, including the box. The main Pirate is Stede Bonnet, *The Gentleman Pirate*. The Priest and Bonnet carry on an intellectual conversation leaving the Priest the idea he will be spared. He is made to walk the plank and dies.

Doctor Bug - Historical Character

Patterned after a real, live, witch doctor that I met in Beaufort, South Carolina, Doctor Bug introduces Garrett to the world of the black arts. We never know if the good Doctor is a part of the solution or a part of the problem.

Stede Bonnet - Historical Character – Hanged

AKA *The Gentleman Pirate*, Stede Bonnet retired from the King's Guard, was an owner of a large estate in the Barbados where he lived with his wife. He was cultured, well groomed, wore fancy clothing and a peniwig. He was known to frequent Charleston alone and with Edward Teach, (aka Blackbeard). In mid 1718, he was captured by Colonel William Rhett. He was put on trail, found guilty, put in prison and sentenced to death. On November 12, 1718, Bonnet was hung at low waters mark at White Point Gardens, now called the Battery.

Cardinal Guscipi Vassilli - Fictional Character

Chief curator of Vatican Musea, representative of the Pope at the auction.

Robert "Bob" Grant - Fictional Character

A former military special forces officer, he was well-suited to design a security team to protect Garrett. His business was special event planning, logistics and security.

Beautiful Young Woman - Fictional Character

Garrett's personal secretary during the auction. She was added as a distraction for Garrett and for the reader.

DEDICATION

To...God, the Father, from whom all things come.
1 Corinthians 8:6

Thank you to: Mike Parker for taking a chance on an untested writer; Sybil, my lovely wife, whose persistence and support paid off; Judy Powell grammarian, speller extraordinaire and encourager; a variety of women who shared my life and provided support to keep writing, particularly Rose who started this merry-go-round; Tom Robbins his writing style influenced me even though I never met the man; and anyone willing to pay money to read this book.

Please note that a substantial portion of the profit derived for the sale of this book will go to support programs that help feed Widows in India and Orphans in Africa as we are admonished to do in James 1:27

...look after the orphans and widows in their distress.

Additionally, my family (everyone of them) and anyone that I promised I would dedicate this story to. And, I must mention Mary Holland (RIP) wife of my half-brother, Billy Holland (RIP). I told her if I ever finished the story and it was published, I would dedicate it to her.

Thank you all.

Also Available From

WORDCRAFTS PRESS

Obedience
   by Michael Potts

When Kings Clash
   by J.E. Lowder

The Scavengers
   by Mike Parker

Odd Man Outlaw
   by K.M. Zahrt

Maggie's Refrain
   by Marcia Ware

The Awakening of Leeowyn Blake
   by Mary Parker

Home
   By Eleni McKnight

www.wordcrafts.net